Fiona Shillito was born in Yorkshire and moved to Northamptonshire at a young age with her family. She was a primary school teacher for several years and has also worked as a copywriter. She is now a full-time writer.

Fiona Shillito lives in Somerset with her husband and their two daughters.

THE COLOURS OF THE DAY

Between the wars, in the lush countryside of Southern France, Anna's parents become lovers. When their idyll is shattered amidst bitter recriminations, there is a marriage, then exile, then poverty — the ultimate test of love. For Anna too there is passion — but she is forced into a loveless marriage and her daughter must never know who her real father is. Though Anna lives her life with courage and determination, it is a life built on a tissue of lies, and the repercussions of her actions echo down the years. Secrets may never be spoken, but diaries and letters can be time bombs of truth waiting to explode.

FIONA SHILLITO

---◆---

THE COLOURS
OF THE DAY

Complete and Unabridged

ULVERSCROFT

First published in Great Britain in 2000 by
Headline Book Publishing
London

First Large Print Edition
published 2001
by arrangement with
Headline Book Publishing
a division of
Hodder Headline Group
London

The moral right of the author has been asserted

British Library CIP Data

Shillito, Fiona
    The colours of the day.—Large print ed.—
    Ulverscroft large print series: general fiction
    1. Mother and daughters 2. France, Southern
    3. Large type books
    I. Title
    823.9′2 [F]

    ISBN 0–7089–4425–6

Published by
F. A. Thorpe (Publishing)
Anstey, Leicestershire

Set by Words & Graphics Ltd.
Anstey, Leicestershire
Printed and bound in Great Britain by
T. J. International Ltd., Padstow, Cornwall

This book is printed on acid-free paper

With grateful thanks to my agents Helenka Fuglewicz and Ros Edwards, for their faith in me as a writer, to Julia Forrest for her diligence and to my husband and daughters for their support.

Prologue

In after years it was the tea-time terrace they remembered most. The terrace where, at the end of long ungoverned days throughout each summer, they would congregate. With each passing year it seemed there was one more of them and Maman was one year more bitter.

There was music, from a gramophone, dance and song cranked up, scratching at the afternoons. There was Maman, playing the English lady, dressed in crêpe de chine and pouring tea. Always tea at this time of day, and small sweet cakes, cloying on the tongue. There were evenings, when the children lay in bed and knew, as if by instinct, the footsteps. They knew the adult voices, Maman and Papa, Monsieur Becque, and other visitors — of whom there were many. They knew the nuances of Maman's voice pitched according to her mood, or by the quantity of wine that flowed from crystal glasses. The clink of drink, a familiar sound beneath their open windows.

The children knew breakfasts, before the adults appeared, the morning ritual of fruit and wild-birdsong. There was laughter and love, there was teasing and rivalry, there were tears and, running through and over every conversation, the sound of the wind through the tall trees mingled with the roll of shoreline breakers. They knew it all.

La Roche was Philippe's house. Philippe Breton, 'un homme fatal', or so it would appear, who had married his beautiful, vivacious English bride, Elspeth Bourne, a shopkeeper's daughter from Canterbury. Soon, and in quick succession they had children, Cathryn, Olivier, Babette, Mary, Duncan, Alicia, Blanche, Edward and Millie. Meanwhile Philippe had affairs.

When Mary was young she almost believed her mother when she said she had only to look at Papa and there was another baby on its way; but when Cathryn met Bryn she found there was more to it than that.

1

Summer 1929

Mary

Peaches on a green table and the sun slams down hard beyond the cool of the little tea terrace. Maman binds Blanche's small hand, and speaks half in French, half in English; she speaks so quietly that, although I cannot see her face, I know she is angry.

'*Tiens!* I told you to take more care of her. What were you thinking of, Mary, to let her out of your sight? She is only four!' Maman's straw hat is tilted and her whole body turned away from me. She is absorbed, preoccupied with Blanche. Blanche's sobs, which began when her awful screaming stopped, finally hiccough to a snuffle. Edward, whose fault I say it was, stands naked in the heat, his small hands feeding black grapes into his rosebud mouth. His pretty face is stained and smeared with the grime of the day mingled with tears and grape juice.

'I told you,' Maman repeats, quieter still. I sit on the terrace wall above her, and swing my sixteen-year-old legs.

3

'*Ce n'est pas de ma faute,*' I mutter, my teeth clenched, my eyes screwed up against more than sunlight.

'*Non?* You were supposed to be in charge. Papa and I, *nous sommes très fatigués.* The maid . . . you know the maid has given notice.'

I think of the sounds last night, the arguing, the smash of a wine glass in the fireplace, Maman screaming at Papa. It is not only the maid who is missing today. I shrug. We all know where Papa might be — in one of his bolt holes in Marseille or perhaps he's gone into Toulon, I'm sure he has gambling friends there. One thing's for certain: we won't be sending out any search parties. Papa will be back. It is not the first time.

Maman swings round to face me as Cathryn comes up from the garden to the terrace. She is carrying Edward's clothes but drops them and stoops to sweep him into her arms, kissing the curls around his hot, sticky face. 'Yum! You smell delicious.' She swings him above her head and he pees with excitement. A tiny god peeing a tiny golden fountain against the sun. Cathryn laughs. '*Tu es très méchant. Petit cochon.*'

She holds him close, astride one hip. Her lovely fair hair hangs loose and damp around her face, she is fashionably brown and

4

unfashionably freckled, as are we all. I know she has been swimming in the bay. She has that look about her, the one she has when she's been with *him*. Her face is sleepy, as though she's looking inside her own head and not out at the world at all, and her big shapely body moves lazily. When she's like this it's as if she's the only person on the terrace that Life with a capital 'L' is really happening to. I feel dull and inadequate. I think about the English artist down in the cottage for the summer again. He is very handsome. I know what they do. Haven't I been the one who has kept watch for them these past weeks, covering for Cathryn's absences, telling lies for her. Maman may have had her suspicions but is too exhausted to do, or say, anything.

Even Cathryn cannot ignore the tension between Maman and me and she glances in my direction, and then at Blanche where she rests her head, pale and tearstained against Maman's shoulder. A small frown gathers between Cathryn's winged fair eyebrows. 'What's happening? What's the matter with little Blanche? *Ah, ma pauvre petite.*' Cathryn sucks in her breath as she sees blood seeping through Blanche's bandages.

'That's Mary's fault.' Maman glares at me as she begins to collect together the silver scissors, salve and bandages with one hand; she holds Blanche close with the other and kisses the top of her head.

'Tell Maman it's not my fault.' I appeal to Cathryn for help. 'Tell her, Cathryn. It was Edward. He picked up the broken glass, he gave it to her. I can't be with them all the time. It simply isn't fair!'

My voice rises to an angry wail — I know that soon it will be my turn to cry. Cathryn looks across at me, she's very beautiful, very calm. In her blue cotton dress it's as though she is made of the stuff of the day itself. The first of Maman and Papa's brood, she has inherited the beauty of them both, leaving me little, but then I am only Papa's child, not Maman's. Where Cathryn and Maman are tall, stately and fair, with the full-blown beauty of an English rose, I am small, dark and straight-haired. Sometimes when I'm dressing I watch my grey eyes in the mirror, under their straight black eyebrows, the lashes black as soot, and tell myself I am not ugly, but interesting, very interesting. That's what Monsieur Becque said the day he came looking for Cathryn and she wasn't here to meet him.

Maman was busy in the kitchen with Cook and sent me out with some iced tea to talk to Monsieur on the tea terrace until Cathryn

6

should come. I walked the long way round, out of the servants' door and through the high-walled kitchen gardens, hoping Cathryn might arrive before me but she didn't, which was a good thing after all, because Monsieur Becque was standing looking out towards the sea when I came up onto the terrace and I was terrified that if he turned his head he might spot Cathryn coming back through the trees from the Englishman's cottage.

So I handed him his drink and, by standing with my back to the house, I managed to manoeuvre him round so he was looking away from the trees. It would seem that being Cath's spy and confidante is teaching me cunning. I pointed out the doves up on the roof; how pretty their whiteness is against the terracotta tiles, how they make me think of innocence on wings. Monsieur Becque looked amused, but I babbled on, telling him what a fine view of the sea there is from Maman's balcony window and saying how much I would like a balcony, and I told him of Papa's plans to build a new wing, but I think it would spoil the proportions of the house.

I was talking too fast and I hoped Becque would not notice how often I turned to look for Cathryn, to try to warn her not to come straight up through the trees, but to go round

7

the other way, along the beach and up the steep little path to the barns. I needn't have worried — after a time Monsieur Becque stood up to go. He kissed my hand and laughed softly as I tried to pull away.

'Thank you for your company and your opinions of La Roche and its architecture,' he said. 'I agree, such an elegant house should not have ugly additions. Your comments were most entertaining.' He patronises me so much. I would like to strike him. Then, as he was walking away, he turned and said, 'One day, Mary, someone will love you very deeply. You have such an interesting little face, very interesting,' and he left. But I didn't really believe him.

Olivier teases me about my looks. I hate him. He was the one who told me I'm not really Maman's daughter, that after Cathryn, and then the twins Olivier and Babette were born, Maman didn't want more children. Olivier told me dirty stories about how a man and a woman can have babies and not have babies. He told me Maman was wicked and an unnatural wife and refused to have Papa in her bed and that was to stop her having any more babies, because she wouldn't do the other things to stop them and Papa was so angry he went out 'whoring', that's what Olivier called it, and one night Papa came home with me wrapped in a white sheet in a basket and he said to Maman, 'Here, if you won't have any of your own, you must look after this one. It is at least mine.' Olivier says she took pity on me and she took me in. I'm one of Papa's bastards and she took pity on me. That's what Olivier says. After that Maman had the other babies, Duncan, Alicia, Blanche and Edward. But now it's the maid whose belly is rounding and Papa has that look on his face, like a smug cockerel. Olivier says Papa will 'put it into anything', but I think Olivier's as bad and he showed me some dirty pictures.

I hate Olivier for everything, but mainly because he told me I wasn't Maman's child. I hate him most for that. It must be true. Why else would Maman hate me so? Why else would I be her scapegoat? Why else do I look so different from the rest of them?

I made Olivier tell me who my real mother was. I caught him coming up from the cellar one evening when Maman and Papa were out. I threatened to tell Papa about the wine Olivier's taken from the cellars and about the stupid village girls he goes with on Saturday mornings when Papa thinks he's having his piano lessons. I scratched his face, I wanted to scratch his eyes out. I hounded him and hounded him until he told me. My mother

9

wasn't a maid. The joke is that my real mother's from a better family than Maman's. Maman is only a shopkeeper's daughter. Olivier said my real mother came from a good family beyond the village. Her family sent her away when they knew about me. Then the whole of my mother's family moved away and forgave her and took her back in but they wouldn't have me. I was going to be put in an orphanage. So, when Papa heard about it he was very brave, because my real mother's father was threatening to shoot him, but he went to them and insisted on looking after me. Papa loves me. He's wicked in other ways but I think Papa was a good man for that.

But I hate Olivier, I hate the way he and Babette are always laughing together in corners. I hate that they are twins and have each other. Cathy and I are close, but it's not the same as Olivier and Babette. When I told Olivier I didn't believe his stories about me, Babette told me to go and ask any of the staff, they all know it's true. Olivier goes out and talks to the stablehands, I hear them laughing together, telling each other smut and rudeness. Maman says Olivier's running wild and Babette's almost as bad, but Maman's too tired to do anything about them and Papa doesn't seem to care. I think they both really know about Cathryn and her English painter, but they're too wrapped up in their own problems to put a stop to it.

Papa hopes Cathryn will marry soon, a rich man, a man with lands to add to our own. That is why he invites Monsieur Becque to come when Cathryn's around. Becque has driven over several times for tea. He finds our family a little strange, a little eccentric, with our taste for art and paintings and books; the laughter and conversation, the wild arguments and fierceness that ebbs and flows around our table bewilder him, but I know he also finds Cathryn's heavy beauty irresistible. He ignores her biting sarcasms, and interprets her antagonism as a passion for him which she is trying to hide from him. He couldn't be more wrong. He should hear the things she says to me when we're lying in the dark in our room. She's so sharp and funny about him.

Cathryn has that dreamy look on her face. She must be thinking about the Englishman again. She should be more careful because I know Maman has seen the look too, I can tell by the way she clears her throat and says briskly, 'Cathryn, can't you tell Mary. She really should be more responsible. I've tried but she's hopeless.'

Cathryn gives her head a little shake; her expression changes. She looks at me now, her

11

pity mingling with what I hope is gratitude for all I've done for her this summer, for her and Bryn the Englishman. She knows I tell Maman lies for her, she's told me what to say when she wants to be with him. Almost imperceptibly she shakes her head at me, lays a slim finger along her chin. It is our signal. She's going to say something to make Maman believe that Cathryn is on her side. I mustn't be hurt by it.

Cathryn looks at me severely and says, 'But Mary, if you were supposed to be looking after the littles, then you were supposed to be looking after them.' She shrugs and pouts as Edward twists fat fists into her mass of hair, curling now along her neck and shoulders as it dries in the heat. She won't wear her hair bobbed. She's too proud of its beauty, just as she's too aware of her lovely body to hide it with bust binders and the pretence of no curves between shoulder and thigh. It would be impossible anyway. Whereas I'm the perfect shape for the latest fashions, but me, I am not allowed to wear them, Maman still dresses me like a child. I wish I looked like the film actress Clara Bow, it might be fun to be called the 'It Girl'.

Cathryn always laughs when I tell her that. She says I would look better in a smoking jacket or lounge suit, like the ones in the copy of *Vogue* Papa brought home the last time he went to Marseille. That might be fun too, to wear a bow tie and a white shirt, and smart trousers — what a shock Cook would get! Or to be allowed to go to a *soirée* in one of the new bias-cut frocks, they're so beautiful. If only Maman would let me have some fabric and try my hand, I'm sure I could make something. Perhaps I could be like Coco Chanel, dressed all in black. A little black dress. How *avant garde*, how grown-up that would be. But no. Maman says no, I'm too young. I come out of my reverie. Cathryn is walking off the terrace towards the house door.

'Shall I take Edward in for his bath, Maman?' she says. She is hoping to distract Maman, to wheedle her way round her. She says, 'I'll bathe him tonight if you like, Maman. I can see you're tired.'

As Cathryn moves I catch the faint smell of fresh sweat and sea on her skin; and I know that for all the love I bear her and, at this time in our lives, it is a very great love, momentarily I hate her. She is so beautiful, so implacable, so much older than I. So in control. Her soft cotton dress blows a little in the cool breeze which has snaked onto the terrace. Suddenly Cathryn's face looks like a crumpled paper bag, she drops Edward

13

abruptly into my arms. I sag beneath his unexpected weight and he whimpers as Cathryn runs to the terrace parapet over which she vomits violently onto the garden below. When she stops it is as if the usual afternoon sounds have all ceased. Then they begin again; the birdsong and the wind through the trees, the distant call of the waves out on the shore.

Maman speaks. Her voice sounds strange, and when I glance at her I look away again quickly. Her eyes have such a strange hard glitter they frighten me.

'Well, well, Cathryn. I think we had better have a talk.' Maman's voice is harsh; she's forgotten her refined accent as she barks at me, 'Mary, take Edward and Blanche inside.'

Cathryn

I am still shivering from the fit of sickness. The terrace is cold after the heat of the sun, and the warmth of the waves and the sand where Bryn and I have been lying naked together for the past hour. He is a beautiful man. A big heavy man, strong and muscular. The dark hair on his chest and legs is close curled, that of his head and his beard glossy as a blackbird's wing, with the same blue-black shine when the sun lights it. He is

14

a golden bronze all over.

The little cove is completely private and he loves to lie there when he's not working. Naked. Divine. It's how I first saw him, we needed no further introductions. I'd never seen a naked man before and yet his ease with his own body made things so easy for me, so deliciously easy. I felt no shame, no repugnance as Maman had informed me I would. It just seems that Bryn is a part of nature and he's taught me that I am, too. When I look into his eyes I feel I could drown in them for ever; their clear changing grey-green is like the sea in the early mornings. If I stand here, rest my arms on the terrace parapet, think my own thoughts, blot out Maman and Mary and the littles, I can still see Bryn, stepping naked from amongst the trees.

Today he was like a mythical creature, so powerful. I ache to be with him. I ache to touch him, for him to touch me. To touch me. Everywhere. It's like a frenzy in my blood. I've never seen anyone more in tune with themselves, so . . . unabashed. He's here in my head all the time. He speaks as he walks towards me across the hot white sand and at first I can't hear him, it is as if I can only use one sense at a time and my breathing is God knows where. What happens next is what always happens when we're together. I cannot resist him. I have no wish to resist him. Why should I resist him? Already his manhood has risen, I take its strength in my two hands, his mouth is on mine, hot and feverish. His fingers fumble with buttons before he wrenches my dress down off my shoulders. We roll together onto the heat of the sand and his mouth comes down and covers my breasts with kisses. Today he was more urgent than I've ever known him, it was like a kind of madness. It was over almost too quickly for me and my back is raked with his fingernails, I can still feel the pain. It gives me pleasure.

'Cathryn, can't you tell Mary — she's hopeless.' Maman, acid and mean, breaks in on my thoughts, some trouble with Mary and the littles, Blanche has cut her hand. Poor Mary, it's not her fault, it's Maman's for throwing the glass at Papa and then not clearing the debris away. I heard them, both drunk again. How can two people become like that? Did they ever feel about each other as Bryn and I do? No. Maman has told me she hates the 'Act of Union', as she terms it. I'm different. I've never known a more glorious summer.

I decide to placate Maman and bend to lift Edward, I offer to take him in for his bath, but then a dreadful thing happens.

16

I have been sick. I think about the maid being sick and I am forced to acknowledge at last, with an awful clarity, why my body is changing shape. What will happen to me? What will I tell Maman? I turn to face her and realise that Mary, dear sweet Mary, knows too.

Maman's voice sends a chill through me: it has that hard quality that terrifies us all. All except Papa. Without turning from me she tells Mary to take Blanche and Edward indoors.

Mary does as she is told and takes the littles inside, throwing a look of such anguish towards me as she walks past that, in spite of my fear, I almost smile. I make to brush past Maman and knock some peaches off the little green table. Everything I observe seems very clear, very sharply defined. The blue of my dress, the pale green of the table, the soft blush on the peaches as they roll to the edge of the table and I watch them fall. Slowly, so slowly. It seems they'll never land, but of course they do and their softness squashes to a pulp as they reach, at last, the stones beneath the table.

Then I hear Maman's voice again. I close my eyes against her, put my hands to my ears but she drags them down. Her hands on mine are birds' claws. I feel her breath on my face,

17

smell the stale wine from the night before, mingled with milky tea and I retch. She slaps me hard across the face and we look at one another aghast. She begins to cry. Her lovely mouth makes an ugly shape and she sobs as she speaks.

'Oh, Cathryn. No. Not that. Not you. Oh Cath, you silly little fool! Tell me it's not true.' She reaches for her handkerchief, wipes its lace-edged inadequacy across her eyes, pushes her hat back off her face and it falls to the ground, next to the peach mess. 'It's too late for me, but you! You could have had so much. You could have brought so much to this family. Do you want to be like me, dragged down year after year with one baby after another? There are ways to stop it happening — I was going to tell you. Although I find them all distasteful I had hoped to tell you before you married Monsieur Becque.' She glances up at me where I'm standing, still with my hand to the cheek she slapped. Almost hopefully she breathes, 'It is Monsieur Becque, isn't it?'

'Monsieur Becque? I loathe the man.' Hysteria is beginning to swell inside my head, I feel a pulse beating in my neck, I shout at Maman, 'I don't even call him by his first name! How could I possibly make love to him!'

'Cathryn! Please restrain yourself. We don't use words like that — especially when the littles might hear.'

Maman is looking at me as though she's measuring me up for a new dress. 'You won't be able to marry him now. Didn't you know he's in love with you?'

I stifle a snort of laughter. 'How can you say that, Maman? You know it's not true. I was just a bargaining tool, a 'good marriage', securing everyone's social position, making sure the peasantry don't get their hands on any land or money. It's positively mediaeval! You must be crazy if you think love comes into it.'

Maman frowns. Her face is very white and her fingers play ceaselessly with the lace edge on her handkerchief. 'It was a good arrangement. Believe me, Cathryn, it's not a bad thing to have social standing. I should know. Where would I be now if I hadn't met your papa?'

She looks pathetic slumped in her chair. It's a novelty to see Maman looking vulnerable, and a hideous desire to be cruel, to pay her back for slapping me, grips me as I snipe, 'Well, I'm not like you. I wouldn't marry someone just for a position in life — and look where it's got you! You're not happy! Were you ever happy?'

19

I'm instantly ashamed of myself. Maman's eyes fill again; she is looking away, beyond me out toward the sea. 'Oh Cathryn, if only you knew *how* happy. Philippe . . . ' her voice breaks, but she wipes away her tears with the back of her hand and continues. 'Philippe was the best, most wonderful man. What was I? Just a shopkeeper's daughter, but your Papa loved me. Loved me for myself. He used to say I was the most beautiful woman he'd ever met. We used to dance, Cathryn. Your Papa was a good dancer. He would come calling and Ma and Pa let him take me out places I'd never even dreamed of. He even took me to the Ritz in London. My parents were so happy for me. They couldn't believe how lucky I was. I was a beautiful bride.'

She's on a well-worn track now. I've heard this story so many times I'm not really listening, but today the story doesn't stop where it usually does; she continues and the more she does, the more I wish she wouldn't.

'Philippe had told me about La Roche. He made it sound so wonderful I couldn't wait to see it, and the day after we were married when he brought me here, I could scarcely believe how lovely it all was. I couldn't believe it was all mine. I was exhausted after the excitement of the wedding, so on our wedding night he was gentle and didn't make demands on me. He said he understood. He said he would wait. Then after the travelling I told him I was in no state to . . . to do . . . that, and in the early days he didn't press me and even agreed to let me have my own room. He was very kind, but after a week or two he began to come to my room every night. In the end, of course, I had to give in. If only we hadn't had to . . . ' She falters. She's remembered I'm here. A huge sigh shudders through Maman's body. She is rallying, her empty stare flickers into sharper focus and she stands up briskly. We are both embarrassed.

Maman retreats behind her *grande dame* façade again and pours us each some tea. It's bitter and cold but I drink mine to give me something to do. Maman is watching me with narrowed eyes.

'What are we going to do about you, Cathryn? Who is the father?'

I shake my head.

'You won't tell me?'

'No, Maman. I won't tell you.'

'Why not? Are you ashamed of him? Please God, don't tell me it's one of the stablehands.'

'No, Maman, it's not one of the stable-hands.'

'Then, who?'

'I'm not saying.'

'Not saying? Perhaps you don't know who it is,' she throws at me.

Anger fuelled by my love for Bryn burns in me. 'How dare you, Maman! How dare you say that!' I shout at her.

She shrugs and sits down. 'So, tell me who it is. It isn't Monsieur Becque, it isn't one of the stablehands. You don't know anyone from the village.' She sweeps a hand through her hair making it stand in ugly spikes round her face and I know before she speaks that she's guessed. 'Oh dear God. It's the Englishman, isn't it? It's the painter.' I say nothing but I know I don't have to, my face will be telling her all she needs to know. 'I'm right, aren't I? Well, that's that, my girl. He won't be able to afford to marry you. Now he's had his fun, no doubt he wouldn't want to marry you anyway.' I'm speechless with pain, but she's ploughing on like a ship in full sail.

'Becque would have married you. He won't now! You're what I believe is referred to as damaged goods.' There's an edge to her voice that makes me uneasy. She is on the verge of hysteria. All I want to do is to find Bryn. I don't want to be here. I don't want to have to deal with Maman and what I know, from bitter experience, is turning into one of her outbursts. I half turn towards the terrace steps, the garden is mellow and so beautiful in the late-afternoon light, but Maman's voice scrapes my nerves as she gets to her feet and swings me round to face her.

'Damaged goods!' Her voice is rising, she's been like this more frequently recently. Her eyes are glittering bright in her white haggard face. She's like marble and emeralds, cold and hard. I back away from her, my head reeling with her words. 'Damaged goods' — what does she think I am? Something to be bought and sold? I am the eldest daughter. I am a commodity. The truth hurts, almost more than the physical pain as she grabs at my wrists, her nails digging into the flesh. I've never been more than a commodity; she and Papa only want me to marry that fool Becque to buy themselves more property and more land. Well, thank God, I've foiled that little plan. Though fear hangs about at the edges of my mind. What does a girl in my position do?

'Maman, you're hurting me,' I plead, but she doesn't release her hold. If anything she holds tighter as a look of cunning creeps across her face. Barely above a whisper, she asks, 'How many weeks is it since you had your monthly visitor? if you're not too far on, we may fool Monsieur Becque.'

I gape at her in horror, I think I may be going to be sick again.

'Maman, you can't mean it,' but she's not looking at me. She's looking somewhere beyond my right shoulder as if she can read the words she's speaking.

'We could have an immediate wedding and,' her attention comes back to me, she glares at my stomach, 'that,' she waves a finger in my belly's direction, 'that thing that you've so wantonly conceived could be passed off as his. Yes! That's it, that's what we must do. Don't you think so? That would be for the best, wouldn't it?' She lets go of me. I step away from her. My skin feels clammy. I speak carefully, unsure if what I am saying will make sense to her in the state she's in.

'Maman, I can't pretend to Monsieur Becque. I won't do it. I may not love him, but I couldn't do that to him. It wouldn't be right. It would be utterly abhorrent.'

'I hardly think you're in a position to find anything more abhorrent, Cathryn, than what you've already done.'

'I'm not staying to listen to this.' I start down the terrace steps, but she comes after me. We reach the bottom of the small flight almost simultaneously. I turn to run towards the trees, but she's surprisingly fast, and too quick for me. She's already grabbed my arm. Her grasp is very strong and now I'm really afraid of her. She looks almost mad — her

24

face is bright and it's so exultant.

'You're not getting away from me, Cathryn. You'll stay here and we'll sort this mess out. You'll do as you're damn well told. We can't have the family disgraced.'

'What's the family got to do with it?' I feel trapped and suffocated.

'Of course the family has everything to do with it. We can't have a scandal in the village. We're well thought of. There must be no disgrace; we could never hold our heads up again. I insist absolutely, Cathryn, you will do as you're told.' Her voice sinks to a passionate hiss. 'There will be no disgrace.'

Her hands move up to my shoulders and she looks into my face, thrusting her head near. I move my head away from her stench and from the corner of my eye glimpse Mary's small worried face at our bedroom window. Then she has gone and Maman propels me back up the steps to the terrace but I shrink from her and I know I'm going to cry. I hate seeing Maman like this and I'm tired, so terribly tired I can barely concentrate on what she is saying.

'You will invite Monsieur Becque here tomorrow, you will be nice to him, you will be extremely nice to him. Do you understand what I'm saying?' She glances over her shoulder making sure we're unobserved before she whispers. 'You will, in short, seduce him.'

I shake my head. I can't believe what I'm hearing, but she's continuing, 'You'll seduce him, in one of the barns. You will take him for a walk around the estate and out along the shore. Then you'll suggest he might like to see some of the older buildings — it's very pleasant up by the barns. You can go up the steps from the beach. No one will see you. When you reach the big barn you'll invite him inside and take him to the hay-loft. After all, it would seem you know how to do that kind of thing. You'll seduce him and, after a week or so, you'll tell him the child is his and that will be that.'

'You're mad. I won't do it — I *can't* do it.'

'Why not? You slut, you've already done it with one man! What difference will another make to you?'

Tears are rolling down my face. I'm gulping for air. How can she be like this with me? How can she say such things?

'You will marry Monsieur Becque and all will be well. There will be no shame, this will be our secret.'

'No, Maman,' I wail. 'I cannot marry Monsieur Becque. Never! I detest him.'

That's when she hits me again, the second blow harder than the first. 'You have no choice, my girl. I repeat, I will not have disgrace brought on our good name, and neither will your Papa. He couldn't stand the shame.'

My face is sticky with crying but her words, not the blow, are what send my senses reeling. 'Disgrace! Shame!' I shriek, spitting the words at her, not caring about the consequences. 'And what about Papa? What if the world knew how he had made his money? He pretends to be a gentleman but face it, Maman, he's a gambler. We wouldn't be living here if it wasn't for his incredible luck. He's just a gambler and a womaniser. What about his latest conquest — the *maid*! Won't *that* bring disgrace on the family?'

Maman's bosom heaves and I can hear her breath coming ragged and fast as she glowers at me. She bares her teeth in what could almost be a smile. 'Papa? Don't bring him into this. He is a man, they cannot help themselves.'

'That's not what you said to him last night,' I blurt between huge shuddering sobs.

'You shouldn't have been listening!' She almost screams the words at me, her head thrown back. I remember how her thick fair mane used to fall loose from its pins; her shingled hair still standing in spikes fails to carry the same majestic effect.

'How could I help listening. We all heard you,' I fling at her. 'Mary, Alicia, the littles, all of us. I should think the whole village heard you. You were like a pair of howling cats. You're loathsome, both of you.'

'Careful, Cathryn, be very careful of what you say. You're in no position to give me cheek. Listen to me, listen to what I tell you. You don't know anything about the ways of men, they're different from women. They're brutes, with the ravening natures of brutes. They have dark urges, they can't help themselves — they're naturally depraved. The sexual act is necessary to them. It's us women who must suffer their desires. By nature we're pure and wholesome, we get led astray: it's our duty to allow the men to do what they will with us, but only within the sacred bonds of marriage. Anything else is . . . foul.'

Spittle has gathered at the corners of her mouth. She sits back into her chair and regards me, her head cocked to one side, her long neck reminding me of the swans down on the lake, how they coil their necks back ready to strike. 'You,' she hisses. 'You!' she repeats, warming to her theme. 'You're no worse than an animal. An animal in its own dirt and filth. What you did is unnatural. Or perhaps,' she adds on a sudden note of hope, 'the Englishman — perhaps he forced himself on you? That's it, isn't it, Cathryn? That's what happened. Tell me that it's true — he forced you to it, didn't he? My poor darling girl.' She claws at my hand. Utterly repelled, I shake her off. I enjoy telling her,

'No, Maman, he did not force me. I gave myself to him,' and I add with great emphasis the one word, *'willingly.'* Oh, how willing I was. How shocked Maman would be if she only knew. Maman has blanched, her hand is to her mouth.

Only later do I realise that, had Bryn taken me by force, rather than me giving myself of my own free will to him, it would have been preferable to Maman's mind. This ludicrous notion strikes me so strongly that I lie in my bath and laugh so much that Mary comes running in to see if I'm all right and quite well in the head. But now, on the terrace, only a deep and bitter rage fills me as I say, between teeth clenched so hard my jaw is aching, 'I love him. I love the father of this — *baby.'* I bring the word out triumphantly. Baby. My baby, and the saying of the word lends me strength, and the rage miraculously subsides. I am amazed and utterly overwhelmed by a sudden surge of love for the tiny creature growing inside me. I am not angry. I am not afraid. This is a baby. This is

Bryn's baby; together out of love we made a new life. I am to be a mother.

'You say you gave yourself willingly? You say you love him, the father? What the devil do you know? You silly little girl!'

Once I would have been furious with her for that, now I find myself looking at her as if I am walled in with sheets of glass. Nothing she can say at this moment will hurt me. Bryn is my lover and the father of my child; my thoughts and my whole being are centred in him. Maman is an outside force; she means no more to me than a hyena howling in the desert. Knowing I have Bryn's child growing in me I feel I can face anything. I stand looking down at Maman who is sitting back in her chair. She looks up at me querulous and tired. 'What is it, Cathryn? What are you thinking?' I am thinking she looks suddenly old, but thank God she no longer looks crazed.

'Cathryn, we mustn't fight about this. We must work together.' She almost smiles and holds out her arms to me and in spite of myself, in spite of everything, I go to her and I kneel at her feet. There is no point in not doing so.

'Cathryn,' she murmurs against my hair. '*Ma chérie*, what are we to do? Do you really love this man?'

I nod my head and feel the silkiness of her skirt against my overheated cheek. It makes me think of being small, of being held in safety on Maman's lap, of being six years old again, when Nanny had beaten me and Maman had sacked her from the nursery, and I begin to cry quietly.

'Will he marry you?' Her hand moves slowly over my hair.

'I don't know.'

'Does he know about the child?' I sense the tension in her communicating itself through the pressure of her fingers on my shoulders.

I shake my head and sit back from Maman. 'How can he know about it when it's only now that I've realised myself?' Seeing my tears she hands me her handkerchief.

'How long have you known the English-man?'

I get to my feet and walk away from her, drying my eyes. 'Not very long.'

'This summer only? Last summer?' My mind swims. I think about last summer and of how I would catch glimpses of Bryn through the trees, or once at Papa's study door when he came to pay his rent. I had been on the stairs and I saw Bryn, like a shadow in the cool darkness at the end of the hall beyond the library. Mary had come through the front door, letting in a blaze of light and I saw his profile, his white teeth as he turned and smiled, but I had shrunk down against the shelter of the banisters, creeping back up to the turn in the stairs, putting my finger to my lips, warning Mary not to let anyone know I was there until he had gone. I can't believe I was too shy even to speak. Is this what they call growing up? Maman's voice is droning on.

'I told Philippe we didn't need the rent on the cottage, but he wouldn't listen to me. This is his fault.'

'It's nobody's fault.'

'No? Not even yours? How have you been able to be with him?'

I say nothing. Maman looks up at me. 'If you don't tell me, I'll ask Mary.' Her mouth has set again in a tight, straight line.

I hand back her handkerchief and say, 'No, leave Mary out of this, you mustn't ask her. Not Mary, it isn't fair.'

'But she does know?' Maman is on her feet, she is looking excited again.

'No, she doesn't know.'

'I think you're lying, Cathryn. She's helped you, hasn't she? The little minx.'

'Leave her alone, Maman, it's nothing to do with her.'

'I can always find out you know. I can beat it out of her.'

'You wouldn't!'

'Oh, but I would.' She takes a step towards the door into the house. I move in front of her, and am aware that Mary has come to stand quietly behind the heavy cream curtains; my ears follow her swift progress as she slides out of their folds and runs lightly across the dining room's parquet floor, then over the Aubusson, back onto wood, then through the servants' door to the kitchen — it sighs shut behind her.

Maman is watching me closely as I say, 'Yes, Mary knows — but does it really matter any more? The harm, if harm it is, has been done. Don't be angry with her, Maman. She only helped me because she loves me and I love her. She was only doing what she thought I wanted.'

As if it's suddenly inconsequential Maman seems to lose interest. 'God knows why you love her. You know she's one of your father's bastards? I only took her in out of pity and,' she pauses, 'and because he forced me to it. Said he'd tell the whole neighbourhood I was unnatural if I didn't.' She passes a delicate hand across her brow. The gesture irritates me. How dare she disparage Mary as she does.

'I love Mary. I don't care about who she is or where she came from. She may only be my half-sister, but I don't care. She means more to me than Babette and Olivier — she's worth ten of them,' I fling at her.

Maman sits down in her chair and reaches for my hand, pulling me down beside her. There is a wistfulness about her as she murmurs, 'Shush now, Cathryn, you're behaving like a little child, and you to be a mother yourself. My God,' she sighs, 'another bastard child, and your father has sired another one on the maid. No doubt all in good time we'll be bringing that one up too. Oh, Cathryn, what are we to do?'

We sit for a while without speaking. The air is growing cool and I shiver. Maman notices and stands up, holding out her hand to me. 'Come along, we mustn't let you catch a chill, it won't be good for the baby. You need a hot bath. We can discuss your future after supper this evening,' and she kisses my cheek lightly, her lips not quite healing the hurt where earlier her hand had wounded.

Mary
From our bedroom I can hear Cathryn laughing. She's been in the bathroom for a long time, ever since she and Maman came in from the terrace. Their voices frightened me — such anger in Maman's, and to hear it turned against Cathryn, I can't bear it. And

yet when they came in I looked down into the stairwell and saw them crossing the hall and they were arm in arm, Maman with that special look on her face that only Cathryn ever receives from her.

Cathryn is laughing again. I go and knock softly on the bathroom door. When she doesn't answer I try the handle; the heavy door swings open. Cathryn is lying up to her neck in scented water in the big claw-footed bathtub, her head's back and she's laughing. She sits up, with water streaming off her shoulders when I walk in. 'Don't look so scared.' She smiles.

'I heard you laughing — are you all right?'

'Not soft in the head? Come on in, Mary, you can soap my back if you like.' I sit on the edge of the bath as she hands me the big bar of lavender-scented soap and leans forward.

'Why were you laughing? Are you all right?' I bend over her and begin to soap her shoulders: they feel soft and slightly fleshy, warm beneath my hands. I notice there are long scratches running from her shoulders to her waist, and a curious shudder passes through me. I cannot go on looking at her, so I continue to soap her back with my head turned away.

'Am I all right? In the head — yes.' She reaches for a towel and stands up.

'I haven't finished,' I protest.

'Never mind. I'll turn into a prune if I stay in here much longer.' Her long legs, slightly heavy at the thigh and tapering to fine ankles, swing over the edge of the bath and I'm transfixed by the sight of her breasts. Always so much larger and rounder than mine they swing forward, blue-veined and heavy and, beneath them, the curve of her belly is high and rounded. I let out a small sigh. Cathryn turns her head, sees me looking and soft colour steals into her face. She drops the towel and stands defiantly with her hands above her head. 'You might as well know what a pregnant woman looks like, it'll be your turn one day.'

'Oh — Cathryn,' I whisper and my hand creeps to my mouth. 'What have you done?'

She laughs again, 'I've fucked, that's what I've done. That's what Bryn calls it and it's *wonderful!* Chuck me my clothes, there's a darling.'

'Fucked'. The word passes along all my nerve-endings. I feel heat travel swiftly over my body, an image of Bryn and Cathryn doing *that.* I shut it off and I shut off that other sensation, the one that seems to squeeze my brain. Jealousy. I go through to the dressing room and return with Cathryn's clothes.

'But Maman always said ... ' I'm dumbfounded. I begin again. 'Maman always said it was something to be endured, that the man must have his way and women must endure.'

'Yes, I know what Maman always said, but she's *wrong!* So wrong. Oh Mary, it's wonderful. It's the best thing that's ever happened to me. It makes me feel so alive I want him all over again the minute we've stopped. When I'm not with him I can't stop thinking about it, and when I am with him I can't stop thinking about it. He's eating me up and it's wonderful.' Cathryn's blonde tousled head comes out from the folds of her green silk dress and she laughs. Her dress makes a soft susurration as it slides over her rounded body. Lately, since she's known Bryn, she hasn't bothered with camisole or knickers.

I'm temporarily speechless. I trail her from the bathroom to our bedroom. Its large open spaces are filled with the golden evening light. She sits on the end of her bed and begins to brush and plait her long, curling hair. She looks like a ripening fruit; there is more than her usual languor tonight about her movements. The opalescent evening plays across all the surfaces of her face and body as I kneel on the bed behind her and reach out to take

37

over the plaiting of her hair. It feels thick and heavy under my fingers, slightly coarse like the hair of a colt. I almost feel it has a life of its own. I continue to plait her hair in silence. I can feel the heat of her body and smell the sweetness of the lavender soap mingling with her own body scent. Through the open window I can hear the sound of the sea, sweet rippling birdsong and the comforting rattle of china. Cook is laying the table in the dining room below.

I finish Cath's hair and take the silver-backed brush over to the dressing table. Cathryn's eyes sparkle as she looks across at me. 'What's the matter, sweetheart? Cat got your tongue?'

I blurt, 'But Cath, doesn't it make you a *whore* if you enjoy it?'

Her sudden giggle is infectious, 'If it does, then all I can say is Hooray for whores!' And she begins to dance around the room. As I hear the last of the bathwater gurgle down the drain, she stands still for an instant, all her usual indolence has left her. She is holding herself in, tapping her feet, holding her arms down by her sides, looking down at her own body. She reminds me of the humming tops we had when we were little, there is such energy in her. Then she darts off across the room whirling and chanting, 'Hooray for whores! Hooray for whores!' Her hair is working itself loose, breaking from its restraining plait into a huge golden halo; she's spinning till all I see is a column of green and gold and soon I've joined her and we're swooping around in a mad tarantella shouting and whooping, 'Hooray for whores! Hooray for fucking!' until we collapse in each other's arms onto Cath's soft white bed and wait for our laughter to subside.

Cath recovers first. She strokes my hair back off my hot forehead and sits up. I lie for a while looking up at her. 'What *are* you going to do, Cathy?' I ask at last. She lifts her lovely shoulders, and pulls a little *moue*. 'I don't quite know.' She replaits her hair and her mouth is set in a line I've never known before. It makes her look eerily like Maman and, now she has stopped laughing, I realise she looks strained. 'I don't know,' she repeats.

'It's terrible that you have to have a baby because of it.'

Cath's face has gone very pale. 'Maman said she's heard there are ways of stopping it. Bryn said he'd make sure there wasn't a baby.'

I think of my conversations with Olivier. 'Don't you know how?'

Her voice is hard. 'All I know is Bryn said he'd make sure. Seems he was wrong.'

'But he'll marry you, Cath?' I see the strained look deepen, the golden evening seems turned to lead and some of that lead is sitting in my stomach, but I persist.

'Would you marry him if he asked you to?'

Again she shrugs, 'If he does ask then, yes, I suppose I will.'

'Don't you love him?' I'm horrified by the thought she could do what she has done if she didn't love him.

She reaches out a hand and strokes my arm. 'Don't look so miserable, Mary, of course I love him,' she smiles. 'Of course I do.'

There's no time to say any more before the supper gong sounds through the house and Maman puts her head in at the door. She speaks as if there is nothing wrong, and looks almost her normal self. 'Come along, girls, Cook's sounded the gong twice. Have you seen Alicia anywhere?'

We shake our heads in silence, awestruck by the possibility that Maman could have heard us. She stands like a statue out on the landing and waits for us to precede her downstairs. There's no time for further talk and besides, Cook is crossing the hall on her way out for the evening. It would never do to let her hear any more scandal. Maman shoots her a steely look for daring to use the front door, but says nothing. Cook ignores her and lets herself out into the freshness of the evening, I wish I could go with her.

Olivier, Babette and Duncan haven't come in for supper. Maman is angry, I can tell, but preoccupied as she is with Cathryn and with Papa and the maid she says nothing and in silence we begin to eat. I discover I'm finding it hard to swallow. I keep thinking about Cathryn and Bryn. I keep thinking about how awful it is to have to have a baby every time you've done . . . that. But I also know that Maman's right — there are ways to stop it. I've heard the village girls talking — I've suffered Olivier's filthy talk. If only he'd talked to Cathryn instead of me, this needn't have happened. I push my soup away untouched.

Even Blanche and Edward seem to know that it would not be wise to make their usual childish babble. Just as the silence is stretching itself to a point where I think none of us will be able to utter a sound ever again, Alicia, who has arrived late at table asks, 'Maman, what is fucking? What's a whore?'

Maman lays down her soup spoon. 'I beg your pardon?' Her voice is like a whole lake freezing.

'I asked what fu — '

'I heard what you said. Go immediately to the washroom and wash your dirty little mouth out. How dare you use such words at my table!'

Alicia's eyes are huge and guileless.

'Maman, she doesn't know,' Cathryn intervenes.

'Aha! I might have known. So it was you who put such filth into her mind. Was it Cathryn who told you those words?'

Alicia nods, her short blonde curls bob against her small neck.

Cathryn explodes. 'You rat!' She grabs Alicia by her thin brown arm and shakes her till her hair flies in a mop round her small bewildered face. 'Where were you? Where were you hiding, sneaking, listening? You toad!'

'Cathryn! Let her go!' This from Maman. Cathryn drops Alicia's arm and stands up. I can see she's trembling all over, her hands are fists on the damask tablecloth.

'Sit down, Cathryn. You have not been given permission to leave the room.' Maman isn't even looking at Cathryn; she has resumed drinking her soup almost as if nothing has happened.

Cathryn sinks back into her seat. 'Where were you?' she hisses at Alicia.

'I — I was in your bedroom cupboard getting my doll. I'd put her to bed there. I heard you and Mary talking.' Alicia rubs her arm but doesn't cry. Alicia hardly ever cries. I feel ill. We hear a scuffle in the hallway and Babette, Olivier and Duncan erupt into the room talking and laughing. Their laughter stops abruptly as Maman raps her spoon on the table leaving a greasy brown stain.

I look at its ugliness on the white tablecloth and hear our mother's voice as she snaps, 'How many times have I told you not to enter a room speaking! You know I consider it the height of vulgarity. You could have been interrupting an important conversation.'

'But no one was saying a word, Maman!' grins Olivier, Babette's giggle is cut short by Maman's, 'That is hardly the point. Where on earth have you all been? How dare you be so late?'

Caught in Maman's glacial stare the three miscreants shuffle to their places. Babette and Olivier are still nudging each other. They love upsetting Maman's sense of propriety but Duncan is blushing and looks as if he would rather be somewhere else.

Olivier lifts his soup spoon, glances round the table, and decides an apology might be a good idea. 'I say, Maman. No need to take on. Sorry to be late. We were teaching Duncan to sail out in the bay, forgot the time completely.' Even he, usually so ebullient, so insensitive, is finally brought to a standstill by the atmosphere in that room. It's like a thick suffocating blanket. Olivier's fair eyebrows rise, he looks round the table at each of us in turn, his pale-lashed eyes goggling. He lowers his spoon. 'I say, what is going on?'

I feel unreal. I think this is not happening, it's like watching a play. Maman stands up, I think she looks very beautiful tonight, her eyes seem enormous in her thin face. She has played the grand lady for so long now she carries it off really well.

'Cathryn, you had better come with me to Papa's study. Babette, will you be kind enough to bring us a tray with some salads on it. The rest of you, if you are not going to finish your soup there's a cold collation on the sideboard and then, when you have finished, I'm afraid you'll have to clear away for yourselves. I have allowed Cook the evening off, and the maid . . . ' she falters, 'well, you all know about the maid.'

Olivier sniggers, but one look from Maman is sufficient to quell even him tonight.

Cathryn
I've told him. Maman said last night that I mustn't tell him. It was a terrible, terrible evening but at last I persuaded her to accept that short of being bound, gagged and

44

knocked senseless there was nothing on earth that would induce me to marry Monsieur Becque, but now she's laying plans to have me sent away. She's going to write to Cousin Ada in Canterbury. I'd been awake almost all night, and early this morning I crept out of the house and came down through the woods before anyone else was up, before anyone would miss me.

Bryn was working in his little studio at the back of the cottage. He's working on a painting of the village. He wasn't very pleased to see me at first. He hates to be interrupted whilst he's working, but he invited me in and suggested we went upstairs. I shook my head, so we sat amongst the debris of his last night's meal.

'So if it's not fucking that you want, why are you here? I thought that was why you'd come?' He looked at me in that way he has, his eyes brilliant with his want for me, his mouth, his lovely mouth, smiling, just a little. He put his hand out to touch me and it was like being touched with fire, but I pulled away.

Bryn looked at me more closely. 'What's the matter, Cathryn? You look ill. You look as if you've hardly slept.' His eyes had gone grey, like stormclouds out over the sea and his brows came together, in a deep frown.

45

I didn't know how to say the right words so I said stupidly, 'I haven't slept well, but I'm not ill.'

'Why didn't you sleep? Is there something wrong?' He put an arm round me, but again I pulled away and he looked at me with his heavy brows drawn together, and that funny little sideways lift he gets on his mouth when he's anxious. 'What's happening, Cath? Don't you want me any more? Is that why you've come — to tell me that?'

'No.' I had to swallow hard before I could continue. 'No, I've come to tell you something else.'

Bryn took my hands, not looking at me, playing with my fingers. 'Oh God. It's Monsieur Becque, isn't it. Has he proposed to you at last?'

I shook my head. 'No it's not Monsieur Becque. It never will be Monsieur Becque.'

Bryn stood up then, looking down at me, one hand on the back of his neck, the other in his pocket. He seemed to fill the space between me and the door, and blocked the light so that I could hardly see his face.

'Don't make it difficult for me. Please don't play games with me. It's someone else, isn't it? You've met someone else. Your parents have found someone more suitable than Becque. Cath, don't do this to me,

46

please.' His voice was soft and urgent. I'd never seen him like that before. There was panic in his voice as he said, 'I can't give you what anyone from your social circle can give you. If you want to live the way you're used to living, you'll have to marry someone else.' Then he reached for my hands and kissed them in turn. 'I don't want to lose you, Cath, but you know I can't offer you anything. You knew that right at the beginning. It was fun and fondness of each other at the beginning and nothing more. But I've realised in these past few weeks that I don't want to be without you in my life. I love you, Cathryn.'

I could have flown out of his studio and across the sea. I could have run for miles and miles and miles. I could have fought any number of giants. I've read in books that people's hearts sing with happiness and never believed it, but it's true. I felt so light and free and so utterly happy. He had said it. He loves me, and when I spoke the words, 'I love you too, Bryn,' and knew it to be the absolute truth, we just stood and looked and looked at each other, until I felt there was nothing I didn't know about his dear face.

Then all at once we were kissing and laughing and crying all at the same time, and Bryn held me close and safe and said above my head, 'Well, that's a relief. So why all the drama? Why are you here so early? Couldn't you wait to tell me?' He tipped my chin up and kissed my mouth again but then I couldn't kiss him back. I was so full of misery: our lovely moment spoilt so soon. I pushed him away and couldn't look at him, and my words sounded awful and clumsy. 'Bryn, there's a baby.'

'A baby! Oh Christ! Are you sure?' He looked so fierce I turned for the door, but he caught me back and held me close against his chest and he was stroking my face as he murmured, 'It's all right, Cath. It'll be all right,' but he had turned very white. 'You really are certain?'

I nodded. 'What are we going to do?'

He held me by the shoulders, his thumbs digging into my flesh and he didn't let go until I looked at him. 'I don't know, but we'll manage. I promise you, Cath. I'll not let you down.' It was very warm in the room and from outside I could just faintly hear the sea. The smell of his paints was beginning to make me feel nauseous. As he kissed me hard on the mouth, I felt his tears wet against my cheek, and I knew then how much I mean to him. If he loves me as he says he does, we'll find a way.

Before we could say any more there was a terrific knocking on the door, and without

48

any ceremony it was flung open so hard it crashed back against the wall bringing Maman, like a whirlwind with it. To his credit Bryn didn't flinch or let go of me as she began a tirade of abuse.

'Cathryn! I expected I'd find you here, you little slut! I told you to keep away from him, but no, you won't listen, will you. You won't learn. You whore! You're like a dog returning to its own mess.'

I heard Bryn gasp. I'd told him of Maman's outbursts on several occasions, but unless one has faced her in this mood, it's impossible to think anyone so outwardly regal could be like this. Bryn's hand tightened on my arm as he said, 'Madame Breton, this house may be your property, but I pay your husband a good rent for its use and for my privacy. Kindly leave.'

'Leave! Leave? How dare you, young man! If anyone is to leave it's my daughter. Cathryn, get back up to the house. I want to talk to Mr Williams in private.'

Made bold because Bryn was with me, I stood my ground. 'Whatever you've got to say, Maman, you can say it in front of me. Bryn and I have no secrets.'

I'd given her a shock; the linking of my name to his was almost more than she could stand. She stared at me and her lip trembled slightly, but it was only seconds before she was back in full flow.

'Very well, Cathryn, if you really want to stay you must be prepared for some home truths. Mr Williams,' she spat out his name as though its taste offended her, 'Mr Williams, you are a no-good. A down and out. A thorough-going reprobate! You come here for the summer on trust, and what do you do? You molest our daughter. You have, I do not doubt, thrust your attentions upon her, tricking her into believing you really cared for her. I do not suppose for one moment that she's the only young woman in this area with whom you have had associations. You have brought shame and disgrace upon our family, you have turned my beautiful, beautiful girl into a slut and you're damn lucky her Papa is not at home or he would have had you horsewhipped. Do you hear me? I find you utterly loathsome. Cathryn will be going away at the end of this week. Until then I forbid you to see her. Come along, Cathryn, we are leaving.'

Bryn was wonderful. He just stood and let her finish. He kept his hand on mine throughout the whole thing and was like a rock. A beautiful immovable rock. When Maman's shrieking finally subsided Bryn spoke. He was amazing, and so dignified.

'Madame, you are of course fully entitled to your opinion of me, but I think you do your daughter a great disservice. We are in love with each other, and if you and your husband will permit us to marry, I shall endeavour to keep Cathryn and the child safe and protected.'

'And just what do you propose to live on? I know when my husband leased the cottage to you, you made it quite plain that you only had sufficient funds for the rent through the summer and I believe you told my husband that your own parents have cut you off without a penny.'

'That's perfectly true, Madame. They don't believe in people making a living through the arts. My father's an industrial giant, or so he would have everyone believe. He wanted me to continue the family business — when I refused he turned me out without a penny. So much for his reputation as a benevolent benefactor.'

'I think you are in no position to criticise your elders and betters, sir! You have ruined our eldest daughter with your philandering ways. She was to have made a good marriage. If we were to allow her to come to you, she would be poor beyond reason.'

'Philandering ways!' I exclaimed, unable to prevent myself. 'Philandering ways? Listen to yourself, Maman, how can you say that? What about Papa and his women — *that's* philandering. At least Bryn and I love one another. At least my child will be born out of love.'

'And without money!' The door slammed behind her. Bryn kissed me and we clung to each other, but her words kept sounding in my head.

2

August 1998

Anna steps into the old library at La Roche and nods her head in silent salute to the portraits of her grandparents, Philippe and Elspeth. They look perfect hanging side by side above the fireplace. Anna was delighted when she came across them only last week, stored with several other family artifacts in a large packing case, down in the cellars, and quite unharmed. Buying La Roche, repossessing it as of her family right, has long been a dream of Anna's, and finding these treasures has set the seal on her feeling that it is only right that she should at last be living there. La Roche is her home.

Anna studies the Bretons' portraits with pleasure. Though she has only known her grandparents in their later lives, and the portraits are representations of youth, she recognised them instantly. The artist has caught Philippe's roguish air perfectly and Elspeth is a tall commanding figure, whose huge green eyes and creamy skin had been of such startling radiance as to completely

53

...vate the young Philippe.

Anna gives the rest of the room a satisfied glance. It is polished and gleaming and, on the walls between the bookcases, are further images of life at La Roche in the 1920s and 1930s. Anna has been lucky finding such a treasure trove of ancestral photographs and smaller paintings. Amongst them are the aunts and uncles she never really knew. There is Duncan sailing his yacht; Blanche and Edward and Alicia grinning like monkeys from between the bars of Elspeth's balcony. There is dear Aunt Mary as a solemn-faced little girl pushing a smiling ten-year-old Cathryn on a swing.

Anna steps closer and looks at Cathryn, her mother. There is little in her face that Anna recognises, other than the large eyes and fine flyaway eyebrows. Next to the swing photograph is one of Philippe with a huge fish on the end of a line. Next to that is one of the entire family including a woman in a white apron. They are picnicking in the bay. Anna decides the woman in the apron must be Cook; she has a vague memory of Cook as an old lady who made Anna crème brûlée when she visited La Roche as a child.

Anna walks from one picture to another — 'visiting her ancestors'. She stops in front of her favourite, a half-completed water colour of an adolescent Mary surrounded by a whirl of flying white doves. Anna stands for a moment contemplating this last image; her father's signature has been scribbled in the corner. How clever of Bryn to capture that expression, that elusive look of almost childlike wonder. Even as an elderly woman there had been times when Mary still wore that look. There are no doves now at La Roche.

Anna sighs and leaves the room, crosses the hall and, leaving the house by the garden door, walks down through the trees to the cottage on the edge of La Roche's grounds. She and Jean-Baptiste will spend all their summers here. It has taken longer than she expected to put La Roche to rights, but at last it is complete, and already she has some late bookings for autumn holidaymakers. Next summer she should begin to make enough profit to employ staff. Anna imagines with contentment the winters ahead, when she and Jean will live in the main house, repair any damage done by the summer visitors and sit in the library during the long evenings in front of a log fire.

Anna unlocks her cottage door and wanders around the neat interior, opening the heavy wooden window shutters, flinging them wide to allow the passage of soft air. The inside of the cottage is oppressive after the heat of the morning but she loves its small space. It gives her pleasure to think of her father Bryn, working in his studio there and of her mother Cathryn, slipping down through the trees to meet him. In the days when her mother must have been lovable. In the days before her mother changed. Anna likes to think of Mary keeping guard, making sure that Elspeth the matriarch didn't know, until the inevitable happened and all hell was let loose, on the tea terrace up at the main house. It must have been a terrible afternoon, all those years ago.

Anna stops in the act of straightening a cushion, and thinks about her morning. She has spent much of it working in the kitchen garden, the last part of the house and grounds to be tackled. Everything else is neat and well ordered. Though many of the barns and outhouses have been sold off, the house and its grounds have been well restored to the loveliness of Philippe and Elspeth's heyday. With Jean-Baptiste's help Anna will harvest this year's small crop and clear more ground ready for next summer. It will be good to provide her paying guests with fresh produce. At fifty-nine, Jean Baptiste is vigorous and strong. His ancestors and her ancestors worked together and some of them lived together; and some slept together. Jean even has a look of Grandfather Philippe's portrait.

Harvesting onions under the hot sun and close to the earth, Anna had found herself thinking about her own adult daughter, Francesca. Anna's mind had travelled, like the rhythm of her work moving forwards and back, up and down the rows, up and down the years. Francesca's name and Francesca's voice beat in Anna's head and she cursed under her breath, and broke off from her work to look around her. Jean has never met her daughter Francesca.

Anna watched Jean for a while where he was working peacefully and methodically, busy at the other end of the garden. She would not think about Francesca. She would think instead about Philippe and Elspeth. Anna knows that an ancestor sold onions and that Philippe, whose origins he preferred to keep a little obscure, would rather that people had not known. Elspeth on the other hand had been proud, emphasising that Philippe had risen to dizzy heights of wealth from nothing; she would tell the story and spread her hands in what she liked to think of as a Gallic gesture, though she herself came from Canterbury and had met Philippe on a day's excursion to the races. Race courses were places where Philippe was always happy to go, and mostly even happier when he returned. One way or another, Philippe's was a success story.

With the sun beating on her back, Anna thought about Cathryn and Bryn, and about her own brother, Greg. She thought about her love for Jean, a relative and yet not so close as to cause any kind of a scandal in the village, or anywhere else in her world, because of her decision to live with him. However, when her mind began to wander again unchecked, she dragged her attention back to concentrate with an avid thoroughness on the onions as she pulled each one from the cracked orange earth. Deliberately she observed the minutiae, the onions' skins like pearled silk, not paper. Labour's sweat salt had beaded her upper lip and palms, as her working fingers laid the long, dry, grey stalks to plait into short, thick ropes. This was the first harvest. She had read how to plant but not how to plait the onions. Where had this knowledge come from? It seemed to her a kind of instinct, a sixth sense.

Anna knows that as a boy, Jean had met Greg, such a very long time ago. She knows they met out in New Zealand, and that Jean's father and Greg had worked together on her Uncle Olivier's farm out there. Then Greg had left as abruptly as he had arrived. Anna also knows that Jean remembers the shock that reverberated around the farm after the tragic news of Greg's death filtered through from England. Anna and Jean had talked of it soon after they met. Anna knows too that, though Jean was only a nine-year-old child at the time, he remembers vividly the tall auburn-haired young man, the paleness of his skin in such contrast to his hair, Jean has told her he was fascinated by Greg's beauty. Anna wiped the back of her hand across her eyes and forced her thoughts back to the vegetable garden.

Only a few days ago, working side by side in the garden with Jean, Anna had thought she might be in paradise. Today she was less sure. Paradise might after all be only an illusion. Last night she had received a telephone call from her daughter. She had thought Francesca was in America when in fact she was back in England. Francesca had been at her most brittle and dangerous. With hardly any preliminary greeting she had launched straight into an attack.

'Am I right in thinking that your lovely granddaughter, my darling child Megan, is coming out to France?'

'You know perfectly well that Megan's coming next week, Francesca. Are you all right? Your voice sounds very hoarse.'

Francesca had been impatient. 'I'm fine, don't fuss. Megan's coming for an exhibition, isn't she? She's putting on one of her exhibitions?'

Already Francesca had eroded Anna's patience. 'Yes, you know that perfectly well too.'

'Is she intending to stay at La Roche?'

In spite of herself Anna's spirits lifted. It might, perhaps, be good to see Francesca after so long apart. 'Did you want to come too, darling? Is this what this is all about?'

'All what's about?' Francesca's terse voice was not encouraging.

'All this hinting and not saying what's on your mind. I wish you'd tell me if you want to come. You know you're always welcome.'

'No, Mum, I don't know that I am welcome. I never know that I'm welcome. All I know is Meg's always been more welcome than me.'

Anna had denied the truth. 'That simply isn't true, Frankie, and you know it.'

'Well, I don't want to come. I just want to be sure Megan is actually going to stay with you at La Roche.'

'Yes, she is.'

'Good, then I'll send my present to Jean with her, shall I?'

Anna had been surprised and touched.

60

'That's very kind of you, dear. Why are you sending him a present?'

'Just to welcome him officially as your lover. He has moved in with you now, hasn't he?'

Anna had sighed. 'Again, you know perfectly well that he has. He moved in last month.'

'And you're really truly happy?'

Anna was puzzled. It was so uncharacteristic of Francesca to care about her welfare. 'Would you mind telling me what all this is about?' she demanded. 'I'm not in the mood for your silly games.'

Francesca had laughed, a short laugh with little mirth in it, cut short by a barking cough. When she was able to speak again she said, 'It's not a game, Mum. This is for real. Shall I tell you what I'm sending Jean? I'm sending Greg's diary. I've owned it for a long time, and now I think it's time someone else had it.'

'His diary? I didn't know — '

'What — that it still existed? Well, unfortunate as it may seem, it does exist. It was in Mary's attic. I think Jean may find it makes interesting reading, don't you?' And Francesca's receiver had been replaced before Anna could reply.

Today Anna found it difficult to be with Jean. She had worked well away from him, hoping he would not notice her distress. She supposed that if anyone was going to spoil her present happiness, it was only right and fitting that it should be Francesca. It was, after all, no more or less than she deserved. What was the saying? Pigeons come home to roost. Well, Francesca had told her, in one brief phone call, that Megan would be bringing a few of those 'pigeons' with her. The problem now was what to do about them.

At the end of the morning Anna had straightened her back, easing herself upright. Small, like her grandfather Philippe, much smaller than her mother Cathryn had been, a slightly plump but shapely figure in her baggy shorts and old sun-bleached T-shirt, Anna lifted her head and smiled at Jean-Baptiste. Sweat-streaked, in an old blue singlet, he raised a lazy earth-covered hand, waving and returning her smile with a questioning smile of his own, his finely moulded mouth lifting at the corners, giving his face an almost Puckish expression. Anna's reticence during the morning had been puzzling and her smile couldn't hide something self-absorbed in her eyes. She had been strange and awkward with him since Francesca's call. He wished Anna would tell him what had been said. When she did meet his gaze, Jean was intensely aware of her watching him carefully, almost sorrowfully.

Anna bent back again to the onions and beneath her wide-brimmed hat flies buzzed and the humid air carried the scent of pine resin. As Anna lifted the next bulging onion globes against her bare browned legs Jean crossed the garden to her side and kissed her beneath her hat. She had allowed herself to lean into his hand as he stroked her neck, sliding up to the silvery curls at the nape and back round to the hollow between her breasts. His pink, sharp tongue had said, 'I love you,' as he bent to kiss her. Paradise was precious.

★ ★ ★

Anna walks now into the kitchen and makes a pot of tea. Jean will be in from the garden soon. He will be thirsty — he enjoys the English habit of a cup of tea. Megan will be here next week, and please God let everything be well.

3

La Roche
July 18, 1998

Dearest Megan,

You won't believe it. I've met a relative! Just when I thought there were hardly any of us left. He's called Jean-Baptiste Antoine. I'd been talking with the painters one day in April and decided to take tea on the little terrace at the back of the house. It's where we had tea when we were children. After the heat of the day it's such a lovely place to be. You can see all the way down to the sea and the scent of the pines is all around. It's very, very hot out here but so beautiful. I want you to see it all. I want you to know what La Roche is and has been to all of us. You really must come and visit us when you have your exhibition next month — August will be scorching — I hope you can stand the heat.

However, I digress! I was just sitting having a moment or two to myself when Jean walked onto the terrace. Naturally, I was completely flustered. You may think,

64

'Aha! Gran and her vanity!' and I did look a mess — hair just anywhere and probably quite sweat-streaked, too — but to tell the truth I was quite scared by the arrival of this stranger . . . I blustered a bit; 'How the hell did you get in?' I said, very indignant and in my best French. I think he realised he'd startled me, because he was extremely courteous and apologised and shook my hand, saying, 'I lived here for a while as a teenager. I was the gardener's son when the house was part of a girls' school.' And then, Oh Megan, this is the good bit! He said. 'My grandfather owned the house at one time — you may have heard of him, and we said together, 'His name was Philippe Breton.'

You may call me a silly old fool, but it was like coming home meeting Jean. He even looks a bit like Grandpa Philippe. Same dark curly hair, greying at the temples, same brown eyes which are usually 'merry' — a word not often used but exactly right for Jean. Laughter lines — a wide mouth. Not quite conventionally handsome, the nose a little too long, the white teeth just a little crooked. As you've probably guessed, another of the old cad's early conquests gave birth to Jean's father. She was a married woman and managed to pass the baby off as her husband's. It was only when her husband died and she was an old lady that she told Jean's father the truth about his parentage and Jean's father tried to lay a claim to La Roche, but of course it had been sold off by then and Grandpa Philippe would have nothing to do with Jean's father, though apparently he did later pay for Jean's education in a sort of belated sense of duty.

I hope you're following all this! I sometimes wonder how many more relatives there are in this part of France! I keep expecting them to crawl out of the woodwork. Philippe was certainly a busy man.

Anna stops writing and wonders how she can so condemn the man who was her grandfather. In comparison with herself, surely Philippe lived a fairly blameless life. She longs to tear down all the pretence and to spell out the truth about Cathryn, about herself, about Francesca, but she knows she cannot. It would be to tear down the whole structure of her life so she bites her lip and continues the letter.

Anyway, the upshot of our meeting was that Jean and I have been together every day, as often as we can, ever since, and last night over supper we agreed to turn La Roche into a partnership. It's been proving almost too much for me on my own, but with Jean's help it will be a going concern far sooner.

'Why am I lying to myself!' Again she puts down her pen and gazes out of the window. *Because you always do,* says her conscience. She sighs and presses her fingers to her temples before picking up the pen again and continuing the letter.

I have a confession to make — I'm head over heels in love with Jean, and apparently he is with me! I hope you understand, darling Megan, it's been a long two years without anyone, Millie and Leo would understand, of that I am totally convinced. They were two of the most generous people I ever knew and it is time I moved on and put the past to rest.

Good luck with the exhibition, it sounds very exciting. I'm longing to see it. Please say you'll come and stay when you're over here.

Love and kisses, Anna — Gran,

PS I've written to your mother too.

Love — A.

Ma came round last night like an avenging angel, bringing almost the final piece of the jigsaw. It came as no real surprise, I think I've known since I was fourteen and, if there is such a thing as tribal memory I probably knew before then. Ma didn't expect me to read the diary, just to deliver it. She's a coward. If it matters so much to her, why didn't she do it last time she met up with Granny Anna? She'd packed the diary carefully and built the whole thing up into such a big mystery it made me suspicious. So when she'd gone I opened the package and read what was inside and now I don't know what to do. All I can think of is the tragedy of those poor young people. Whatever happened happened, and nothing now will ever undo that. Anna is still Anna and I still love her and so should Ma. Anna has been to hell and back for her.

Ma's a wreck, all Indian silk scarves and clanking bangles, reeks of cigarettes or possibly even weed under all that makeup and perfume, had her latest in tow, he's quite a bit younger than her. She's coughing a lot and has lost some weight. She doesn't take enough care of herself.

Still I'd like to paint her sometime, her face is so interesting. So utterly lived in. There are times when she actually bears an uncanny resemblance to Mary, I think it's the dark hair and skin, but those eyes! I've never known eyes quite like them. Mary used to say they were like Bryn's.

I remember thinking at Mary's funeral how strange it was, that of all that huge family there was only Anna and Millie left. That was when Millie and Anna and Leo all shared their lives in the big house up at Clifton. To hell with Ma and her scheming. Anna deserves some happiness.

Anna
It's early evening. Jean and I have changed our clothes and eaten our meal — omelettes and salad again in the garden. I should make more effort, we both should, but it suits us and it's become our habit to sit out on most evenings watching the bats beginning to hunt and listening to La Roche's night sounds. A citronella candle burns low on the table between us, only just keeping mosquitoes at bay. The moon is rising over the sea and the air is soft; the perfume of night-scented stocks and tobacco plants mingles with the scent of the candle. Beyond the garden gate the larger

69

trees cast huge inky shadows and the main house is hidden from view by the night. The earth gives out the heat and scent of the day and somewhere an owl calls. This should be bliss.

'Anna, this is glorious.' Jean stretches luxuriously and reaches for his cigarettes, offering me one but I shake my head as I begin clearing the table.

'I'll do that when we've had coffee.' Jean places a large restraining hand over mine. I feel the hardness of his fingers. I don't want to lose him. He looks into my face. I wonder how much it reveals.

'What's the matter, Anna?'

'Nothing.'

'You've been quiet all day. Was it Francesca last night? She upset you, didn't she? I knew when you came from the phone.'

'It's all right, Jean, it's nothing.'

'Then perhaps I'll make some coffee.' He walks lightly away into the house. He knows I've had a difficult relationship with Francesca; I know he hopes one day I'll be able to talk about it. I have hoped so too. Jean is a patient man. By the time he returns I have fought for and regained my composure and we go on making desultory conversation.

Jean stirs his coffee. 'I've left the sitting-room light on to give us some light out

70

here, but I can still hardly see you. Shall we go in?'

'Soon. It's peaceful out here.'

'It's peaceful in the house.'

'I was just thinking whilst you made the coffee, how lucky I am living here. I've always felt safe here.'

'Safe?' Jean looks at me quizzically, he's so quick, so intuitive. 'Why wouldn't you be safe?'

That was foolish. I try a shrug and sip my coffee. 'No reason, it was a silly thing to say. I'm tired — I think I may go to bed soon.'

'Alone again?'

'I'm sorry, Jean. Do you mind very much if we don't tonight?'

'Yes,' he grins. 'But it will be all the better for waiting. Samuel will keep me company.'

'Samuel?'

'I started reading Samuel Pepys last night when you'd gone to bed.'

'Really? In English, or French?'

'English. I thought it may improve my vocabulary.'

I'm glad of the opportunity to laugh. Jean's English is superb. 'You don't need your vocabulary improving. Are you enjoying it?'

'It's absolutely fascinating. I wonder if, when Pepys wrote it, he guessed that people would be reading his diary over three hundred years later. I don't suppose many people write diaries with that end in view!'

It's like a slap in the face. I get to my feet. I have to put some space between us. I begin gathering plates together, not looking at Jean, clattering knives and forks to the ground. 'Damn!'

Jean stoops to pick up the fallen cutlery. I don't want him to touch me; I don't want him to know how much I'm trembling. 'Steady, Anna, it's all right. It's only a bit of cutlery, there's nothing broken.'

'No. There's nothing broken.' *Not yet.* I brush past the table, the candle gutters and goes out and I almost run into the house, knowing I've left Jean staring after me. Jean collects the debris from the meal and follows me indoors.

'Anna, are you okay? Where are you?' He walks into the kitchen and I reach out and take the pile of dirty dishes from him. I'm still trembling.

'I'm sorry, Jean. I don't know what happened out there, I suppose I'm a bit het up. Francesca . . . Francesca said something last night . . . and I think perhaps Megan shouldn't come here after all.'

'But why, *chérie*? You love Megan.' Jean looks at me carefully. He stands very close and reaches out a muscular arm. His hand

72

takes one of mine and strokes it; he turns it and kisses each of my fingers. When I don't respond he drops my hand. 'Are you okay?' he asks again and I hear the hurt in his voice.

'Yes, I'm fine. Just a bit tired.' I smile and Jean reaches for me and draws me to him.

'Perhaps you think your granddaughter won't like an ugly old bear like me?' he murmurs against my neck. With an effort of will I concentrate on Jean. Francesca and her odious little gift will not come between us. Somehow I'll talk to Megan. I'll think of something. Haven't I dealt with worse crises than this before? If I hadn't, there would be no diary. I kiss Jean full on the mouth. He pulls back and looks at me wide-eyed.

'So! You're feeling better?' There is relief and tenderness in his voice. 'I think your daughter is a naughty girl to make her maman so *distraite*.'

'She's hardly a girl, and she should know better! I don't want to think about Frankie just now.' I reach up and kiss Jean again.

'Or Megan?' His strong brown hand creeps inside my sweater.

'Or Megan.'

'So everything is all right now and you want her to come here?'

'Jean, be quiet, don't talk.'

'I just wanted to know.' His lips are against my ear.

'I just need a few early nights and I'll be fine.'

'Anna, don't tease. Are we going to make love or not?'

'We're going to make love and then I'm going to bed.'

Jean's dark eyebrows lift. 'Then you're going to bed. After?' and I smile, thinking this is how things should be. It's how things have been since I met Jean — easy, light-hearted and affectionate. How can I deny him, yet as his hand slides along my shoulders and plays with my hair I sense Jean is still unsure if this is what I really want, my mood has apparently changed so suddenly. Dear Jean, he knows there is a great deal in my past that I have not told him. He knows the things I have chosen to tell him, and I'm certain he guesses some of the things I have not told him, but he does not know everything. He lives so wholeheartedly in the present. If only I could learn to live that way too. I have been trying. He murmurs, against my mouth, 'Why bother about bed!'

Holding each other we stumble through the kitchen and into the living room, unfastening each other's clothing as we go, until we're both naked. We roll together onto the softness of the couch which receives and accommodates us.

As Jean lowers his strong stocky body to meet mine, and we begin to move together I think briefly of Francesca's phone call before all thought is obliterated and I sink gratefully into the place where I am nothing and there is no thought. The scent of the flowers in the room is all that haunts the margins of my mind.

★ ★ ★

Much later Jean, sleeping soundly beside Anna in their wide bed, fails to wake when she starts from a dream with Greg's name on her lips, but in the morning's early hours the sound of Anna sobbing in her sleep rouses him and leaves him troubled.

4

Cathryn

I keep dreaming of endings. I see Mary
turning away from me. I see myself falling
into the sea from a great height. I see Bryn
receding into the distance and, when a new
day begins, I am uneasy for half the morning.
Leaving La Roche was every bit as hard as I
expected it to be. I am travelling into the
unknown; it's the end of an era, almost the
end of a decade. Soon it will be autumn, then
Christmas in a foreign land and what will
1930 bring trailing in its wake? I must remain
optimistic. La Roche is not the only place in
the world where I can be happy.

Leaving La Roche with Bryn, I could
hardly bear to look at Mary. She ran beside
the car for as long as she could, all the way
down the drive, but of course at last the car
outpaced her and she was left behind and
then I couldn't bear to look any more, and I
couldn't talk to Bryn, or Papa. I was crying so
much. When Papa saw us off on the train I
cried all over again. I must have looked such
a wreck. I cried almost all the way to Paris,
but Bryn was lovely and very patient and

didn't mind that some of the other passengers were staring at us. In fact, he told one nosy old woman to mind her own business and that I was his wife and in an emotional state because of my 'interesting condition'; and he winked at me and looked so comical I couldn't help laughing because of the expression on the old besom's face.

Paris was good — it always is good, but I'm so tired and feel so sick so much of the time that I'm afraid a lot of it was wasted on me. Bryn enjoyed it, but some nights he went out and I just went to bed. He said he didn't mind and I believe him. He sometimes had too much to drink, but I don't care. At least I know he's not chasing other women. How do I know? Because I trust Bryn and because Papa has given me such good lessons in how to recognise a man who's up to no good.

Maman didn't agree with it, Bryn didn't really want to take it, but it was Papa who gave us enough money for a small honeymoon and I'm so glad that he did. Papa was right — a holiday was what I needed after the past weeks with Maman alternately ranting and raving at me or being sentimentally loving and suffocating.

Dear Papa has been so good and kind. Bryn had insisted that he should be the one to tell Papa about us, and he told me to come

77

to him the moment Papa returned from his jaunt with the maid. Bryn said it was important that he told Papa about the baby before Maman could have her say and poison Papa against us, but I thought we should tell Papa together. Bryn had laughed and said, 'Cath! You don't really think he'd horsewhip me, do you? It's a bit old fashioned even for your parents, isn't it?'

I had laughed too, but a whisper of doubt clung tight enough to make us both afraid when we went to Papa's study door. I had been in the rose garden when I heard a car coming down the drive. I got up and hurried round the side of the house in time to see a car I didn't recognise pull up, throwing gravel out from under its large wheels. Papa climbed out, looking terrible — grey, haggard and exhausted. Goodness knows what kind of a life the maid had been leading him. He was embarrassed when he saw me, but I ran to him and hugged him and said I was glad he was home. He embraced me and kissed me and called me his good girl and then I began to cry.

Papa slipped an arm round my waist and walked me towards the front door, saying, 'Now, Cathryn, what is all this about? You mustn't cry about your Papa who is just a silly old fool and should know better than to go wandering off. Come along, *chérie*, wipe your eyes. It's all right, I'm home now. Come and look at Papa's new car — isn't it fine? I got it from a friend in Toulon.' He took a step back towards the car, some of the old spark beginning to shine in his eyes as he said, 'Well, actually I won it.'

That made me cry all the more. Dear, silly Papa — will he never stop? 'Oh Papa!' I wailed, 'I love you, Papa.'

'Yes, yes, my darling and I love you.' He patted my arm and handed me a clean white handkerchief from his trouser pocket. When I still could not stop crying he looked sharply towards Maman's window. 'What's the matter, Cath? Has your mother been unkind to you?'

I hesitated and couldn't help hanging my head, but he lifted my chin and made me look at him. 'Cath, tell me what's been happening. Where is everyone else?'

My heart was beginning to bang hard under my ribs. I knew now was the moment to tell Papa about the baby or lose the opportunity altogether. My mind raced. Should I tell him without Bryn? No, I mustn't, or Papa would think Bryn a coward, and Bryn would be angry with me. So I blurted, 'Papa, everyone else is out, they're fishing and sailing and visiting, but please,

79

Papa, go to your study and wait for me there. Please.'

'But, Cathryn . . . ' he had begun to protest but I cut in, 'Please, Papa, it's very important. Indulge me a little.' I left him staring after me and ran from him, down through the trees to Bryn's cottage. I prayed, *Please let him be indoors and not out somewhere painting.* I ran through the tangle of little garden at the front of the cottage and pounded on the door, Bryn's head appeared from the bedroom window above me.

'Come down, Bryn, Papa's back!' I called up to him. His head disappeared and a moment later he was standing beside me, paintstained and wild-haired, 'You can't go looking like that!' I gasped.

Bryn shrugged, 'Why not? It's what I look like.'

'But, Bryn, it won't help us.' I was almost frantic.

'No? Perhaps you're right.' He went back inside and I followed, hanging about in the studio, looking out at the light over the sea. I could hear Bryn moving about overhead. I willed him to hurry, but he didn't seem to feel my urgency.

He came into the room, looking clean in a faded shirt and with his hair brushed. He was carrying a half-finished water colour and asked, 'What do you think of this?'

I shouted, 'Bryn, for God's sake! I haven't got time to look at that now. We must go and see Papa, before Maman and the others get back.' But he looked so crestfallen I took the painting from him, and found I was looking at a likeness of Mary. She was on the terrace, with a swirl of doves lifting round her upturned face. He'd made her almost pretty. I felt a sudden stab of jealousy, gone as soon as it arrived. He'd never painted me. He was looking at me curiously. 'What's the matter, Cathy?'

'You've never painted me.' I put the painting down. Bryn caught me by the shoulders, laughed and kissed me. 'Too busy doing other things,' he murmured against my face, his hands moving down over my back to my thighs. I pushed him away. I'd never felt angry with him before; it was a new feeling. It was a surprise, and a shock. I flashed at him, 'It's precisely because of 'other things' we've got to see Papa. You're scared of him, aren't you! That's why you're making all these delays.' I hated myself. I knew I sounded like Maman. Bryn stepped away and stared at me, his face like stone.

'No. I'm not scared, Cathryn. I just love you and I wanted to show you the picture because I want to share things with you.

That's why we want to marry each other, isn't it?'

'I suppose so. That and because there's a baby.' Why couldn't I stop? I didn't mean it. I was hurting him. I could see it in his eyes and his hand was at his mouth.

'Stop it, Cath. Don't do this.'

'Do what?' I snarled. Was I enjoying the fight? I seemed to be, it was making me feel powerful.

'Don't be fierce like this, Cath. It isn't right. We love each other.'

I looked at him standing in his studio, surrounded by his paints and his paintings, canvases from the summer's work stacked against the wall, the familiar smell of the paints rising round us. He wasn't looking at me, he was looking at his painting of Mary. Already he had forgotten we were fighting; already he was preoccupied with his work. Irritation gave way to my love for him and my anger drained away. I touched his sleeve.

'Shall we go now and tell Papa?'

Bryn nodded and smiled as he kissed my forehead as if I was a child, his lips soft and warm against my skin. We held hands, saying little, all the way to the house, and by the time we reached Papa's study neither of us was feeling very brave. Bryn kissed me and whispered, 'I'll go in first. You come in when I call you.'

'Are you sure?'

'Quite sure.' He squeezed my hand, knocked on Papa's study door and then Papa's call, 'Come in, Cathryn,' was cut short by Bryn's disappearance into the room and the door closed behind him.

I pressed my ear to the heavy wooden panelling, but it was too thick to hear anything clearly, not even the two men's intonation. I cursed and paced up and down the hall straining to hear the family's return, feeling sick but whether from nerves or because of the baby I wasn't sure. I stopped pacing and slid down the wall with my back against it, my feet braced against the door. Suddenly the door opened and Papa was gazing down at me. He didn't look angry, he looked sad. His dark eyes were so sad I wanted to cry.

'Papa?'

'Cath. You had better come into the study.' His voice was quiet, resigned. I'd rather he had been angry; at least with anger I would have had something to fight against, but this sorrow was a terrible thing. He bent down, held out his hand and helped me to my feet. I straightened my dress, aware of its tightness across my breasts, its pull against my belly.

Papa's eyes flickered over me and he turned away into his study saying, 'Come in and sit down. Close the door. There's a good girl.'

I wanted to run after him and catch at his coat. I wanted him to smile at me and give me bonbons and call me his silly pet names. I wanted to be just me and Papa walking by the sea, and for there to be no one and nothing to come between us. I had transgressed. Childhood was behind me. I sat down.

Bryn, who had risen to his feet when I came into the room, was sitting now with his back to the tall open window. The light behind him was so bright I could not read his expression. Papa sat behind his desk between us, one hand cupping his chin, his fingers stroking his little short beard and looking all the time from one to the other of us. None of us spoke. Then Papa said, 'Well, Cathryn. Bryn has told me the facts of the way things are between you.' I held my breath. Papa had said, 'Bryn', not 'Mr Williams'.

'So, Cathryn. It's true — there is to be a baby. I can see no reason why Bryn should lie about that. Is it also true that you love Bryn?'

'Yes, Papa.'

'You don't sound very sure. What if I was to send him away from here? Order him off? Perhaps even pay him never to come here again. What then?'

'Sir!' 'Papa!' We were both on our feet. For the first time since Papa had called me into the room he smiled.

'Aha! Both offended and on the defensive. Good. I can see neither of you is taking this lightly. Sit down, both of you. Please, Bryn, don't be offended. I had to know how you really feel about my girl. Darling Cathy, forgive me for my little ruse. I had to find out if you really truly love Bryn.'

'Oh Papa, I do. He's wonderful.'

Papa's eyebrows rose. 'Wonderful, you say! I don't know about that. Is it wonderful to give a woman a baby before one marries her?' There was an uneasy silence. Papa stood up and came round from behind his desk, his hands in his pockets. 'Bryn.'

'Sir?'

'Would you give me a moment or two alone with my daughter. I will send her out to you presently. You may wait in the little orchard at this side of the house if you wish — no one will see you there. No one ever uses it but me.' Papa indicated the long window.

'Do I climb out?'

Papa nodded. 'I often do, if I do not wish to be observed,' and, as he smiled at Bryn, I felt my eyes widen.

Bryn left, turning to look anxiously at me

before stepping out over the low windowsill, and loping lightly out of sight. Then Papa came across to me and sat holding my hands. 'So, Cathryn. You do love him. But will he make you happy?'

'Don't you like him, Papa?'

'I like him very much, though God knows I should have had him shot for what he's done to you.'

'But Papa, he hasn't *done* anything to me. I acquiesced.'

Papa looked at me sharply, and some of the sadness left his eyes as he began to laugh. 'Cathryn! If your Maman heard you say that she would make you wash out your mouth.'

'Yes, Papa.'

'Do not be saucy with me, Cathryn. Your Maman does know about the child?'

I nodded.

'And she is not happy?'

'Papa, you do not have to ask.'

He stood up and paced the room. 'No, I do not have to ask and you have still not answered my question. Does this man, Bryn, make you happy?'

'Oh yes, Papa. Very happy.'

'Happy enough to leave here and live far away with him?'

I looked at the sunlight flooding the peaceful familiar room, Papa, small and very dear to me and beginning to put on weight. He was lighting his pipe; his hands shielding the match shook slightly, he was not looking directly at me. 'You do realise you will not be able to live here?'

'Not live here? Why not, Papa? Bryn and I could move into the cottage together.' Even as I said it I knew it was impossible.

'No, Cathryn, you could not and I think you know why you could not.' Still he wasn't looking at me. He drew on his pipe and tipped his face up to the ceiling, I watched in horror as two tears slid from under his lowered lashes. 'You could not live here, Cathryn, my darling, because of . . . ' he stopped speaking.

'Maman? Scandal? Gossips talking about me?'

'All of that, and more. Cathryn, darling girl, you will have to go away from here. I think you will have to live in England and I think that will be hard for you to do.'

A kind of terror gripped me. I felt cold all over. 'No, Papa! You can't make us do that. We've done nothing wrong. It would be like a punishment. It would be like exile. We could live elsewhere in France.'

'No, Cathryn.' Papa wiped his eyes with one of his fine linen handkerchiefs, but still there were tears. Papa blew his nose hard before he continued, speaking quietly, 'You could not live in France. Bryn has little money, but he does have a small house in England. It will be a roof over your heads.'

My brain whirled. A small house? How small? Where was it? What did it look like? Were there servants? I put a hand to my head. But Papa took it down and held it, looking into my face, saying, 'Listen to me, Cathy. If you really love Bryn and he loves you, then it will be all right. It will be better than all right.'

I felt frantic. I tried again. 'Papa, tell me this is another test to prove I love him.'

He shook his head. 'No, darling, it is not a test and I want you to know it is not easy for me either. But it is necessary and we must hold onto the main factor in all of this and that is that you and Bryn do love one another. Of that I have no doubt. Let us hope and pray that it is enough to bring you through some of the difficult times ahead. Alas! I am sure you realise marriage is not always an easy thing. Not an easy thing at all.' He sighed and his smile this time did not reach his eyes but he said, 'Come along, little one. You mustn't look so crestfallen. We'll dry our eyes and we shall make the most of this. You must let Papa spoil you before you leave. You won't be going for ever. Perhaps one day you will be able to come back, when all the fuss has died down.'

Papa drew me to my feet and we stood by the window with our arms around each other's waists and all the time I was looking at the bright garden, but I wasn't seeing it.

★   ★   ★

Now we're here in Calais and tomorrow we're really leaving. I'm going to miss France so much. I shan't miss Maman, but I will miss Mary and the littles. I shall miss Papa terribly, too, even with all his faults. I just thank God I inherited some of Maman's careful ways. Papa gave me money for clothes and wanted me to spend it all on extravagances like hats but I told him, where Bryn and I are going to live there'll be precious little use for hats, and I shall have to save the money until I see just what I will need. Bryn doesn't really like the fact that Papa has paid for so much, but under the circumstances he knows that we have few choices, and I do rejoice that he's stayed by me through all this.

It wasn't the same for the maid. She hasn't got a man at all now, and when her baby's born she won't have that either. Thank God Papa returned from his madness with her.

He'll save Mary from some of Maman's worst excesses; he'll stop her from turning Mary into a drudge. Papa's such a strange mix of good and bad. He's persuaded, if that's the right word to use for the kind of hideous blackmail he's indulged in, he's persuaded Maman to take on the maid's child when it's born.

It was revolting. The three of us were together on the terrace and I was reading. I think they'd almost forgotten I was there. The others were all out on the beach. I sometimes think Maman is completely crazy, but Papa pointed out that if the baby isn't taken in it will grow up as a bastard with no money to its name. Maman yelled at him that she thought it wouldn't be such a bad thing, especially as it's the child of a bastard. Papa shouted at her that if she would only give him the gratification he wanted he wouldn't need to go looking anywhere else and I tried to leave the terrace, but Maman screamed at me to stay where I was because I might as well know what married life was all about. Then Papa said I could go if I wanted to, but I could still hear them from down in the rose garden. Papa was telling Maman that, even if she wouldn't take the child in, he would still oversee its growing up and in the end Maman said the only way she'd take it in would be if

Papa promised to send the maid right away and she'll never be spoken of again. So that's what will happen, because that's what's been decided. And the maid? She gets no say at all in the matter. Her baby will be taken away from her. She won't know the rabbity feel of its new little limbs, or the softness of its hair, or the tight grasp of its tiny fingers. They'll all be taken away from her.

The day after Maman and Papa's fight was my wedding day. A quick ceremony. Not the fairytale I always imagined. Mary was my only bridesmaid. Papa gave me away and Bryn's best man was a local fisherman he sometimes goes drinking with.

I wore my old cream silk dress, and some cream and pink roses from the garden in my hair. Papa wanted to buy me something new, but I wanted to wear the dress because it's what I wore the first time I saw Bryn. The littles weren't allowed to come, though Alicia and Duncan begged and begged to be allowed, and Maman didn't come because she claimed she's too exhausted. I'd always thought when I was a little girl, that Maman would be so interested in my dress and arranging flowers and all the things a girl dreams about, bridesmaids and tulle by the yard, all that sort of thing and a mother who cries elegantly into lace hankies. So when she didn't come to the church I didn't know whether to be pleased or sad. She could have ruined the day by being there, like some great dark cloud sitting on my sunshine. But without her it felt so odd, so — she managed to steal some of my happiness after all.

Olivier and Babette chose to be out for the day, probably with Olivier's disreputable 'drinking and copulating friends' as Mary calls them. It would not surprise me; those two are a law to themselves nowadays. There was no wedding feast arranged so Papa, Bryn, Mary and I went back to the cottage and Bryn gave Mary the half-finished picture of her and laughed when she blushed and stammered her thanks. He said, 'Mary, it's usual to give the bridesmaid a gift. I only wish it could have been more,' and her eyes were shining as if he'd given her a gold bracelet, or something really expensive. She's so sweet and so easily satisfied. Papa looked at the painting and said he thought it was excellent, but perhaps for the time being it should be kept out of Maman's sight. Then we all went out to the beach and Bryn made a fire and we cooked the sardines that were a wedding gift from the fisherman. We ate with our fingers and drank a lot of wine and afterwards we danced, Papa had brought the gramophone down from the house. So Mary and Papa were our first guests and it was all the wedding feast I wanted. Maman won't get the better of me. Bryn and I don't need any one else, we're happy.

In the past weeks Babette has been courted by Monsieur Becque. He has been coming to the house when I have been out. If he knew what Babette was really like he wouldn't touch her with a barge pole. Maman had been able to inform Monsieur of my whereabouts so we have not had the embarrassment of meeting each other. Olivier is not happy about Babette and Monsieur Becque, and I'm not at all sure that Babette is, if she were more honest. She hates him almost as much as I do but wants her hands on his money. Olivier sulks and is talking of emigrating to New Zealand; he says there's good money to be made out there but Maman and Papa won't hear of it, at least until he's twenty-one and they're talking of sending him to university in England.

Papa was right. Bryn and I have no choice but to live in England. Papa has settled some money on us, we're to do as we are told and go away and not return until the baby has been born and the estate workers will have forgotten about exactly when Bryn and I were married. There is to be no scandal. So that is a relief to Maman.

I'm afraid of going to England. Maman is English, but she came from Canterbury. Bryn and I are to live in his house in a place called Yorkshire. He's shown me where it is on the map. He says it's very beautiful, but it can be very cold. We won't have any servants, only a woman from the village to clean once a week and Bryn's sister will come and show me how to cook, he says. I have so much to learn, but I have made up my mind I will do it for Bryn.

If I didn't love Bryn so much, if I wasn't having his baby, if I hadn't met him . . . Perhaps I would have found someone else to love? But as the days are passing I'm more and more sure there could not be anyone else. Bryn says we'll come back to La Roche in the summers. Papa says yes. Maman says no. Perhaps she'll forgive me, perhaps one day I'll be able to come back. I can hardly bear to think I won't; sometimes I feel I can't bear the pain. Yet I must for Bryn's sake.

It's so strange to think that my baby and the maid's baby will be born within weeks of each other. It will be my new half-sister or brother but if Maman has her way I'll never see it. It's too cruel. I won't think about it.

Bryn and I will be all right. We'll make ourselves a good life, we won't always be poor and, when this baby is born, we'll be our own family. If the baby's a girl, she'll be Anna, if it's a boy he'll be called Gregory. I'm growing bigger, growing clumsier. I was afraid as I changed and grew bigger that Bryn wouldn't love me any more but he adores my shape, can't get enough of me. He says he wants to paint me like this, but I won't let him. It would not be a pretty painting. At nights we lie together and he takes my huge full breasts in his mouth and cradles my buttocks in his big strong hands. I should be glad that he still wants me, but he's greedy for me — too greedy. I feel so tired. All I want is sleep. I want to be with Mary and I want to sleep. Tomorrow we leave this horrid little hotel and sail to England. The money Papa has settled on us should last long enough for Bryn to finish this summer's paintings and exhibit them. He has contacts in London and in a place called Leeds. He will be famous one day, I know it.

★   ★   ★

Anna wakes alone in her bed, thankful that Jean has gone out. She needs time to think, time to be alone to work out what to do. It's Sunday morning and the cottage is quiet. Without turning over Anna knows Jean has been up for some time. She puts her hand out to his side of the bed, it feels cold. The house feels empty.

Anna sits up; the air is cool on her arms and upper body though her legs and feet are warm beneath the duvet. Paws, her grey kitten, has come upstairs and jumped onto the bed. Her purring is a comfort as she kneads the bedclothes, turning round and round before she finally settles, resting her small head against Anna's thigh. The bed headboard sticks into the middle of Anna's back; she reaches round arranging pillows, pulling Jean's discarded dressing gown round her — it steadies her to wear it. The night has been full of dreams, but now they've slipped away, leaving only the sensation that fear was here. Anna feels heavy and stupid with too little rest. Her throat is sore, there are damp patches on her pillow. Has she been crying? Why would she cry. Why wouldn't she cry. If Francesca succeeds in getting the diary to Jean, God only knows what his reaction will be. Anna doesn't know him well enough. She wanted to know him better before she told him. Francesca doesn't know what it was like, how can she possibly know.

When Anna was an adolescent growing into young womanhood, there were times when she was so filled with happiness she thought she might fly apart. There was so much she wanted to do and see. There had

96

been times when life seemed such an adventure she felt she really might burst with the hugeness of it all, until it had all come crashing down around her. Once she had thought those days would never come again; throughout her adult life she had caught haphazardly at threads and wisps of happiness, but with Jean, Anna had recognised a completeness. How dare Francesca threaten her.

Through the half-open window the sound of the local crow colony beginning a fight disturbs Anna's thoughts. The birds quarrel with each other metallically from the trees surrounding the garden, their wings rustle and flap like black silk umbrellas. Anna climbs out of bed and stands by the window to watch the ragged explosion of their flight and the ensuing aerial battle. Paws raises her head and mews fretfully. Anna is overwhelmed by a sudden longing for England. A longing for Sunday mornings, of dog-walkers and Sunday-morning paper buyers leaving their houses and going down to the corner shop, leaving behind them their rumpled beds and the smell of coffee brewing and bacon cooking and the prospect of a day spent mowing grass and visiting friends. She is filled with a rare melancholy and dashes her hand across her eyes. Millie and Leo and her life in Clifton have gone. She is not the person she was then. She is not the person she was all those years ago in Yorkshire with Greg, two children running wild around the village, allies against their mother Cathryn.

Impatiently Anna throws off Jean's dressing gown, washes and dresses for the day and goes downstairs. Jean has left a note for her on the kitchen table. She smiles, saving the treat of reading it until she has put out yesterday's rubbish. Walking barefoot out of the back door she steps round the side of the cottage into shadow. Shaded by the largest trees on the estate, this side of the cottage is always cool at this time in the morning.

As the cold strikes up through her feet Anna is held by a memory so sharp, it hurts like a knife. Her father, Bryn, is leaving. Anna is seven years old standing on the road outside Moorland Cottage in her bare feet. The road is cold and hard and her feet hurt, but that's nothing compared with the pain in her heart. Bryn is going away. She has known for a long time that all is not well between Cathryn and Bryn. All winter and the following spring Anna had known there were tensions and fears between her parents. All summer she had tried her childish best to keep the worst of their battles away from Greg, less than a year her junior. Anna was the elder, it was her duty to protect Greg. At nights she told him stories until he slept. She told him stories and cuddled him close to block out the terror of the sound of her parents fighting and the fear of the sounds of breaking china and broken hearts.

One morning she woke early and lay listening to the house around her. It had been late when she had gone to sleep, with Greg's head against her side, his soft breathing and the warm animal smell of him a comfort against the adult world. Her father and mother had fought long and hard that evening, and even when Anna had at last slept, her mother's abusing, screaming voice had torn into her dreams. Now in the paleness of the morning Anna knew something was different. Something was dreadfully wrong.

It was too early for anyone to be up and about, and yet she had quite clearly heard the sound of the stairs creaking, the sound of the door at the foot of the stairs opening and closing, and fear sliced through her mind. In that instant she knew what she had known and forbidden herself to know all that horrible year. Bryn was going away. Her lovely father, her protector from Cathryn's worse excesses of temper. The man who made her laugh, who made her feel so special, who made magic for her with his paintings and drawings. The man she loved more than anyone else in the world was going away without a word to tell her so.

Anna can see it all so clearly, she can hear it all so well, she drops the bag of rubbish she is carrying and puts her hands over her ears. It is reality. It is what happened. Her sharp high cry.

'Daddy! Daddy! My Daddy!'

Bryn, turning, his face gaunt with grief. His grey eyes like two chips of granite. 'Anna! No! You mustn't . . . I can't . . . ' His voice incoherent and breaking on the words as she began to run towards him before the mists off the moors closed in on him and, when the mist swirled again, he had gone and she stood alone on the road beyond the gate to their house. She had still been standing there an hour later when her mother found her. She was unable to speak for a week afterwards. The doctor, an enlightened man, diagnosed severe shock and recommended complete rest. There had been intervals when Anna was aware of Greg sitting by her bed. Of Greg asleep curled beside her, of her mother looking at her sorrowfully and tiptoeing away, of her mother with a bottle or a glass almost permanently in her hand. That was the first time Anna had known that fear and grief can paralyse both mind and body.

Anna shuts her mind like a box and picks up the bag of rubbish. Some of it has fallen onto the path. She shoves it back into the bag and rams the bag hard into the dustbin, slamming down the lid. Returning to the cottage she finds it is possible to go back, whistling and brave into the kitchen. It is possible to look at the morning sunshine striping the tiled floor and feel glad to be alive.

Anna picks up Jean's note from the kitchen table, and looks at his large scrawling slightly angular handwriting which is so much a part of him that she smiles as she reads.

8 a.m. Couldn't stay in bed any longer. Didn't want to disturb you because I think you had a bad night? Gone for a swim in the bay. Join me if you like. If not I'll be home soon — see you at breakfast. Je t'adore. PS I love you!!!!

Anna reads the brief note several times, as if it might impart something of great importance to her. At length, deciding that it does, she folds it neatly and puts it into the pocket of her shorts, where for the rest of the day it gives her hope whenever she thinks of it. She glances at the clock — almost nine-thirty. Jean is taking a long time over his swim, or perhaps he has recognised that some time alone might be what she needs. She talks to her small grey cat as it winds itself around her feet. 'Some time alone is never possible when you're around, is it?' She bends to stroke the cat's small hard head and it rubs itself with gratitude against her. She picks Paws up and holds the comfort of her soft body close, murmuring nonsense into the cat's ear.

'Whoever are you talking to?' Jean's curly head appears at the open kitchen window, and he laughs when he sees the cat in Anna's arms. She puts the cat down with a final stroke, as Jean comes into the kitchen, kisses Anna lightly and takes the kettle.

'Come on, my love,' he says. 'I'll make the tea. It was glorious in the sea this morning — you should have come. It would have blown a few cobwebs away.'

Anna goes over to the fridge and opens it. 'I like my cobwebs. Leave them alone. Do you fancy bacon and eggs this morning?'

'I certainly do, but what's this? We hardly ever have bacon and eggs — are we practising for the English visitors? Or just for Megan? That is,' he is cautious, 'that's if you still want her to come. We could ring her today and put her off if you do not feel up to it.'

Anna busies herself at the stove. She speaks without turning to look at Jean. 'I don't think we can put her off. She's got the exhibition, it's very important to her — a big opportunity. She's hardly going to cancel that and besides, she'd think it very offhand if I told her she wasn't welcome here.'

'But you'd like to? She could stay somewhere else.'

'It will be all right. Come and eat your breakfast. It's going to go cold.'

'Why am I being filled with cholesterol, which smells too delicious to resist.' Jean kisses the back of Anna's neck. His body feels warm against her. Anna twists round and kisses him quickly.

'Because I love you and I wanted to give you something nice for breakfast. Sit down and we'll eat.'

Jean sits at the small café table in one corner of the kitchen. He looks sleek and fit, his skin gleams with health. 'So, my *chérie* loves me?'

'I do. Oh yes I do,' but Anna turns her head away as she places his plate in front of him. Paws sits by the open back door. The crows have flown elsewhere and the cat chatters her teeth in futile anger at swallows skimming low overhead, their high-pitched cries giving Anna the opportunity of a diversion. 'I adore that sound, don't you? So much more cheerful than crows.'

'I suppose it is.' Jean waves a fork loaded with bacon. 'Aren't you having some of this?'

'Yes. Of course.' Anna returns to the stove and slides unwanted bacon and egg onto her own plate. She'll have to tell Jean. Today. Though she has eaten nothing since the night before, she is not hungry. Jean is watching Anna intently as she comes to sit opposite him.

'Are you sure you're all right, Anna? I thought you seemed *distraite* in the middle of the night. You were crying.'

Anna pours coffee. 'I'm fine. Just a bad dream, all gone now.' She forces a smile. Jean thinks she looks tired this morning and a little frail, but her smile lights her face and he's reassured as she continues, 'Really, Jean, you don't have to worry about me. Are the bacon and eggs okay? Mine are.'

'They're absolutely gorgeous. I don't know why we don't have them more often, though I wasn't sure you were enjoying yours? You seem to be playing with them. If you can't finish them, I can. Swimming's given me an appetite.' He cuts into a rasher of bacon before asking, 'What *did* make you decide to cook this morning?'

'I don't know really. Just some sort of nostalgia thing. I was watching the crows and they made me think of England. Finish mine if you like.' Anna pushes her less than half emptied plate over to Jean.

'You don't regret being out here?'

'No, not at all. It's just sometimes, especially on Sunday mornings, I get a bit nostalgic.'

Jean takes a mouthful of food from Anna's rejected plate. Egg runs down his chin and he wipes it away cheerfully with the back of his hand. 'Well hoorah,' his voice is mockingly English, 'Hoo-jolly-rah for England and hoo-jolly-rah for bacon and eggs! Though I'm sorry you don't want yours. Have some bread instead?' He cuts a thick slice, but Anna shakes her head. Jean raises his eyebrows. 'Nostalgia? Want to talk to me about it?'

'Not really, darling. Nostalgia isn't a country you dwell in, is it? It's one of the things I love most about you.'

'Oh really?' He puts his head on one side, teasing. 'I thought perhaps I have other attractions. It certainly seemed that way last night. And of course I'm a very good worker on the estate.' He pats her arm as he passes on the way to the sink with the empty plates. 'The bacon and eggs were superb, *Madame*, and now if you'll excuse me I shall shower and change and then perhaps we can go out somewhere for the day. Maybe take with us that other English institution — *le pique-nique?*' He stands by the door and looks back at her. The sun makes a halo of her hair, he finds her extraordinarily lovely. 'I wish you would have something to eat. Are you quite certain you don't want to talk?'

She nods her head, blows him a kiss. 'Quite sure.'

When Jean has gone up to the bathroom, Anna waits before creeping on legs that shake to the foot of the stairs. She stands taut and still; her heart is pounding and she realises she is holding her breath. From upstairs she can hear Jean splashing and singing in the shower. Swiftly she crosses the living room and reaches for the phone. She dials Megan's number. Far away in Megan's London flat Anna hears the phone ringing. She counts twenty, thirty times. No reply. She replaces the receiver. What could she have said?

5

Mary

Since Cathryn and Bryn married they have
been to La Roche four times. Every time it
was when Maman was absent in Canterbury,
visiting her sister Ada. Papa allowed Bryn and
Cath to use the cottage. It was all quite
exciting: all the clandestine messages, and the
arrival, making sure Maman really had left.
We had a near-miss once when Maman was
delayed setting off. Papa paid for them to
come here. I know how much he misses Cath.
He talks to me. Sometimes in the evenings
when the others are in bed, he and I walk
together through the grounds and down by
the shore. I think he respects me. I think he
understands why, at the ancient age of
twenty-five, I've still not married. It's not that
I haven't been asked, but I won't make a
loveless marriage. After Monsieur Becque
and Babette made such a fiasco of their
marriage, after Maman's and Papa's marriage, after seeing how even people that I
thought were as much in love as Cathryn and
Bryn have turned out, I'm going to bide my
time. I think Papa at least respects me for

that. Besides, with the world in such turmoil I would not want to marry. I wouldn't want to bring children into such a turbulent terrible time. They say there'll be war in Europe; such awful hideous things are happening to the Jewish people. Hitler is seizing power whenever and wherever he can. The world doesn't feel safe any more.

It's almost nine years since Cathryn married Bryn. She's not a carefree young woman any more and nor am I a child. At twenty-five, who is? Just eleven months after Anna's birth, Greg was born. Since then there have been no more children. Cathryn wrote in a letter to make me laugh that she had found out, at last, all the things Maman wouldn't tell her about. She made it funny; she wrote and said it was just as well, because she and Bryn couldn't keep away from each other and the cottage was too tiny to contemplate having any more children. That was when she used to write often, when I was still so lonely without her. I used to treasure her letters for weeks. I still have some of them. I'm an appalling hoarder — I can't bear to throw things away, especially family things, but I'm not sure that I'll keep the letter that came today. It's so sad.

I haven't seen Cath for two years now but I could see last time how much she had changed. I think she's become hard and bitter and, for much of the time when she was last here, she made me think of Maman. It was the way she spoke to Bryn, the same ice-cold tone Maman uses when she talks to Papa. I couldn't bear it, to hear her talk to Bryn like that. He's not a bad man. He loves the children, I think he still loves Cath — there was still something soft in the way he looked at her. You can always tell what's between a man and a woman when they look at each other. So, whatever was in Bryn's eyes wasn't in Cathryn's any more. It didn't seem right, when I know how much she used to adore him. He's still so attractive, big and good-looking and so full of life, despite all their hardship.

I felt uneasy too about Anna. It seemed to me there was the sound of suppressed rage in Cathryn's voice whenever she spoke to the child; it upset me so much I braved Cathryn's temper and asked her about it. At first she flared up at me and told me to mind my own business. We were walking down on the shore, shoeless and paddling as we did when we were children. Cath stopped walking and shouted at me.

'You've no right to interfere, Mary. They're my children. You don't know what Anna's really like.'

Once I would have murmured an apology and walked away, hoping to make it up with Cathryn later, but her attitude that summer had been depressing and angering me. She was showing all the worst sides of her nature. Or perhaps I was growing up, noticing how often she uses people for her own ends, not loving her any the less, but seeing her at last without the childish scales of adulation over my eyes. So I shouted back.

'So, tell me what Anna is really like. Why is she so awful, that you can't love her?'

Cath stamped away from me, kicking at the water, churning up a foam. I ignored her and went to sit on one of the beach's large flat stones. I sat still and quiet and admired the glistening sand crusting my damp feet and ankles, like a pair of strange slippers. I used to love that when I was a child. Sometimes, when I was little, although it was strictly forbidden I used to run down onto the beach alone. It was even more forbidden to swim alone but I used to strip all my clothes off and wallow naked in the shallow waves. Then I would roll in the sand until I was coated all over. I used to pretend my real mother was a mermaid and my silvery sandy coating was what a mermaid's half-earthly child would look like.

I stopped daydreaming; Cathryn was

walking back towards me. She was waving and calling my name. When she saw me watching her she broke into a lumbering half-run. She was out of breath by the time she reached my side and she almost collapsed onto my rock seat. Her face was red and shining and her hair, long since cut into a ragged bob, was damp against her skin.

'Are you all right?' I was quite alarmed; I hadn't realised how unfit she had become.

It took a moment to recover her breath before Cathryn said, 'I'm fine. A bit out of condition. I don't run anywhere very much these days. Haven't played tennis for years. Don't ride. Don't walk, unless it's for a purpose. The only exercise I get is housework. Why shouldn't I be fine?'

My patience was worn thin. 'Cath, stop it. I've heard it all before. I'm sorry for you, but it gets tedious.'

She sat back and regarded me, her winged eyebrows raised, amusement mingled with sarcasm in her voice. 'Well, well, little sister, you have turned into a tiger.'

'Oh Cath, I'm sorry.' I put a hand on her knee.

She didn't move my hand away, instead she took hold of it and my eyes filled with tears for all the times we'd walked together round the estate, Cath, my big sister, leading me by the hand. I thought of when we had picked so many of the garden flowers, excited by the hugeness of the bright bouquets we had made, and how bewildered we were that Maman was not pleased with our gift, two little girls clutching sweaty palms against her anger: and I thought of us holding hands secretly in the dark between our two beds so often when Maman and Papa shouted at each other, but I blinked back my tears.

'I'm sorry, Cath,' I said. 'I don't mean to be unkind.'

She squeezed my hand and let it drop. She smiled. 'Neither do I. You wanted to know about Anna.'

'It doesn't matter. It's not really my business.'

'I want to tell you though. It would be a relief to tell you. If you'll listen. I feel so guilty about Anna. You're right — I don't like her. She demands of me all the time. Right from the day she was born she has demanded. From her conception Anna has demanded. That Bryn and I should marry, that I had to leave here. That was a demand.'

'But that's not Anna's fault,' I protested.

Cath's face was a mask as she said, 'Intellectually I know that. Emotionally I don't. I cannot connect with her. She was a difficult birth. She never seemed to sleep. She wanted to feed constantly. She sapped my energy and she stopped me being able to communicate with Bryn. I was too exhausted all the time.'

'But you had Greg so soon afterwards,' I blurted.

Cathryn gave me an odd little smile. 'Well, maybe Bryn and I communicated sometimes at a certain animal level. That's always been one of our problems.'

I felt my colour come up but said, 'But if you were so tired all the time, why have another child?'

Cath yawned and stretched. 'We thought it was a good idea. We thought to have them close together so they would be companions for each other as they grew older. I just thank the Lord Greg was never any trouble. He's always slept and fed at the right intervals, he's always been quiet and no trouble at all.'

'And that makes him lovable and Anna not?'

'For God's sake, Mary, stop preaching at me! It's the way I am, and the way things are.' Cath stood up. 'Can't you see how things are for me? My whole life seems to be turning into a mistake and I don't know what to do about it.' She began to walk away, but I made one more attempt.

'You could do all sorts about it, Cath. The

children need you, and Bryn needs you. You could make it work.'

She turned and looked down at me. 'Maybe some people could. But I'm not one of those people, Mary. There's too much for me to do. I can't and won't do it. I suppose I'm just an unnatural mother. I don't like my own child and I know everyone says she's such a dear sweetheart, and, I suppose, you will say you would love her if she were yours, but I resent her so much. After all, if it wasn't for Anna perhaps I would have been living a life of luxury by now, married to some rich French or English aristo. My looks have faded. I drink too much. I'm beginning to hate my husband. I know it isn't all Bryn's fault. He has tried with his paintings, but perhaps he should have tried something else sooner, before the lack of money became a real problem. So perhaps, Mary, you can see I do have some trials.'

I left her to walk back up to the house alone. I had said too much. I had interfered, and Cath's answer had done nothing to stop me worrying about Anna. We patched it up before the family returned to England, but they haven't been back since. I write to Anna, I send her letters and drawings as often as I can. I hope Cathryn lets her have them.

I've read and reread Cath's letter that came

this morning. I've carried it with me all day. I've read it over and over; the paper is so thin, such poor quality, already it's crumpled and worn and smudged with my crying. I took it to the kitchen garden, it's one of the few places where Maman wouldn't think to look for me.

I still can't believe it, in spite of all the warning signs last time they were here. I still can't believe it. How could she do that? How could he? And what about the children, poor darlings? What's to become of them?

Moorland Cottage
April 4, 1938

My dearest Mary,

This is probably one of the hardest letters I'll ever have to write. I scarcely know where to begin. Perhaps the blunt and plain truth is the easiest. Bryn has left us. Six months ago. I'm sorry I didn't tell you earlier but I didn't know how to tell you, of all people. I know how much you like Bryn and, when I think of all the times that you were our good kind guardian and kept Maman away from the truth for us, how much we were in love, how exciting and thrilling it all was — I can scarcely believe it's come to this.

We argued constantly and more bitterly than I ever thought we could. It was more than arguing, Mary, it was ghastly. It was just like Maman and Papa all over again, screaming at each other, throwing things, me really wanting to smash Bryn's face in, I can't think how it ever got so bad, but it did. I hated him, hated everything about him. His voice, his walk, his smell, even the sound of him breathing. Though there was never another woman involved. It hurts unbearably to think about — but I have to tell someone — I don't know where all the love went to, but bit by bit over the years it's been drained away until I couldn't stand the sight of him.

You don't know what it's been like, living here in this godforsaken place with no company and no entertainment and every year expecting Bryn to make it as an international artist and every year him only selling to the summer visitors and being turned down all the time by snooty London galleries and him getting more and more defeated and spending money travelling to and fro for no gains. We've had to make a living taking in people on walking tours of the area and selling our own produce where and how we could. I slaved in the garden. I looked after the visitors. I did the washing and the ironing and made meals. I can't recall when I last read a book or went out for an evening. Ironic to think I once thought I knew nothing about keeping a home — well, believe me, Mary, I know now and you're so wise not to have married, so wise to go on living with Maman and Papa, it's nothing compared with the rigours of the life I've had to lead. The children have behaved like little more than hooligans and seem to take a vicious delight in ganging up against me — they're as thick as thieves. I've hardly a decent rag to wear and sometimes we've had to go to bed hungry. Bryn's parents wouldn't give him a penny. Like Maman they've never even seen the children, yet unlike Maman they only live a few miles away. If it were not for the money Papa sent, we would have been destitute long ago. I did try offering language lessons in the local village, but I'm afraid none of the local people want to know. After all, why would they learn to speak French? You can't talk to sheep in French!

You're probably wondering why it was Bryn who left and why I stayed. All I can say is it would have been either of us sooner or later. He just made the decision faster than I did and left me, literally holding the babies. The night before he left we had a hideous scene, worse than any that had gone before. It makes me feel ill to even think about it and when I got up in the morning he'd gone. No note. Nothing.

I'm just beginning to feel halfway human again. I thank God we have good neighbours or I don't know what would have happened to the children. I'm ashamed to say I was useless. The bottle seemed to be the easiest way out of the pain. I should have learned from Maman's and Papa's experiences that it isn't! God forgive me I've been a dreadful mother, but I could only see my own hurt.

Anna behaved abominably when Bryn first went away. I actually thought she might be going out of her mind with her dreadful tantrums. She's behaved like a spoiled brat, no help whatsoever and the trouble I've had with her wetting the bed! Trying to dry sheets up here in the winter is no joke. Anyway, I think we're through the worst of it. She's been dry at nights for the last couple of weeks and has stopped her everlasting questions. Greg says less, but I know he's hurt.

I sometimes wonder what the past nine years have been about. I've had plenty of time to think and, sometimes, I wonder if

Bryn ever really cared, but of course he did. Who else would have withstood my ceaseless nagging for as long as he did. I just wish I could put the clock back and start again. I wonder now just what we did have in common. We never really had time to find out if the attraction was much more than physical and just two young people enjoying life before we were bound up into marriage and having to make the best of it. And we did try, Mary, we really did, but the trying wasn't enough. Bryn doesn't mind deprivation. I do — desperately — and as the years have gone by I've realised I only managed to love Bryn when he was cheerful, I wasn't strong enough for him when he was low-spirited and he needs so much more love than I was prepared to give him. I wanted parties and fun, while he was quite happy with his work, and his preoccupation when he's involved with his work always made me feel ignored and unwanted. So, you see, Mary, what a sad and sorry state we had come to. It is difficult to come to terms with, but in the end I think I just wasn't grown-up enough for poor Bryn.

I envy you your freedom, though I've got no more or less than I deserve and I find, to my astonishment, that after all I do wish

Bryn well. I don't want him back, but I wish him well. Can you understand that? Who knows, perhaps without us Bryn will become the artist he always said he was. As I said at the beginning of this letter, this is the blunt and plain truth and, unfortunately, that is sometimes unpalatable.

Think of me, darling, as I think of you, Your loving sister, Cath.

Mary stops reading and refolds the letter. She has come to a decision. Papa must know of this — how else is Cathryn to survive with two children, both under the age of nine and Cath with no way of earning a living? Mary slips unobserved out of the kitchen garden and walks down past Bryn's cottage to the seashore. The little house looks forlorn and deserted. Perhaps if Maman wouldn't allow Cath up at the house, she might soften and allow her at least a respite in the cottage, if it would not be too painful for Cath to stay there. Mary comes out from the trees onto the shore and ponders the possibilities of the family coming to live at La Roche. What would Maman say? Does she still hate Cathryn? She hasn't seen her for nine years, she always claims she wants to know nothing of the children and yet, Mary knows that every birthday and every Christmas, the children, though not Cathryn, have received a card. Cathryn has written and told her so.

With Olivier in New Zealand and the recently divorced Babette on her way to join him, Duncan and Alicia away in Oxford and London for much of the time, and a governess to look after the younger children, Maman finds time hanging heavy on her hands. In recent years she has lost much of her fire; she reads a lot and sleeps a lot and eats too much. The governess has proved not only ugly — Maman chose her most carefully — but also extremely efficient, and kind.

A small flame of excitement ignites in Mary. To have Cathryn back here would be wonderful. The children would have instant companions in Blanche, Edward and Millie. Cathryn would be able to rest and possibly be able to formulate some kind of plans for her future.

Mary walks along the shore and considers, not for the first time, how strange it is that Millie and Anna were born within weeks of one another. After the trauma of taking in Millie, the maid's child, when the family had lived through one of La Roche's darkest times when Papa and Maman had not even screamed at one another but the house had been filled with tension like a thick smog, a curious thing had happened. Maman had grown to love Millie and had proved unexpectedly easy to persuade that Mary should come out of the nursery to take lessons in typing and book-keeping, as other young women were doing, with a view to earning her own living. Meanwhile Mary has done much to help Papa with the managing of the estate in the past few years.

Mary resents the way Maman loads affection on Millie, one of Papa's bastards like herself, and yet doted on and spoiled by Maman. Spoiled and loved by all she comes into contact with, Millie is a pretty and charming child, grey-eyed with thick fair silky hair and the kind of face which looks as if it could break into mirth at any moment and frequently does. She is everyone's darling and even Mary cannot help loving her with a zeal which never fails to astound her.

Perhaps if Mary had been a less serious child, perhaps if she had had the gift of ready laughter, things would have been different for her. Mary bends to observe her own reflection in a shallow rock pool. Her dark hair falls forward around her small, olive-skinned face. Her strange dark-grey eyes under their straight black brows stare back at her until a slight movement somewhere off to her left catches her attention and she looks up to see a man coming along the shoreline towards her. With some agitation she recognises Bryn. It is as if Cathryn's letter has somehow conjured him here. Instantly Mary is on her feet. A hand creeps protectively toward the pocket of her baggy khaki shorts where she has stowed Cathryn's letter.

Bryn has seen her now, his head is up. He is running, bounding towards her. He runs with surprising grace for one so large. The sky behind him is a bright, clear blue and little waves break at his feet. His heavy black hair, which lifts around his broad, handsome face, Mary notes with surprise is tinged with the first frostings of silver, and though he has shaved his beard, there is a few days' stubble on his chin. Bryn's once-powerful body has turned a little to fat. His trouser legs are rolled to above the knee and he is wearing a threadbare dark-blue sweater. All of these details Mary takes in, in one searing glance. Her chest feels unaccountably tight and she stands braced, her small feet planted hard on the sand. A tremor runs through her which she fights to subdue before Bryn reaches her.

He waves and calls to her, his face lighting in a smile but the wind whips his voice away, breaking up the words. Mary leans forward straining to hear him and then he is next to her, has lifted her off her feet and kissed her cheek. 'Mary! It's so good to see you. I'm glad I found you before any of the others see me.' He replaces her on the sand and she stands beside him, scarcely reaching his shoulder. With her face tipped up she says, 'I had a letter from Cath.'

'Good. I'm glad.'

'She told me what happened, that you left.'

'Don't blame me, Mary. Please don't blame me.'

Mary regards him thoughtfully.

'Don't look at me like that. I hate the way you seem to be able to see right into people!' Bryn turns his head away and looks out towards the horizon.

'How did you get here, Bryn?' Her voice is tremulous.

'Boat, walking, hitching a lift where I could.'

'Where have you been? Cathryn said in her letter you'd left home six months ago.'

'I did. I went down to London for a while, after that I hardly know where I've been or what I've been doing. It's been bad, Mary, but I think I'm through the worst of it. About a couple of weeks ago I found that things were beginning to make sense again and I knew I had to come and find you.'

'Have you eaten?'

Bryn shrugs, and passes a shaky hand across his face. 'I — uhm — I'm not sure.'

'I'll get you something from the house. Do you want to come up to La Roche?'

Bryn hesitates. When he looks down at her, Mary can see the strain in his eyes; the fine lines around them have bitten deeper than she remembered them, and to her horror there is such stark grief looking out at her that she almost flinches. 'Oh God help me, Mary.' His broad, capable-looking hands touch his forehead, his long, splayed fingers, which Anna has inherited, rake through his hair and he blinks hard, swallowing, tilting his big head up towards the sky and biting at his lower lip.

Mary steps forward and puts her arms round Bryn; her head is against his chest and in spite of herself she is happy. She can feel the solidity of him, hear his heart beating and his breathing as it shakes with the effort of quenching tears and, as Mary's small hand timidly strokes his back, slows to a quiet, even pace. He strokes her hair and kisses the top of her head. 'I'm all right, Mary. Truly I am. It's just,' he clears his throat, 'it's just that I miss them all so much. I thought you could tell them where I am.'

Mary straightens her body and with it her mind, steps back from Bryn and holds his hand, but lightly. 'Go back to them, Bryn. Cath is unhappy. Anna's distraught, Greg is missing you. Go back. You *must!* Papa will give you the money to go back.'

Bryn sits on a flat rock, and looks up at her, squinting against the sun. 'Are you really so confident? Do you think Cathryn would have me back? Is that what she said in her letter?' His voice is toneless and without hope, and when Mary does not reply he frowns. 'It wouldn't work. Whatever Cath and I had once — and you know how happy we were — bless you, you were our little lookout, whatever we had has gone.' He fondles Mary's hand absentmindedly and strokes her fingers. She holds her breath, but with his eyes on the sea he drops her hand. 'I can't go back. Cathryn was right — I am useless, useless and without talent. What do I know about art? What do I know about painting? All these years I've been fooling myself, dragging Cathryn down and down. When,' he looks back over his shoulder towards the trees where La Roche's squared-off outline can just be seen, 'she could have lived here, married a rich Frenchman. She was a lady when I met her. I've turned her into a drudge. I'm going to Spain, Mary.'

The words hang in the clear air, then as their full implication bites into her conscious-ness Mary blurts, 'But the war — there's a war out there!'

126

Bryn smiles, but his mouth twists and his deep voice catches as he says, 'That's why I'm going. Something has to be done. There's work a man can do out there. I can go and help. I'll stay in the cottage tonight if I may, and in the morning I'll be gone. Tell Cathryn where I am. Tell her she must come here, I know your father will look after her.'

Mary stuffs her hands in the pockets of her shorts, and digs a sandalled foot into the sand. For a moment she says nothing, then as she begins to cry she raises her head. 'Wait here, I'll get you some food.'

*   *   *

It's Monday morning. Jean has driven into town to the supermarché and Anna is walking alone on the beach. The seashore is a different landscape. Bleached sky and shifted horizons hold no reference points. The sea sucks at Anna's bare feet and sands run backwards. She stands only yards away from where Mary and Bryn stood on that April morning. Perhaps if she was able to turn her head swiftly enough she might catch a fleeting glimpse of a small fine-boned woman and a heavily built, handsome man in dark clothes. If she did, she would know and love them both.

Anna walks up from the edge of the sea and sits on the flat rock where her father sat so many mornings ago. Another day gone and still she has not made her confession to Jean. Three times yesterday she attempted to ring Megan. Over and over again she made up her mind to tell Jean what he would know soon enough, and each time she had taken fright.

With a sigh Anna settles on the rock and looks around her. As light splinters off the sea she is a bewildered child again. Aunt Millie, only one month older than Anna, has gone back to the house sulking. They have had an argument, but Greg is running towards her, laughing and teasing. He is her brother. She loves him but eight-year-old Anna is confused. He has kissed her. Twice. Hard on the mouth. It was one day when they were in the barn looking for hens' eggs. 'Brothers and sisters don't kiss like that,' she had said. 'That's proper kissing like grown-ups do. Like they do on the films.'

'I don't care. I like it. I'm going to do it again.' His lips had been warm and tasted of aniseed. He had laughed and run away from her.

Mama comes up from a swim in the bay, shaking water out of her thick hair. She is looking better than she has since Daddy left. It is the end of the summer. Granny Elspeth agreed to let them stay in the cottage. It has been wonderful; there has been fun and laughter and tea on the terrace at the back of La Roche. Grandpa Philippe is lovely, so jolly. Granny Elspeth is all right, she's tall and big like Mama but rather slow and quiet and she seems much older than Grandpa. Blanche and Edward are good at jokes and have taught Anna and Greg how to sail, taking a small dinghy out and tacking round the bay.

The sun and sea and fresh air have turned Anna a wonderful golden brown and even Greg, whose skin is usually so pale and creamy, looks honey brown and freckles have appeared all over the bridge of his nose. Tomorrow it will all be over. Tomorrow they will go back to England. They won't hear the high-pitched calls of the seagulls any more or the shrieking skim of swallows. Mama has found a job, in a place called Northampton-shire. She is to be a nanny in a country house. Mama says it is a house not unlike La Roche. She will look after some children whose mother died last month. The children are only small. Cathryn and her children will not live in the big house — they will live in a house called Keeper's Cottage. Cathryn will go to work every day; the children in her care will have a different nurse at night. That is what Mama calls 'the arrangement' and Anna is pleased. It means she and Greg will have their own mother all to themselves at home in the nights. Since they have been at La Roche Mama has been kinder, softer, less angry and though at times Anna is still afraid of Mama, she could not bear to be without her as well as without Bryn.

Like magic, the loveliness of La Roche and its surrounding woods and beaches have had a powerful healing effect on Anna, but still when she thinks too hard about Bryn she feels as if a huge hole has been torn in her insides and she thinks sometimes it may never get put back together again. There is loneliness and darkness when she thinks about him, so mostly she doesn't think about him.

Aunt Mary is building sandcastles with Blanche and Edward. Anna is drawing pictures in the sand with the edge of her spade. Greg has finished his and decorated it with seaweed and pebbles — it's a recognisable portrait of La Roche. Now Greg dances in front of Anna and tells her when they are both grown up he and she will be married. They'll live in La Roche, it's the place where they belong.

'Don't be silly, Greg. Brothers and sisters can't marry each other, can they, Mama?'

Cathryn, lying face down on the sand

beside her daughter, turns her head and squints into the sun. 'Of course brothers and sisters can't marry each other. Whatever next! And I doubt if you'll be living here.'

'I love La Roche. We'll come back and visit won't we, Mama?' Cathryn turns her head away; she thinks about the unease in Europe and of Bryn somewhere out there, she doesn't know where. Her voice is harsh when she replies, 'I'm not sure about that, Anna.'

When Anna makes no reply, Cathryn turns back to look at her. For a moment she is contrite, she should not have spoken to the child like that, but Anna never fails to bring out the worst in her. Anna is picking at a scab on her knee and staring out to sea. Automatically Cathryn says, 'Don't do that, Anna. You'll make it bleed.' She taps at the child's hand where it picks and picks at the scab. Anna's eyes are very bright but she says nothing before she runs away along the beach. Seeing the child's distress Aunt Mary follows Anna slowly before catching up with her to walk hand in hand back to the house.

'It's all right, Anna, you'll come back and see us next summer.' Comforting the child, Mary reiterates, 'You can come back.' Unseen, she crosses her fingers, thinks about

Hitler, thinks about the way the world is, wonders where Bryn is now.

Anna tugs at Mary's skirt. 'Aunt Mary, why aren't you married?'

Mary's laugh bubbles from between her parted lips and she looks at Anna with her lovely clear grey eyes. 'Because, *ma petite*, the right man for me married someone else.' She pats the child's head and turns away.

They have reached the tea terrace. Mary goes towards the garden door, but Anna regards Mary with wonder and calls after her retreating back, 'Is there only one right person for each of us, Aunt Mary?'

'Eight years old and asking such questions!' Mary tries *légerdemain*.

'But is there?' Anna follows Mary and tugs at her sleeve, looking up into her face.

Aunt Mary looks back at her, solemn-faced. 'I believe so, *chérie*. For me, at least, that's the truth. I met a man once. No one else will ever match him. So,' she spreads her hands upturned in a half-comic gesture, 'I have chosen not to take second best!' Aunt Mary is lovely. Anna loves Aunt Mary almost as much as she loves her father. Although Anna still misses Bryn she doesn't think Greg does any more.

Adult Anna shifts and looks around her as a cool breeze plays off the sea. The day will be hot by noon. She must go and work in the garden. Jean will be back soon.

6

Keeper's Cottage,
Brockley House
April, 1947

Darling Mary,

I'm writing for two reasons, the first to let you know that James and I have decided to live together. Don't be too horrified, will you, darling, but we daren't marry for fear that I would be committing bigamy. After all, although it's nine years since Bryn left and four since I heard anything of him, he could still be alive. 'Lieutenant Williams missing, presumed dead' and as you know, no further news. Am I a widow? Am I not? It doesn't seem to matter to James. Since he came back to Brockley House after the war we have been thrown together so much, particularly during this last winter, that I believe we've grown to love each other. So many people's lives have been overturned by the war that I'm certain I shall withstand any scandal in the village attached to my living with James. After all, at thirty-six I'd like to think I can stand up for myself better than I could when all that beastly trouble blew up over me and Bryn. It all seems so long ago now. I feel quite fearful at times for Anna — it's because I can't help remembering myself at her age, and particularly remembering how power-fully I felt about Bryn.

I've taken the coward's route and I know it's foolish and I can hear you, Mary, telling me so, but all I've been able to do is warn her. I've told her not to go near men. I simply can't bring myself to tell her about me and her father. I can't let her know she was almost a bastard. What would have happened, I wonder, if Papa hadn't settled all that money on us? What would have happened to me? Would I have been forced into giving Anna away? Perhaps it would have been better. She's never asked about Bryn and me, but I think she must have wondered. Even after all these years it still causes me anguish.

Anyway, enough of all that. It's behind me and it's so wonderful to have come through it all and into calm waters. James is marvellous, but unfortunately, the children (my children! — James's are fine about the whole thing, probably because they're so much younger and I've been their nanny and governess for most of their lives) but my children, particularly Anna, are less certain of James than I am. Anna keeps declaring she will not move out of Keeper's Cottage to the big house. James is indulgent and says that at seventeen, if that's what she wants, then that's what she shall have. Personally I think he's mad! We could be making some money from the rent of Keeper's Cottage — goodness knows the big house needs some money spending on it.

Mind you, James was so clever during the war persuading the powers-that-be not to take it over. He's got such a lot of influence in high places! At least it's not had all sorts of horrible conversions done to it like poor old La Roche. I heard from Millie last week that La Roche is going to be turned into some kind of annexe to a girls' ghastly boarding school. I can't believe it, don't even want to think about it. Nothing we can do about it, of course, since Maman and Papa divorced and they sold up. I don't suppose we'll see any of the money now. It's horrible, Duncan being killed in action and then Maman and Alicia in the Blitz, and they thought they'd come to England for safety! It was a grisly, grisly time. I couldn't get messages to the rest of you, I don't think I'd ever felt so isolated and all the years with Maman fighting and arguing with her and battling for the right to be recognised — none of it seemed to matter any more. I don't know how you felt about it, Mary — she treated you worse than any of us — perhaps best not to dig up those sort of feelings.

Suffice to say the Blitz was fearful, they'd only been with us the week before. I thank God almost daily that Blanche and Edward and Millie were all safely stowed out in the country. I see them all from time to time, very grown-up and getting on with their lives. Of course, Millie is going back to France to be with Papa, so perhaps you may see her shortly.

How's dear old Marseille now? You must be enjoying yourself hugely working as an assistant in your friend's hotel. What a relief after your little bit of fun as a Resistance worker. No sign of a permanent manfriend yet? I suppose you were too busy during the war, but darling Mary, don't leave it too late. After all, we're none of us getting any younger and I must say it's wonderful to be with James. Mind you, I always thought you were a dark horse, and it may amuse you to know that I really did sometimes think you might even have a secret pash for Bryn! Still, what did any of us know? We were only young, so very young. Not much older than Anna and Greg.

Anyway, I know it's a long time since I last wrote to you but now I come to the second reason for my letter. Would you be willing to have Anna to live with you for a short while? At least until James and I have settled in together. Living as you do alone, I'm sure it would do Anna good to have an older woman to keep an eye on her. I'm afraid she can be very wilful and, loath though I am to admit it, in spite of all my endeavours we almost had some trouble with some of the airmen based in the area. She's becoming quite a beauty. I know you would be a good companion to her — perhaps you could even get her a little job? The language would be no problem, of course, as I've kept all the children fully bi-lingual.

So, dearest Mary, will you do this for me? Just until things have settled down a bit here. I hope all is well with you and perhaps we might meet up again before too much longer. If you do agree to have Anna we could talk on the telephone about arrangements. I won't be able to bring her out myself to you — there's too much to do here.

Much love, as always, Cathryn.

Mary finishes reading the letter, fingering the heavy cream paper where it lies on her desk and lifts her coffee cup. This early-morning break is one of her favourite parts of the day. A chance to be alone from the rush and noise of the hotel. To be herself for a brief spell, before members of her staff come knocking on her door with endless queries. She savours the taste of the hot sweet coffee, so good after the ersatz rubbish of the war years. She glances again at Cathryn's letter. Can Cathryn really have forgotten that Anna does know about her parents' rushed marriage? How like her to remove from her memory anything that is uncomfortable to live with. Just as now she is so blatantly trying to remove Anna from her life, presumably because, reading between the lines, she too is becoming uncomfortable to live with.

Mary sits in her office in one of Marseille's finest hotels, and surveys her tiny kingdom. It is typical of Cathryn to denigrate what she is doing. 'Working as an assistant'! Mary runs a hand through her hair and laughs; she knows that Cathryn is perfectly aware that Mary is the hotel manager, and as for the thought that she had a 'little bit of fun as a Résistante' ... seeing friends, other members of The Group, shot dead, their chests starred with machine-gun bullets. Taking constant risks herself. Helping the forgers in secret printing rooms, learning to counterfeit documents, riding her bicycle through suburbs carrying messages hidden beneath baskets of fruit and vegetables, always with the fear of discovery, and its undoubtedly fatal consequences hanging over her. Hiding for weeks on end, and always on the move. None of these would she class as 'a bit of fun', but she had learned that she was resourceful and resilient; she had survived so much.

Typical of Cathryn too to look for any port in a storm, but more often than not that port is Mary. She knows she should be angry, but on reflection feels absurdly pleased at the prospect of seeing Anna again. She must have grown so much in the last nine years and, as Cathryn says, into a beauty. Why else would Cathryn be so worried about her daughter's chastity? What was the real reason for wanting to move Anna out of the way? The servicemen had left — could it be that the 'marvellous' James might have been showing an unhealthy interest in the girl? Or was it simply that Cathryn wanted to move a lodger into Keeper's Cottage and present Anna with no alternative on her return other than to move into the big house?

Mary stands up and stretches her neat body; she reaches for and lights a cigarette. If

Anna is coming here, perhaps Mary should be circumspect about her current lover and meet him less often. It is certain that he won't be able to come to the apartment. Perhaps this is the opportunity she's been waiting for; it is time he left anyway. Mary has grown tired of him, as sooner or later she has tired of all her lovers except Bryn. She thinks of Bryn, of how he came back to her in secret at intervals throughout the war, how they met in strange places at strange times. What would Cathryn say if she knew? What does it matter now? Bryn has gone. It's over with. Finished for them all. There is no more Bryn. The news she had always known she would hear one day had come from Cathryn in the briefest of letters; Lieutenant Williams was missing, presumed dead. It had been a hot day. The sun had blazed, the sky had been the most beautiful shade of opalescent blue; somewhere in the room a geranium sent out its suffocating bitter aroma, and Mary had felt her heart turn to ice.

She remembers everything about Bryn, but most of all she remembers their last meeting. How they spent that one complete week in a member of The Group's apartment on the outskirts of Lyon. It was crazy, it was madness, they ran so many risks, but it was such heaven to be together. They danced, they drank contraband brandy and champagne, they lay awake for hours making love, it was ecstasy to be together; it was torture to think of being parted. So they had lived every moment to the full, sleeping hardly at all.

Mary will carry with her to the end of her life, the memory of telling Bryn at last, murmuring against his naked chest that she was in love with him. She did not care, did not mind at all that he spoke no words of love to her, but told her silly things instead about the quality of her voice and the shapeliness of her feet. To have held him, to have made love to him was enough.

She sat naked and joyous for him and he painted her portrait. Whilst he painted she told him of how, once, finding her looking at Bryn's bridesmaid's gift to her, the painting of her with the terrace doves, Papa had laughed, saying, 'Bryn's captured your soul, Mary. It's a beautiful painting. It's a good job he's gone away. A painting like that makes me think you might have captured a little bit of Bryn's soul too!' When she told him that, Bryn put down his brushes and smiled at her. 'Are you fishing for compliments?'

Mary shook her head, laughing up at him. 'I never do. It's rarely worth the effort. You have finished the painting?'

'I have finished it.'

'Will I like it?'

'I hope so.'

'Can I stand up now, can I see the picture? What would Papa think of it?'

'I think, considering the subject-matter, your Papa should never see this!' Bryn had grinned and stepped away from the canvas. Without waiting to put on her gown, her dark hair falling in a soft cloak onto her shoulders, Mary padded barefoot towards him, teasing and saying, 'So, you have made me beautiful? Would Papa think you had captured my soul? Or have I captured yours?' She came round to the front of the canvas and stood quite still as her heart began to pound and she found she was shaking as she breathed a long, soft, 'Oh!' She tried to speak, but Bryn put a hardened rough finger to her lips. Looking into her eyes he said, 'Hush, Mary,' and, lifting her small naked body easily against him, he carried her across the room to the bed where he wrapped her in her silk shawl and, without making love for a long time they lay entwined and peaceful in each other's arms.

They had woken the next day to their last morning together and when at last Bryn could stay no longer and had torn himself away, taking part of her with him for ever, they had both wept. When he departed, he left the portrait with her. It was as if they had known it would be their last time together.

In the four years since she heard of Bryn's death, Mary has been tempted several times to take a lover, sometimes a man, sometimes a woman, though no one ultimately fills the need in her soul that Bryn had done. So, by choice she mostly lives alone without loneliness, but it will be good to be with Anna for a while. Mary will enjoy showing her Marseille. They might even drive out to look at La Roche one day.

That Cathryn should contemplate sending Anna to her at the beginning of the season amuses Mary greatly. An attractive girl amongst so many tourists . . .

7

By eleven o'clock the sun in the enclosed kitchen garden is unbearably hot. Anna has broken a fingernail; she curses and nibbles at the offending ragged edge enjoying the damp taste of earth. It is a very long time since she last bit her nails. It was her Aunt Mary, during those months she spent in Marseille, who taught her not to bite them, painting them with bitter aloes to make her stop, laughing at Anna when she forgot and grimaced at the bitter taste. During those months Mary and Anna's strong alliance was forged.

Anna walks slowly up to the main house and into the kitchen, where she rinses her hands and opens the fridge. Pouring herself a glass of orange juice she perches on the edge of the large pine table. It's the same table that used to stand in the dining room, the table where Cathryn and Mary and Alicia sat on the night when Cathryn's pregnancy was discovered. The table at which so many family celebrations, crises and discussions have taken place. Anna reaches for the notched grooves beneath the table top, her long fingers tracing her own and Greg's initials. They carved them on that last evening at La Roche. It was the last mark Greg ever made at the house, and only Anna knows the initials are there.

Anna's memory is as vivid as a painting. It was 1938, the end of the magic healing summer at La Roche. She was eight years old, sitting hidden by the heavy white folds of the long damask table-cloth beneath the table with Greg, and listening to the adults, Mary and Cathryn sitting together, drinking wine, the night before Cathryn took her family back to England to begin their new life at Brockley.

It was the first time Anna became aware that adults are capable of deception, and the first time she realised, with the clear uncluttered perception of a child, that Aunt Mary loved Bryn more than Mama had ever done. It was something about the way she said his name, something about the way she took a little breath whenever his name was mentioned.

The sound of a bottle being opened had held Greg and Anna silent and still in their cavern beneath the table. Granny Elspeth had seen them to bed, but when Millie had suggested a last game of hide and seek, Greg and Blanche, Edward, Millie and Anna had crept along the house's upper corridors and slipped in and out of shadows and across pools of evening light with glee. What could any adult do to them? It was their last night at La Roche — even Mama would be laughing and kind if she found them. Granny Elspeth and Grandpa Philippe were out with friends and only Cathryn and Mary remained to be wary of. So, when Anna and Greg found themselves hiding together beneath the table and heard footsteps enter the room, a glance between them had said faster than any spoken word ever could that it would be prudent to remain quiet until the adults had gone. Then the conversation had begun and held Anna and Greg in such thrall they could not have moved if they wanted to.

'I'll be sorry to see you all go. I think Maman will be too.'

'Do you really think so, Mary? I thought Maman was just tolerating our presence here. I mean, I know she likes the children, but it's me, isn't it? She's never really forgiven me.'

('What for?' Anna mouths at Greg, who shakes his head and puts a finger to his lips. The carpet smells of dust. Anna thinks she might sneeze and rubs her nose hard. Greg sticks out his tongue.)

'Don't be silly. You know she cares about you.'

'But does she really? She's never forgiven

me for Bryn, never forgiven me for having to make an early marriage. She wanted me to marry old Becque, you know.'

('Greg, what does she mean? Who was old Becque?' Anna breathes the words into Greg's ear and his hair tickles her nose, but he puts his hand over her mouth. His palm tastes of salt when she licks it. He pulls his hand away and sniffs it. 'Your tongue smells of toothpaste.' His breath is hot on her ear.)

Mary was smiling, Anna could hear it in her voice. 'But you didn't marry Becque. Poor old Babette married him — and a fat lot of good it did her.' There is the sound of wine being poured, the children can hear its trickle as it enters the glasses and Anna has such an urgent need to pee that she wets her pyjamas. She wriggles away from Greg, ashamed that he might see the dark stain on the carpet, but he is absorbed in the conversation overhead.

'You got away, Cath, and you married Bryn and you *were* happy once, weren't you?'

'Yes, we were happy, very happy. But it's over. I'm twenty-eight, a mother of two, with no husband. I'm lucky to have found a job.'

'You sound bitter.'

'Not really, not any more. We couldn't have gone on. I do wonder where Bryn is sometimes and I even catch myself wondering if he's safe, but no more than I would wonder

148

about any old friend. Isn't it strange, all that passion burned out to nothing. At least, it was passion on my side.'

'It was passion on both sides.' Mary's voice has got that odd little catch in it that Anna has heard before, but no one else ever seems to hear it. 'He loved you very much. He wouldn't look at anyone else, and even when he left you it wasn't to go to anyone else, was it?'

'You sound as if you wish he might have looked at you, little sister.' Cathryn's voice is light and there's laughter in it.

'How can you say that? Don't be so ridiculous. You know I was never interested in Bryn — if I was, why would I have kept a lookout for you? Have some more wine? I'm going to.'

'Not for me, darling. I've had two already and I'm feeling a bit tipsy. If I drink any more I'll have a foul headache tomorrow. It'll be bad enough travelling with the brats.'

'Perhaps if I'd put my mind to it, I could have taken Bryn from you,' Mary laughs. Is she getting drunk? Her voice sounds funny, but Cathryn doesn't seem to notice, and she laughs too. Anna sees her legs go out of sight and hears the clump of her feet as she puts them up on the table. Anna can see the back legs of her mother's chair tipped at exactly the angle she always tells Anna is dangerous.

'Oh Mary, you were only sixteen and you really weren't his type. He always used to say what a strange little thing you were; you never seemed to laugh like you do now. Far too serious for him in those days — he loved to laugh, he was a happy man. He and I laughed a lot at first, until our differences began to be too apparent. He wanted a simple life and I couldn't cope. Maman was right all along. What a silly little fool I was.'

'You weren't. You were in love.'

'In love? That old chestnut. It didn't do any good, did it? In love wasn't enough when life began to wear Bryn down. Life and me and the children. Did he love me, do you think? I sometimes wonder if it was just the money that he wanted all along. He promised I wouldn't get pregnant, you know, Mary, and yet I did. I sometimes think it was just a plot to get his hands on the money.'

('What does she mean?' Anna pleads with Greg, whose face has gone sharp with interest.)

'Don't be silly.' Mary's voice is crisp. 'Of course it wasn't a plot. You told me yourself when Papa offered to buy him off how hurt Bryn was. Anna was an accident — accidents happen.'

('What does she mean I'm an accident?'

Anna tugs at Greg's sleeve. He leans and whispers in her ear, 'She means you're a bastard, like Millie. Never mind, Anna,' and he kisses her on the cheek before exclaiming, 'Pooh! Anna, you smell of pee!') And so they were discovered, and Anna was dimly aware of Aunt Mary's anguished gaze as the two were hauled out from beneath the table.

'Anna! You've wet yourself, you naughty girl. And what were you doing there anyway?' Her mother's voice is hard and blustering. Above the children's heads she mouths, 'Do you think they understood?'

'Don't be unkind, Cath, I expect they were only playing.' Mary is soft and warm and anxious. She shrugs in response to Cathryn's question. 'Come on, Anna sweetheart, shall Mary take you and get you some clean jamas?'

'You fuss too much, Mary. She should be left to shiver in those, it'd serve her right the little toad.' Cathryn glares at Anna and leaves the room.

Later, unable to sleep, Anna slips from her own bed along the corridor to Mary's room and climbs in beside her. Mary turns in her sleep and wakes to find Anna's curling hair tickling her face. 'What's the matter, sweetheart? Why can't you sleep?'

'I don't want to go back to England

tomorrow, Auntie Mary. I want to stay here with you.'

Mary kisses the top of the little girl's head. 'You'll be back next summer, darling. Granny Elspeth says you and Greg can come back for a holiday.'

'That's nice.' Anna smiles in the darkness and curls closer to Mary. It is very warm in Mary's bed and the two are just falling asleep when Anna remembers why she came to find Mary. 'Mary, what's a bastard? I heard Uncle Edward call someone a lucky bastard the other day and Granny Elspeth told him to go and wash his mouth out; and Greg says I'm a bastard. Is it a bad word?'

At first Anna thinks Mary has gone to sleep and hasn't heard her, but after a while her voice comes through the darkness, very soft and soothing. 'A bastard is someone very special, Anna. I'm one and Millie's one and you're sort of one and we're three of the most specialest people I know. A great many kings have fathered bastards. If you look up bastard in a dictionary, it will only tell you words about people's parents not being married, but it won't tell you the feelings those parents had for each other. Never forget, Anna, your parents loved each other once — very, very much.'

8

Anna's small grey cat has found her way up from the cottage into La Roche's kitchen. She startles Anna as she leaps on the table beside her, making her spill orange juice onto her shorts; it trickles stickily down her bare legs. 'Damn you, Paws, you nearly gave me a heart attack!' She fetches a cloth and wipes her legs, leaving a sleek trail on the dusty bloom of pollens from the garden. The cat has followed her to the sink and butts against her. 'For God's sake, leave me alone!' Anna swipes at the cat with the cloth. Surprised and aggrieved, Paws growls and runs to the door, looking back at Anna with bristling fur and startled eyes.

'Oh hell. I'm sorry. Come on, Paws, come back here.' Anna squats and holds out her hand palm up, balancing on the balls of her feet, coaxing, 'Come on, puss. It's too hot out there, come on, I'll get you some water.' She runs water in a shallow dish and places it on the floor. Sitting in a patch of shade on the cool terracotta tiles, with her legs stretched out in front of her, Anna eases her back against a cupboard door and fondles the cat's ears, as Paws laps forgivingly at the water.

If only Jean had never come to La Roche, she could have had moments like this for the rest of her life. Innocence was in the sun falling on the tiles, the polished wood of the table, the motes of dust floating in the light from the open door. The scents of the garden eddy into the room on currents of warm air. She had been content before Jean came. Content but not joyful. If he went away she could find contentment again. She could live alone. Alone. The word sounds in her head. She had been alone since Millie and Leo; sometimes she had been alone *with* Millie and Leo. There were people she knew in the village, there were one or two friends from England who would visit, but on the whole she was alone. Her history made it hard to make new friends. Tears slide beneath her closed eyelids. It's very quiet in the room. Paws finishes drinking and pads on silent feet to sit on the threshold.

Outside a lone bird whistles. The strange peace of hundreds of cicadas shivering the air closes in, holding Anna immobile in the heat of the afternoon. She feels as though she is waiting for something, but is unsure of what and she wishes, as she has wished for most of her life, that things had been different in the spring and summer of 1947.

How glad Anna had been when Mama decided to send her away to Marseille. Cathryn had said, 'After all, you're seventeen, darling — it's time you gained some polish, and to practise your French will be wonderful.' The thought of spending some time with Mary had pleased Anna. She remembered Mary, smiling down at her that last day on the beach, and she remembered Mary's quiet voice telling her they were both special people.

Mama didn't think Anna was special. Mama's lover, James, was finding Anna interesting in a way that frightened and appalled the young girl; he had never actually touched her but it was like living with a poisonous spider — Anna felt it would only be a matter of time. She felt too she had no one to turn to, not even Greg. He had changed.

Greg, who had always been so close to her he felt like part of her own skin, had been strange and aloof all winter. He had gone back to school after Christmas with hardly a backward glance; there had been no hugs, no funny private code words. It was as though some part of her that she had not even known existed had been hacked away. So it might be pleasant to be with Mary, to be made to feel special again. Besides, now that the war was over it would be good to see something of the world. To work for money would be good too. She would be one of the grown-ups at last.

Lonelier than she had ever been in her life, Anna had taken to spending time with the other young people of the village. She and Cathryn had had furious arguments, Cathryn declaring that she was little better than a slut hanging around outside the pub, and Anna flaring with rage and the bitterness of the unloved that she had no one else to be with, James's children were too young for her and Greg was away at school. What else was she supposed to do with her time? Cathryn had slapped her, as she seemed to be doing increasingly often, and left the room.

Anna was under no illusions that James's unwanted attentions had gone unnoticed by Mama. Less welcome was the thought of being removed from the company of the young men of the village, but when Mama wrote to Mary, she and Anna were both delighted when Mary replied saying she would be pleased to have Anna for the summer.

Mama had told Anna she would be 'safe' with Aunt Mary; that she was certain Mary would keep her away from men, was certain that Mary never had anything to do with them.

'Mary lives like a nun, hardly surprising really with her looks.' Mama had tossed her own head of frizzled curls.

* * *

Travelling alone for the first time, Anna had left the peace and rural tranquillity of Northamptonshire for the bright lights and brilliant sunshine of Marseille; she had been almost sick with fear and anticipation. Speaking to no one on the flight out, hoping desperately to appear sophisticated in her thin cotton dress and the cheap little hat that Mama had sworn was fashionable, Anna arrived in a state of high tension.

There was no one to greet her at Nice airport and Anna struggled through customs with her suitcase, half terrified that the *douanier* would stop her when she said she had nothing to declare. The unaccustomed press of people and the noise and roar of the airport tore at her nerves. Her heart beat distressingly fast and nausea gripped her stomach. She had suffered stage fright once as a child, pushed onto the makeshift stage of her village school to play a good fairy at Sleeping Beauty's christening. She had felt then as she felt now, that the ground in front of her might at any moment give way.

Nothing was safe, nothing predictable. She should never have come. Mama had been wrong to send her. It didn't matter that the sky was the freshest blue she had ever seen, that the sun was shining, or that the clamour of French voices called 'home' to something deep inside her. She was alone and petrified until, from out of a sea of faces, a fashionably dressed young woman appeared, running in high heels, too high to run in at all. Waving and smiling and calling Anna's name in a voice that Anna remembered, and remembered with such unexpected affection that she burst into embarrassing tears.

'Anna! Darling! I'm so sorry, *c'est un embouteillage* — a traffic jam. I'm so sorry to be late. Don't cry, *chérie*.' And Anna had found herself enfolded in a warm embrace, kissed lightly on both cheeks and whisked into Mary's waiting car.

Driving through the shimmering heat of Southern France, Mary had chattered lightly of family details, of her work, of La Roche, breaking off to compliment Anna on how much she had grown up — 'and as tall as me,' Mary had laughed, 'which isn't very tall at all.'

Anna's apprehension had melted away under the warmth of her aunt's personality and she found herself responding eagerly,

158

sometimes in French, sometimes in English, sliding to her delight, effortlessly between the two languages and all the time she drank in and marvelled at Mary's appearance. Anna's childhood memory of Mary had been so at variance with Mama's description, it was pure pleasure for Anna to discover her memory had not played her false.

Watching Mary's lively face and enjoying her bright chatter, Anna had suddenly divined how very jealous of Mary Mama must be to so malign her. Mary was lovely, Mary had a life all her very own. Anna would like a life like that, not like poor Mama, stuck with dull old James, knowing all the time that her little sister was apparently having so much more fun. Anna almost felt sorry for her mother; where Mary's well-groomed hair shone with no trace of grey, Mama's was dull and yellowed. Mary's figure showed no sign of running to fat as Mama's had done, and as for Mary's laugh, it was surely the happiest sound Anna had ever heard.

Sitting now on the kitchen floor, Anna opens her eyes. An intense wave of longing to be with Mary again, of renewed sorrow for her death threatens to engulf her. If only it was Mary's laughter she could hear, not just a bird calling somewhere out on the shore. Light footsteps in the entrance hall interrupt

Anna's thoughts. She had meant to be ready for Jean, to have worked out some plan, possibly even to have decided what to tell him — and what not to tell. Now he has caught her day dreaming. Anna scrambles to her feet picking up her empty glass, pretending to wash it.

'Hi! I'm back!' Jean bends to kiss Anna's cheek, 'My God, you're white as a sheet. You look as though you've seen a ghost!'

Anna forces a laugh and returns Jean's kiss; his skin feels warm beneath her lips and the slight stubble of his jaw grazes her cheek. 'You startled me, that's all. I was thinking of Mary.'

Jean regards her steadily. 'Mary? But she's been dead for quite a while now.'

'I know she has, but I still think about her from time to time.'

'You must do, she was a good friend to you.'

'She was. I miss her.' Anna sees an opening and, with the feeling she is stepping into space she frames her question, 'Don't you miss relatives who have died? I want to talk to you about something — '

Jean smiles. 'I didn't have many relatives in the first place to die!' Then he sees Anna's intent gaze and stops. 'Sorry that was unpardonable — it was unthinking of me. You

160

have . . . too many — and I think I interrupted you?'

Anna's heart beats as if she has run a marathon. She steadies herself against the sink — the time for telling has passed. 'It doesn't matter. Let's put the shopping away.' She begins to unpack the baskets of groceries which Jean has brought back from the town. A fly buzzes low across the kitchen and Anna attempts to swat it with the flat of her hand, knocking over a carton of cream. 'Oh! Shit! Bloody hell!'

'Hey, take it easy, Anna. It doesn't matter, it's only spilled a little. I'll wipe it up.'

'Leave it. I'll do it.'

'Okay, okay. Don't get so fierce.'

Anna fetches a cloth and wipes the spilled cream; her hair has come loose around her flushed face. 'I'm sorry, Jean. Really, I am sorry, I'll snap out of it.'

Jean chooses to say nothing more until the shopping has all been stowed away. From time to time he steals covert glances at Anna; he thinks she is looking very tired and appears to be lost in her own thoughts. Still neither of them speaks until, reaching into the fridge Jean produces a bottle of beer. 'Would you like some of this? We could go and sit out in the shade and drink it, if you like?'

'That would be nice.' Anna speaks as

politely as if Jean were a stranger whilst she watches his familiar hands open the bottle and pour them each a glass.

'Come on, darling, come and talk to me.' Jean holds out a glass to her. Anna watches the sunlight caught in the deep amber of her beer.

'What shall we talk about?' She sips quickly at her drink. It is very cool. Slightly bitter. She drinks again. A longer drink this time.

'Well, what would you like to talk about?'

Anna laughs. A sudden laugh. Too shrill. 'Don't say that! It's the biggest conversation killer ever.'

Jean puts a lazy arm across her shoulders, nuzzling the top of her head. 'I suppose it is. I love the smell of your hair. You're a very pretty woman. No — you're a very beautiful woman.'

'Aha! Your English is becoming superlative!'

Jean grins. 'And your jokes are becoming feeble!'

'Like my mind.' Anna puts an arm round Jean's waist. Banter is easy, it's something you can do with one part of your brain whilst another part races about like a rat in a trap — if you've had sufficient practice — but for how long? They walk together into the garden and round the side of the house, their feet crunching in unison on the light gravel of the paths Anna has had reinstated.

Jean has brought an extra bottle of beer from the fridge. Lodging it in the shadow of a lavender bush he lowers himself to the shaded front doorstep, holding out his free hand to Anna, smiling up at her, saying, 'Come live with me, and be my love.'

As she sits down beside him Anna automatically caps the line, 'And we will some new pleasures prove.'

'John Donne. How wonderful to have someone writing poetry for you. If I could, I would write poetry for you, Anna, but I'm a practical man. It takes a romantic to write poetry.'

'I like you to be practical.'

'You wouldn't want me to write poetry for you?' Jean teases, but there is something in Anna's expression that is disturbing him.

'I've told you I like you to be practical.'

Jean watches her, wondering at her remoteness. It's as if she has slipped away from him — somehow she has made herself inaccessible. Though the sun is shining as brightly as ever, the air seems cooler. Feeling he is on precarious ground Jean ventures, against his better judgement, 'Has anyone ever written poetry for you?'

'It was a very long time ago.'

'You weren't happy?' Jean looks at his beer

glass. What's the matter with him this afternoon — has the drink gone to his head? He puts his glass down. 'Sorry. None of my business,' but Anna is looking directly at him. She has come back to him, he senses she is completely there when she reaches for his hand and kisses it gently.

'But it is your business, Jean,' she murmurs. 'It has to be your business. I would have told you sooner or later anyway.' She is blinking rapidly, scrubbing at her eyes with the hem of her T-shirt. She folds her hands in her lap displaying a composure she does not feel. When she speaks her voice is so low, Jean has to bend close to hear her.

'There was a lover who wrote poetry to me. He wrote poetry and I loved him very, very much. I adored him. He was everything in the world to me. Then . . . ' Anna pauses for so long that Jean glances at her; her face is turned in profile, her hat and her hair hide her expression, but he can see that her lower lip is trembling.

'How old were you?'

Anna moves restlessly next to Jean, she bites her lip. Again there is such a long pause that Jean is unsure whether she has heard him. She is not looking at him, she is looking at the sunlight falling in slices between the trees. When she begins to speak again she appears to have come to a decision. Her voice is strong and confident; she speaks as though she is telling a story that she has known and rehearsed for a long time.

'I was seventeen. It was the summer of 1947 — harvest-time at Brockley. I'd been with Mary since the spring. Mama had sent me to France . . . for various reasons. It was heady stuff for a young girl, leading such a sophisticated life, particularly then. There were smart dinners out when Mary was off duty (she managed one of the swishest hotels in Marseille). Sometimes we went to the theatre and sometimes there were fabulous bathing parties. Millie used to drive over and join us whenever she could. She was working as a photographer's assistant. I think she was missing her brother Edward who had got married rather quickly, and there had been another sister called Blanche who died in a road accident. One way or another, poor Millie had been the one left behind and there was a strong streak of rebellion in her. She was much more worldly wise than me; she fascinated me with her fashionable clothes and her taste for expensive food. She gave me my first cigarette and my first glass of wine. As for Mary, in spite of the age difference between us, we had a lot in common. In fact, the three of us were practically inseparable.

Mary had been kind to me when I was little, and Millie had grown out of the sulks she used to have when we were younger — it was like unexpectedly discovering I had two wonderful sisters. Mind you, Mary kept Millie and me on the straight and narrow. She told me she was under strict orders from Mama to keep an eye on me and, as for Millie, *somebody* had to keep an eye on her!

'From the instant Mary took the hideous hat Mama had made me wear to travel to France, and threw it in the bin, declaring it wasn't fit for a donkey to be seen in, I adored her. She took me shopping, she never forced me to do anything, not even tidy my room, and because I didn't *have* to do things of course I soon learned to look after myself. After a few weeks I began to realise I was capable of making my own decisions. Because I didn't have to be a child any more, I began to grow up.'

Anna pauses and sips at her beer. Jean smiles, and interjects, 'And that's when you met your poetry-writing lover?' He watches her tense as she replies, and her voice has become hard and flat, 'I only wish it was. There were men, of course, who were interested. I was young and I was pretty, there were whole evenings of dancing and very occasionally parties into the early hours, but

166

Mary made sure there was never anything more than flirtation. Nonetheless it was an intoxicating freedom for a girl from the country. I was earning my own money. I loved the work — I liked meeting all the people coming into Reception in the hotel. I liked seeing them transformed during their stay, from looking white and tired to relaxed and happy and bronzed; it was like a magic trick and I felt in some way I was part of it. I was happy, happier than I'd been for years.

'Then, at the end of July a letter came from Cathryn — Mama. She'd changed her mind about me being away. Perhaps one of my postcards home had said too much about what a good time I was having. Whatever the cause, it suddenly wasn't convenient to Mama any more for me to be in France. There was too much work for her in the house and the farm had to be managed as well.'

'So she called you home?'

'I suppose she thought it would be safer for me to be at home, than dancing in Marseille. She had been paranoid about me 'getting into trouble' with the local boys, she'd thought the airmen based nearby during the war were after me, and now I had made her frantic about the possibility of holidaymakers, but I think what she really thought was that the main danger — James, my sort of stepfather — was out of the way. He'd been getting horribly greasy and making all kinds of suggestive comments before Mama sent me packing to Marseille.

'Anyway, James had started being away a lot of the time and Mama was having problems with staff. Something to do with wages and James not giving her enough money to deal with it all. Brockley was quite a big estate to look after and there was no way my mother could run it all herself. The sensible thing to do would have been to sell up and move to something smaller, but James wasn't given to doing sensible things. Neither was Mama.

'To be fair to James, I don't think he could really have given her any more help unless of course he'd come home from time to time. They did sell up soon after the next Christmas, by which time they only had enough left for a smallish house in London. But in that summer James was hoping to save the farm by making a profit on the harvest. It was incredible — the weather had been so wonderful, endless days of sunshine and the harvest was the best for years, but he left Mama to deal with it all. It was a crazy thing to do, but I think he was too busy up in Town living a bachelor existence. James wasn't exactly a stable character, and he was already having other affairs. I suppose I should have felt sorry for Mama but all I could think of was how she had an unfortunate habit of driving her menfolk away and how she was going to wreck my lovely time in France dragging me back to be a country bumpkin.

'Mama's letter came, the royal summons. Mary telephoned Mama straight away, begging her to at least let me stay on until the end of the season, but Mama was adamant. She said the harvest was important and she needed every pair of hands she could get. So, in spite of all Mary's pleas, I had to go. Had to leave Mary and her wise and clever ways, and Millie's lively friendship, the fun of working as receptionist in the hotel, the flattery of all those holidaymaking young men and go back to Northamptonshire and Brockley House and the threat of sleazy James arriving at any minute.

'Northamptonshire has little to recommend it. It must surely be one of the most suffocating counties in England. No sea coast, no vast views. English Midlands. Claustrophobia for a young girl who's just had her first taste of excitement.

'At first I tried to tell myself it wasn't too bad; at least James wasn't around with his awful braying voice and clammy hands.

Mama looked awful, worn out and worried; the contrast between her and Mary wasn't just physical either. Mama tried to treat me like a child again — you can imagine how much that rankled. I thought I was so grown up, but I probably behaved like a spoiled brat and I know Mama was regretting bringing me home. I was worse than useless. I was so determined to be a pain in the arse. Instead of helping with the work I'd get up early and either take myself off for a walk or saddle up one of the horses and disappear for most of the day. Needless to say, Mama and I had endless rows. Looking back I feel sorry for her. At the time I hated her for ruining my life.

'What did I know? I was about to really wreck it. Without any help from her.

'I missed Mary and Millie dreadfully. James's children were less than useless as companions; they were only young and only ever talked to each other, unless they absolutely had to communicate with someone else. So I had no real female companionship, and as for Greg . . . I hardly recognised Greg. In the few months I'd been away he'd grown up so much; he'd been doing a lot of work on the farm and he'd grown big and strong — he seemed much older than when I'd left. Greg and I had always been so close as children, but the previous Christmas he'd started being moody and difficult to communicate with. Now it seemed impossible. He never stayed around me for very long and there was some kind of tension between us. I didn't know what it was at first . . . ' Anna's voice trails away. Beneath her hat, her face feels hot and flushed.

'You must have been very lonely.' Jean turns her hand over and plants a kiss in the palm.

'I was.'

'And this is when you met your poet?'

'It's when I became pregnant with Francesca.'

A tremor has started somewhere deep inside Anna, a thrumming along the nerves and interconnections of her body's telegraph system. She thinks she might shatter like broken glass, or the sudden shock of dark birds that erupts flapping and beating its way over the woods, making them both jump. The crows circle cawing, loud and coarse in the peace of the day before they resettle in the rafts of the treetops.

Neither Anna nor Jean speak. A tension is growing in Jean too. The whole afternoon will soon swell and vibrate with it, expanding to the blue dome of the sky and quieting even the waves on the seashore. The sun has

171

moved round and is beating down on them. It is very hot, but neither Jean nor Anna mentions moving into the shade. The heat is becoming unbearably oppressive. Anna shifts uneasily — she doesn't think that she can finish this after all. The combination of heat and beer and tension is making her feel ill, but still she doesn't make a move towards the shade.

Anna wishes profoundly that they were down at the cottage, Jean practising his meditation, or reading, whilst she potters in the cottage. She wishes that Megan had not written telling her about the exhibition. She wishes that Francesca had not phoned with her threats. Anna tries to swallow, but her throat is constricted. Jean's eyes are closed and his long lashes make shadows across his high cheekbones. A tic is running in his jaw. He continues to hold her hand, but his is still, and holding tight enough to hurt.

'Anna, you don't have to tell me. You really don't have to tell me. It will make no difference to the way I feel about you. Why do you want to tell me?'

Tears are beginning to roll down Anna's face and her voice comes in convulsive gasps. 'I want to tell you . . . because when you see Megan . . . you'll know, and even if you didn't, Francesca . . . Francesca would make sure . . . that you did. I . . . I truly believe that she hates me, but I love her . . . and I love you and . . . I want you to go on loving me . . . but if you don't I'll understand.'

Her voice has sunk to a hoarse whisper and, oh God, Anna wants to run, to get up and run and hide. She should never have begun this conversation. It didn't have to happen.

Jean looks directly at Anna. He smiles very sweetly and leans in under her hat and kisses her, cradling her face with his hard, strong fingers. 'I love you, Anna, and if you're going to tell me that Francesca was illegitimate, that's okay. Is Francesca trying to wreak some kind of belated vengeance on you? Because if she is she'll have me to answer to!

'I'm only sorry for you, my darling, that it was that bastard James. You're telling me he raped you, aren't you? Is that what it was?' and as she sobs without replying, he murmurs, 'Oh my poor, poor Anna. It really doesn't matter to me that Charles wasn't Megan's grandfather. I'm illegitimate myself. I'm just so terribly, terribly sorry for you, about James. It must have been unimaginably awful.' He takes her by the hand. 'Come on, darling, let's go into the shade. It's far too hot out here, you're looking ill. My lovely Anna, I love you so much. It was a long time ago. You must try and put it all behind you. You've had other relationships since and if Charles could deal with it then I'm sure I can. Charles did know, I suppose? Not that it's any of my business. It really makes no difference to you and me.' He stands and looks down at her.

When Anna makes no move but sits staring at him wordlessly, he becomes less sure of himself.

'*Merde!* I've guessed wrong. I've made things worse for you, haven't I, poor darling?' Jean looks down at her, his face so contorted with pity for her pain, that a yelp of hysteria escapes from Anna.

'Oh Jean! Don't look at me like that. You must be imagining all sorts of terrible things. I wasn't raped. By anyone.' Anna stands up. She is very small next to Jean. 'You were right, Charles wasn't Megan's grandfather, but it wasn't James either.' She draws a soft breath before almost shouting the words. 'It was Greg. It was my brother.'

The day shifts and spreads out around her like ripples in a pool.

9

Extract from Greg's diary —

Christmas 1946

I miss Anna. She's here, but somehow we can't be together. Since I came home from school this holiday I can't seem to speak to her like I used to be able to. I don't know what it is, but we're funny with each other. Prickly, antagonistic. Not easy like we were. I heard her out by the stables. She was calling and calling our special owl call, but I couldn't answer her. It seemed suddenly silly and childish, then a strange thing happened. She got a real owl answering her — at least, I suppose it was a real owl. She must have thought it was me to begin with, but then there were two of them calling. For an age after she came in I could hear them calling and answering, calling and answering. They're like Anna and I used to be. I imagined their unseen ashy wings and imagined my soul flying out to be with them living in the darkness without speech.

August 4, 1947
Anna came back last week. France has
made her different or perhaps I'm the one
that's different. She's beautiful. I hadn't
realised before. I'm her brother — I
shouldn't have thoughts about her like I
do, but I just want to touch her all the
time. Her skin's like warm brown velvet, or
toast and honey. That's what she is — toast
and honey — all golden and browns. When
she stands out in the fields talking to the
men I watch. She's like a part of the
landscape. Solid and golden — like all this
summer's been and now she's here I know
what I've been waiting for. I know now
what it was between us at Christmas. What
I dream about at night is her. She's filling
me up and eating me away at the same
time. I'm in a kind of delicious agony.
Can't bear to be in the same room as her.
Can't bear to be away from her. Her eyes
are . . .

The diary entry is not completed. Perhaps
Cathryn looked into Greg's room, perhaps
the younger children ran past shouting and
fighting. Perhaps it was Anna herself.

August 6
Anna and I have been brother and sister all

176

our lives. She was good to me before Papa went away; she tried to protect me from all the hurt of Mama and Papa and their fights. She is my older sister, she is not to be thought about the way I think about her. I took the horse-whip to myself out in the barn this morning. I hate myself. I must not feel the way I do about her, it's so wrong. I don't know what to do. I have to leave the room whenever she comes into it.

August 7
Anna is my sister. Anna and I have the same parents. I love Anna like a brother. She is forbidden fruit. I want to hit every other man who looks at her. I should horse-whip myself again but it was ineffectual and I'm too afraid of the pain. Anna is my sister, she is my sister and that's all there is to it.

August 8
Went into the town on the bus. Mama didn't know where I'd gone. Got drunk, wanted to pick up a real prostitute, there were none about but one of the local girls took me back to her house. Her parents were out. I gave it to her. It was what she wanted. She'd done it before, that much

was obvious. She showed me what to do. So I suppose I'm a man now. I didn't feel anything other than cheated somehow. Came home in the evening, still drunk. Mama was furious. Anna nowhere to be seen.

August 10
Had the same girl again last night, she was hanging about down at the pub. It was better this time. I wasn't drunk. She's called Sally — we got drunk together after on her dad's port. Then she pulled up her dress and we were going to do it again but she asked if I had any sisters and I couldn't do it any more and she kicked me out. Said I was a nancy boy. Came in late, had to sleep in the barn. Mama had locked me out. She was furious again, but I don't care. At least this way I don't have to think about Anna.

August 11
Anna saw me going to catch the bus after work. I thought I'd go see Sal again and try to patch it up. At least she stops me thinking about Anna, but then Anna walked down the lane past the bus stop and we talked. It was good, it was like before Papa left except I had to hold onto the

fence behind the bus stop to prevent myself from collapsing, my legs felt as if they didn't belong to me, but I don't think Anna noticed. When she stands next to me, she's tiny. I hadn't noticed before and she smelled so nice. Clean and sweet — I think she'd just washed her hair. When the bus came she got on it too and instead of going to see Sal I went to the pictures with Anna. We laughed a lot and I bought us both some fish and chips on the way home. Perhaps I can put all these sex thoughts about her out of my head and we can be friends. Real friends. But it's more than sex, I know that now after Sal. That was sex — this is something else. Anna just fills up my thoughts all the time.

August 12
Anna very odd with me today. She wouldn't talk about the film last night when Mama asked at breakfast; she went funny and left. Haven't seen her all day but she came back this evening after tea. Said she'd been off on the horse. Mama was angry, said she'd brought Anna back to work, not mess about on horses. Both of us forbidden to go out. I hadn't the stomach to go see Sal again anyway, so Anna and I sat with each other a long time this evening

talking a bit and reading. I think I'm getting this whole thing in perspective. She's my sister.

August 14
Mama relented a bit and let us play tennis in the evening over at the vicarage, with the vicar and his daughter, Doris — a big lumpy girl, nothing like Anna. I could hardly bear to look at Anna so I played badly, having such wicked thoughts the vicar would be horrified. I thought of a poem. I wish I could give the poem to Anna

> *Your racquet splices air,*
> *later we'll make love.*
> *My fingertips will know*
> *what they already know —*
> *the bones and sinews that are you.*
> *My racquet strings rebound.*
> *I have not touched you — yet.*
> *You zap the ball.*
> *Dead centre.*

August 15
I hardly dare write what's happened. If anyone ever finds this it will be terrible but I must tell someone. I'm not a Catholic — can't confess to a priest, this diary's my

only salvation. I feel as if a hot brand's burning into my mind. I was walking in the spinney after working in the fields all day, it was still very hot and she was there. There were poppies bound in her hair and cornflowers and wheat stalks; she'd made herself a crown like we used to do when we were little. She looked like a pagan goddess; her dress was open at the neck, she was sitting with her feet in the stream and her legs were scratched and bleeding a bit from the wheat stubble. I went and stood behind her, where I could see the swell of her breasts inside her open dress and she leaned back against my legs and looked up at me. She was laughing, she was going to say something then it happened — I bent down and kissed her, smack on the mouth, and I put my hand on the weight of one of her breasts. She didn't pull away. She didn't move my hand away. She kissed me back and, when we'd stopped kissing she tugged me down to sit beside her. We didn't speak a word, but she looked at me like a startled deer and then her arms went round me and we were tearing at each other's clothes. We were in the stream together and on the bank together and I was in her and she gave and gave and gave until we were both crying and shaking and terrified. I wanted to write all that happened, so I don't forget, but I can't bring myself to write any more. Anyway, how could I forget — and what are we going to do now?

September 2
There's been no time to write in here. Anna and I have been together whenever and wherever we can. It's been mad. It's been wonderful. It's crazy. I gave her the tennis poem, she loved it. It made her laugh. She said she'd been thinking the same things on the night we played tennis. She said I was a prophet.

Our delicious secret nearly found out by Mama last night. She came looking for us out in the barn — Anna heard her just in time. She hid behind the old tractor while I pretended to be looking for something over by the door to distract Mama. 'Where's Anna?' Mama asks. 'I'm not sure,' I mumble. 'Gone down to the village, I think.' 'What, at this time of night? That girl's getting into bad ways,' says Mama. Then the greatest joke — Mama looks me up and down and says, 'Do your flies up, for goodness sake, Greg. How many times have I told you not to pee out here. It's just laziness. You're not one of the workmen, you know,' and off she flounces. Anna crept out from behind the tractor and we laughed so much we cried. I love her.

September 4 1947
I'm devastated. Anna says we mustn't let it happen again. When I go back to school tomorrow she says that must be an end to it. She says she won't even write; we've got to stop thinking about each other that way and go back to being brother and sister properly. I can't bear it. Told her I'd run away from school to be with her in London. She starts her new job next week.

September 20
I hate it here. I hate school, I want to be with Anna. The swifts and swallows are still here, they make me think of her. Air's so crisp and cool this morning it's like biting into an apple — that makes me think of her too. She wrote a letter last week about a man called Charles at the office. He's taken her to a concert and he's taken her to dinner. I think she thought her letter would make me laugh. It didn't. I just feel jealous. He'd better not have kissed her. I can't bear to think of that.

September 25
Jenkins and I gated. Went on a bender last night. Nearly told him about Anna, thank God I didn't. Not quite drunk enough. Ross, MR Ross, *sir*! sent me out for a run this a.m., the bastard. Air was like cold water. I could hardly breathe and my head's got steam hammers in it. Heard the church clock strike the hour on my way back — made me think of Brockley. Made me think of Anna. Sod it all, I just want to be with her but I'm not going to write back to that stupid letter of hers. It felt as if she was just showing off.

October 24
I know it's a terrible risk but I just want to write everything in here that's happened. No short cuts, no abbreviations. Everything just as I remember it. First the sound of Brockley Church clock. How it sounded as Anna came into the house — it's such a part of living here that sometimes I don't even notice it, but as soon as she came back into the house it was like a light switching on and I felt as if I noticed everything. Every single thing became hugely important. She looked lovely, she was wearing a soft brown dress and it suited her. It made me think of a tiny bird.

She's done her hair differently. When she saw me she was surprised and said to Mama that she hadn't known I was home for half-term. She blushed when she said it and Mama remarked that she was looking very flushed and was she all right and Anna said yes, it was just coming into the warm house from outside and then she wouldn't look at me, so I knew she was lying when she said it was all over between us. She talked a lot at dinner about this man called Charles. She's been out with him quite often since she wrote to me. He is apparently to be in charge of the office she works in and she asked Mama if she could bring him here some time soon and Mama looked all sort of knowing and said yes of course she could, she'd be pleased to meet him and James, who's here for once, hurrumphed a bit into his moustache and said yes that was all right and of course they'd like to meet him, and I hated Charles without even meeting him. I think James has the hots for Anna, the old sleaze.

After the meal we all sat for a while in the dining room and talked and then I said I thought I'd just go out and talk to the horses for a bit and tried to signal to Anna to come too but she wouldn't even look at me. By the time I came back in she'd gone up to bed and when I tried her door it was locked.

Next morning I was up early but Anna was up before me and had gone out on Pagan. By the time she got back I'd cut my losses and gone for a walk down to the village.

Even without all the trees turning colour I'd know what time of year it is from the babble of the starlings, those ceaseless notes and that falling whistle. I wish I could draw that sound, sweet and swooping because from now on, from this day it will always make me think of Anna. There are smaller birds too, constant squeaking staccato notes and chirring undertones. I'm not an ornithologist, I can't identify each one but they formed a tapestry, weaving their background to what happened. It's as if the whole world has a different meaning now.

I'd mooched round the village — had a couple of pints — was walking back and there was Anna coming towards me along the lane. It was just as if the light had all been beaten out like flat gold all around her and there was a cloud of midges shimmering around her hair like a sort of halo. She looked so wonderful. She walked right up to me and said, 'What are we going to do?

I'll have to go back to London.' I asked her what she meant and she said, 'This,' and stood up on her toes and kissed me. It was like having everything drawn out of me. She put her two hands on either side of my face and we stayed there and for one crazy fragile moment we didn't care who saw us.

When we'd stopped kissing she took my hand and without either of us saying anything we went off into the little side wood. We still didn't talk until we were right in amongst the trees and it was as if they were all lit from underneath, the reds and golds made the trees like huge lanterns. Then we kissed each other again and again and I mumbled into her hair that I thought she hadn't wanted me any more and she said she's crazy about me and hasn't stopped thinking about me all the time she's been away and she hadn't wanted this to happen. I asked her who the hell Charles is and she said he's a man who's taken an interest in her but I'm not to be jealous. She's tried to be interested in him, tried to stop herself from loving me. She said it — LOVING me — then she took my hand and slid it inside her shirt and I felt the warmth and softness of her breast and she was kissing me all the time and it was incredible. We were laughing and undoing our own and each other's clothes like a pair of lunatics. We were there in the wood completely naked and the birds were still calling and there was no one else around and we lay on my coat and under hers and we made love and she felt so wonderful. It didn't go on for long — I was too excited, but Anna didn't seem to mind. We just lay in each other's arms afterwards and the leaves kept falling on the ground. I could hear them pattering every few seconds and the sweet smell of decay was in my nose for hours afterwards.

Anna left the wood first. She got back into her clothes and tidied her hair. I pulled some leaves out of it. I've still got them — I'm going to press them in the back of here. After five minutes I followed her and we spent the afternoon ostentatiously separately, and made sure we didn't sit near each other at dinner. It made me laugh watching Anna pretending to flirt with old James over the pudding.

Oh God — I know what we're doing is wrong in the eyes of the Law and the Church, but how can it be? We love each other. I can't believe there'll be hell and damnation to pay for this.

All that was two days ago and now Anna has just been here in my room. It was a risk but we were fairly certain no one would be in the house for a few hours. Mama is up in London with James for the day. So Anna came to me and we made love again here in my room, and it was wonderful, better than it's ever been. We've done it three times this afternoon. She came in just to talk. She's so full of fun and ideas and we were laughing at something funny she'd just said and it was like electricity racing between us. It was just so amazing to lie in a bed together. Her body is so beautiful. If only we could go away somewhere where nobody knows us. We could live together. No one would need to know who we are.

We fell asleep and Mama nearly found us — she'd come back on an earlier train than James. Anna had to hide under my bed when Mama came in all tired and grubby from the journey. She poked her head in at the door of my room, asked where Anna was. I said I'd no idea — she went off to have her bath and Anna crawled out from under the bed. By the time it was teatime there was Anna all neat and tidy and serving cake just like she'd been baking it all afternoon.

Anna says she'll write to me when I'm back at school. I've promised to write back this time, I didn't know how much I'd hurt her by not writing. I can't bear to think of her crying and on her own. She says she loves me. She says she's never felt so alive.

December 29

In place of Gold
Penny for every lonely thought,
penny for every stone unturned
penny for presents never bought,
penny for all the bridges burned
penny for speeches never made,
penny for all the love unearned
penny for music left unplayed,
penny for memories unshared
penny for living in the shade,
penny for the soul laid bare
penny for all the silent cries,
penny for things left undeclared.
He spins the tight-rope of his lies.
She could be rich, she could be wise.

Charles and Anna went back to London today. I'm so afraid that Charles will ask Anna to marry him. My love for her hurts so much. We're together as often as we dare. When we move to London next month it's going to be harder; the house is smaller, there's less privacy. I sometimes think James's brats suspect something is

190

going on, but they say nothing. James has chosen the house we'll live in. Anna came home for Christmas. Charles was with her. Her last letter before she came here said I had to try to forget her in 'that way' and she was bringing Charles with her to make it easier. Anna is going to move out of her 'broom cupboard flat', as she calls it, and come back to live with the family when we get to London. I wish she wouldn't; it makes things more difficult for us.

I don't like Charles, he's a bit of a glamour boy — all that easy charm. I don't trust him. I think he might be in love with Anna. When he was here I thought I would never be on my own with her, which is what she intended by inviting him here. I know it is, but she's been with me almost more often than ever before. We're part of each other, we need each other, there's a bond between us that nothing will break.

One night she came to my room and we did it nearly all night — it was exciting, dangerous, knowing that man Charles was only in the next room. Christmas Eve was wonderful. Anna and I managed to sneak out of the house and we went to the woods; it was cold, but it didn't matter. I held her inside my coat and we did it against a tree. No one knew where we were and when we came back it was getting dark. Anna looked amazing, all dark-eyed and pink-cheeked — she has the most incredible skin. Anna, Anna, Anna. I love writing her name. Anna, ANNA, ANNA!!

10

Anna is asleep at La Roche in the little
room that used to be Millie's. Jean has gone
back down to the cottage and the moon is
up. Jean — dear, trustworthy, reliable Jean,
the unshockable, the one who has recited to
Anna his ideals and philosophies for only
living in the present, for not carrying guilt
with her for any past incidents in her life,
this same Jean has withdrawn into a taciturn
and shaken shell. He has retired to the
cottage for the night, leaving Anna alone at
La Roche.

The afternoon has been one of the hardest,
most exhausting Anna has had to endure for
a very long time. In the hush that had
followed Anna's disclosure neither she nor
Jean had spoken, and the constraint between
them had gone on filling up the afternoon
until Anna thought she might never be able to
speak again. On legs like lead she had walked
blindly back into the house.

When, at last, Jean came in search of her,
he discovered her sitting motionless on the
tea terrace at the back of the house.

'I thought I might find you here.' He

hesitated on the steps down into the garden.

'Did you?' Anna's voice was flat and her head averted.

'It's one of your favourite places, isn't it?'

'Yes.'

'Anna . . . what you have told me about Greg . . . why didn't you say anything before?'

'Because I didn't think it would matter to you.'

'So why now?'

'Because Francesca was threatening to 'blow the gaffe'. Apparently Greg wrote a diary, and when he died it was amongst the things Olivier sent back from New Zealand. He passed it on to my Aunt Mary. She must have hidden it — Mary never could throw things away. And then, unluckily, my daughter Francesca found it. She's sending it with Megan, with instructions to hand it only to you. I panicked and thought that perhaps it would matter to you, after all. By the look of you, I was right.'

Jean had remained silent, looking out over the garden to the almost hidden shoreline. Anna glanced up and away from the set of his jaw; the small frown that made him look so bewildered hurt her too much.

After a while Jean said, 'I remember Greg. You know I do, we've already discussed him, but you didn't tell me . . . It was alcohol, wasn't it?'

'That killed him? Yes.' *No, it was me.*

'He was very kind to me. He used to sing silly made-up songs to me and played with me when he was free from work. Olivier worked him hard. Too hard. I recollect my father saying for a young boy he worked too hard and drank too much. There were some days he couldn't get up to work. Olivier used to shout at him. Did he know about Francesca?'

He never drank too much before. I did that to him.

'Yes.'

'That's why he went to New Zealand?'

'Yes. It's all right, Jean — if you want to leave me, I will understand. I just want you to know I haven't deliberately set out to deceive you. I simply believed this was something that had no relevance to you and me.'

'Who else knows?'

'Mary did, and Millie did.'

'Did Charles know?' The note of censure in Jean's voice was a shock. Anna turned very white, but Jean persisted. 'He didn't know, did he?'

'I couldn't tell him, Jean. I was a pathetic, stupid girl, living a lie, hoping no one would ever know, hoping to get away with so much.

You don't know what it was like. I was so frightened. I'd never been so frightened in my life, and I missed Greg so much! I hadn't known how much loving someone could hurt. I hadn't thought he would go away.' Jean stepped towards her, but she flashed at him, 'I'm not expecting pity. I don't *want* pity! I just wanted you to understand that my only motive was fear. Times were so different then. To be having an illegitimate child was bad enough, but that the child was my own brother's was unthinkable.'

'When did Francesca find out? Has she always known?'

'Does it matter?' Anna was enormously tired.

'I think it does.'

Why should I tell you? What right have you to question me? You have every right to question me, I've deceived you too. 'She's known since she was twenty-one.'

'You didn't tell her until she was twenty-one!' Jean's voice is an explosion in the quiet on the terrace.

'I didn't tell her. She found out. I always thought it was an unlucky guess. I didn't know how until the other day. She's had Greg's diary all these years, I thought perhaps it was something she had pieced together for herself.'

196

'Twenty-one before she knew? Merde! I'm not surprised she wants to hurt you.'

'I thought you didn't judge people.' Anna's voice was cold, but her head was down on her arms on the green table and her hair was falling across her face. Her voice was muffled when she spoke again. 'How dare you stand there judging me, Jean. I was only seventeen when it happened. I had no idea what to do. I've paid for what Greg and I did over and over again, and sometimes, just living hasn't been easy, and sometimes loving Francesca hasn't been easy, but I did what I thought was best. I went on doing what I thought was best all the years Francesca was growing up. You should know yourself it's hard enough to tell a child its parents are not who they believed them to be. Try telling a child their father should really be their uncle. When do you do it? When they're ten? When they're twelve? *When?* There simply isn't a right time to impart that sort of information.'

'You said Millie and Mary knew. What about Leo? Did you tell him?'

'Yes.'

'You told him — but you couldn't tell me?'

Jean had said nothing more but turned on his heel and walked away from her across the lawn and down through the trees. When she lifted her head Anna found she was alone, apart from a young crow which had settled uneasily on the low wall beside her. Ugly and ungainly, its feathers blown backwards by a sudden buffet of wind, the crow sat like a badly made black feather-duster seeming to watch Anna from one malevolent eye. Anna hated the way it hunched its back and shifted itself, rustling a little before the next gust of wind lifted it, raising its wings for the short flight to the grass below the terrace where it bounced as though its legs and feet were made of rubber. Anna stood up, clapping her hands and shouting, 'Shoo!' but the ghastly bird only fluttered a short distance before stopping to cast another malicious glance in her direction. Anna turned her back and went into the house, closing the door tightly behind her.

Unable to face Jean again that day Anna had stayed up at La Roche and gone to bed early in Millie's old room. Sometime past midnight she had fallen into a disturbed sleep.

She is dreaming it is cold and wet and has rained for hours. The ground gives back glassy reflections and the air is so full of moisture it will surely never be dry again. Walking out into the rain is like entering a box of water. Above, below, all round her there is water, permeating and saturating every leaf and every blade of grass. Within seconds her clothes are weighed down by the wetness and breathing is like drinking. Her head is throbbing and her legs ache from trying to walk on the strange wet surface of the road; the middle of her back feels as though someone has taken a baseball bat to it. Her mother, Cathryn, glides along the pavement in a boat. She is waving and smiling, she is sailing through the corridors and empty rooms of La Roche and the voices of family members echo along the walls. Anna is running, running towards Bryn. She hears a voice calling to her. It isn't Bryn's voice, it's Charles's. Anna is awake. The single sheet over her legs is weighing her down; she fights free of it and sits up.

Her arms around her drawn-up knees Anna listens, holding her breath to listen. It was Charles calling her — she heard his voice quite distinctly, and then the slamming of the door onto the terrace. Anna sits very still, straining and straining to hear. Some of Millie's childhood belongings have survived the changes to La Roche. Anna has recently returned them to this room from the attics. She can make out their shapes in the pale light; they offer some small comfort. Millie's initials are scratched into the glass in a corner of the window pane. Anna remembers her doing it, taking Grandmother Elspeth's diamond ring from her dressing table and tiptoeing along the corridor, pulling Anna along giggling with breathless haste, for fear that Elspeth should come upstairs and find them.

Anna's back hurts, she holds herself so rigidly. Again she thinks she has heard Charles calling her name. A rapid flash of heat passes over her entire body before Anna shivers and, reaching for the old-fashioned quilted counterpane at the bottom of the bed, she pulls it up around her shoulders. Climbing out of the narrow bed, hesitating as it creaks beneath her slight weight, she creeps to the open window and peers cautiously down onto the little terrace. There is a man standing directly below her. It cannot be Charles who is standing there. Charles never came to La Roche. Anna feels sick; her legs do not belong to her. The man looks up and in the moonlight she sees with horror that it is Greg. Greg, not as he was when she last saw him, twenty years old on a slab in the morgue, verdict death from acute alcoholic poisoning, but a man of her own age stands below her and smiles before pointing an accusing finger. 'It was your fault, Anna, all your fault,' and she wakes up to the reality of sunlight flooding the room and Jean bringing

200

her brioche and coffee, the morning post and her cat.

'Hi.' He does not bend to kiss her. 'You look tired this morning, and I think you were having a bad dream?' He sits cautiously on the edge of the bed, placing the tray of food into her hands. They do not quite hold each other's gaze. 'Are you okay?' Jean reaches out a tentative hand and holds the small hummocks beneath the quilt where Anna's feet rest.

She looks at him nervously. 'Yes, I'm fine. I didn't expect to see you this morning. When you walked off and left me yesterday afternoon I didn't think you'd still be around this morning.'

'I went because I didn't know what else to say to you, so I went. I have had a long night in which to think about you. You must have been very brave. Francesca is wrong to hate you,' but he is looking at his hands, not at her.

'Don't patronise me, Jean. Please.'

Jean stands up and then sits down again, away from her on a hard little chair. 'I wasn't. I'm trying to understand. I really am trying, Anna.'

Outside the day is heating up, but Anna has no inclination to be a part of it. She bites back a cutting retort and plays with her food.

Jean stands by the window with his back to her. He says, 'I don't want to drag everything up again, but will you just answer something?'

Anna's hand is at her throat. She feels cold and sick. 'I'll try.'

'If you felt Francesca's paternity had no relevance to us, why did Francesca's threat make you panic? If you lived with Leo all those years and he knew, why did you feel you couldn't tell me? You said yesterday you would have told me eventually. Is that true? Would you have ever told me if Francesca had not done this?'

If she doesn't breathe deeply, Anna is not sure that she won't faint. She searches for the truth. It has to be the truth that she gives to Jean. She says slowly, 'I can only tell you that I hope I would have told you — eventually. I wanted to be sure I knew you well enough, but I wasn't sure that even you would be able to understand. Leo left for a long time when he first knew. Are you going to leave?'

Jean's smile is ragged. 'I should like to try to stay. I should like to try to understand. If you want to tell me about it, it would be good,' and after a hesitation he adds, 'but if you don't then that's all right too.'

Anna pushes her breakfast to one side. The brioche tastes like cottonwool; her throat is too dry to swallow her coffee; her head feels as if it is divided into compartments. Some are in darkness, some are blocked, but each one will give access to the next if she can just find the key. After a few minutes she begins to talk as she has not talked for years.

'Christmas that year was terrible, beautiful and terrible. I went to watch the local children in their Nativity play — it was Mama's idea of parish work. I watched the little boys with tea towels on their heads, shuffling round in their old curtain cloaks, with tinsel and gold cardboard crowns on their heads. There was a Virgin Mary, a small dark-haired girl, with her doll baby. I watched the play and tried to feel something about God and that what Greg and I were doing was wrong. I'd tried twice to stop it, but every time I saw him I just fell more in love with him. My need to be with him was becoming like an illness, an addiction. I even brought Charles to Brockley for Christmas to try and put some distance between myself and Greg, but somehow it only made things worse.

'I knew I was pregnant the day before the family moved from Northamptonshire to London, I'd been throwing up for weeks, thinking it was just nerves, having the affair with Greg had made me very tense, very 'wired'! Then there was Charles always after me, always wanting me to make love to him. I liked Charles, but not in the same way I felt about Greg. Greg was everything to me. I was only eighteen, he was seventeen. What the hell did we know about anything — except, of course, that what we were doing was wrong, so wrong.' Her breath escapes in a shuddering sob. 'I married Charles through deception. I was so terrified I didn't know what else to do.'

'Anna. Stop this. You don't have to tell me any more.'

Anna sits up, holding her head erect and her spine very straight. 'But I *do*. If we're to stand any chance, I think I do.'

In the peace of Millie's room Anna talks for a long time, and Jean listens, allowing her to talk without interruption until at last, when she has talked herself almost to a standstill, she says, 'It's no good saying now, if this had happened or if that had happened, things would have been different. Things happen and that's the way they are — stuck, unchangeable — and now you know everything, and I don't know what we'll do about it.' She lies back on the pillows, exhausted.

Jean, who has been studying his hands, raises his head to reply, but Anna has closed her eyes. Jean and Anna and the little grey cat sit on in silence whilst the sun's fingers shift along the bedroom wall. When he is certain that Anna has fallen asleep, Jean removes the breakfast tray and slips quietly from the room.

11

When Anna left Brockley at the end of that
summer with Greg, she had moved to
Chelsea and started working in the office of
Stock, Matthews and Browning Solicitors. As
soon as he saw her, Charles Browning, a
young bright partner in the firm, had wanted
her. It was a warm September day. Charles
had passed the typing pool and noted the
presence of a new girl; soft tanned arms, crisp
white blouse, narrow waist in a smart grey
flannel skirt, all made an instantaneous
impression on him. He had whistled beneath
his breath and raised wry eyebrows as he
walked into the office he shared with an older
colleague.

'Pa didn't say we'd taken on any new staff.
New secretary in the pool's a pretty little
thing, George, did you interview her?'

'No, it was my dad.'

'Always did have an eye for a filly. Think I'll
get her to come up and do some filing or
something. I want to have a closer look at
her.'

George Matthews had smiled. 'When will
you stop seeing the typing pool as your own

private fishing rights, Charlie! My dad should have told you this girl's only here as a temporary measure, filling in till Doreen gets back.'

'Well then, I'd better not waste much time! What's her name?'

'Anna Williams. She'll be around for a while so there's no hurry. Dad wants her to work on Reception and your pa agrees. She's no ordinary girl — he says she's got an excellent social manner, and speaks fluent French — useful with Dad's Parisian trips. He's hoping when she's found her feet a bit she might be able to work as his translator — chaperoned, of course! She's a clever girl, did well at school, been working out in the South of France most of the summer. It's given her a little 'je ne sais quoi', apparently.'

Charles had grinned. 'I'll bet it has!'

So Anna had met Charles. He had summoned her to his office that first afternoon with the excuse that some files needed sorting. She had obeyed the summons and was puzzled to discover that there were no files to sort, but that she was being offered a cup of tea and an iced bun. She had looked at Charles enquiringly.

'Mr Browning, I think I ought to go back downstairs,' she said. 'Senior Mr Matthews wouldn't like it if he saw me in here drinking tea.'

Charles smiled. Anna liked his smile — it reminded her of a naughty child. He said, 'Don't worry. He likes the new staff to feel welcome. Besides,' he grinned, 'he's gone out for the afternoon.' The moment he said it, Charles knew he had made a mistake. Anna's colour came up and she walked to the door, making a formal speech as she went.

'Mr Browning, please don't think I am being insolent, but I am here to work. I really must get on.'

Charles reached the door handle before she did and held out a hand, at once stopping her from leaving and gesturing to a seat. 'Do sit down please, Miss Williams. If you think I'm going to molest you, I can assure you I'm not. I just wanted to make a friendly gesture. Bad start. So, I apologise unreservedly. Do please sit down. Seriously, please, sit down. I do genuinely like to get to know junior members of staff. Besides, I gather we will be working together from time to time.'

'Will we?' Anna had still been wary, though she allowed Charles to take her by the elbow and propel her to a seat, and found herself taking the cup of tea and plate which he placed in her hands.

'It's more than likely we'll have to work

208

together from time to time. Everyone does here. Relax. Drink your tea and eat your bun and tell me something about yourself. Why are you working here?'

Anna sipped the tea. It was tepid and the bun when she bit it was slightly stale. She said, 'I'm working here because my mother and stepfather thought it might be a good idea. They didn't want me to go back to France.'

'Are your parents living nearby?'

Anna put down her empty cup. 'My stepfather comes up to London quite often.'

'But you're not living with them?'

She shook her head and Charles laughed. 'You really are very good at self-preservation, but I could get your address from the files if I really wanted to.'

'I suppose you could.' She put her hand over her teacup and shook her head as Charles offered more tea.

'Are you sharing with anyone?'

What a persistent man. Thank goodness France had given her some experience in fending off unwanted attentions. Anna stood up to leave, saying almost politely, 'I don't really want to answer any more of these questions, Mr Browning. I really do have some work to do.'

'Aha! So you *are* living on your own.

Perhaps you're too prickly a person to share easily?'

Anna had flashed at him, 'How dare you be so personal! I live on my own because I want to live on my own!' She had run from the room.

A few minutes later, George Matthews appeared beside her desk in the typing pool. He had leaned down to speak to her, keeping his head close to hers so that the other girls would not hear what he was saying. 'Miss Williams, I'm really sorry about Charles Browning's behaviour. He told me what happened. It shan't happen again.'

Anna's smile was tight-lipped and she continued typing as she said, 'Thank you, Mr Matthews, but I would rather have heard that from Mr Browning himself.'

When she left work that evening Charles was waiting for her. He held out his hand. 'Miss Williams, I just wanted to apologise. I behaved badly. Will you forgive me?'

Anna had taken the outstretched hand, saying, 'I don't bear grudges. Thank you, Mr Browning.' Charles had watched her go before saying to George Matthews who had come up beside him, 'Stunning! Absolutely stunning!'

In spite of, or perhaps because of Charles Browning's apology, Anna found herself summoned to his office to do unnecessary filing every day of her first working week. As he had promised, there had been no repeat of his previous behaviour, and he had been kind and courteous, but Anna still felt resentful. She wished she could be with Greg. She cried nightly over her denial of him and, when she thought of the way in which she had told him so brusquely they could not be together, she cried again. She burned to reverse her decision not to see him, but knew if she did she would not have the strength to resist him. At nights she dreamed of being back in France with Mary, or walking in the woods at Brockley with Greg. Waking to the loneliness of her flat was a daily numbness. She felt she had been hired under false pretences, despite senior Mr Matthews's promise that when Doreen returned from holiday, Anna's job would be the one for which she had been hired, and that it was useful to have a settling-in period.

Anna had been on the point of giving in her notice when two things occurred. The first was the return of Doreen, the second was that Charles invited her out to a concert and dinner. He asked her twice before loneliness made her accept. The prospect of yet another night eating warmed-up scraps cooked on a single burner cooker was more than she could bear. Besides, despite his obvious interest in her, Charles was not obnoxious as James had been; he was witty and urbane. Ten years younger than Charles, Anna could not help being flattered by his attentions, and he was the only person she had met in the whole of that long and dismal first week who had actually made her not only smile but laugh out loud.

Although Anna had told Greg she would not write to him, her aching need to contact him was becoming unbearable. Anna told herself, and almost believed, that a long letter detailing what she and Charles had eaten and what the concert was like would salve some of the hurt she had inflicted on Greg, and he would know she was not after all hostile to him; the letter would make him laugh and Greg would be pleased for her that she had found a friend. Anna convinced herself that it would also serve to strengthen her avowal that there was to be nothing other than true sibling friendship between them. She hoped that Greg would see she was moving away from him and know he must put the summer behind him.

It was a Saturday afternoon and Anna's first weekend alone. She had spent her morning cleaning and tidying her tiny one-room flat. She had enjoyed the feeling of independence generated by the task, but she was less certain of herself as she ventured to the local shops in search of food and some writing paper. She had hesitated in the stationer's, wanting to send something special to Greg. Examining the various writing papers on display Anna had been panicked by the shopkeeper's enquiries. Could he help her? Was there something in particular she was looking for? She had seized on a pad of good-quality paper, knowing she could not really afford the luxury of its heavy creaminess, and the price of the half-dozen matching envelopes had made her wince. She would have to be careful in the next week not to ladder her nylons, she certainly would not be able to afford any more, but the paper was worth it. It would add to the message she was sending out to Greg, that she was happy and faring well.

On her return from her expedition Anna had waved in what she hoped was a cheerful and confident manner to the couple from the flat below hers, and felt absurdly pleased when they returned her greeting. She had cooked herself a single rabbit joint for her lunch; she had borne it home from the shops in triumph but, uncertain of what to do with it when she got home, she had looked with some anxiety at the battered old recipe book

213

given to her by Cathryn. Leafing through the pages, she could only find a recipe for rabbit stew or roast rabbit, so she decided to roast the rabbit joint and had subsequently been dismayed by the small charcoal brick which it had apparently become. Bread and cheese had been her lunch, as it would be her supper, but at least Charles had fed her well the previous evening at a small restaurant in Soho. She had felt very daring, very grown-up.

Sitting on her bed writing to Greg, Anna bit her lip as she formed careful words on the thick heavy paper. Her body ached to be next to Greg's body and with a quiet despair she acknowledged that no matter how hard she struggled to deny it, her body would remember what she forbade her mind to even contemplate. Her pen pressed so deeply into the paper it blotted, a sudden heavy dark-blue haemorrhage of ink. Tears threatened, as she crumpled the sheet of precious paper and began afresh forming the determinedly cheerful words, closing her mind to the echo of Greg's voice, hesitant and husky in her memory. Charles's kiss goodnight had been assured and firm as if he expected no rebuttal. Anna had been grateful that he did not press her any further but left her with a wave and a smile at her front door. She had, in retrospect, enjoyed her evening. It had been a pleasant diversion, but Charles's company was a pale shadow of the pleasure she felt when she was with Greg.

She completed the letter, signing it with an almost formal, *your sister Anna*. Should she underline the word *sister*? She should, but she could not. She folded the paper and slid it into an envelope, wrote Greg's name and school address and fetched a light jacket from a row of hooks by the door. She had just put on her jacket when the doorbell shrilled and Charles's voice, whose carrying and well-rounded vowels were unmistakable, sounded clearly through the cheap pine door.

'Anna, it's me. I thought your mother might have warned you not to open your door to strangers,' a self-denigrating laugh was followed by a practised pause, 'but it's such a lovely afternoon, I wondered if you'd like a ride out of town?'

A feeling akin to panic swept over Anna. She did not want this. She should not have gone out with him. She wasn't so young and foolish as not to recognise when a man was interested in her. Keeping very still, she stood behind the closed door. Perhaps Charles would go away, but the bell rang again. 'Anna, are you in there?' Then the voices of the couple she had seen this morning. 'Is everything all right? Can we help at all?'

'No, no, that's all right. I just wondered if my friend was at home.'

'Well, we saw her this morning, didn't we, Bill?'

'Yes, we did. I saw her going back to her flat at about midday. Do you think she's been taken ill?'

'No, no — I'm sure she's probably slipped out somewhere.'

'Or perhaps she's lying down?'

Unable to bear the discussion as to her possible whereabouts any longer, Anna opened the door. 'Come in, Charles.'

His fair eyebrows were raised but he said nothing, as with a gracious but dismissive smile to the couple on the landing Charles entered the flat. When he was safely inside, he asked with just the faintest hint of amusement in his voice: 'Where were you? Hiding behind the sofa?'

'I was dozing.'

Charles's keen glance travelled round the room and back to Anna. 'In your jacket?' He smiled down at her.

Anna blushed. 'No. I — I just didn't want to answer the door. I was going to go to the post box with this.' She indicated the letter still clutched in her hand.

'Why didn't you want to answer the door?

You're not afraid of me, are you?' His smile was appealing, almost boyish.

'No.' She laughed nervously, unsure of herself. 'No, I'm not afraid of you. I'm sorry, Charles, it was rude of me. I just wanted to be on my own.'

'Really? I thought you told me last night over dinner you were tired of being on your own?'

Anna blushed again; she felt horribly gauche. If it were not for Greg, she might feel pleased to be pursued by someone as obviously charming and good-looking as Charles, but she felt nothing as his hand lightly brushed against her arm.

'Sorry, Anna, I'm being pushy, aren't I. Shall I go?'

'No. Stay, now you're here. It was good of you to come and . . . it would be nice to have a ride out to the country. Thank you, Charles.'

'Aha! Now I see why old man Matthews hired you. You do have the most delightful social manner.' His voice had a crisp, defensive edge.

'Please don't be like that. I've been appallingly rude to you. Can we start again? Would you like a cup of tea?' After all, she had to work with the man.

He shook his head, smiling. 'What a dear

quaint girl you are. No, no tea thank you, but perhaps we could start again. Will you come for a ride in my car, Miss Williams?' He proffered an arm which Anna took, trying to cover her unwillingness with repartee.

'Yes. Thank you, Mr Browning. I should like that.'

He patted her hand and opened the door. 'Good, then let us proceed! This really is a jolly little flat.'

He cast another look round as Anna extricated herself from his grasp, glad of the excuse of locking the door.

'Please don't try and be kind about it,' she said over her shoulder, 'It's all a girl on my pay can afford.'

'But you really have made it very pleasant. I do mean that, Anna, most sincerely. I'm not trying to flatter you.'

Anna was aware of his breath on her hair in the tiny space of the landing. 'Well then, that really is kind of you, Charles.'

He grinned suddenly. 'Come on, let's get out of here. We'll post your letter on the way. Is it an important one?'

'It's to my brother.' Anna slipped the letter into her pocket, relieved to be ahead of Charles on the steep, uncarpeted stairs.

'Your brother? I didn't know you have a brother. Older or younger?'

'Younger, just a little bit.'

'And are you very close?'

'We used to be close,' *liar, liar, your soul's on fire,* 'but he's away at school now.'

'Well, it's nice that you write to him. What a very nice big sister you must be.'

They had reached the ground floor. Anna held the letter tightly in her pocket and stepped out onto the street, a cooling wind breathing a blessing on her heated face.

Anna

It's October. It's half-term. I didn't need to check on the calendar — I know when Greg's holidays fall. I've done such a wicked thing. I told Mr Matthews I was feeling unwell, I telephoned this morning to say I thought it was the flu and I would rather go home to Brockley than stay in London. I knew he wouldn't argue; he likes me. I know it was wrong, but I'm already damned. Damned as surely as Faustus and travelling by train to what should be heaven, but may send me to hell.

I've tried so hard; I have done so well. Charles has been good to me. He is good to be with, but I know I'm only using him. I should have left well alone. What happened with Greg should never have happened in the first place. When I left for London that should have been an end to it, but I couldn't bear his silence. After I wrote telling him about Charles there was nothing. No response at all. I watched the post for days. When I try to ring him at school I always get a message, 'Gregory is at tea, at sport, at chapel,' anywhere that makes him unable to speak to his sister, and he never rings back. He's like a sickness, a fever — I just want to be with him. I'm finding it harder and harder to go on without him. It's growing more difficult to appear normal and get through each day at work, and then there's Charles. I should never have started something I know I can't finish.

Charles just doesn't compare and he's becoming too persistent. He's so much older than me, he's a charming man, handsome, debonair — but I'm in love with a beautiful, beautiful boy. I'm in love with everything about Greg. Really in love, so deeply in love it's as if everything inside me is being expanded, opening up to possibilities I was so unaware of it doesn't seem true. When I'm with him I feel so completely alive and when I'm without him it's like being more than half-dead.

I love Greg so much it's like having my soul magnified and held up like a mirror in front of me. We know each other — down through the bones and the blood and the sinews we know each other. I'm terrified. I'm exhilarated. The whole world turns in one word from him; it's like knowing everything and knowing nothing. I only have to think of him and I can hardly stand.

What could I do? I was drawn to Brockley as if I have no will of my own. I have no strength left to fight this thing. So I pretended to be sick, to have the flu and I took a week off work and I'm travelling by train through the brown and gold of the countryside away from the grey of London and the noise. How peaceful dull Northamptonshire seems, and no one else in this carriage knows my secret. My dangerous, precious secret.

12

After Anna's return from Brockley, Charles
had sensed a change in her. She had been less
willing to see him after work, claiming that
she was still tired from the flu. At first he had
acquiesced willingly enough to a break in
their weekly visits to cinemas or concerts and
tête à tête lunches. Charles had felt for some
time that Anna was beginning to cost him
more than he was willing to afford on a girl
from whom he was receiving precious little in
return. He was a man of the world, he had
needs, and Anna was not fulfilling those
needs as previous women friends had so often
been willing to do. That it was her difference
from those other women that had attracted
him to her in the first place Charles had
almost forgotten, so after a fortnight of trivial
outings with other more apparently suitable
attachments, Charles was surprised to realise
that he still wanted Anna. He knew he was
not in love with her, but nonetheless there
was something about her that haunted his
dreams and his waking thoughts; she had an
elusive quality that both intrigued and
unsettled him. It had been there when they

first met; it was stronger now after her recent visit to Brockley. It pleased Charles to think of it as her fey quality. Of course she was still very young, possibly even a virgin still, but that made her all the more alluring.

Working late together one Friday evening in November, Charles had leaned across the desk and asked Anna, 'Would you like to come home this weekend and meet my mother?'

Anna's eyes were wide. 'I'm not sure.'

Charles had laughed, sitting back in his chair. 'It's all right, Anna, I'm not proposing marriage. I just thought you might like to come down to the country. Fresh air and all that. No strings attached. I won't even kiss you if you don't want me to. Though I have missed you. George is coming and a few of my old friends. It could be fun. Pa would be happy to have you along — I know how much he likes you.'

'Is it a special occasion?'

'Would that make a difference?'

Anna had smiled. 'It might.'

'All right then, let me think.' He steepled his hands, looking at the ceiling, then back at her. 'I'm racking my brains. I know! It's ten days after my mother's birthday and twenty-seven before mine. Does that make it special enough?'

Anna had laughed. It was very lonely in her room at weekends. Charles was good company. He had said he wouldn't even kiss her. 'Okay,' she said. 'I'll come — thank you, Charles, and . . . Happy Unbirthday!'

Anna

Charles came to the flat early this morning. I had my case packed and ready. I'm so glad Mama said I could bring him home with me for Christmas. I wrote to Greg. It's done. I told him that when Charles and I come down for Christmas there's to be no more between us. Greg is no fool, he'll know why I've brought Charles with me. I know I'm using him, I know it's wrong, but he's like an insurance policy, otherwise I don't know why I would continue to be with Charles. After the weekend party at his parents' house I had more than a few offers. The problem is, most of them weren't of friendship. They all seemed to want more of me; I think Charles wants more of me, but he is patient and he is kind. Perhaps if we go on long enough together I could grow to love him. His parents are good people, they obviously adore him. His mother's anxious for him to be married — that much I discerned from her less than subtle questioning. Who am I

224

kidding, I can't make love to anyone. Not after Greg.

The future looks hideously grim and barren. I won't be able to continue with Charles. I'll stop after Christmas — sooner or later he will want me. His patience won't last for ever. I should let him know he's never going to get anywhere with me. I should leave my job and go out to France and live with Mary. We could be two spinsters together in France. But no, I'm here playing the smart young thing, travelling the road to Brockley in Charles's wonderful old Chrysler. I hate myself.

We're here. The car turns into the drive. The front door is opening. Mama is on the step to greet us. How pleased she looks. She thinks her daughter is going to make a good marriage. Oh Mama, if only you knew. My heart jolts. Greg is standing behind her. I saw the paleness of his face, like a sickle moon in the shadows and he's gone, slipping away to his room, but not before I've seen his eyes. I still love him.

★   ★   ★

Christmas is over. It was wonderful, it was difficult, it was exhilarating and I'm so afraid now that all I'll have is memories. There can't

225

ever be any more running across the back fields to the wood as if we were little again and knowing when we get there that we're not. It's all finished. It has to be.

The farm's been sold before all was a total loss and James has managed to pull some more of his everlasting strings and now has a job in the City. Mama and he have come out of the mess quite well. James is such a spiv, I don't know how she puts up with him. He and Mama and the family moved up to London last week, to a small house but in a nice area. I join them tomorrow. Mama put pressure on. They won't go on helping with my rent here, so this is the last night I spend on my own in this ghastly flat, but I feel as though a noose is tightening round my neck. I don't know what will happen next.

Millie has been in London for a few days, it was so good to see her. She slept on the couch, but last night she couldn't sleep. I heard her get up and I could see her silhouetted against the window.

I said, 'What's the matter, Millie?'

'Sorry, sweetheart, did I wake you?'

'No, it's okay, I wasn't sleeping really.' I slipped out of bed and lit the gas fire — it was very cold in the flat. Millie came to me with my dressing gown and wrapped it round me.

'Get back into bed, Anna,' she said. 'I'll

make us a hot drink.' I was crying before I knew I was going to. 'Hey, come on, Anna.' Her sweet round face was all concern. She patted my pillows and held back the covers for me. 'Let's get you cosy. I'm sorry I woke you.' She held my hand and stroked my hair off my face, offering me her own large white handkerchief. 'Here, blow your nose.' She smiled, and stroked my hand and still I went on crying. When at last I stopped, Millie was standing beside me with two mugs of warm milk. 'I'm afraid it means no tea in the morning.' She squeezed into the bed next to me. 'Shift up.' Her hip and her thigh rested against mine. I could feel the heaviness of her flesh; it was a comfort. 'Better now?'

I sniffed. 'Yes. Sorry, Millie. I don't know what all that was about.'

'I think I do.'

I felt cold crawl on my skin. 'Why?'

Millie sipped her drink; when she looked at me there was a faint white moustache of milk on her upper lip. She was watching me closely. 'You're going to have a baby, aren't you?'

'How did you know?' There was no point in denial.

'Sweetheart, look at yourself — vomiting every morning, big-eyed, big-breasted, too thin, not eating enough, eating too much, and so distracted. This isn't the Anna I know. So I put two and two together. What are you going to do? Will Charles marry you?'

'*Charles?*' The sound of his name and the unconcealed surprise in my voice hung in the air between us; it took me a second to come to my senses, but I was too late to cover my tracks.

'Well, of course, Charles. My God! Is it someone else?'

The room had become over-warm, the milk was slightly sour. Millie's body was trapping me against the wall. I felt sweat break out under my arms and between my breasts. Millie took my mug from me and slipped swiftly out of the bed. She looked alarmed. 'Hell, Anna! Are you going to be sick?'

I lay back on the pillows, feeling weak and dizzy. 'No.'

'I'll turn the fire off.' She darted across the room and bent to the fire. As the gas popped she asked, 'Do you want to talk — or not? Perhaps you should just go to sleep. I'm sorry if I said too much.'

I couldn't speak at all at first, my mind was too full. I didn't know what order to put the words in. I didn't know how much Millie would understand, but Millie listened to all of it. She listened all the way through from beginning to end. There was a great deal to tell. I started by telling her that Greg was very afraid I will marry Charles. I ended by telling her something terrible has happened and I'm going to have Greg's baby. When I finished talking it was her turn to say nothing at all. She just held me and we cried until we both fell asleep.

This morning Millie had to leave for France, where Grandpa Philippe is expecting her. Neither of us ate much breakfast. We spoke in disjointed sentences. Millie says I should marry Charles, but I don't think I could go through with all that would be necessary, not after Greg. Not after Charles almost attacked me at New Year. My fault and, because of it, it may be too late. Charles and I are hardly speaking. I've never felt so desperate in my life. I feel as if my world is closing down. I feel as if I can hardly breathe I'm so scared of what Greg and I have done.

13

Charles had looked forward to Christmas at Brockley. He had hoped it would at last put his relationship with Anna on a footing as lovers and he had been hurt and bewildered by her aloofness. She had been odd and withdrawn when she was with him, which wasn't often because she kept slipping off somewhere leaving him alone with James and Cathryn. Charles had liked Cathryn, who had been at her best, making him feel as welcome as she could, instigating party games and singing round the piano in the evenings, keeping up a cheerful flow of conversation, making sure he was comfortable. Charles had been glad of her company, she was an attractive woman despite being a trifle overweight. If it had not been for Cathryn he might have left early. So Christmas had passed and New Year was spent with Charles's parents, if only because to change plans would create too many problems and involve too many explanations.

Away from Brockley Anna had been warmer towards Charles, but still he was wondering if perhaps the New Year should after all be a new beginning. He should cut his losses and stop seeing Anna; he might even ask Pa for a transfer to one of Stock, Matthews and Browning's other offices, then he would not have to see her at all and whatever it was that drew him to her would no longer be a problem. A clean break was needed. There were plenty of other women who would be glad to go out with Charles. As for Anna, Charles had begun to suspect she had a lover in Brockley, and had challenged her during a brief walk together on New Year's Day. They were entering a small wood and Anna who had been talking quite animatedly became quiet.

'What's the matter now, Anna?'

'Sorry, Charles? What do you mean by 'now'?' She sounded defensive.

'Ever since we went to Brockley, you've been different. I'm beginning to think it was a mistake for us to spend the Christmas season together. It's hardly been what one would describe as festive, has it?'

'Are you unhappy?' This with a questioning tone, but Charles sensed no real interest.

'You could say that,' he snapped. 'I feel like a fish out of water. You're either not around or if you are, you just don't seem interested in me. When we were at Brockley, where the hell did you keep disappearing to?'

'I'm sorry, Charles, I just had a lot of catching up to do with old friends.'

'Well, couldn't I meet your old friends?'

'You wouldn't like them.'

'How do you know? You thought you wouldn't like my friends, but you do.'

'My friends are all so much younger than you, you'd have been bored.'

Irritation rose in Charles. 'For Christ's sake, Anna. I'm bored as it is. I was bored at Brockley and I'm bored here. I'm beginning to think you've got another man tucked away somewhere.'

Anna had flushed. 'A man! Don't be ridiculous, Charles, you know I like you.'

She had kissed his cheek and was terrified when he grabbed her hand and held her to him, breathing hard, his face white and his eyes wild. She could feel his excitement against her and shrank from him. 'God, Anna! You're so unfair!' He had kissed her savagely on the mouth, with such violence she felt his teeth graze her lips, and his hands clawed and grasped at her thick clothing until he was able to shove one hand against her breast, squeezing so hard she cried out and tried to push him away.

Charles's free hand had yanked at her hair as he dragged her heavily to the ground, lying on top of her, trying to force himself between her legs. Anna had bitten and kicked and lashed out at Charles, filled with such rage she felt she might actually kill him. Her head was banged hard against the ground and through flashes of pain she saw the flat of his hand raised above her. That was when she screamed, once with no words and then as loudly as she could. 'Don't hit me! Don't you dare to hit me!'

That was when Charles rolled away from her and got to his feet. He wouldn't look at her, but held out a hand to help her up. Anna ignored the hand and staggered to her feet, straightening her clothes, feeling her lip with tentative fingers. Her head ached and she felt numb with shock.

Charles muttered, 'Oh hell! I'm sorry. I really am. Please believe me. You're enough to drive a man mad. You don't know what you do to me.' He held out his arms, and stepped towards her. It was very cold and very quiet in the wood. 'Come here. Don't look at me like that. Please.'

'I don't want you to touch me, Charles.' Anna had stood apart from him, a small determined figure, with hands deep in the pockets of her heavy woollen coat. She would not let him know how deeply shaken his attack had left her. She squeezed her hands so tightly she found later that the nails had bitten into her palms.

'I'm sorry, Anna. Please forgive me. It's just . . . it's . . . you drive me crazy. I've been patient. I've held back, but I don't know how much longer I can go on waiting for you.'

Her voice was quiet, she looked at her feet. 'You're talking about making it. You think I would, after . . . after *that*?' Her glance went involuntarily to the patch of ground where he had pushed her down.

Charles groaned and said, 'Making it as you call it. Having sex, making love. Why not, Anna? It's something that men and women do.'

'Well, I'm sorry, Charles, but I'm not the making it kind. Perhaps we'd better call a halt to this whole thing.'

'Funny you should say that,' Charles flung at her. 'It's been on my mind too. I'm transferring to another office. We needn't see each other at all. It will be better that way.'

'I think you're absolutely right. Believe me. Nothing would please me more.'

The return to London and subsequently to work had been tense and difficult. They had passed each other in the corridor with scarcely an acknowledgement. It was common knowledge that Mr Browning Junior was seeking a transfer.

* ★ ★ ★

Charles's transfer took longer than he expected and when, in late January, he noticed that Anna was pale and withdrawn, with huge dark shadows beneath her eyes he surprised himself because he was worried about her. The quality of her work had fallen off to such an extent that his father had called Charles into his office.

'Charles, sit down. I want to ask you something. I'll come straight to the point. Something's gone wrong between you and the Williams girl, hasn't it? You both left in such a rush after New Year, your mother and I were quite concerned.'

'It's nothing, Pa. None of your business really, if you don't mind my saying so. Damn it, I am twenty-seven!'

'The trouble is, it *is* my business. Matthews has been putting some pressure on me, you know I owe him money. He's fond of Anna, but apparently she's not coming up to scratch at all. Did a translation for him yesterday, and even he spotted the most howling errors all over the bally thing. He had to send it back. If it goes on he's not sure he can continue to employ her. Now I may be speaking out of turn here, old boy, but your mother and I know you've had a falling-out. I think the

235

girl's upset, missing you. That sort of thing gets to the fillies. You haven't been yourself lately either and Matthews doesn't like everyone being so unsettled . . . so if you could make it up with Anna, make her happy again and all that, we could all settle down again and the firm can get on with its business. There are junior members of staff who have been talking about you and it's not good for morale.'

Charles gaped at his father. 'Is there some sort of blackmail going on? You want me to make it up with Anna so Matthews doesn't chuck you out, is that it?'

'More or less the top and bottom of it, old son. Trouble is, if I go — you could go too.'

'But what hold has he got on you, Pa? And why the need to keep Anna happy?'

Charles's father spread his hands in an elaborate apologetic gesture. 'I should have told you before. Anna is the stepdaughter, or as near as damn it, of one of Cyril Matthews's old school chums. If Anna loses her job it means she'll have to be supported by her parents and seemingly they're moving to prevent financial embarrassment — the chap didn't have the ability or sufficient interest to run that farm they had, not after the war — too much money owed, too few men to work the land, so he's pulled out

236

while they've still got some funds left: but if the girl can bring her own money into the house it will help them — you get the picture? It would be damned embarrassing for Cyril if she has to go. Apparently this chap pulled a lot of strings for him during the war. Cyril owes him several favours, and I owe Cyril several hundred pounds.'

'And bigger fleas have lesser fleas upon their backs to bite them.' Charles's fair eyebrows drew together as he added, 'Good God, Pa! I can't have a fling with a girl just because of that.'

'I don't really think you have much choice, Charlie, not if we all want to keep our jobs. It needn't be permanent, just till the girl pulls out of her moodiness.'

'So — you're seriously suggesting I should see her again?'

Henry Browning did something with his face, Charles thought it might be a smile but it looked more like a grimace, as his father said, 'Up to you, old boy. Do you fancy a drink after work? I'll meet you in the Lamb.'

The following day Charles left a note on Anna's desk, a polite request to meet over lunch.

He was pleased when she complied. 'I almost didn't expect you to come.'

Anna had smiled, covering her tension, 'I

thought perhaps we should be friends.'

'Are you all right, Anna? You've not been looking at all well recently.'

She had flushed and replied that she had been under the weather with a cold, unable to sleep properly, and also the move into her mother's house had been tiring and, she added after a second's pause, she had been missing him.

Charles invited her out to dinner. Anna not only accepted but, when he collected her from the new family house, she made it very plain that on their return the rest of the family would be out, visiting friends for the whole weekend. She had looked at him so brazenly Charles was stunned. Surely this was not the same unresponsive girl he had known before. During the meal she drank far more than she usually did, laughing and flirting quite outrageously so, by the time they arrived home, Charles was in a fever of anticipation. Nor was he disappointed when Anna led him up the stairs, reaching the landing, turning to kiss him with such ferocity it felt more like rage than seduction. Charles had been overwhelmed as, laughing and excited, he returned her kisses, saying, 'Easy, Anna, we've got all night,' but already she had stepped into her bedroom, dragging off her clothes until she stood naked in front of him, beckoning, teasing, lying back on her bed. Drunk and apparently wanton she drew Charles to her.

Charles had had other lovers: that Anna clearly knew what she was doing made her all the more intriguing. He liked a woman who took the lead, but Anna's wild lovemaking was a total surprise. Afterwards Charles lay sweating and dazed as Anna rolled away from him to the other side of the bed. He turned his head to look at her and then down at the long scratchmarks on his shoulders and chest. 'Jesus, Anna! You're a tigress! I always suspected you might be — they say it's always the quiet ones.' He laughed, low in his throat, and reached out for her, but she had already slipped away to the bathroom and Charles could hear water running. He didn't really mind, post coital cuddles could be such a bore. By the time Anna returned he was already asleep.

After that Charles had been thrilled and more than eager when Anna suggested they spend several more nights as 'Mr and Mrs Smith' in a small hotel. Each time Anna had been more than slightly drunk, but Charles didn't mind; he positively revelled in the ferocity of her approach. He had never known such violence in a woman nor anyone so fierce, and Anna's complete lack

239

of tenderness only served to excite him the more, driving him to swift ecstasy.

Then, as quickly as she had warmed to Charles, Anna's mood changed. It was not that she was unfriendly, but the passion had gone. She bewildered him by seeming after all to want tenderness and to be held and caressed, and if Charles suggested lovemaking she would make an excuse.

Utterly perplexed, Charles had begun to wonder again if Anna was after all the right girl for him. Though he still enjoyed her company her sudden unwillingness to allow him the comforts of her body was more than irksome. Besides, Charles had always found that once a girl had been with him for any length of time he grew bored, and there were many other women who attracted him more than Anna. Indeed, that her mother was one of them made visits to the house increasingly difficult. He told himself that Anna had never really regained her looks since Christmas, she really hadn't been the same girl; at times she looked almost gaunt. Why he had been interested in her in the first place he was no longer sure; her abandoned passion had been exciting but now that was apparently over, it was perhaps time to end the relationship. Hopefully this time old man Matthews would find Anna's work didn't suffer and Charles would be a free man once more. So when, staying one weekend at his parents' house, Anna had come to him in the garden and told him falteringly that she was expecting a baby, Charles had been filled with dismay.

'But . . . how?'

Anna had looked at him in surprise. 'What do you mean how?'

'We were always so careful.'

'Something must have gone wrong. Things can go wrong — can't they?'

'Well, yes, but . . . Oh God, Anna. What do you want to do about it?'

'I hoped you might . . . '

'What — marry you!'

She had nodded with deadened eyes and an averted face. In the dull light of a late January afternoon she looked ill and her skin was a grey-green. Charles drew in a breath. 'Is it my baby?'

Anna's hand was at her mouth; she was so pale he thought she might be going to faint, but she raised her head and squared her shoulders. Staring into the distance beyond the end of the garden she said softly, 'What are you saying? What are you accusing me of?'

He walked a few paces from her and came back, his step sounding loud in the cold air. 'Oh God, I don't know, Anna. It wouldn't be the first time a chap had been landed with another chap's baby.'

She had turned away from him then and begun to run towards the house. When he caught up with her she was crying. 'Anna, I'm sorry.' He was holding her. 'I'm so sorry. That was unforgivable. Of course the baby's mine.' He turned her face towards him and was deeply shocked to see an ugly mask of silent grief, the mouth turned down and froglike, with running nose and eyes so tightly closed as to make the lashes almost invisible. Hectic white and red patches blotched her skin. 'Oh, Anna!' He scooped her into his arms and carried her into the house.

14

Two days after Charles and Anna had announced their intention to marry, Cathryn received a phone call from Greg's school. Was he at home? When, with some alarm, Cathryn had replied he was not, there followed a series of frantic phone calls to police and friends and long hours of waiting. No one had seen Greg or heard anything from him. Anna had been so distraught that Cathryn had seriously feared for her health, but it was Anna who located Greg. She had woken in the middle of the night with a total certainty of his whereabouts. She had been dreaming of Brockley and of the outhouses: she knew Greg was there waiting for her.

With no other thought than reaching him, she scrawled a note for James and Cathryn and, slipping swiftly into her clothes, crept from the house and into James's car. She had not driven for some time and with a pounding heart she backed carefully out onto the road, only switching on the headlights when she was some yards from the house. The car picked up speed and, as the miles of night-time drummed past, lit only occasionally by other travellers' headlamps, Anna held the steering wheel and allowed herself to enjoy the feeling of power beneath her feet. By one o'clock fatigue combined with a fear that what she was doing was foolhardy, had set in and she was having to battle a sensation of defeat. Supposing Greg was not at Brockley, what would she do then? Perhaps she should turn round now and just go back home.

Trying to read the dial of her watch in the headlights of a lorry coming towards her, on the opposite side of the road, Anna's attention wavered just at the same moment as a large grey cat leaped out of the hedge on her nearside. With a shriek Anna spun her wheel, swerving violently towards the lorry and away again. With the lorry's horn blasting her ears, Anna straightened course and pulled the car to a standstill. She switched off the engine and climbed out of the car. The chill of the night struck her, making her teeth chatter violently. The moon was behind a bank of clouds. It was very dark and, after the lorry had thundered away over the next hill, silence closed in. Of the cat there was no sign. Anna climbed back into the car, locking the door after her. She sat clutching her arms tightly round herself, rocking gently, until her breathing slowed. A vision of the oncoming lorry flashed through her mind, and in the headlights she saw not the cat but Greg's face. Anna gritted her teeth and re-started the car's engine.

At two in the morning she reached Brockley House and turned the car into the drive, passing Keeper's Cottage, standing empty and closed, and cautiously approached the main house. It too was still standing empty. Thank goodness the new owners would not be moving in for another few weeks. Everything looked shuttered and dark; it was hard to think she had ever lived there. A full moon had come out from behind the clouds and hung above the house and farm, scattering its eerie light as a blue-white frosting. Anna parked the car and climbed out. Pulling her thick coat tightly round her against the cold, she began to walk towards the outhouses, her feet crunching loudly on the gravel. She called Greg's name softly twice, but growing afraid of the night she called more loudly. From somewhere nearby there came a muffled answering whimper and Anna swung round in the direction of the sound.

'Anna? Is that you?' Greg's voice, sounding hardly above a croak but recognisably his, travelled towards her. She had found him, just as she had dreamed him, dishevelled and dirty, crouching in one of the outhouses. He was drunk and exhausted, a curled ball of misery huddled in a corner. Moonlight filtered through gaps in the weather boarding, striping him with white light. She had run across the uneven ground to him and squatted, holding him, whispering his name, kissing his face, and his precious hands over and over again. 'Oh Greg! Oh, my darling! What are you doing here?'

His voice was thick with drink. 'I wanted to get away from you. I wanted to be where we used to be happy. Why did you do it, Anna? Why did you do this to me? Why are you marrying that man? I hate him. Why don't you hate him too? Don't marry him, Anna. Don't. Please . . . ' His voice stopped on a choking sob. Anna continued holding him, stroking his hair, rocking him gently and, when his voice came again it was like a puzzled child's. 'Why are you marrying him? Do you love him?'

'I'm marrying him because I have no choice.'

'What do you mean?'

She had cradled his head against her, crouching in the dust beside him, sobbing as she said, 'I've got to marry him. I'm going to have a baby.'

'A baby? You?' Greg looked at her warily

before he reached for and grabbed her, his fingers catching at her hair, twisting into it, tighter and tighter until pain made her cry out. Tears ran down his face, leaving tracks in the dirt. 'Tell me it's not his baby, Anna. Look at me and tell me. *Tell me*. It's mine, it has to be mine!' His frantic lips were on hers, mingling his tears with her own until she broke free. Her mind felt numb as he repeated, with his face so close to hers she could feel his drink-stained breath on her cheek as he hissed, 'Tell me it's mine. My baby. Not his. You haven't done *that* with him. You haven't been to bed with him. Ever.'

She put her hands on his, trying to free herself from his grip and gasped, 'I had no choice. I had to go to bed with him.'

'You dirty bitch! You whore! Slut!' Greg had pushed her away from him, so hard that she fell sideways to the floor, while he huddled with his head down on his knees and his face hidden from her, sobbing as he muttered, 'I don't want to speak to you, Anna. I don't want to touch you. You're destroying me.'

'Greg, don't. Please don't say that.'

'Don't? *Don't!?* You've broken my heart, Anna — that's what you've done.'

She crawled back to his side. 'And mine is breaking too. You must believe that. I didn't know what to do. I'm so frightened, Greg. I wish you could be with me. It's all I want. I have such bad dreams and sometimes I don't know if the dreams are real or not. When I wake up I'm so afraid.'

When Greg lifted his head, his face in the thin moonlight was such a mass of shadows and white planes she couldn't see his eyes, but he was more alert now.

'Why do you have bad dreams?'

But she had withdrawn into herself. 'It doesn't matter. I can't tell you.'

'You can tell me, Anna. We've always told each other everything.'

'Not this. I can't tell you this.'

'Then why are you here?'

'I came to make sure you were all right.'

'Huh! Well, you've seen me now — so just go away, Anna. Just fucking go away and marry bloody Charles and have your fucking baby. I hate you.' He crouched deeper into his corner, turning his back.

For a long time Anna sat and shivered and watched Greg. Neither of them said anything until, speaking from somewhere deep inside her, the words coming as though on a thread drawn out of her against her will, Anna heard her own voice saying, 'It isn't Charles's baby. You were right. It *is* yours. Yours and mine and that's why I have bad dreams, Greg.

We're brother and sister — brothers and sisters aren't meant to have babies together. God knows what the baby will be like.' Her voice lowered to a whisper as she said, 'What have we made, Greg?'

'Oh God.' Greg sat staring at her, then he shook his head. 'Don't say that. You mustn't say that. You mustn't think that. Oh Christ! Anna. Oh darling, sweetheart. Oh God. No.'

'Don't hate me, darling, please don't hate me. I didn't know what to do. I had to make Charles think it was his — that's why I had to go to bed with him. Do you understand now?'

'Anna, darling, come here.' Greg's arms were tight round her.

They had clung to each other, unaware of time passing. Afterwards Anna could not have said if it had been minutes or hours before Greg murmured, 'Perhaps you should get rid of it? Get rid of it and don't marry Charles.'

Anna stayed close to him, holding him as she said, 'I can't get rid of it, Greg. I'm too afraid to get rid of it. Afraid of what it would do to my body and afraid of taking a life.'

Greg kissed her hair and said nothing, but as she began to shiver he stroked her back and held her tighter, saying, 'We could have gone away together. No one would have known.'

'But it would have ruined your life, Greg.'

'No, darling, that's already been done.' He shambled to his feet. 'Sorry. I'm going to be sick.' He disappeared round the side of the building. Outside, a pale grey light was beginning to show beyond the house, over the woods. When Greg came back Anna was standing waiting, looking out across the farmyard through a thin veil of rain that had begun to blow off the fields towards her. Light beads of moisture clung to Greg's hair. Anna spoke automatically. 'Come back inside, you'll get soaked.' He came and stood beside her, not touching her. They stood in silence, looking out at the growing light then, when a violent shudder ran over Greg's body, Anna ran to the car and returned with a car rug. 'Here,' she held it out to him. When he didn't move she said, 'Take it, for God's sake. Wrap yourself in it, you'll catch your death of cold.' She threw the rug round his shoulders and, stretching up to his height, she wrapped him tenderly and held him gently for the last time. Reaching up, wiping the tears from his face with her fingertips she whispered, 'I've got the car. I could take you somewhere. Let me take you somewhere.'

'No, I'll be all right. I'm going to Marseille for a while to stay at Aunt Mary's — she's already said I can. I've got some money. I'll go there first and then I think I'll go away somewhere. Right away. I can't live in England.'

She stepped away from him, her hands stuffed into her pockets, her chin tilted down so he couldn't quite see her eyes. 'Where will you go after Mary's?'

'Probably New Zealand, when it can be arranged. I'll contact Olivier and Babette.'

Anna had nodded. 'I understand. Will you write to me?'

'I don't know. Please go now, Anna.'

She had touched his arm and left him there alone in the growing dawn, a tall figure, bizarre in his tightly held car rug, watching her climb into the car. 'I love you, Anna.' His voice had carried through the soft rain.

Anna had at last arrived home. Climbing stiffly from the car, looking up at James's and Cathryn's window she was relieved to see the curtains still drawn. She had slipped into the house and destroyed the note she had left, pinning another to her bedroom door, requesting not to be disturbed; she had a headache and had gone back to bed. Shutting her door quietly she lay down and slept until past noon.

That evening she concocted a tale to say she had heard from Greg; he was staying with a friend but he did not want her to say where.

What was one more lie amongst so many? His teachers had been baffled. Though head-strong at times, Greg had, on the whole, been a good pupil and likely to do well enough to go on to university. Why he should run away had been a total mystery.

15

Mary

So, I arrived late last night for Anna's wedding and now I am sitting in a cold February church and I am glad for Anna that the snow has stopped and cleared away. Other than that, there seems little else to be glad about with the exception that Papa is thrilled I am here, and I am pleased to see him. He is giving Anna away. It was my suggestion when Cathryn telephoned to say Anna was declaring she could not possibly be given away by James. They will look delightful — Papa silver-haired and so distinguished and Anna like a pale fairy.

I am watching Charles whom I do not yet know but, no doubt, he will be an impeccable bridegroom and he will turn his fair curled head to watch and wait for his ethereal bride. As organ music lifts and rolls around this little church, Charles glances around at the assembled families and friends, nodding affably as he catches each one's eye. He seems relaxed and happy. I know he doesn't know the truth, and I knew when I saw her briefly last night that Anna doesn't know that

I know the truth. I fear for Anna if Charles ever finds out he's been duped. Pray God he does not, and that Anna and he will manage and will work hard to make a good life together.

Cathryn told me that Charles hopes the child will bring him and Anna closer, and I think this is not the best start to a marriage, but have said nothing. I see Charles's parents smile reassuringly at him; they are pleased for him. I know at first they were shocked that there would be a baby so soon after the marriage, but because Charles is pleased they are pleased. His father and he will have smoked cigars and toasted each other in brandy. 'Well done, my boy,' his father will have said, raising his glass. 'Continuing the family line! That's the stuff. She's a lovely girl and it's high time you settled down.'

Cathryn tells me Charles's mother has always been fond of Anna; she has even confided in Cathryn that, of all Charles's 'girlfriends' (how euphemistic the English can be), Anna is the one of whom she most approved. Hell's teeth and *merde*! If she knew the truth 'approval' would not be the word. I rather think Mrs Browning has enjoyed the conspiracy of silence about the baby. I also suspect she has shocked herself because she feels no shame. Cathryn says

Mrs Browning seems quite excited that Charles is to be a father. All the taboos of an early baby have passed her by. I expect, unlike Cathryn, she is thinking it will be fun to be a grandmother and, now the two young people are to be safely married, in a few weeks' time she will have the pleasure of informing her friends that she is to be a grandmother. Oh Lord, if they all knew the truth, what a different scenario Anna would now be facing!

I must not think like this, it is too destructive. For Anna's sake we must keep up the pretence, but my heart aches when I think of Greg. Such a mess. What to do about it. When he came to me in Marseille he looked so broken and defeated I wanted to weep for him, and I did in private. I could kill them both. I love them both so much — how could they have done this to themselves! But who has the right to judge anyone else? Certainly not me. I bow my head, try to concentrate my thoughts on a prayer for Anna's future. A prayer for Greg. I tried so hard to dissuade him from going to Olivier. I haven't seen Olivier for years but he has such a high turnover in farmhands I can't believe he's a reformed character and Greg is such a sensitive soul, God alone knows how he's going to cope with Olivier's temperamental excesses. Ha! What a fine phrase for an out-and-out nasty piece of work. I begged Greg to reconsider, to stay on in Marseille but he was adamant. He wanted a passage out. He said living in Marseille was too close to home. He has precious little money, he has no training. He must do something with his life. He has sworn me to secrecy. I must pray for him. I must concentrate.

Cathryn

Here we all are. Almost all. The family. Growing smaller. Dwindling. Mary could at least have worn a hat, but she is looking very lovely in that jade-green suit; how serious she looks today. Perhaps, like me, she's wondering exactly where Greg is at this moment. I haven't had time to talk to her properly. Perhaps at the reception, or after it, before she flies back to France we'll have a chance to talk.

At least we know now that Greg is safe. I've heard from Olivier and Babette, Anna was right. Greg has been staying with a friend, but he's now in touch with them and has every intention of going out to New Zealand to live and work on their farm. How could he do that to me? To tell Olivier, of all people, what he was doing and not me. I know Greg is close to Anna and can't stand Charles, but to run away because she's marrying the fellow is a ridiculously dramatic act. Whatever put him into the state of mind that he should run away? Although his headmaster said nothing about it, I suspect something's been going on at school — too much pressure, not enough leniency, that and impending university. It has to be that. Why on earth didn't he talk to me? Can't the boy see what he's done to us all? It's such a stupid selfish thing to do. He's not been home at all. I can't bear to think I may never see him again, I won't think about it. I just wish I knew why he'd gone. Now of all times. Surely he'd want to be here for Anna's wedding, they've always been so close. Surely he couldn't be jealous? It's too ridiculous to think about. I won't think about it.

Mary's smiling at me. I smile back. I must put on a show. I smile and smile at Charles's relatives; my face is aching with smiling. I smile at the rest of the family. Edward and his pretty little French wife, and Millie, no older than Anna herself but sensible enough to have kept out of trouble. I used to think she would grow tall but she's small like Anna, but plump and blonde. Greg should have been here. His absence is so difficult to explain. But at least now I can tell Papa that Greg is safe. Papa will ask everlasting questions. How can I explain what I don't even know? If it were not for the baby I would have suggested we call off this wedding. Perhaps I should have made Anna and Charles go away and have a small wedding somewhere, just the two of them and a witness, like Bryn and I did. All this business with Greg has upset me so much. It's all been such a muddle since I knew Anna was pregnant.

From the moment Anna moved back into the house I knew all was far from well with her. I listened to the early-morning rushes to the bathroom. I heard Anna crying, I watched her carefully and felt I was watching a lingering faded image unwind. Like mother, like daughter, I suppose. I've dreamed so often and so vividly of Bryn, my nerves feel flayed and jagged; even now, after all these years, the resonances are too painful. I waited for Anna to tell me and when she didn't, I confronted her, and the scene between us was angrier than I intended and so hedged around with bitter ghosts I could hardly cope.

We were alone in the house one Saturday afternoon. Anna had been sleeping, curled into a chair, one leg tucked beneath her, her head resting on her arm, like she used to do when she was a child. I always liked her better asleep than awake. Asleep she looked sweet. When she woke up she saw me staring at her, it was too late to pretend I wasn't.

'What is it, Mama?' She stood up stiffly, stretching out her arms and legs.

I could see already her figure was changing. Anger made me blurt, 'I think you know what it is. Whose child is it?'

Anna sat down, crumpling back into the chair as though I had hit her. I knew how cold my voice was as I said, 'Don't try and deny it. You are going to have a baby, aren't you?'

She nodded but said nothing. She can be so insolent and I was growing angrier, as I demanded: 'When were you going to tell me?'

'I — I don't know.'

'Does anyone else know?'

'Only Millie.'

I was astounded. Why should Anna confide in Millie of all people? 'Millie! Not the father? I take it the father is Charles? I can think of no other candidate.'

Anna didn't reply but walked to the French doors and looked out over the garden. Just an excuse not to look at me. She can't have been looking at anything as it was already dark.

I persisted, 'Will Charles marry you?'

'I don't know. I haven't said anything to him.'

'But he should be told. Does he love you?'

'I don't know.'

Phrases seemed to roll off my tongue so easily. 'You gave yourself to him and you don't know if he loves you. My God! What is the world coming to? Anna, you should be ashamed of yourself.'

'Oh, believe me, Mama, I am!' Anna swung round, she looked ill. 'You don't know how ashamed.'

She came away from the window and tried to brush past me, but I caught her by the arm. 'Don't walk out on me, young lady. This needs talking about. When is Charles going to be told?'

She stood looking coolly down at my hand holding her arm, but she didn't struggle as she said, 'Next weekend. We're going down to his parents' together. I shall tell him when we're there.'

'Do you love him?'

When Anna didn't reply, I stormed at her, 'You silly cheap little fool.'

'You'll be calling me damaged goods next!' Anna snapped back at me. Her chin lifted, her eyes were narrowed and she looked momentarily almost snakelike; she looked momentarily like Maman. How the past is always ready to trip us.

My head span, but I managed to say, 'No. 'Damaged goods' is not a phrase I much care for,' but I let go of Anna's arm. Suddenly anger seemed so utterly pointless. As my daughter walked out of the room I called after her: 'Promise me you will tell Charles next weekend. The sooner we can do something about this, the better. Surely he'll marry you?'

Anna came back and stood in the doorway. The likeness to Maman had gone; she looked absurdly young and she spoke quietly. 'You're not to say anything to him when he comes here tonight, Mama. I'll never forgive you if you do.'

I could not help insisting, 'You must promise me you will tell him.'

'Yes. Next weekend. I've told you I will.'

A terrible thought occurred to me. 'What will you do if he doesn't want to marry you?'

Anna shrugged. 'I don't quite know. And please don't suggest abortion. I couldn't do that. I just couldn't.'

Her face was white and her lips trembled. To my horror I heard myself saying, 'Is there anyone else you know who would be willing to take you on? Who could perhaps be persuaded.'

Anna was crying as she said, 'Mama, don't, that's horrible. It's a revolting thought.'

She stood leaning against the doorframe and just for a moment I felt very close to her as I said, 'Yes, it is. Horrible and revolting

261

and deceitful. I'm sorry. Let's hope Charles will do the decent thing.' But she had left the room before I finished the sentence. Thank goodness Charles has done the decent thing.

Whether or not Charles and Anna really love each other, at least they will have a better start in married life than I did with Bryn. Charles is established, well educated and has a career with good prospects.

I've been struggling with the thought all morning that Bryn would have wanted to be here today. Damn Anna, all this business has stirred up too many memories and made me revoltingly introspective. James is speaking; he's squeezing my hand, whispering that it's not every day your oldest child gets married. I may not love James any more, but he's a good friend. He's stood by me these last weeks, and it's been so hard, I've had so much to contend with.

The vicar is signalling to the organist, there is a movement by the church door, we're on our feet as Anna and Papa enter the church.

16

This is the morning Anna has waited for. Not longed for, just waited for. Since that last meeting with Greg at Brockley she has been locked into herself in a desperation of loneliness that nothing will alleviate. The rest of the world has carried on its daily round whilst she has been alone at the bottom of a pit whose sides she has no hope of climbing. She is walled in by her own fears, and sees others as though through a mist. They speak, they smile and wave. They come and go. They are all in slow motion. She looks in the mirror and sees pain staring out through eyes which are no longer her own but those of a wounded beast and, like a beast, she gives herself over, when she is alone, to deep howling cries that seem to drag themselves from her gut and go crawling along the walls of her room.

Constantly at her shoulder there are small furry black creatures with grinning simian faces. They shriek and howl at her at nights and reach long bony fingers into the interstices of her mind. During the days she is able to keep them at bay; if she doesn't tread on any cracks in pavements, if she doesn't walk in the shadow of trees, if she sings a certain song at a certain time of day, if she doesn't close her eyes . . . if . . . if . . . Charles has been a rock, a lighthouse, a haven. Greg has left. She will not think about Greg, will not think about the expression on his dirty, ashen face when she told him she was to marry Charles, or when she told him she was having a baby.

Cathryn has attributed her daughter's quietness to a pregnancy fraught with bad health, and is relieved that at last Charles will be the one to care for and protect her. Cathryn has never found Anna easy and these past weeks have been some of the most difficult either has had to endure. The baby will be born in wedlock — this is what matters to Cathryn, and to James.

Anna's head is aching beneath its heavy veil. She has fought with as much of her feeble strength as she could muster not to wear white; the creatures howl with laughter at the very thought of it, they gibber and point and leap in front of her. If she is very clever and very careful they won't come near her, they cannot touch her. She whispers secret incantations as the dressmaker crawls around her on hands and knees, her mouth full of pins. The creatures are growing larger.

Anna must repeat the words, or they will reach out and touch her.

'Oops, sorry, love.' The dressmaker has caught her with a pin. 'What was that you were saying?'

Anna sees the dressmaker's round moonish face and draws in a sudden sharp breath, whether with relief or for air is unclear.

'Are you all right, Miss Williams?' The dressmaker's expression is sly. 'It's all right, you won't be the first of my ladies to be getting married in a slightly larger frock than they'd usually wear, my dear,' and she winks.

Anna stands mute and sullen, unable to communicate with the dressmaker as she is tugged and pulled and white silk is swathed over the firm rounding of Anna's belly. 'Let's hope you don't put on any more weight before the do, Miss Williams.' She puts her head on one side and observes the effect of the dress and her words, and Anna shrinks from the woman's fat pink hands. If Greg cannot touch her, neither must anyone else. No one must touch her, no one at all. Making love to Charles had been a dread necessity. She had come away from each encounter to baths as hot as she could bear them and had scrubbed and scrubbed at her face and body. Now no one would touch her.

Anna is walking down the aisle on Grandpa

Philippe's arm; she is wearing the white dress, she is wearing the veil and for the first time the baby inside her kicks. Anna pauses only fractionally in her glide to the altar and Charles turns to smile at her. Today he is not Charles, he is the largest and grimiest of the creatures. Sick and faint, Anna takes her marriage vows, and she and the creature who is not Charles pass back down the aisle through a grinning jeering mob.

Outside the church the air is cooler. Anna stands, mute and terrified, beside Charles, who bends to kiss her. She sees his face advancing on hers, sees his slightly uneven teeth, smells the whisky on his breath and blacks out.

Charles has caught her as she swayed; he and Mary have taken her back inside the church porch. Aunt Mary is bending over her, holding her hand. Charles hovers anxiously and, outside the church, concerned faces peer at Anna.

Mary stands up. 'It's all right.' She is brisk. 'It is all right, everyone — she's come round. Perhaps we could do the photographs later, at the hotel?' This to the photographer. 'It might be a good idea if everyone went on to the hotel now.' There is a concerted movement towards the church gates amongst murmuring and backward glances. Mary leaves Anna for a moment to call to Cathryn, 'I'll see to Anna, Cath. You go on, keep everyone happy at the hotel — yes?'

Cathryn nods assent. Now there is only Mary waiting with Charles and Anna. Charles sits beside Anna holding her hand. 'I knew it would be too much for you. We should have had a register office do. It wouldn't have mattered.'

Mary is watching Anna. 'Charles, why don't you go and ask the driver to bring the car round to the gate. We'll wait here until you come back.'

When Charles has gone, she speaks rapidly and urgently to Anna. 'Greg's at my place in Marseille, did you know?'

Anna's eyes are wide in her pale face; she thinks of the last time she saw Greg, as he watched the car pull out of Brockley's farmyard. She says miserably, 'He said he was coming to you. Is he all right?'

'As well as can be expected.'

'You know about us, don't you?'

'Yes, my lamb, I do.'

'You're not blaming me, are you?'

'No. I know about love. It is not always the most convenient of companions.'

'You know about the baby?'

'Yes, I do. About Greg . . . clearly Charles does not know?'

'What don't I know?' Charles steps into the porch blocking weak sunlight.

Mary stands up and kisses him on the cheek. 'What it is like to be a young bride with all this attention on one.'

'That's true enough.' He turns to Anna. 'Feeling well enough to move now, my dear?'

'Yes, thank you, Charles. May I rest for a while when we reach the hotel?'

'Of course, darling. I'll try and keep the guests happy.'

The little party moves slowly towards the waiting car.

★ ★ ★

It is very peaceful in the hotel bedroom and Anna sleeps for a while. When she wakes up, Millie, not Charles, is sitting beside her. Millie smiles and strokes Anna's hand. 'Are you all right, darling?'

Tears slide from beneath Anna's eyelids. 'Millie! It's so good to see you. I'm glad you're here.'

Millie kisses her cheek. 'You gave us all a fright, passing out like that. Is it the baby?'

Anna's mouth is a tight hard line; she weeps so much, tears roll down her cheeks and onto her neck. Millie pats at her hand awkwardly. 'Sorry. I'm always so clumsy,

268

always say the wrong things.'

'Well, you didn't say the wrong thing when you told me to get Charles to marry me. I did what you said. It worked and here I am a married lady,' but Anna goes on weeping.

Millie's expression is bleak. 'Perhaps I did say the wrong thing. You're not happy, are you?'

'I'm in torture, Millie, and that's the truth. I can't stop thinking about Greg and what I've done to him. I miss him so much. Making love with Charles was awful. How am I going to manage that for the rest of my life? And when I told him about the baby and he almost didn't believe me, I'd have given in gladly then, I'd have given in and gone away, but when he saw I was crying he thought it was because he'd been horrible to me and I let him believe it, I'm so weak. I'm a coward! I should have gone away like Greg did. I shouldn't have done this.'

'And how would you have managed — a single woman with a baby. You'd have had no job, you'd have had no money, or even worse they'd have taken the baby away from you and you'd never ever have seen it again. At least this way you have something of Greg to hold on to. It's better this way. I'm sure of it, Anna.'

'Perhaps it would be better not to have

something of Greg, but I'm too afraid to have an abortion.'

'You can't do that, it would be a sin!'

'And isn't it already a sin to have done what I have done?' Anna sobs, placing a hand on her belly. As though in answer she feels faint flutterings; an image of a trapped bird presents itself. 'I have bad dreams about the baby. I dream it's a monster or even a minotaur and it's inside me, Millie, it's growing. With every day that passes it's getting bigger.'

'Anna, you mustn't think like that. It will be all right.'

Anna struggles to sit up. 'What am I going to do, Millie?' Millie is startled by the wildness of her eyes.

'What do you mean, what are you going to do? You're going to be a fine married lady with a beautiful baby, perhaps born somewhat soon.'

Anna climbs off the bed and walks about the room; her crumpled wedding dress drags along the carpet behind her, and her dishevelled hair hangs around her pale face. 'I don't love Charles.' She speaks with her back turned to Millie. 'I almost think I hate him. I've done a terrible, terrible thing. I've married him under false pretences. Can't you go to prison for that? Oh God, I wish someone would put me in prison, then I'd be punished.'

Millie hurries to Anna and puts an arm round her. 'Come on, sweetheart, you're talking wildly. Come and sit down again.' Gently she guides her back towards the bed.

The hotel bedroom is pleasant, with white walls and white muslin at the windows. The early dusk of a February afternoon is beginning to close in and Millie has switched on a small bedside lamp; its soft glow illuminates the area around the bed, leaving the rest of the room in shadow. Anna's hands are two tight fists and her eyes are very bright and hard as she sits down in a small basket chair beside the bed and looks up at Millie. 'What am I going to do? It's the most awful mess . . . ' She turns her head away. 'Charles is the only one who would have me, but now I've married him and I know I don't love him. Greg's gone away, the baby will probably be hideously deformed, and it will be my punishment to look after it with a man I don't love for the rest of my days!'

Millie holds out her arms and Anna falters a moment before standing up and stepping into their enfolding kindness. Millie holds her close and strokes and smooths her back as they both begin to cry. Millie whispers and rocks and whispers and rocks. 'It won't be deformed. It will be all right. Time will pass. You'll grow to love Charles, I'm sure of it. He cares about you. You must let Greg go from your life. If you don't, you'll only hurt yourself. You'll only hurt him.' On and on. The words falling into and over each other in a rhythm like running water. Soothing. Healing. How long they stand like that neither of them knows, but gradually their tears subside and a knock on the door makes them spring apart.

The door opens and Charles strolls in. 'Darling, are you all right now? Feeling better?' He slips a proprietory arm around Anna's waist, then looks from Anna to Millie and back again, before saying crisply, 'Perhaps you'd better tidy yourself, Anna. Really, Millie, you mustn't tire her, you can see she's not well.'

Millie murmurs an apology and returns to the other guests. Charles and Anna stand and stare at each other. 'Has Millie tired you, Anna?'

Anna shakes her head. 'She's good to me.'

'Is she? I wonder.'

Anna looks at her bridegroom and watches the gulf between them widen as he says, 'You look terrible. What has Millie been saying to upset you? You've obviously been crying.'

Anna glances at herself in the dressing-table mirror, her makeup is streaked and her face heavily blotched. 'Oh, God! Do I have to come downstairs, Charles?'

He says, 'Well, I rather think you do, Anna. People are really quite concerned and of course, they don't all know about the baby. And neither do we want them to, do we, dear? Not yet, anyway. Perhaps you should change into your going-away outfit. Your dress is in a terrible state. I'll expect you in five minutes.' He strides to the door, but on the point of leaving the room, he turns and crosses swiftly to her side, kissing her lightly on the cheek. 'Anna, I do care about you, you know. It's just — well, appearances. We must try to keep our guests happy, mustn't we, darling?' Then he has gone.

Blankly Anna reaches down her neat little suit from where it waits on its hanger. She slips out of the sham of her white dress and rinses her face at the hand basin; she combs her hair and applies lipstick. She puts on her suit and goes downstairs.

'Here she is!' Charles's father greets her with a hug. 'Come along, my dear. We've all been so worried about you — are you all right, my sweetheart?' Without waiting for an answer he calls out, 'Look everybody, here she is and none the worse for wear!' He squeezes her arm and murmurs, 'That's my girl, keep smiling.' There is laughter, there is champagne. Anna moves through the afternoon in a daze until at last it is over. Millie, almost the last to leave, kisses Anna's cold, tired cheek and whispers, 'I'll be in touch, I won't let you down, Anna.'

17

Dear Mary,

I'm glad I decided to stay on here in England. Cathryn and James have invited us all to share a Bed and Breakfast holiday with them for a week and I think the rest is doing Anna a lot of good. To be out of London is just what she needs. Charles hasn't been able to come because of work, but he'll be down at the weekend. The weather here is good and Anna is able to spend a lot of time sitting out in the orchard. To tell you the truth, Mary, I'm very worried about her. She sits all day and stares at the blossom and at the sky, but if anyone speaks to her she seems almost not to notice. When she speaks at all it's as though her voice is coming from somewhere else.

In London I have spent as much time as possible with dear Anna. I go to see her in the flat when Charles is out at work. I've found as much information as I can on

275

genetics and heredity and I take biology books to the flat. We read them together and then I take them away again before Charles comes home. I've taken too much time off from my studies, I know, but if it were not for me I don't know what Anna would do. I think Charles hates me always being there; he said he thought I make Anna worse, but I'm convinced she's so ill she doesn't know half the time what's going on. Charles said if I didn't spend so much time with Anna she wouldn't be so introspective, that's what he said. What does he know? She's moving further and further away from reality and no one seems able to stop her. As the time for her baby to be born is getting nearer she's withdrawing more and more into herself. You'd hardly recognise her, she's so pale, and I'm sure beneath the bulk of the baby she's actually got very thin.

I know from things she's said to me that she and Charles don't ever make love — they've even got separate bedrooms now! At first it was because of the baby she persuaded him to leave her alone, saying it might hurt the child. Now he just leaves her alone. I think he might even have another woman somewhere.

It's not that he's deliberately unkind. He

gives her everything he can, materially. It's just that he doesn't seem to understand her, or to want to help, but I suppose the not making love suits poor Anna anyway.

I keep wondering if it would be possible to stay on here indefinitely and maybe complete my photographic course over here. Do you think Papa would agree to it? I'd like to be near Anna if possible. I think she needs me.

In spite of inviting us here Cathryn is dreadful; she's absolutely useless as a mother. She doesn't seem to want to help Anna at all. Not that there's much communication between them. When they're in a room together it feels as if someone has opened a door directly to the North Pole! I wonder really why Cathryn asked us here but I think perhaps even she can't avoid duty — and, of course, shared costs do help to have a decent break!!

Anna has said that when the baby is born she doesn't want her mother to go to their flat to help with the first few days and weeks. I've tried to persuade her that she must have someone, but she's in such a weak condition she doesn't seem to want to see sense. I know how fond Anna is of you, dearest Mary, and if you could arrange to be with her when the baby comes I'm certain it would help her so much. If I'm honest and face things, I do fear for Anna's mental health. There are days when she can be very strange. Anna's few friends from the office have stopped visiting. The last time they were at the flat Anna screamed abuse at them and began to throw things. I don't think Charles really understands her and I am very much afraid that the marriage was a huge mistake on both sides. I feel responsible for that because, as I told you before, it was partly my suggestion.

Sorry to write such a depressing letter, but I couldn't think who else to turn to.

Love as always, Millie.

Florence
June 6, 1948

Dearest Millie,

You letter took some time to reach me as it had to be redirected twice. Thank you for writing. I'm so sorry to hear of Anna's problems. I have always known how very fond you are of her and it must be difficult for you when you see she is not very well, but are you really so sure it's the best thing for you to be there so much of the time?

As for Charles hating you being there, he probably does. He doesn't know the baby isn't his. He thinks he is the father of this child and, from what little I know of him, he seemed after the initial shock to have become rather keen on the idea of fatherhood, so to have another female about the place keeping him from his wife cannot be helping the situation. Newly married couples like to spend some time alone together, you know — especially ones who are going to have a child so early in their marriage. After all, they're going to have precious little time on their own once the baby arrives. It seems to me essential for everyone's wellbeing that, whether or not it is right to do so, we cannot question that the best thing for Anna is that Charles should go on believing this is his baby. What is done 'is done and cannot be undone'. Ultimately, who knows, Anna may come to see it that way too — and yes, I know you put the idea into Anna's head of 'persuading Charles', but my dear child I really don't think you should feel guilty for the consequences. Anna approached Charles, he complied and they are both capable of making up their own minds about things.

Dearest Millie, please do not think I'm being horrid, but maybe Charles is right. Maybe if it were not for your continual presence, Anna would make more of an effort and pull herself together. After all, surely if she is as ill as you say she is, Charles would have done something about it? He would get the doctor, he isn't an unfeeling man. Which brings me to the next point in your letter — if Charles and Anna are having separate bedrooms, even though Anna confided that to you, it's really no one else's business but their own. I really do feel you've allowed yourself to become far too involved. If Anna makes the effort, I am sure she and Charles will be able to make a go of this. Greg has had the grace and good sense to leave well alone; now we must allow Anna to do the same.

I have heard nothing from Anna herself that would indicate she thinks she made the wrong decision when she married Charles. She does not write often but when she does, her letters seem full of the flat and how well Charles is doing with his new promotion. She actually seems quite proud to be his wife. I must, I suppose, admit that even as I write, it is occurring to me that for a mother-to-be, she mentions the baby never at all, which is strange, or perhaps not. Perhaps she cannot help being concerned about the child, or perhaps she thinks Aunt Mary, the spinster, might not be interested in layettes and frilly shawls! With regard to her being withdrawn, you must remember, Millie, Anna is still very young herself. Perhaps she's worried about how good a mother she'll be and, of course, she must be worried about the birth itself. Never having been through a labour and birth, I should imagine the idea of it is a bit daunting, to say the least! Even without the worry of the baby being unwell — or worse. Millie, it simply does not do to dwell on these things. Whatever will be will be. Then, and only if we are needed, will be the time to give as much help as we can offer.

Your comments about Cathryn being a hopeless mother — well haven't I known that for ever and a day? Especially where Anna was concerned. It was always Greg who Cathryn preferred. She'll probably change once the baby's born. Though I'm not sure that even I believe that, but maybe one of the reasons she's not getting on very well with Anna just now is that she, Cathryn, has difficulty seeing herself in the role of grandmother. After all, she's still only in her late thirties herself! Thank God she does not know the truth about Anna and Greg and you certainly must not tell her — ever.

Darling Millie, please don't be annoyed if I haven't given you exactly the answers you hoped for, but I would suggest that perhaps you may have become a little too involved and, perhaps, to put some distance between yourself and Charles and Anna would be helpful for all parties? If you still really feel Anna needs to see me I shall be in London at the end of July, probably just in time for the baby's arrival — though these things happen in their own time. I'm honestly sorry I can't be more helpful.

Truly I send you all the best and give Anna my love,

Mary.

Millie receives this letter with a kind of despair. It is some weeks since she and Anna returned to London from Oxfordshire and the rest and relaxation and clean country air have lost their benefits to Anna. Millie had seen Anna the previous evening at the flat, and the pallor of her skin drawn tight across her cheekbones and the purple shadows, like two thumb-prints beneath her eyes, had distressed and frightened Millie. Her suggestion that Anna should see a doctor had been met with a stony stare. When Millie asked where Charles was, Anna had replied in a wooden voice that Charles was out for the evening and unlikely to be in until late. If Millie didn't mind, would she please go back to her digs and drop the latch on her way out. Anna was going to bed.

Reading Mary's letter Millie runs a hand through her hair, making it stand like a cockscomb in fair peaks. It is clear that Mary thinks she is making a mountain out of a molehill. Charles doesn't seem to care about the state of his wife, and to top everything off, a strongly worded letter has arrived from Philippe who has been suggesting in his last few letters that, at eighteen years old, it is time that Millie returned to France and resumed her studies. He cannot afford to allow her to stay indefinitely in England with Cathryn and the other relatives. They must all be growing tired of her, especially as the baby is to be born soon and, in short, if she does not return in the next month she will find her allowance has been severely cut.

Anna

For days and days now I've been so utterly weary, even the process of thinking has become too great an effort and every day has been like a film looped and looped again. Millie comes and goes; today she said Grandpa Philippe wants her back in France or she loses her allowance. Charles is almost never here. My fault. I have driven him off. I have told lie upon lie until I can scarcely remember what is truth and what is not.

Charles wants the child to be called Henry after his own father, he seems not to think it could be a girl. He seems not to think. His voice, his mannerisms — everything about him repels me. If it were not for the baby I cannot believe we would be together at all. He says I should see a doctor and looks at me with his great sheep's eyes telling me it must be wrong to be the way I am. I tell him that I've seen the doctor and I tell him that she says the baby and I are fine. I've resorted to subterfuge more than once, Charles has driven me to the doctor's surgery and waited to watch me going in. So I go in and I pretend to read the leaflets and the notices in there so the receptionist doesn't ask any questions, and when I hear Charles drive away I wait a minute or two longer and then I leave. I won't see a doctor! A doctor would know I had done wrong, he would know this is my brother's child — I just know he would.

When Charles comes home in the evenings I tell him that the doctor says I'm fine and will see me again soon. He drinks his whisky and makes our meal. I eat a small amount of it to keep him quiet. Charles is very busy, the baby will mean we need more money so he works a great deal. When he's not working he sleeps, or he goes out. I suggested separate rooms so we don't disturb each other. He looked miserable and said he hoped after the baby comes things will be different. More lies — I said I hope so too. I have tried to make love to him. It almost works if I have had a drink, until I see Greg's face in my head and it goes wrong. Twice at the beginning it went so wrong that Charles hit me. It was my fault. It's all my fault. He said it was a warning. Then he cried. It was degrading, it was the most degrading thing that ever happened to me. He said he was sorry and he hasn't hit me again, but I am very afraid he might, one day. So sometimes I let him come into my room and do what he wants to do with me, but I don't think he enjoys it any more than I do.

I wish I could hear something of Greg. If I just knew he was all right, perhaps I would be at least content.

One day drifts into the next without any differences. Everything I do, everything I say, I have no recollection of only minutes after, and there's never *never* a moment of peace and stillness inside my head except at nights. Every night I go to bed and I'm so exhausted, to lie down and sleep is bliss; my only escape is to go into that deep black hole. It's becoming like an addiction. Perhaps soon I might fall into it and never come out again.

Mary
The café interior was dimly lit, the only natural light coming from a small window set high in one of the side walls and the remainder from low-wattage electric lighting, making the interior strange and cavernous. Each small table was draped with a shabby white cloth with a smaller, black faded to grey cloth placed diagonally across it. On top of each black cloth was a posy of imitation silk roses in black, and carnations in grey, sitting in cheap cut-glass vases. Red napkins had been teased unwillingly into the shape of fans. Across ebony curtain poles, which framed blank windowless walls, red swathes of curtains had been hung. The whole thing made me think of a Victorian funeral. In this bizarre setting I met Millie.

Perhaps because of the setting, the café being Millie's choice and, I thought, reflecting her tendency to enjoy the 'dramatic' (it only occurred to me afterwards that it may have had more to do with lack of expense), I still did not give sufficient credence to what she was saying about Anna.

I saw Millie off at the airport and she was tearful. Today I went to see Anna and tonight I must telephone Millie and apologise for not believing her and then reassure her that I will do everything I can to make sure poor, dear Anna is all right.

It is perfectly obvious that something is indeed terribly wrong with Anna, and no one seems to know what on earth to do. I've talked to Cathryn on the telephone; she didn't seem to be particularly interested but said she'd come up to London at the weekend if I insist.

When I reached the flat Charles let me in. He has changed a great deal since the wedding. He's less ebullient, less sure of himself. Even his hair looked flatter. 'Anna's sleeping,' were his first words, then as if recollecting his manners, 'Sorry, Mary. It was good of you to come.'

I followed him into the flat. It's a nice place — clean and airy, quite large. Charles and I talked inconsequential small talk whilst he made coffee. We stood in the kitchen drinking the coffee — which was good, hot and strong.

'You make good coffee,' I said.

'Thank you. Would you like to come and sit down in the lounge? How was Florence?'

I followed him into the living room. It was untidy, but clean. He pushed a pile of papers and magazines off the sofa. 'Sit down.'

'How is Anna?' I sat down and looked round for somewhere to put my cup. There didn't seem to be anywhere so I held it on my knee, but Charles didn't seem to notice. His shoulders had tensed at the mention of Anna's name.

'I don't know how Anna is.'

'What do you mean, you don't know?'

'I mean just that. She won't tell me — it's as if she's blocking me out.'

'Has she seen a doctor?'

'Yes, she goes each week.'

'Have you spoken to the doctor?'

He looked at me as if I had accused him of something. 'Well, no. One doesn't like to interfere. I mean, it's up to the woman, isn't it?'

I shrugged, and looked at Charles. He's thinner than I remember him, his collar looks too big on his neck. He kept glancing at me and then looking away. 'Charles, why don't you tell me what's wrong? Perhaps I can help.'

'I don't think you can.' He seemed about to say something else when Anna walked into the room. She came straight to me and put her arms round me; behind the bulk of the baby she is frighteningly thin. Her shoulders have gone to almost nothing and her arms and legs seem to stick off at each corner of her body. She was wrapped in an old flannelette dressing gown with her hair hanging in a tangled mane round her poor little face. I can't bear to think of her sweet face looking like that. Her eyes are huge but hooded. She's like a little walking ghost. Over my shoulder she spoke to Charles, 'Why didn't you tell me Mary was here?'

'I wanted you to go on sleeping. Both you and the baby need rest.'

'I'm always sleeping, you should have woken me.'

'I'll make some tea.' I excused myself and went to the kitchen but my agitation was so great I found myself staring blankly at the kettle as if it was an object I'd never seen before. I stood still, gripping the edge of the sink, listening to the rise and fall of their voices, circling each other like snarling dogs. Then a door slammed and Anna was standing in the kitchen beside me. I forced my mouth into a smile. 'Would you like a cup of tea?'

'Please.' Already she had lost her energy.

'Would you like me to wash your hair?'

'That would be nice.' Her hand went uncertainly in the direction of her hair but never reached it. She left her hand hovering in mid-air then let it fall back to her side as if it didn't belong to her.

'Perhaps you're too tired today? Perhaps I'll come back early tomorrow and do it?'

'Please.'

'Anna, have you seen a doctor?'

Her expression was almost crafty. 'No. I lie to Charles. I don't want a doctor near me.'

'What about the baby? It's July, the child will be born soon. Have you made arrangements?'

'I don't want to talk about it, Mary. If you're going to be like this you can leave.' She was shouting but the effort exhausted her and she slumped onto the kitchen stool.

'I'm not going anywhere, young lady, until you've eaten something.' She looked at me with hostility in her eyes but said nothing before swaying out of the room. I noticed her ankles are so thin I wondered how they hold her up.

Somehow I concentrated on finding and preparing eggs. I found a pan, I beat milk and eggs together. I found a white loaf of bread and cut slices, putting them under the grill. I found a tray but no cloth; on it I placed a drink of milk, toast and scrambled eggs. I took them to the lounge where Anna lay dozing on the sofa, her limbs flung out haphazardly and her mounded belly rising and falling. She looked grotesque, but as she sat up there was a glimpse of the old Anna in her smile. 'Thank you, Mary. Sorry I was rude.'

'Don't worry about it. When you've eaten that I'm going to run you a bath. I'll stay until you're ready for bed. Then I must go.' Her face clouded over. 'It's all right, Anna. I'll be back in the morning.'

'Thank you.' She ate her meal but said no more and neither did I. I was too afraid of upsetting her again.

I ran her bathwater and found a clean nightgown. Whilst she was in the bath I searched rapidly through the small drawer in the telephone table. There was an address book. The entries were in handwriting I did not recognise, so it must have been Charles's writing. There was a doctor's name. I reached for my own handbag, scribbling the number into my diary. I could hear Anna letting the water out of the bath. When she emerged from the bathroom I was in the kitchen filling a hot-water bottle.

'I know it's summer, but I thought this might be a comfort. It's not too hot.'

Anna actually smiled. 'Oh Mary! How kind.'

I tucked her into bed, kissed her forehead with a promise to be back the next day and let myself out of the flat and went straight to the nearest phone box.

Cathryn

Damn Mary with her interfering ways. First it's Millie making a fuss about Anna, now she's gone back to France and I have Mary, with her blessed, 'Why don't you come up to London and take care of Anna?' She has the audacity to ask. No more than twenty-four hours in England and she's trying to organise everyone. Perhaps I should have told her the truth, I've never liked Anna very much, and since this child has been on the way I consider that she's been behaving like a complete imbecile. She's driving Charles away. She's just so selfish!

Poor Charles has no one to confide in but me. He says she won't let him anywhere near her, and he's so much of a man it must be an agony for him. At least Bryn and I were able to be something to each other during the time we were together, even if in the end the sex was really all we had left. Even now when I think of Bryn I think about the way he would hold me, but it's no use going down that particular avenue. There's something about Charles when he looks at me that makes me think of Bryn . . . After all, he and I are so much closer in age than he and Anna. I must admit with James away so much I have been so glad of Charles's company, and he has been happy with mine. He is almost at his wits' end with Anna — and who can blame him, poor lamb? What sort of a wife is she being? She spends all day in her dressing gown, waddling about the flat like some revolting duck with her great bloated stomach above her stick-like legs. As for her face, you could fit it into a teacup. She's an absolute mess. I have tried to help. Now Mary seems to think she can do better than me. Well, let her try and good luck to her. Heaven only knows what sort of a mother Anna thinks she's going to be.

Anna
It's happening. I felt it begin, first a creeping pain in my back, then a running, fluttering round from my back to my front. Like a ribbon, like a rope and it's happening. The monster's coming out. If I lie here quiet and still. If I don't tell anyone, perhaps it will stop. Perhaps it will stay where it is. Perhaps I can stay here on the cool bathroom floor and be this thing's prison for ever and ever. The pain is worse and the room has heaved over to one side and back again. The monster is punishing me. It wants to get out. I shan't let it out — the world mustn't see what it is that I've grown inside me. I wish Millie was here, she could help me to make it stay where it is.

293

Not Millie. She's gone. Mary's come in her place. I was glad. I wanted to see her, I want her back here. Now. But now it's the time, it's come and I'm afraid. I'm on my own in the flat. I've been watching the birds. I can see them well from up here. They cruise about the sky. In great flocks like flakes of ash. Rising off a fire. My back is on fire. When I go, I wonder if my soul will go up like that? I wonder if I'll join Papa. He'll be pleased to see me. Will it be like not being a single lone bird? Or even those in twos or threes? But those great massed formations like I used to imagine ocean currents. Papa told me about them. Swinging across each other in multilayers. Like this pain. It swings me over and up. I don't know what I'm doing. I'm on a rack. I'd like the birds to be the last thing I see. The monster is pushing. My belly and back are on fire. If I hold my legs. If I scream. I am screaming. I can hear it in my brain. I know what my brain looks like. Its passage-ways in red and black. The monster has to come through passages in red and black. I'm frightened. I'm frightened. I'm frightened.

Mary
When I leave Anna I go straight to the nearest telephone box, from where I ring Cathryn

who, as I expected, is no use at all. Then I ring the doctor who says she'll call as soon as she can. Restless and unsure of what to do next I decide exercise will do me good and I start walking back to my hotel. I'm on my way there, walking through the streets, enjoying the smell of wet London all around me, when some instinct, an inner voice, tells me that Anna is in trouble. I know she needs me and needs me urgently. I don't hesitate to hail a taxi and, scrambling in, I tell the man to drive as fast as possible.

'What's up, missis? Is there a fire?'

'No, not a fire, but I'll pay you double if you get me there in the next five minutes,' I tell him. I half expect him to respond with a 'Blimey!' but he doesn't and we're on our way. Even though it's July it's a cool grey day. We arrive outside Anna's and Charles's building and I leap out of the taxi, pay the man double as I promised, tell him to keep the change and race past the doorman. The lift is waiting and I dive into it like something possessed. As soon as I step out I can hear her. I fly down the corridor to the front door as fast as I can. Poor kid, she's screaming and yelling. She must be terrified. The hair on the back of my neck is up. There isn't another soul around. I try the door — thank heavens it's not locked.

After all the noise there is a complete and unearthly stillness as I step into the tiny entrance vestibule. 'Anna?' I open the door into the lounge. It looks peaceful and welcoming. The flowers I'd brought earlier in the day perfume the room. 'Anna? Where are you?' I am answered by a scream more animal than human; it seems to split the air and I'm rooted to the spot. She screams again and I'm running towards the sound.

'Anna! Anna! Where are you?' Her next scream leads me to the bathroom and she's there, crouching in the empty bath, clinging to the taps and her head's thrown back with her hair all plastered down. I can see the tendons in her neck and she's bellowing. I'm as frightened as she is, but I mustn't let her see that I am. I stand where she can see me. I'm trembling.

'It's all right, lamb, it's all right. Anna, I'm here.'

Her eyes frighten me more than anything else. She looks at me and through me — there's absolutely no recognition at all. 'Darling, it's Mary. I'm here. Come on, sweetheart. Let me help you.'

I don't really know what to do, but I kick off my shoes and climb into the bath behind her, thinking that at least I can support her weight, and then I see it, the baby's head.

It's there, and with a swift flicker of movement I'm holding Anna's baby. It slips from between her thighs like a little fish, it's so sudden and so slippery I cry out for fear of dropping it. It's a girl. Anna is whimpering and shuddering; her knees are drawn up.

A woman's voice calls through the flat, 'Hello? Anyone at home? It's Doctor Gatton, the door was . . . Oh my lord! Are you all right?' The woman's face appears round the bathroom door. She comes swiftly into the room. I am sobbing as, from my kneeling position in the bath I whisper, 'Thank God you're here.'

'Thank God indeed,' she murmurs and steps forward.

★　★　★

Anna is asleep in the next room, sedated by the doctor who says she will call in again later. Dr Gatton says she would like to talk to me, so we leave Anna to sleep and take Francesca Hope, Anna's beautiful baby, into the sitting room in her Moses basket.

I make us both a cup of tea and we sit together on the couch with the baby sleeping peacefully between us. I can't stop looking at her tiny hands, they are so perfect and so complete, right down to the minute fingernails.

'You did good work today, Miss Breton.'

I am ridiculously pleased. I feel exhilarated. 'Please call me Mary. I don't know what I'd have done if you hadn't arrived when you did.'

'I'm so glad you called me earlier today — your timing couldn't have been better. I must admit I'm more than somewhat embarrassed as I hadn't even known that Miss Williams — Mrs Browning — was expecting a child. It's months since I saw her. She registered with me when she first moved to London, but I don't think I've seen her since then.'

'So you don't really know her?'

'Why do you ask?'

Exhilaration drains out of me. If I say the wrong thing now, it could be more damaging than helpful to Anna. I suddenly perceive with great clarity that Charles has not spoken to a doctor for this very reason. The thought of having Anna pronounced as mentally unstable and possibly even committed to some asylum is too stark to contemplate and yet if we do not do something soon it may be too late.

Dr Gatton is waiting for me to say something. I choose my words carefully.

298

'I'm worried about my niece. I gather she's been very unlike herself recently. Obviously not eating properly and not looking after herself.'

'I can see that. I take it there is a husband?'

'Yes, there is.' I try to keep my voice neutral, but I cannot help my face.

'Do I take it you don't approve of him?'

'It isn't that I approve or disapprove.'

'But you're fond of your niece?'

'Very.'

'Then I hope you don't think it impertinent of me to suggest this, but would you or some other female relative be able to keep an eye on her for a while? I think she's going to need quite a lot of help in the next few weeks.'

'Is there something seriously wrong with her?'

'I think she may be suffering from malnutrition. She's neglected herself quite alarmingly and having the baby will have weakened her considerably. I'm rather concerned about her mental condition, too. That's particularly why I'd like someone to stay with her. It's not normal practice to sedate new mothers but I found all that strange business of not wanting to look at the child and saying she thought it might be deformed extremely worrying. She needs careful handling, I think.'

'Of course I'll stay.' I'll deal with Charles, he'll probably be only too glad of someone to look after Anna. Mentally I put my own life in abeyance and look down at Francesca Hope asleep in her Moses basket. It's a long time since I've been this close to a new baby. Her tiny face is smooth and soft, she hasn't got that crumpled look of so many newborn babies. She has a fuzz of dark hair and her hands are two miniature starfish. She's a beautiful baby. It will be a pleasure to step aside from my work for a while. It's my firm intention to stay for as long as Anna needs me. I'm well overdue for some leave and my place is here.

After the doctor has left I try telephoning Charles but he's nowhere to be found, not at the office nor anywhere else that I can think of, Cathryn's the same. I telephone Millie who is so delighted with the news that she can't stop crying. I reassure her as best I can that I will look after Anna.

It's midnight and Charles still hasn't come home. Dr Gatton has called back with some formula feed for Francesca Hope and between us we have fed her. Anna is still sleeping, though when I looked in on her she was muttering something about Greg.

I make myself a bed on the couch and

bring Francesca's cot into the room so that I'll hear her when she wakes. I lie and look at her for over an hour before I fall asleep.

* * *

The sky has scribbled clouds across the September morning, and a light wind shudders over the grass making an undulation from left to right across Anna's line of sight. She is aware of it without looking directly at it. It is as subtle as the shifting of light, the grass flattening from dark to light and dark again, like a wave rolling in off the sea. The air is clear and white and so full of a clean feeling there's energy in it like steel wires buoying Anna up.

She and Mary are sitting near the sea close to La Roche. They can see the boundary walls from here and the gateway to the drive. The two women and the baby are staying in a small rented house a few miles along the coast from La Roche. Francesca Hope lies on a soft picnic rug between Anna and Mary, shielded from the breeze and the bright light by a parasol. They finished eating an hour ago, and Francesca has slept since her last feed. She is on her side sleeping now, one small fist curled tight to her face, the other held half-open as though caught in a tiny gracious wave to an adoring public.

Anna also lies on her side, propped on one elbow, and looks at her sleeping child. She adjusts the tiny sun hat covering the fine wisps of dark hair. This morning Francesca had smiled her first smile and Anna's heart had turned over with such total overwhelming love it almost took her breath away. The dark blue gaze of her baby held her bewitched and in love as she leaned in over the side of the cot. There was recognition in those eyes and then Francesca had smiled.

Anna gets up and fetches a light blanket from the pram at her side, settling the soft folds gently round Francesca, tucking it securely round her little form.

'Do you think it's too cool for her? Shall we move off?' Mary says, watching Anna as she rolls over onto her back, stretching her tanned legs luxuriously, settling into the softness of the rug. She has filled out in the last two weeks; the bones in her wrists no longer make her hands appear too heavy for them to support, and there is firm flesh on her legs.

'Let's stay a moment or two longer, it's so lovely here. I'm so glad Charles agreed to the holiday, but I think it's time Francesca and I went back to London.'

'Are you sure, *chérie*?' Mary glances over

at Anna. She looks relaxed and calm, the bruises of tiredness beneath her eyes have all but gone. Mary says, 'Another week would do no harm. Shall I ring Charles this evening and tell him we want another week? It would do you good. After all, you're only just on your feet.'

'It would be nice.' Anna's voice is wistful. She speaks with her eyes closed. 'Perhaps you're right.'

After a lull in which Mary thinks Anna has fallen asleep, Anna says, 'I'll never be able to thank you enough for what you've done, Mary. You saved me.'

'Nonsense! It would have happened anyway.'

Anna breathes deeply, opening her eyes, looking at Mary's profile above her. 'I don't think so. Living in the flat all that time, never going anywhere, afraid of my own shadow.'

Mary smiles. 'Not any more, thank goodness. You had me worried.' A pause. 'Charles was worried too, I think. He just didn't know how to show it. You mustn't blame him.'

Anna says, 'I don't. I never blame him. Not even when he hits me.'

Mary looks at her then. 'He hits you? When does he hit you?'

Anna sits up, hunching forward, wrapping

her arms protectively round herself and looks away from Mary. 'Not often, just a couple of times. I wouldn't make love to him properly. It was my fault.'

Mary reaches for her hand. 'It is never justified, Anna. You must not try to justify it. I had no idea.'

Anna shrugs. 'It's all right. It won't happen again. He promised me.'

A fine line has appeared between Mary's dark eyebrows. 'And I thought at base he was a kind man.'

'He is. I owe him a lot.'

Mary searches in her bag for a cigarette and lights it, drawing on it hard. 'Are you sure it will be all right? You could stay with me.'

Anna shakes her head. 'No, I couldn't. You've got your own life to lead. You've taken enough time over me already. I've made my bed and it's up to me to lie in it.'

'If ever you need me, you will say so, won't you? Promise me.' Mary looks at Anna very straight through the smoke from her cigarette.

'I promise.'

'He doesn't know, does he?'

'About Greg? No.' Anna glances down at Francesca. 'No, he doesn't know and he never will.'

Mary plucks at the seed heads of grasses, throwing them away, grinding out her cigarette on the heel of her sandal.

Anna says, 'Mary, I need to tell someone about Greg and me. I need to tell you. We never meant it to happen. I don't just mean Francesca, I mean any of it. It was as if something was compelling us.'

'I know, sweetheart.' Mary looks down the slope of land to where La Roche can just be seen snuggling amongst its protecting trees. 'I know. These things happen, and we're not always strong.'

'Greg didn't write back, did he? When you wrote and told him about Francesca?' Anna is biting her lip.

'No, my love, he didn't write back.'

'Still, he had to know she'd been born.'

'Yes. I think he did.'

Francesca moves and whimpers in her sleep; she is waking up. She makes a small breathy sound before her eyes screw tight shut and her fists flail at the air. Anna scoops her up, opening her shirt, letting the child fight for and find her nipple. Francesca's jaws clamp tight and Anna's face is suffused with pride as she says, 'I love her so much.'

'That's good, chérie, that's good. She is such a beautiful baby.'

18

In her bed at the cottage, Anna turns over restlessly; she is dreaming dreams of long ago. She is walking with Mary in the fields near Brockley. Greg rides past on Pagan, he is grinning at her. 'Feed our baby, Anna, you must feed our baby. She'll die without you. Here — feed her,' and he throws a ragged bundle at her. 'Don't drop her, Anna, she'll break.' Mary catches the bundle and turns to offer it to Anna, but when Anna looks down at what she is holding, she sees not a baby but Charles and he is laughing. Next comes Cathryn and Cathryn is floating above the ground. Her feet are making no contact at all with the long grass in the field; she is soaking wet, her hair plastered to her pallid face and Anna screams, and screams herself awake and sweating.

She reaches for the light and snaps it on. Her familiar room leaps into place, but her heart still hammers and her chest is tight as she fights to control the emotions racing through her. If only Jean were here, but he is not. He has chosen to spend the night up at the main house. She knows he is trying to come to terms with everything she has told him in the past two days, but a constraint lies between them like a thick wall of fog. Somehow she will get through the next few hours. She must make arrangements to stop Megan from coming here. Whatever he may say to the contrary, Anna knows that Jean is shocked to his core. Francesca has done her damage; Anna will ring Francesca and congratulate her. Then she and Jean must answer the question that hangs between them and decide what to do. If Jean will not leave La Roche then Anna supposes she must.

She has made up her mind to go far away from here, from anywhere where she is known, and to live the rest of her life alone. It is the only honourable thing to do. She is not fit to be loved by anyone. That she was loved and protected for so long by Millie and Leo should surely have been enough for her. To expect more from life is nothing short of greed. Anna sits slumped for a moment, lost in thought, before she climbs out of bed and pulls on her dressing gown. She goes quickly to her dressing table and kneels in front of it on the floor. The bare wood of the polished floor is cold to her knees and she eases over onto one leg and one hip, leaning in and reaching a hand into the recess beneath the dressing table. Her hand makes contact with what it is seeking. It knows without the need for sight the exact size and shape of the box that it draws from its hiding place.

Anna sits back on her heels and with the flat of her hand smooths dust off the top of the small green box. The feel is so familiar. It is a wooden box, made for her by Bryn when she was a little girl; painted and decorated with daisies, heavy for its size — somewhere to keep her treasures. She feels the familiar sharp edges, the wood cool to her fingertips. Anna gets to her feet and places the box on the bed. She is never able to make a direct approach to the box, it's something she rarely looks at, but when she does she approaches warily, like a wild animal circling a fire, afraid of hidden dangers. She goes out of the room and downstairs to make a cup of tea. The brandy in the cupboard is tempting, but Anna reaches past it for the tea caddy.

In the kitchen she is tense. The cottage is very quiet — involuntarily she casts a glance towards the ceiling as though the box might somehow know she is coming. The kettle boils, Anna makes tea and mounts the stairs. She slides into bed. Pushing pillows into place around her back and neck, she pulls the box onto her drawn-up knees and lifts up the lid. It opens easily, releasing a faint scent of sandalwood and revealing a scarlet painted interior enclosing a small quantity of letters; the letters which Greg had never sent. They had found them in the shabby little suitcase he had been carrying the day they came across his body, the day he was coming to find her. It had been her name and address on the dirty scrap of paper in Greg's pocket that had brought them to her. He had been on his way to find her when death overtook him, leaving him alone in an alleyway to be discovered by a group of playing children. Anna thinks again of those children, their innocent day so hideously torn apart and she shudders.

She had insisted on going to identify the body alone. Greg. She had not even known he was back in England. Her brother to be viewed in a mortuary, his dead face gaunt and frightful beneath his shock of red hair. She had said yes, that was her brother. They had given her his pathetic belongings and she had gone home on the bus. It was Francesca's first birthday.

Anna takes out the first letter. It is heavily creased, the paper folded and refolded, scarring the once so familiar handwriting, faded now, but Anna knows most of the words by heart. Their strange fragmentation, his slow disintegration are branded into her brain.

April 1948

Anna, I cannot imagine what you're doing now or how you are coping. I wish I had not come here. Uncle Olivier is unlike the rest of the family; there's a cruel streak in him, much worse than Mama can be. There are times when I even miss the old girl. She wrote to me. I will try and write back but I don't know what to tell her. She wrote a 'jolly' letter about the wedding. I didn't want to know about the wedding. She wrote I should have been there and wondered what in the world could have made me miss it. It was 'naughty' of me! As if I had missed a child's tea-party. She said you were upset and fainted. Is that true? She left undertones of things unsaid in her letter. Is Mama onto us? Surely not. She is shrewd sometimes but not that shrewd. I had another letter last week in which she wrote as if I was on holiday and likely to come back. I suppose she ought to be told I'm not coming back. Not yet. Not if I can learn Olivier's way of doing things. He works me hard.

May 3, 1948

Anna, I don't know what to do. I should leave. I should come back home, but I have no will of my own. Mama wrote. She said you are okay. I have sent a postcard, told her I was okay too. I didn't tell her my only companion is a boy called Jean-Baptiste Antoine. He's a nice boy — he seems to like me. We sing songs together. He's here with his father, they're some kind of distant cousins to us. For the most part of each day black space lives inside my head. I want to be with you and I cannot be with you. Life is so hard to do this to us. We should have had the wit to stay away from each other, but that isn't what I regret; my only regret is we had to stop. Now there are only shadows where you used to be. I love you and I wish I could be near you.

May 19
Darling Anna, it gets worse not better. The farm is very beautiful and so is the countryside. I wish I could show it all to you. You would love it, I know you would. Olivier and Babette have made the farmhouse comfortable. If you and I shared the house we wouldn't be like Olivier and Babette. They are like two dried-up sticks. I imagine us living here with no one to know who we really are. They share the house like a proper sister and brother. She is his housekeeper, he runs the farm. I long for you to be here. I long to make love to you.

311

I dreamed last night I was at La Roche. I could see the cream and the terracotta and sunlight trapped against the walls of the house, then there were clouds coming in off the sea and I was writing you a letter. Then, though not immediately apparent, I realised you were sitting in the rose garden, half-shuttered from my view. That's how I feel about you: you're there but you're not there. It's agony to know you and I are in the same world but may never see each other again. I can't bear it and so I drink at night to shut out the pain. Olivier and Babette don't approve of my drinking so I drink in secret. In the dark. In my room.

May 30

I wanted to rush against my shyness
  and shout
that my mouth wasn't working right,
  that my broken brain
has outlived its house and was rusting
  in the rain.
But you wouldn't have believed me.
  The walls that held
us cry instead. The wind is showing
  through
the stained old space where we used to
  be.

July 1948
Anna, why couldn't you have written to me? Why did it have to be Mary who told me? Her letter came, like a sneak thief, so innocent-looking on the outside. Mary's handwriting. I should have known — it had a London postmark. So I opened it and there was the news that I could not share with anyone. I have a daughter. She will grow up and I will not know her. She will not know me. Anna, I can't deal with this much longer. It's tearing me apart. Mary says you have been ill, but are getting better. She did not say what it was but I wish I could have been there to comfort and hold you.

Christmas
Strange to have Christmas at the wrong time of year — the sun is shining, the flowers are out. I wanted to send something to Francesca, but could not think what, so I spent the money on drink instead. It was wrong. Forgive me as I pray every day for God to forgive me.

June 1949
Darling Anna, I'm coming home, I'm coming to you. Olivier has finally kicked me out and who can blame him. I'm ill and

drunk and useless. If I die before we meet I hope remembrance does not pass away as we pass away.

Anna

It is Francesca Hope's third birthday. It is two years beyond Greg. There is to be a party in the afternoon. Charles will try to be home early from the office and his mother will be here in the evening. Mary will be here, and Mama is coming too. Mama and I are at least allies where Francesca is concerned. Mama adores her. James long since became a shadowy figure and then departed Mama's life for ever. I think Mama must have been very difficult for James to live with during the dark time after Greg's death, and James certainly didn't love her enough to support her and stay with her. I realise now Mama must have suffered badly, though we never talk about it. James did the decent thing before he left and made provision for a small monthly income and Mama has the house. James is living with a rich heiress and Mama has quite enjoyed being an independent woman. She's become very smart, regained her figure — she's quite beautiful in a hard sort of way. I know there have been various affairs, but discreetly. Above all, notoriety must be avoided. The matriarch Elspeth's codes of acceptable and non-acceptable behaviour are well entrenched.

Today, unable to sleep, as I am so frequently, I'm up at five, pottering in the kitchen of the new house. It's a time of day I've grown to love. I'm on my own. I can think. Charles has not yet come bothering me, messing up my mind.

We made love last night. Those are wrong words for what it is that we do. I ache all over and move stiffly this morning. My thighs feel heavy and my body is hateful to me. About twice a month we go to bed together. If I refuse he gets violent. If I don't refuse he's still violent. There's no tenderness. I think I must have a sick mind. I can't tell anyone about this but it seems right, it feels as if it's my justified punishment for him to do what he does with my body. It's what I deserve. Outwardly no one would ever know — I make sure of that. I wear my makeup and I wear my smile. I put them both on together in the morning along with the clothes that he buys for me. I know he goes elsewhere for it; I know he has a lover somewhere. We've talked about divorce, but he says it would damage his reputation too much and besides, he loves Francesca even if he doesn't love me. So does Mama.

I see the future stretching in front of me endless and without nourishment. If it were not for Frankie I would have joined Greg that day. I would have taken the bus to the railway station and thrown myself off the bridge. I would have waited until the next express came through and dropped like a stone in front of it and that would have been an end to it all. But there was Frankie at home waiting for her birthday cake and its candle and I couldn't do it. I couldn't leave her — she's all I had left of him. I couldn't do that to Greg — it would have meant abandoning him altogether. Then the blackness began and the nightmares. It's better now we live out here.

I wish Millie was here. She finished her course and is working on *Le Monde*. I hadn't realised she was so good at her work, but already she's gaining a reputation for herself. I love Frankie but I wish there was more to my life. I have acquaintances here but no friends. How can I make friends? What would I tell them about myself that wasn't a lie? So we have get-togethers over morning coffee and afternoon tea, the other mothers and I, but I never let them see who I really am.

It is pleasant out in the country. Charles chose this house after Greg's death. The doctors had suggested that perhaps living in London was not good for me. I needed peace and quiet; I needed to be in pleasant surroundings. Charles commutes daily to London, leaving me and Francesca surrounded by pleasant green fields and pleasant cows and pleasant country walks.

Recently I suggested to Charles that now that Francesca is going to be three, it might be time for me to perhaps at least offer language lessons in the neighbourhood. He blustered and argued that no wife of his needs to go out to work. His is an important job, the neighbours are aware of the importance of his work, and his colleagues in the office would be amazed at the very idea that his wife should have to work.

'I don't have to work for the money, Charles. I have to work for me. Mary works.'

'Mary has to work. She's a spinster.'

'You make the word sound like an insult — and anyway, she doesn't have to work. She could retire tomorrow if she wanted to.'

Charles lowered his newspaper and looked at me in that damning way he has. 'How so?'

'She came into some money last year. Apparently her real mother had had her traced before she died and left her a small fortune. She wasn't the daughter of a maid like Millie, she was the child of a wealthy family. Mama told me all about her.'

'Christ! What a family you come from!'

I tensed, but Charles had gone back to his paper muttering, 'Lucky Mary! So why is she still working?'

'Charles, you're impossible! You know when Mary moved to England last year she said she didn't want to be a lady of leisure. She enjoys what she does, she gets a thrill out of running her catering agency.'

The newspaper rustled ominously and from behind it came a murmured, 'Huh! You mean she needs to think she's important.'

I wanted to tear the newspaper out of his hands and hit him. His voice came again, cool and arrogant, 'Well, am I right or am I not?'

I was finding my own voice hard to control. 'Yes, I suppose you are. Yes, if you like, if you want to see it that way. It makes Mary feel important, it makes her feel she's got something to contribute.' I rallied. 'That's precisely my point. Mary works because she wants to, not because she has to. I want to work too. I worked before Francesca was born.'

There followed one of Charles's heavy with meaning strategic silences, during which I stood looking out of the French windows at the garden, at space, at anything other than Charles, whilst he carefully readjusted his newspaper so I was unable to see his face. When he spoke again his voice was measured.

'Do you think it would be good for your health to work? You know how . . . delicate you are at times. We moved out here for your health's sake.'

'Perhaps if I had more to occupy my mind we wouldn't need to worry about my 'delicate' nature.' I was sullen, angry with myself for steering the conversation so foolishly into dangerous waters.

'You are absolutely not working, Anna, and that's my last word on the matter.' Charles stood up, throwing down his paper and strode out of the house. It was a Sunday, there was nowhere in particular for him to go but I heard the front door open and close and the car, Charles's prize possession, swing out into the road. It was evening before I heard from him again; he was ringing to say he was with friends up in London, and not to expect him before Monday evening.

'But what about Francesca? You didn't say goodbye to her and she's been asking for you all afternoon.'

'I did try to ring you this afternoon but you were out.'

'We'd gone for a walk. What else am I supposed to do, cooped up here with a small child?'

'You tell me, Anna! You tell me!'

The phone went dead. I didn't cry, I was

too weary for crying; instead I put Francesca to bed and spent the evening listening to the radio. By nine o'clock I too had gone to bed. When Francesca woke crying during the night I stumbled to her bedside and lifted her small baby-smelling body into the warmth of my own narrow single bed.

The following evening Charles came home and neither of us mentioned the previous day. It was as if nothing had happened and another crater in our marriage was patched over. I have not mentioned working since then.

Upstairs, Charles and Francesca are still sleeping. In another hour they will both wake, but now I have the house to myself.

Dawn was probably an hour ago. I stand by the kitchen window and look out over my garden, feeling as if I'm in a Vermeer painting. I'm aware of the light falling across my body, my right side in strong shadow; the folds and creases of my housecoat make me wish I could paint at least half as well as Bryn could, but even his meagre talent has passed me by. Two geraniums splash their colour against the wall, one crimson and luminous, the other salmon-pink and smelling faintly bitter. Francesca drew them yesterday, her small chubby hands holding tight to bright wax crayons, the finished picture being recognisably flowers. If I brushed against their leaves they would release their full scent, evocative of the terrace at La Roche, so I don't touch them.

The garden's colours are taking shape; as the light increases I can see that a blue-pink rose has shed its petals — they're glowing against the dark earth. This morning sweet birdsong is winning over the insane cawing of the crows in the big trees at the end of the garden. I look at Francesca's little garden plot of red-hot salvias edged with shells collected and chosen so lovingly from a day at the seaside, and find I'm smiling. I think of the earthy mess we made together planting the seeds. Frankie's fat hands squeezing and squeezing the soil, patting it down too hard, but the flowers have grown as flowers do against the odds.

Charles begins to move about upstairs. I must begin the day, bacon from the fridge, new bread from the bread bin, tea when the kettle has boiled. He'll be wanting his breakfast. I am a housewife, it is 1951 and I am playing house, a young mother with a miraculously beautiful child, an apparently ideal husband and an ideal home, complete with as many electrical gadgets as any young wife could ever want.

★ ★ ★

Anna makes jellies for the afternoon tea-party. It is eleven o'clock on the morning of Francesca's third birthday. Rows of iced teddy, bunny and duck biscuits lie in ordered ranks on a cooling rack, and Anna sings quietly to herself as she pours liquid red jelly into a castle mould. Francesca will enjoy her party, she will love all the pretty food. The telephone starts ringing in the hallway and Anna tips the last of the jelly mixture quickly into the mould before going to answer the phone. From upstairs she can hear Francesca crying, woken from her nap by the shrill ringing, and fractious from broken sleep.

Anna calls up the stairs, 'It's all right, darling. Mummy's coming.' She lifts the receiver with hands still sticky with jelly. 'Hello?' Whoever was ringing has given up and the phone has gone dead. Anna puts the receiver down, curses, and runs lightly upstairs. Francesca's room is warm with morning sun and sleepy child. Anna holds out her arms to Francesca who stops crying and clings to her mother.

'Come on, sweetheart, did the naughty old phone wake Francesca up? It's all right, lie down again. You can go back to sleep.' She eases Francesca back onto the bed but the

322

phone begins to ring again, and Francesca throws demanding small arms around Anna's neck. 'Let go, my lovely. Mummy's got to answer that,' but the child's arms tighten so Anna lifts her onto her hip and descends the stairs to answer the phone, which maddeningly and predictably stops ringing as soon as Anna reaches out a hand towards it.

'Damn.'

'Damn.' Francesca repeats the word and slides down from her perch on Anna's hip. She marches up and down the hall murmuring, 'Damn, damn, damn,' lovingly to herself. This is a new word to be tasted and enjoyed.

'Shhh, Francesca. Come on — Mummy will get you a biscuit,' but the child's voice is getting louder, and when the phone rings again and Anna lifts the receiver she has difficulty in hearing the voice on the other end of the line.

'Would you excuse me for a moment, please.' Anna puts the receiver down on the floor and runs into the kitchen, returning with a teddy bear biscuit for Francesca, who has, with a thoughtful frown, just replaced the receiver on its cradle.

'Oh Francesca!' Anna runs exasperated hands through her hair, making it stand out around her head in a dark halo. 'What am I going to do with you!' but she is laughing as she bends to cuddle the child. The phone rings again.

'Gen!' beams Francesca. 'Phone. Gen.' She jumps around the hall, landing squarely on sturdy legs, balancing easily on short spreading toes. Her face beams.

'Yes, again. Now shush, eat your biscuit and let Mummy answer it this time. Please, darling, be good. Shush.' Anna presses a finger to her own lips and picks up the receiver.

'Mrs Browning?' The voice on the other end of the line is peremptory.

'Yes, yes, I'm sorry we got cut off. I've got a small child . . . ' Anna's voice trails away as the unknown voice cuts across what she is saying. At first Anna can't understand what the woman is telling her. The line is distorted and through the crackles and echoes she is able to discern that someone in a hospital in Cambridge is ringing her, telling her there has been an accident — a serious accident and that she should go to the hospital immediately. The words seem to fuse together into a meaningless mass. There has been an accident, the caller is someone official. The call is coming from a hospital. Anna's legs begin to tremble and the motes of dust floating in the sunlight in the hall momentarily become a thick fog. The colours of the day are wiped away. Anna struggles to make sense of the words that seem to fall at random, making no sense as the unknown voice asks if she is able to hear what it has said to her and repeats the information. Anna stumbles out some words of thanks and puts down the phone. Francesca regards her solemnly.

A loud knocking on the front door combines with the doorbell chimes and Anna reaches out to comfort a now wailing Francesca. Together they answer the door. Anna's legs feel like rubber; her stomach has taken on a life of its own. A policeman and a policewoman are standing on the step. Their sombre blue bulk blots out the light. Cold clutches at Anna as she holds Francesca to her, but exactly who she is protecting she is unsure.

Thoughts of Greg whirl and rip through Anna's mind. The police came like this the day Greg was found — two of them on the step of her small London house, blotting out the sun. Anna steps back from the front door, one hand holding on to Francesca, the other at her own throat. 'What is it? What's the matter? Is it about the accident? Who's been hurt? The hospital rang me but I couldn't understand what they said. It was a bad connection.' She knows she is gabbling, but the words won't stop.

'May we come in, Mrs Browning?' The policeman's voice is soft and concerned.

'Shall I look after the little girl?' The policewoman's face is very young and kind and round. She takes Francesca from Anna and disappears into the kitchen, talking soothingly to the child.

The policeman follows Anna into the sitting room and closes the door. 'I think you should sit down, Mrs Browning. There's been an accident. I'm afraid I have to tell you this, but your husband is rather badly hurt. They say it's touch and go.' He puts one hand to his chin and clears his throat, and before Anna can say anything he continues. 'There is something else, Mrs Browning. I'm really so sorry, but — it's about your mother. Seemingly there was nothing that could be done to save her.'

'My mother!?'

The policeman nods. 'I'm afraid so, Mrs Browning. She died at the scene of the accident.'

'She's dead?' Anna whispers. 'But how? Where?'

The policewoman returns with a cup of tea for Anna, which she takes with trembling hands. She cannot drink the tea. Its smell revolts her. Nothing is real, everything is happening too slowly or too fast. Through the French windows Anna can see Francesca playing happily in the garden; the police-woman has joined her. They are kicking Francesca's big orange ball to each other, the pretty young WPC is incongruous in her dark uniform and heavy shoes.

Anna turns back to the policeman. He is saying, 'They were in a boat on the Cam.' His voice sounds loud in the small room.

'A boat? What boat? Charles . . . are you sure it's Charles?'

The policeman is beginning to feel uncomfortable; he has the advantage of lack of involvement and a very shrewd mind. 'Yes, Mrs Browning. He's conscious, though very ill and was able to give us your address and phone number.'

'But what were they doing together? Why were they out in a boat? I don't understand.'

'Perhaps you'd like to get a coat, Mrs Browning.' The policeman, who has been shifting from foot to foot, steps forward. 'We can take you to the hospital if you'd like.'

Anna stands up. She is still bewildered that Cathryn should be dead, drowned. It makes no sense. Water was her element — she loved to swim. Anna turns in the doorway. 'How did it happen?'

The policeman coughs like a stage policeman before replying. 'We don't have all the details, but it would appear the boat got caught up in the wash of a larger vessel and your mother fell over the side, hitting her head. She was knocked unconscious, your husband tried to save her but it was too late. I'm afraid according to your husband, your mother was already dead. That will have to be confirmed, of course.'

Anna's thoughts are beginning to race. Charles and Cathryn, in a boat on the Cam. He had told her last night that he had a business meeting this morning. He had left earlier than usual, in such a hurry to leave the house, ebullient and yet on edge, calling to her from the open window of his car that she should start Frankie's party without him, he'd get there as soon as he could. All those times he has had to stay overnight in Town, or go to the country on business. Her mother's call late yesterday evening, how light-hearted she had sounded. She wouldn't be round to help out in the morning with the party arrangements; she was awfully sorry, but something had come up. She had made an evasive response to Anna's question as to when she would get to Francesca's party. Anna does not meet the policeman's eyes. She gets to her feet.

The police help Anna to make hurried arrangements with a kind neighbour who will care for Francesca. There will be no birthday party. The policewoman helps Anna with the list of phone numbers to ring, she helps her with the wording of the swift explanation, and onto the next, before words of sympathy, which Anna does not want to hear, can be uttered. Throughout the drive to the hospital the policewoman sits with Anna and smiles and pats her hand occasionally. She stays with her when Anna makes her confirmation that the woman lying beneath the white sheet is indeed Cathryn. Forty-one years old — beautiful, statuesque, shrewd and adulterous in life. In death unspeakably disfigured.

The policewoman takes Anna to the canteen for a cup of tea and they sit silently whilst the realisation seeps into Anna's dulled mind that there will be no more petty jealousies, no more talking, no more sparring, just a steep falling away into a depth too stark to even contemplate. She looks up at the policewoman and says, 'Can someone be a twenty-one-year-old orphan?' and when the policewoman can think of no immediate response Anna adds, 'I don't have a brother any more either. I did have one, but I lost him. Wasn't that careless of me.'

The other young woman takes her by the

arm. 'Come along, Mrs Browning. Don't be upsetting yourself. You've had a nasty shock. Perhaps you'd like to see your husband now? We could go up to the ward and see if they'll let you in for a few minutes, if you like.'

Anna knows only a horrifying coldness gripping tight at the centre of her being. She looks without comprehension at the woman's hand on her arm before she pushes it away and stumbles from the room. She travels endless corridors seeking an outside door. People in white coats, in nurses' uniforms, in outdoor clothes, turn and watch her; and all the time her mind creeps towards the edge of the abyss and skitters away, only to return again and again to the point where panic begins and reality dwindles.

★ ★ ★

'Anna! Are you okay, Anna?' Jean-Baptiste calls up to Anna's open window and hammers on the cottage door. It's well into the morning. Anna wakes with a stiff neck; she's been sleeping propped awkwardly against her pillows. Greg's final letter still lies on the curl of her open hand.

'Anna? Are you there? Are you all right?' Jean's voice is louder as Anna slides from her bed and replaces the letters in their box.

Easing her stiffened joints she leans out of the bedroom window. From here she can see the top of Jean's head. The morning is already hot. 'I'm here. What time is it?'

Jean steps back and looks up at her; a half-smile fights against something in his eyes and Anna flinches, but she says evenly, 'I'll come down.' She pushes the daisy box back into its hiding place beneath the dressing table and makes her way down the stairs aware of aching bones and a heaviness in her step. She unlocks the door and stands back to allow Jean into the house.

'Didn't you have your key?' she asks.

They do not touch.

'I did, but . . . '

'Yes, I know,' she says, walking away from him. 'Cup of tea?'

'Please. I'll make it. You get changed if you want to.'

Without replying Anna goes upstairs, showers and dresses for the day. She can hear Jean moving about downstairs. It's very hot already and Anna is light-headed from lack of sleep. In a detached way she wonders if Jean has come to pack his things. But when she comes downstairs, he is in the kitchen washing his breakfast dishes. He turns and smiles. Almost a proper smile.

'Shall we work in the garden today?'

'Jean. Don't. Don't do this. Things aren't normal any more, you can't pretend that they are. This won't go away. If only Frankie hadn't made that phone call, if only Megan were not coming to stay, we could have continued peacefully and indefinitely. But Megan is coming. Francesca did ring. We can't go on as if nothing has happened.'

'You could ring Megan and ask her not to come,' Jean says.

'It would make no difference. She has to come, she has the exhibition in Toulon.'

'But she doesn't have to come on here afterwards.'

'I'll have to think about it.'

'I wouldn't read the diary.'

'No. I know that.'

'I want things to be right.'

'Yes, I know that too. But I think we can't go on much longer. I think I should leave. It's not a question I'm asking you, Jean. It's something I'm saying.'

The kitchen is quiet and sunlit. Anna moves into the living room and looks around at the warm glowing colours of the furnishings. She and Jean have chosen so many of the things in this room together. The little cottage has been their private world and their haven. Jean follows her and stands in the doorway looking at her looking at the room.

He clears his throat. 'I'll be in the garden if you need me.' Before she can make a reply he has left by the back door.

Anna lies on her bed. From here she can see the brilliant sky, where a flock of seagulls is flying very high. The birds are floating above Anna, silvery white against the blue: each bird's wings makes its own beautiful arced pattern and together they combine into a further pattern, individuals making up the whole and Anna thinks they are like fish on a calm ocean and the whole world is upside down. For a brief span she is with them. With the sun on her face she is someone else and somewhere else. By the time Jean returns to the cottage Anna has fallen asleep. Jean sits watchfully beside her for over an hour. When he leaves she is still sleeping. Jean collects some of his belongings and goes up to the big house, leaving her a note to say where he has gone.

19

Francesca

When the bottom of your world falls out, life changes. I was three years old, but it wasn't until years afterwards that the fragmentary snapshot images fell together to make a complete picture. Before that the images flickered like one of those books where, if you flick the pages fast enough, a moving image appears, but I could never do that. Not so that it was smooth and continuous. My flicker book always jerked and faltered, skipping pages, causing the images to run without sense, or not to run at all. When the film runs smoothly then you have the power to say *That was it — that was the moment, the one that altered everything* — you can say it because you can see where it fits into the pattern and where, without it, the pattern would have been completely different. Or, the pattern might not have existed at all.

I was three years old. It was my birthday. There was going to be a party. The telephone rang. A man and a woman in dark clothes came. I know now they were police, though for years I dreamed them without knowing who they were. My mother went away and when she came back she wasn't like my mother any more. There was going to be a party and the party didn't happen. The funny animal biscuits all went stale and had to be thrown away. Aunt Mary threw them away and whilst she did, she was crying. My mother went out for the day and when she came back she wasn't my mother any more and my father didn't come back at all. There was a coffin. There were two coffins and people in black clothes. After that I didn't have a grandmother and I didn't have a father. They were in two holes in the ground and my mother wasn't like my mother any more. I lived with Mary in a different house. She was there all the time. Sometimes my mother was there and sometimes she wasn't and sometimes we went to see her in a big building with gardens. The gardens were very beautiful but the building smelled strange and I still can't eat boiled cabbage. After the following Christmas my mother came to live with Mary and me, and my mother was my mother again. At least I thought she was.

Mary
It's a Friday evening and darkness presses against the walls of my ancient Somerset

farmhouse. Inside we're peaceful. Anna is upstairs helping seven-year-old Francesca with her bath. Millie, who is here for a much-needed break from her hectic schedule, is helping me fold the ironing. The clock ticks on the wall, its hands pointing to half-past seven. The calendar informs me it's October and it's 1955, but living here I feel timeless. Domestic harmony. Bliss. I've no wish to return to work. I realise I'm happier than I've ever been. I feel I could go on like this for many years.

When Anna comes downstairs she's warm and flushed from bathing Francesca and her long brown hair is escaping in curling wisps around her face. She turns in the doorway and calls up the stairs, 'Night, night, Frankie, sleep tight. Mind those bugs don't bite.' We smile at each other as Francesca's clear voice calls, 'And if they do, bite them back! Night, night, Mummy — nightie, nightie, everyone.'

'Shall I make a pot of tea?' Anna goes through to the kitchen and puts the kettle on.

'Not for me — I'm off to the pub.' Millie stretches her plump arms elaborately before running her fingers through her thick fair hair.

'You didn't say you were going out tonight.' Anna puts her head back round the door.

'Ah well, I don't tell you everything, you

know!' Millie's grey eyes are dancing and she blushes.

'A man?'

'Of course!'

'Not necessarily,' I laugh.

Millie pulls a face at me. 'No, apparently not, Mary!'

'You told her?' This from Anna coming back into the room with a tray of biscuits and a pot of tea.

'Well, why not?' I fold the last sheet and take the ironing blanket off the table. 'After all, I think she's old enough to know!' Millie throws a cushion at me as she goes to fetch her new swing coat. She blows us both an airy kiss and, grabbing her keys, leaves the house. 'Don't wait up for me!'

'Be good,' we chorus.

The room closes back in on itself. I stoop to put more coal on the fire. As Anna pours the tea, I say, 'You seemed surprised that I'd told Millie about my affairs.'

Anna shrugs and pats a place on the settee next to her. 'Not really. Come and sit down. Take the weight off your tootsies. If I know, why shouldn't she?'

'Fair's fair,' I murmur, sinking into the cushions. I'm tired tonight. 'I've got something to ask you. Millie's met a man.'

'Yes, I know, she's just gone to the pub to

meet him.' Anna grins and bites into a biscuit.

'Another man.'

Anna sputters biscuit crumbs. 'Another one! How many does she want?'

'It's not like that,' I say. 'He's another photographer.'

'Sounds interesting. Where did she meet him? Is he French?'

'He's English, she met him by chance on the train.'

'She really should be more careful. She should know by now not to pick up just anybody.'

'Leo isn't just anybody. He's very nice.'

'You've met him?'

'A couple of days ago.'

'And?'

'And he needs a place to stay. He's in a hotel now but he's going to be working locally for a while and it's costing him too much. He's working as a freelance doing a book about Somerset villages and the Levels. He's taken some wonderful pictures already.'

'It sounds as if you have a soft spot for him already!' Anna reaches for another biscuit. I think of the young man Millie introduced me to in the library earlier in the week. I had liked him immediately — slightly built beneath the bulk of his duffel coat but broad at the shoulders, a little over six foot, with soft dark hair and eyes so dark as to be almost black, but, unlike so many brown eyes, totally readable. A man with eyes like that? How could I help but like him!

'Perhaps I do have a soft spot,' I say. 'He's nice-looking and he's very intelligent.'

Anna giggles. 'I do love you, Mary. From 'nice-looking' I shall deduce that you mean extraordinarily attractive. I'm very glad he's intelligent. That just has to be a bonus!'

'Stop teasing. Would you mind him coming here?'

'Of course not. It's your house, Mary, you should decide.'

'Yes, I know, but I wondered if it would bother you having a man in the place.' I feel awkward and much younger than my forty-two years, as I say, 'I was thinking about Charles.'

Anna looks suddenly tired. 'And Greg?'

'Oh God, I'm sorry, Anna. I've caused you pain.'

I feel wretched, but Anna says, 'It's all right, Mary. I've had plenty of time for reflection. There's pain. Of course there's pain, but I think things are in some kind of perspective. If they're not after all this time, when will they ever be?'

I pause before I say, 'So you think you

won't mind a man being here?'

'Mary, I work with men all the time! Every architect in that office is male.' I glance at Anna and see she is smiling as she says, 'It might be pleasant to have a nice man around the place. Besides, if he's working I don't suppose he'll be here much, and neither will I. Personal Assistant to the boss is a pretty tall order.'

I ruffle Anna's hair as I fetch more tea. 'You did well, *chérie*.'

'Yes, didn't I?' Anna tucks her feet up under her. 'What will this man Leo do about a darkroom?'

'I thought he might be able to use the boxroom.'

'Aha! Just as I suspected. You've got it all planned.'

'Then there's the bathroom arrangements — he might not like to see rows of nylons hanging over the bath, so I thought he could have the big bedroom with the bathroom next door and we'll have the other end of the house. It should work quite well.'

'He's not sharing with Millie while she's here?'

'I don't think it is that sort of a relationship. Though you can never tell with Millie.'

Anna raises her eyebrows. 'Ooh! You don't

really approve, do you?'

'Young people nowadays are not so very different from young people in my day. Though of course we had the excuse of the war, and if I am honest I think it made a difference. People took lovers. Life was so much more precarious.' Thinking of Bryn and knowing that Anna's intuitive gaze is on me I rush on. 'Anyway, I think if this Leo will come to stay with us he is a brave man to take us on.'

Anna leans forward and kisses me. 'So do I, Mary. He'll be very welcome. It will be nice to have him here, I'm sure.'

Anna

It's a shock the next day to find Leo on our doorstep, not a middle-aged man as I had thought from Mary's obvious delight with him, but a man of my own age. His photographic gear is piled around him and he has one suitcase. I take an immediate liking to him. His smile is warm and open and his eyes are bright like a particularly alert squirrel's eyes. He holds out a hand for me to shake. I am aware of a firm cool grip on mine as he says, 'Hello, I'm Leo. I hope this is the right address?'

'I'll fetch Mary,' I say, feeling like a child

hiding behind its mother's skirts. 'Mary?' I call her name stepping back off the doorstep into the house, leaving Leo standing outside.

Mary comes running, brushing flour from her hands onto her apron.

'Leo! How lovely you've come.'

She shoots me a quizzical look, and I say slightly too late, 'Sorry, would you like to come in?' I hold the door wider open. I am very aware of his smile.

'I'm not too early?' he says, and his voice catches at something inside me that I thought had died.

'Of course not,' Mary says. 'Come in. I'm afraid Millie's out — buying shoes.' Mary laughs over her shoulder, helping Leo into the house with his things. She's almost flirting with him; I can't blame her. Her face is alive beneath her silvering hair. Behind Leo's head a flock of birds scatters over the empty sky and reassembles along the telegraph wires. He brushes past me and I go on holding the door as weak sunlight breaks through the autumn mist lifting off the river beyond the garden.

Francesca
You can tell a great deal from photographs. I have one of Uncle Leo taken soon after he

first came to live with us all. He is smiling straight into the camera. They say the eyes are the windows of the soul; if that's the case, his whole soul is in his eyes. I know who took the photograph. It wasn't Millie — it was my mother. It's the sort of look that should be censored before it breaks someone's heart.

Mary

Spring has come and things are going to change. Millie stayed on, after all. She gave up her position on *Le Monde* and has thrown in her lot with Leo. They work well together; they are compiling photographs for what I think will be a very beautiful book. They are lovers too. She moved into his room just before Christmas. For a while I thought it would be Anna, but no. Anna is clearly very fond of Leo, but I sense she holds him off at arm's length. However it's been good for Francesca to be brought up in a household that is not exclusively female. Leo is so good with her. She'll miss him when he and Millie go off to London next month. Frankie and Leo spend a lot of time together — she calls him 'uncle'. He invents wonderful games for her and has built a tree-house. They were outside all day yesterday refurbishing it after the winter.

I was in the village post office this morning and know now for a fact that the neighbours have jumped to all kinds of conclusions about Leo. He's apparently keeping us *all* happy in bed. I was behind the seed-packet display, choosing vegetable seeds and some nasturtiums for Frankie. The postmistress hadn't seen me come in with Mrs Marten from along the lane, and began to discuss our business with Mrs Marten in no uncertain terms, calling us all 'half-bloomin' foreign'. I'm not sure who was the more embarrased — her or me when I emerged. Needless to say she made no sale of seed packets, nor will she!

Anna
Two years since Millie and Leo left and they've come to visit as they often do. They're becoming well-to-do. Their partnership is going well. Millie is quite a celebrity — a young woman in such a commanding position, she's quite a rarity. There was even an article about the two of them in the *Tatler*; *'Miss Breton the unconventional society photographer and her handsome escort, also a photographer.'* By unconventional they mean they're unmarried.

I asked Leo if he minds being described as

Millie's escort and he roared with laughter. 'No, I love it! Millie enjoys the limelight, it suits me to be less noticed.'

It's a Saturday morning. Millie and Mary have driven into Bath for a day's gossip and shopping, so Leo and I have caught the train to the seaside with Frankie. Leo and I walk together, leaning a little into the wind. Francesca, nine years old, long-legged in her red coat skips alongside, past the manmade boating lake and four seagulls bobbing disconsolately on the water. Do they know they're on Madeira Cove? I wonder aloud and Leo laughs and swings my hand. Perhaps it was a mistake to agree to come with him, but Frankie was so thrilled to have him here. She adores him and I know how much she misses him between visits; they're always writing and exchanging drawings and photographs. He writes such funny letters to her, and sometimes he writes to me. Letters I'm always pleased to have.

The sea-path winds round the bay backed with tamarisks and stunted laurels; their thick glossy leaves are slightly deformed because of the salt air. A plump woman in black sits on a bench reading a romantic novel. Leo and I agree that, either the woman has a cold or she's weeping — it's hard to know which. Grand Victorian houses march up the

345

hillside; an old woman looks out from one of them, her world shrunk to a room with a balcony and a deckchair for warmer days. Today isn't one of them.

We're having a day at the seaside, Leo, Francesca and I, taking the sea air, wandering along the Prom, being smiled at like any happy family. A handsome family, to judge from our reflected selves in shop windows as we walk down through the town to the seafront. Leo is lovely to be with. He's lovely just to look at. I hadn't realised how much I've missed him since last time he was here, and I hope it doesn't show.

In a café we eat fish and chips with white bread and butter, and drink strong tea poured from a heavy brown teapot into thick white cups. Leo loads three spoonfuls of sugar into his tea and grins, 'I love times like this. Beats the caviar life any day.' I look at him through the steam rising from his cup and can think of no reply. Frankie rides donkeys on the beach. We eat ice cream.

We're on the way home on the train. Francesca has fallen asleep, her head heavy against my shoulder and her weight slumped on my knees. The sea air has made us all sleepy. Leo and I talk quietly.

Without warning Leo leans over and kisses me, hard on the mouth, and releases me only to pull me back to him. He kisses me again, very softly, very sweetly. I want the kiss to go on. I push him away.

'Sorry, Anna. Perhaps I shouldn't have?'

I want him so much I'm frightened. There's been no one for me since Greg and now I'm thinking of loving Millie's lover and I know now it's the thought I've denied ever since I met him. I must be crazy. I look into the darkening evening; we travel on through an unseen countryside. It's started to rain and the rain washing on the windows makes the surface appear insubstantial and fluid like jelly.

Leo takes my hand. 'I am sorry, Anna. Let's just forget it, shall we? It was a nice kiss for a nice day out. Let's leave it at that.'

'I think we should.'

The train rattles on. Neither of us utters a word. By the time we arrive at our stop Frankie is awake and irritable but Millie comes to meet us with the car as she promised. We drive the mile home in torrential rain, shouting to Millie about our day above the noise of a thousand drummers beating a tattoo on the car roof.

When we reach the house Mary flings open the door. The light from the house turns the rain into a million flashing splinters. Shielding Frankie's head we dash to the warmth of the kitchen, but the rain's so heavy that in the short space between car and house we're all drenched.

'Oh, my dears. Come on in. Come on, let me get Francesca into a warm bath and then you two must see to yourselves. Millie and I are going out to the pictures. You don't mind, do you?'

'How can we mind?' Leo smiles, and I love his smile so much I have to look away. 'We've had our outing for the day.' He goes upstairs to change and I don't see him again until Francesca is in bed and Mary and Millie have gone out for the evening.

I've had a hot shower and slipped into a soft jersey and slacks; although it's April it's cool tonight. I think I may spend the evening in my room and avoid Leo, but I discover I'm ravenous. It would be churlish to make myself a meal and not offer food to Leo. It will be awkward to sit and eat with him, but it's a hurdle we have to get over, so we might as well get over it as soon as possible.

I go to the foot of the stairs and call Leo's name quietly. I don't want to wake Frankie. He comes to the head of the stairs; it's obvious he's been asleep — his shirt's half out at his waist and undone at the neck, his long smooth feet are bare and he's wearing an old pair of soft cord trousers. It occurs to me

348

suddenly and with such astounding clarity that I'm surprised I hadn't thought of it before — I'm still young. After Francesca; after Greg's death; after the brutality of Charles, I have become no gender and no age in particular. It is more than that — I have been careful to be no gender and no age. I've known I'm not old, or remotely middle-aged, but neither have I been young. I have been dimly aware of men who may have wanted me, but I've made sure they understood I'm not available and they soon grew tired of a chase that was leading nowhere. Seeing Leo standing above me on the stairs — it's like a revelation. My body is coming alive again and I am more than disturbed. I've been so long in limbo that awakening is almost painful. I feel as exposed as a newly emerged butterfly stretching and drying its wings, unaware of its own fragility.

'What is it?' Leo stands at the top of the stairs grinning down at me and runs a hand through his thick dark hair. It glints with shades of brown amongst the apparent blackness. His smile is lazy and his eyes are very dark.

'Do you want something to eat? I'm making a sandwich if you'd like one.' I'm aware of having to control my voice. I don't meet his eyes.

'Umm, coffee would be good too. I'm coming down.' His voice is a husky stage whisper. As Frankie cries out in her sleep and settles again, Leo tiptoes in an exaggerated fashion down the stairs, making me laugh. He puts a hand on my shoulder; in its light pressure I feel each individual finger. I know his hands as well as I know my own. He smiles. 'Come on, we'll make something to eat together.'

The conversation has returned to our usual friendly everyday level and Leo's hand on my shoulder is no more than a gesture of friendship. I slip from beneath its pressure and head for the kitchen.

He calls after my retreating back, 'Shall I light the fire in the sitting room? It's chilly, we could eat in there if you like.'

'Good idea. I'll make a start on the food.'

By the time Leo returns I've made the sandwiches and poured coffee into a Thermos. I've found fruit cake and apples and I've loaded a tray.

'Lovely! We'll have a picnic.' Leo comes into the kitchen and picks up the tray and I follow him down the hall into the sitting room, trying not to watch the narrowness of his hips. Leo puts the tray on the coffee table and between us we pull the settee up to the fire.

I bend to pour the coffee but Leo is behind me. He puts his hands on my waist and kisses the back of my neck, I freeze. 'Don't, Leo. Oh please don't,' but he's turned me to him and smothered my face and lips with kisses and everything in me is responding. I run my hands over his back, closing my eyes, imagining the way the muscles move and the complex pattern of his skeleton and the blood flowing through his veins to the heart that a few minutes ago I could feel pounding against my ribcage. I stroke the tight curve of his buttocks. He raises his head and smiles at me and I see what I've always seen when he looks at me. I make one final ineffectual attempt to push him away.

Afterwards we lie naked together on the settee. We lie without speaking for a long time. The coals on the fire have sunk and fused to a smouldering mass. I feel their heat along my body as I lie slightly apart from Leo and he reaches out to stroke my back. 'I love you, Anna. I always have.'

I catch and kiss his hand and hold it against my mouth, kissing each of his fingers and his palm, but I'm crying as I say, 'I love you too, Leo, but we can't do this again. We mustn't. It's wrong — it will only lead to misery.'

'It won't. It needn't. Don't cry.' His voice is

an urgent whisper.

I sit up. 'Secrecy is a terrible thing, Leo. You're Millie's man. Not mine.'

'But I could be both — she wouldn't have to know.' His hand strokes my thigh. 'You're so beautiful. I don't just mean your body and your face. I mean you. The essence of you.'

'Leo, it would be so wrong. It's already wrong!' My soul shrinks as I think of Greg; this could be no different. Leo and I would never be able to be together, we won't be able to walk hand in hand any more as friends, there will always be the knowledge of what we've done between us — for ever. What we have done will break Millie's heart. I have lost Leo and I have lost Millie. Millie will never forgive me. My head is aching, there's a dull pain behind my eyes. I thought I would never be a fool again . . . how wrong could I be.

'I had an affair once,' I say, my voice is stiff and formal.

Leo smiles. 'So?' He reaches up and touches my back.

'It was with my brother. Francesca is the result.' I stand up and reach for my clothes without looking at Leo. I say, 'So now tell me I'm beautiful.'

There is a small sound outside the living-room door. Leo sits up, he's not looking at me. Footsteps on the stairs? I drag

352

on my clothes and go to the door. I'm sure I hear Francesca's door closing, but when I go up she is sound asleep. By the time I return downstairs Leo is dressed and Millie and Mary have returned, full of talk about *The Bridge on the River Kwai*; a lively discussion of David Lean's direction follows. Pleading tiredness I slip away to bed. I am aware of Leo watching me as I leave the room, but he does not follow.

Francesca

More pages from my flicker book. There's a photograph taken at a party. Leo has his arm round Millie; one casual masculine hand lies along the line of her hip, his fingers rest on her thigh with an easy pressure. He is smiling straight at the camera. Millie is glowing with pride in her man.

I remember the party, I remember everyone telling my mother how lovely she looked. Everyone said it except for Uncle Leo. He didn't say anything at all. For two days he and my mother had hardly spoken to each other and though I didn't know why two grown-ups would not talk to each other after they had made love, I knew it had something to do with it. I knew they shouldn't have been doing what they did; I knew that Leo was meant to be with Millie.

Flick the pages. Two days before that photograph was taken. My mother and Leo are naked together in the living room whilst Millie and Mary are at the pictures. I know — I saw them. I want a drink of water. I want my mother. I've had a bad dream about the time she was away from me and I feel empty and dark. I want her with me — I need to be with her. I am standing in the room, just inside the door. The room is dark apart from the firelight and I see them together. Leo's hand is on my mother's back. My mother is saying words about her brother. Words I don't understand. Words I think I have forgotten until years and years later. I run from the room and when my mother comes to my bedroom I pretend to be asleep.

Flick again. It is the day after the party. Millie is shouting at Leo. They are in the orchard amongst the daffodils. Millie is shouting terrible bad words about, my mother. Leo is shushing her; over his shoulder he can see me looking out of the window at them. He is trying to hold onto Millie but she hits him and runs away into the house. I hear her come in, then I hear her leaving by the front door.

Leo sits for a long time on my swing; he isn't moving, he isn't doing anything. I hide well back inside my room so he can't see I'm still watching. I hear my mother calling Leo's name and I creep closer to the window. I can see the top of my mother's head. She is walking down through the garden. Leo watches her and, when she gets near he says something, but I can't hear what it is. It's like watching a puppet show. Leo isn't smiling. His face looks funny — sort of twisted up and a funny colour. My mother touches his shoulder but he pushes her hand away and says something angry. I can see he is angry by the way his hands are waving about and his head keeps making little stabbing movements. Then he leaves my mother on her own amongst the daffodils in the orchard and he comes into the house. I can hear him along the landing in the room he shares with Millie. I creep to the door and listen.

I don't know what the sound he is making might be. Then I realise he is crying. Poor Leo. I didn't know men could cry. I go back to my room and I cry too. But I'm not sure why.

Now Millie and Leo are leaving. My mother is not there. Millie has done a lot more shouting. My mother has done a lot of crying. Leo has said nothing. Mary has been white-faced and she has kept crying. I have been alone in Leo's tree-house. I know he won't be back.

Flick again. My mother received some letters from Leo, but I know she never read them. I found the pieces torn up, shredded so only a word here and there could be read. She told me Millie and Leo had to go away to do some work abroad. Leo still wrote to me, but only at Christmas. They didn't come to see us again for a long time. I cried for a long time. Flick — flick. I am bad at school. I hit and bite other children. I am rude to teachers. I swear at the headmistress. My mother is asked to take me somewhere else to school. It is the first time it has happened, but it won't be the last.

20

Mary

I am buying a book for Francesca. For her Christmas gift. Choosing with care in the bookshop off the High Street. I ask for the shop assistant's assistance. What would be suitable for a demanding twelve-year-old with highly developed artistic skills? The girl recommends, in a sulky voice, various tomes, not one of which is suitable. Has she listened to a thing I've said, I wonder. I wish the owner was here. What is he thinking of, to be employing such disinterested staff. However, I thank the girl and turn back into the shop's inner room. I've always liked it in here. The dark mahogany shelves, the peace and stillness, the rows and rows of new stiff covered books, all give me immense pleasure.

Later I shall add to my day's pleasure. I'm going to meet Anna for lunch; she and her fiancé Anthony are Christmas shopping further down the street. Anthony is an unassuming quiet man, tall and well spoken, not a great deal to recommend him. I don't believe Anna is in love with him but he looks after her. He reminds me of a nice quiet dog, the sort that might be used to help the blind, an uncharitable thought and I squash it almost as quickly as it comes into my head.

This evening Frankie is coming home from her first term at boarding school. It was my suggestion that she should go there. I have helped to pay the fees. Though Anna is doing well with her new translation job she still could not have afforded the fees, but it seemed a good solution before Frankie could cause any more disruption.

Anna and Frankie do not get on at all well and, as Francesca grows towards womanhood, I sense things could become even harder for Anna. Frankie has not yet met Anthony. Anna says she has written to her about him but will give Francesca a few days at home before she suggests a meeting. A mistake in my eyes, but . . . who am I these days, but an observer of life. That's my last thought before I notice a man standing above me. The shop is so arranged as to be in terraces; short flights of steps link each stage and the shelves are arranged in such a way that it is possible to see easily from one level to the next.

The man smiles and I smile back. He comes to stand beside me, reaching for the same book as I do, it's a long time since I was propositioned in any way. As our hands meet he lifts his eyebrows and says, 'We would seem to have the same taste.'

'I'm looking for a book for my great-niece,' I say and am gratified when he does not say, 'You look far too youthful to have a great-niece,' but begins instead to ask intelligent searching questions concerning her tastes and interests. Before long we have chosen two lovely volumes on Van Gogh and are leaving the shop together. It is only as I am eating my second portion of steamed pudding, exchanging thoughts and ideas, building a friendship with this rather short, stout and slightly balding schoolmaster that I realise simultaneously that I may have found an unexpected kindred spirit and I've forgotten about Anna. 'Oh Jesus!' I say.

'Something wrong with the pudding?' He is laughing. He has such a nice laugh.

I smile and say, 'No, it's my niece — mother of the great-niece. I'm supposed to have met her for lunch.'

'Aah. A problem. Will she be very angry?' His eyes are full of genuine concern.

'Not angry, but probably worried.'

'Where were you meeting her?'

'At the Swan.'

'The Swan? I know where that is. Shall we go there now?' The bill is paid, coats are fetched and I walk down the street on John's arm, feeling as if I might possibly have come to a safe harbour.

When we reach the Swan I am met by a very strange sight indeed. Anna and Anthony and Leo are all sitting together eating an enormous lunch. Anna turns and waves a hand; she gets to her feet and comes across to meet me. 'Mary, isn't this wonderful! Look who's here! I can't believe it — Leo! After all this time, we just ran into each other in the street. Come and join us and bring your friend too.'

Francesca

More pages of the flicker book. New Year, 1960. I'm twelve. I've been away at school for one term. It's been good. Leo's back. Mummy was going to marry a man called Anthony, then Leo came back and Anthony's gone away. Mummy is happy with Leo and he's happy with her and it's really lovely to see him again. Millie's working in London and abroad and all over the place. She's very busy. She and Leo aren't together any more. They haven't been together for a year now. Leo's living in Bristol.

Everything's changing. Mary's met a man called John. He's a teacher and he comes every day to see her. Can people as old as that be in love? I'm lonely. It was good at school; there are people there who like me. I'm beginning to hate the Christmas decorations, they're looking scruffy now. In the living room, sweet wrappers and small pieces of tangerine peel which have missed the wastepaper basket litter the floor; it looks a mess. Mummy doesn't seem to notice, she's so busy with Leo. A Christmas card has fallen off the door, spoiling the pattern I'd made. No one seems to notice it. No one seems to notice me. I've learned a new word at school. Extraneous. That's me this Christmas.

The days are short and grey and evening comes very early. It's so dark. The ground really is as hard as iron. I walked alone round the village, and the tarmac was all bleached white. Mary says it's because of the salting wagons. I watched a blackbird taking the last of the berries from a bare leafless bush; the bird was so desperate for food it was clinging to twigs too small for its weight, stabbing at the berries with its sharp beak. It kept stretching out its wings, and it was watching me with bright suspicious eyes. I'll make a drawing of it later, the red and the black, and the yellow of its beak. Then Leo came out and found me in the garden on my own. He said he'd like to photograph me with the bird. We went for a walk whilst Mummy vacuumed the living room. Then Leo took us out for some lunch. Lunch was nice. Leo's still my friend, but how do I know he won't go away again? He's not here for me anyway. He's here for Mummy.

Newspaper cutting, 1962
SOCIALITE AND PHOTOGRAPHER TAKES TIME OUT. *Miss Millie Breton, well known amongst the international jet set as both a photographer and friend of many a celebrity, has told reporters she intends to step aside from the 'in-crowd' to re-evaluate her life. She told our reporter today that she intends to become part of a simple community living high in the French Alps following a lifestyle not dissimilar to that of a Tibetan monastery. This follows the recent disclosure that Miss Breton has a drink-related problem . . .*

Mary turns the page; she has read enough. Over the past two years, since Leo and Anna moved in together, visits from Millie have been spaced at wider and wider intervals as her life has speeded along on its increasingly frenetic course. Mary has known for some time that her sister drinks too much. Maman's and Papa's habits had taught her enough to recognise the signs, and Mary nurses to herself the hurt that Millie had not told her where she was going; that she had to

362

find out through the pages of a newspaper was like a slap in the face. She had been too busy with her own life to acknowledge Millie's pain. Mary comes out of her reverie. John is talking to her about a parents' meeting at the school tonight; will she be available to make and serve coffee? Yes, of course she will. She would do anything for John. He is a sweet man, but her thoughts throughout the day fly to her troubled youngest sister. Serving coffee for half the evening with a fixed smile and pleasantries drives Mary to bed early with a migraine.

Moon Child Lodge
Near Briançon
May 1963

Dearest Mary,
   My monthly bulletin to you and John is going to be short because I'm packing! You'll be pleased to know I'm leaving today. I know you've had your doubts about the way of life here but you must realise it suited me and was what I needed for a while. However, I'm completely together now. I feel fit and well and it's wonderful. My life and I are in perspective again and, as a consequence, it's become more than a little claustrophobic here

recently. Although I know it has been good for me, I also know when it's time to go.

I want to start work again soon, but not just yet. I have been out and about with my camera; it is not really allowed under the rules of the Simple Life to own such a thing, but Anna arranged a bank account secretly for me and I went out and bought myself this real beauty of a camera. You'll see what I mean about things becoming claustrophobic when I tell you that when the Leaders here found me with the camera they were none too pleased. However, as I was only photographing flora and fauna in Le Queyras Parc nobody could really make too much of a fuss, apart from the fact that the camera is a costly item and as you know, this is supposed to be a place for the Simple Life. Don't misunderstand me, it has been very, very good for me to be here, but I must tell you that crunch time really came when it was discovered that I'd got to Le Queyras by 'borrowing' one of the Leader's motorbikes. I can't blame them . . . they were not pleased at all! So we've had what I believe is called a free and frank discussion and we've agreed it's time to part company, whilst we can still remain amicable.

I've found work in Italy. Don't laugh, I'm

going to be a waitress in a small guesthouse in Lucca. To work hard in a menial capacity will be good for me, and I get free board and lodgings. Also, I'm not ready to come home just yet. I want to be anonymous for a while longer. That's probably untrue — I want to be anonymous from now on and just stick to what I do best . . . taking photographs, but first I need some cash, so I must earn. I can't rely on Anna's kindness all of the time. I promise I will come back to Blighty eventually.

Meanwhile, love to everyone — Leo, Anna, Frankie, John, Toute La Famille! I love you all! Tell Anna and Leo I'll write to them from Lucca.

Millie.

Telegram from Millie to Anna, late June 1964

Coming Home. STOP. *Meet me at Victoria.* STOP.
3.00 P.M. *Thursday.* STOP.

Anna
I'm waiting for Millie. When she comes off the train it's my job to drive her to Mary's. Leo will be at Mary's when we get back.

That's what we agreed. It's hot and my feet are aching; it's a long time since I was up in London. Leo's taken his car and gone for a long walk before he goes to Mary's. He'll be striding down across the fields by now. He did offer to come with me; we talked about it. I said, 'I'm not sure if Millie will be expecting you to be there.'

He said, 'Don't you think I should come? What do you think she'll think if I'm not there?'

'I don't know, Leo, you must decide,' I said and went outside to wash the car. I washed off the dust and threw great pails full of water so hard the water arced and smacked and boomed against the sides and roof of the car. I spilled it deliberately over my legs and feet, loving the squelch of my feet in my canvas shoes. Then I polished so hard my face was as red as the car and I could see my reflection. It relieved something, for a while.

I'm here now on the platform alone amongst strangers. I feel sticky and grubby. I glance at my watch — I've got time to freshen up before the train gets in. I'm far too early. I go to the Ladies, wash my hands, splash water on my overheated face and look at myself in the mirror. Leo lay on our bed this morning watching me getting ready and I watched him and loved the nape of his neck and his smile. My carefully smoothed-out fringe is already curling in the heat; by the time Millie arrives I know I'll have disintegrated completely. I wonder if my skirt's too short, if my lipstick's too pale though I chose carefully. Details. Displacement activities. What do they really matter? They're just something to think about to stop me thinking about the reality of Millie being here. I return to the platform and watch the hands of the clock.

Leo and I have talked, we've done almost nothing else since Millie's telegram arrived. Even so, I know he's not telling me things. The problem is, I think I know what they are. I also know it wasn't me that came between them in the end, it was her ambition and her obsession with the jet set and the fast life. She's moved away from that life and she's better now. I owe Millie a great deal; we have a history. We all do.

The train is here, she's getting off and waving. She's running towards me. She's lost weight, but she looks well. She's very tanned. She looks wonderful and the years between fall away as she says, 'Hi, kid, have you missed me?' and then we're both crying and I hold on to her as though my life depends on it and don't care that people around us are staring. All I seem capable of saying is the one word, 'Millie' over and over again. We're laughing now, standing apart, looking at each other. She's grinning her lovely lopsided grin and we're walking out of the station arm in arm, getting into my Mini, travelling through London and out to the suburbs. We travel the miles to Somerset and don't stop talking once throughout the journey. As I park the car outside Mary's, and Leo comes bounding down the front steps, I hold my breath, just for a moment.

★ ★ ★

Summer is being disconnected, but gently, nothing too sudden. Just a tug to loosen here and there. Along the high hill, subtle warnings whisper. Grasses bristle like bone-white spears rattling beneath the hand of a passing breeze. Cool mornings rise off land heated less. Sky is crisper. Shadows longer. Up on the high ridge, barbed wire staples a field onto Anna's memory as she sits on the stiff parched grass and looks across to where her daughter lies face down beside her. She looks at Francesca's long limbs and tousled hair, her sullen face which is half turned towards her. If only Frankie would smile more she could be quite beautiful. If she smiled more she would look like Greg; her mouth particularly is like Greg's, Anna feels her throat tighten dangerously. Sixteen years ago now, but still when she looks at Francesca, it can hurt so much.

Anna gets to her feet and walks on so she no longer has to look at Frankie. Anna has to tell her about Millie and Leo. She has to tell Frankie that when she comes home for the next holiday, it will be to Mary and John's house. Leo and Millie and Anna are going to live in Paris for a while. Anna puzzles over how much to tell Francesca. Is she old enough to know the truth about their living arrangements? Or should she allow her to go on believing that because Millie is working with Leo again, and because Anna works as Leo's and Millie's PA, it's convenient to share a house and have an office on the premises?

'It's getting near lunchtime. We could go on down to the pub at the foot of the hill?' When Frankie doesn't reply Anna turns slightly to make sure she is following. Somewhere overhead a lark is singing. The combined scents of sheep and dried summer grass fill the air. Frankie, dressed in a black Beatle sweater and black trousers despite the warmth of the day, is walking with her head down and is looking at her feet, not at the view. Irritation rises in Anna. How can

Francesca be so unlovable? Why does she always have to make things so hard? She will not be made to feel guilty again.

Anna decides there is no possible way in which she can tell Frankie the truth or even half of it. She can't possibly tell her how Leo broke down in tears after a meal one night and how her new living arrangements came into being.

She cannot tell her how Leo and Millie and Anna had gathered in the kitchen in Leo and Anna's flat one evening in July, each having brought ingredients to cook and concoct together dishes of rice and saffron, chicken with sharp lemons and many spices and herbs. They had tasted and joked and commented, sipping a bottle of white wine as they worked. Opening a bottle of red wine Leo had shoved back a heavy lock of dark hair, and raised his glass to the two women, saying, 'I love red wine and I want us to try this with the meal. To hell with convention — why shouldn't we drink what we choose with whom we choose.' His dark eyes glinted. They had raised their glasses in smiling response.

'Hear! hear!' Anna blew him a kiss from where she was cutting up strawberries, the juice spilling onto her fingers.

Millie, busy with an arrangement of crisp

370

light salads of new lettuce and sweet baby tomatoes with fresh basil, almonds and grapes, nodded. 'We shall eat and drink as the gods themselves this evening, my dears. What do you think of my creation?' She held up her dish for the others to see and Leo laughed.

'Millie arranges food as if she's going to photograph it,' and Millie had laughed too, showing even white teeth against the red of her lipstick. Leo invented his own salad dressing and Anna had created a coffee mousse of such delicacy it seemed sacrilege at the end of the meal to be eating such perfection.

'Anna! You can't possibly have a second helping!' Leo's voice had sounded a long way away through Millie's fourth glass of wine, and Anna in a soft red velvet dress leaned towards Leo spooning food into his mouth.

For a long time after the meal, they sat together, sprawled on the sofa, not talking at all. Relaxed and warm in each other's company, half drowsing, smoking Gitanes, listening to Mahler's First Symphony from the record player; the twists and turns of the music as amazing and unexpected as life itself, Anna thought as the fumes of Leo's red wine pulsed heavily through her. How full of love she was for her lover and her youngest aunt who was her best friend. An aunt the same age as oneself was something Anna had long ago stopped trying to explain. Nowadays she introduces Millie as a friend and 'a sort of relative'.

During the last few days whilst Millie had been staying with Leo and Anna in their garden flat, Anna had become increasingly aware of a tension between the three of them; of stolen glances passing between Millie and Leo and embarrassed silences when Anna entered a room, and yet Leo had been more attentive to her than usual. She had been puzzled and as alert as a cat to every nuance of expression passing across Leo's fine aquiline features. Sometimes his eyes were veiled and secretive, sometimes she felt he had withdrawn into a space of his own creating, but mostly when he looked at her he could still communicate more with one glance than any amount of words. Anna closed her eyes as the music came to an end, she was aware of Millie leaning heavily against her, already her shape was filling out again. Leo lit another cigarette. Anna heard the click of his cigarette lighter, heard him inhale deeply and the aromatic thread of smoke wisped across the room towards her.

Millie spoke. 'This is so-oo good.' Now the music had come to an end, the record whispered round and round beneath the needle. 'Damn, the automatic's stuck again. Can't you turn that off, Leo?'

Anna heard his throaty laugh as he said, 'Why me? Lazy girl,' and she knew without opening her eyes that Leo had reached out and touched Millie's hair. She felt Millie shift her weight and heard her intake of breath and wondered just when Leo and Millie would start their affair and what she would do about it.

Anna opened her eyes and watched through a haze of drink as Leo swayed gently on his feet fumbling to replace the record in its protective cardboard sleeve. Millie was watching him too. In the candlelit room Leo's shadow leaped and jumped across the ceiling. He spoke, but his voice was muffled and his words made no sense, then as he turned round from his task both women saw he was crying.

'Oh my God! Leo! What is it?' Anna was on her feet, though the room span, and walking across carpet felt like wading through mud. She wove her way to him and held him close. His arms went round her, holding very tight. She could feel him breathing. His face was warm against hers.

'It's you,' he had sobbed. 'You and Millie. I don't know what to do. I can't go on like this, it's killing me.'

Millie had put down her wine glass and was watching Leo carefully. 'What do you mean, Leo?' She stood up and came to where the other two stood and embraced them both, her perfume thick on the air.

'I mean I'm in love with you. Both of you. I love you both. You mean everything to me, but if I have to choose between you I think I might go mad. It's no good — I shall have to leave.'

Anna stepped back and away, leaving Millie and Leo with their arms around each other. Anna stood quite still looking at them. They looked back at her, their eyes enormous and shadowy in the half-light. The candles swam and flickered in their own pools of light. Two cats skirmished briefly out in the garden, whilst from the kitchen the insistent light thud of a leaking tap marked slow seconds. Anna felt her stomach tighten; she was going to lose Leo. She had known all along it would come to this. She forced herself to speak, the words carefully thought through, but out into the open swiftly before she lost her courage. 'Are you sure you mean that, Leo? Because if you don't and it's Millie you really want, I will leave. I won't make a fuss. I've always known you were only borrowed.'

Leo groaned and let go of Millie.

'Borrowed! Stop it, Anna — didn't you listen? I meant what I said. I *can't* choose! I've fought this and it's driving me insane.' He wiped the back of his hand across his eyes.

Millie's voice was high. 'Perhaps you don't have to choose?' As soon as she had spoken she clapped a hand over her own mouth and giggled. Then Millie's widened eyes met Anna's and a swift, barely perceptible nod of recognition passed between them. Even though a frisson of fear tingled in Anna's spine she said, 'Perhaps Millie's right.' She knew she was trembling; she knew the others would see she was, but she went on, 'It could work.'

Millie nodded breathlessly. 'Don't look like that, Leo. It could work.'

'But how? What are you saying?' Leo seemed bewildered as he looked from one to the other, but he half laughed as Anna began to pace the room. She knew she was drunk but she knew what she was saying.

She turned at the end of the room, her arms raised and said, 'Oh Leo! We're not just talking sex. We're talking loving and living together. Tell him, Millie, because that *is* what we're saying, isn't it?' She began to sway back towards him, half dancing and laughing.

'We could make it work.' Millie caught hold of her and whirled her round, repeating

375

her words; 'We could make it work. We could!' They stopped and held onto each other, laughing and giddy with more than their dance.

'As for the sex . . . Anna and I will take it in turns. Poor Leo, you'll be exhausted!' Millie burst into peals of laughter but stopped abruptly when she saw Leo wasn't laughing, 'I mean it, Leo. We could really make this work. I'm not winding you up and I don't think Anna is either.'

Anna shook her head and stood quiet and solemn in front of Leo. 'It's what we all want, isn't it?'

Leo nodded slowly. 'No jealousy?'

'No jealousy. No greed. Agreed?' Millie's face was alight with almost childlike glee as she poured them each more wine and raised her glass.

'Agreed.'

'Agreed. Could we really make it work? What about the neighbours?' Leo was smiling, and as fear and excitement mingled in almost equal measure, Anna raised her own glass high and drank fast. 'To hell with the neighbours. They can't join in!'

'Anna!' Millie collapsed giggling onto the sofa, pulling Anna down after her.

Leo sat down heavily between them. Silenced by the magnitude of their own thoughts the three sat unspeaking for several minutes. Leo cleared his throat; his speech was slurred as he said, 'We're all drunk tonight. What if you've changed your minds by the morning?'

Anna rested her head sleepily on his shoulder. 'What if you have?'

'Are we going to bed now?' This from Millie.

'Separately?'

Millie was beginning to laugh again — it was infectious. 'What do you think, Anna?'

'No. Not separately, and only to sleep. No choosing tonight. Oh my God — that's going to be weird!'

'Weird and wonderful!'

They had all spent that first night together. There had been no more talk of sex, there had been no talk at all, but they had lain in each others' arms in the calm of each others' presence, until one by one they had drifted into sleep.

Waking late the following day, all three had felt only the completeness of their situation. As water finds its own level, so they had sealed their shared fate. Practicalities could wait, for now.

★ ★ ★

Anna reached the pub before Francesca and waited for her. As Francesca drew level Anna told her to wait whilst she found out if lunch was possible, and went inside. Francesca stood chewing her fingernails, staring around at the hills and the dusty-looking trees. A few cars were parked in the pub car park and the sound of voices came from somewhere behind the building. When Anna returned she was smiling. 'That's fixed. I've ordered sandwiches and cider for us both. Apparently there are picnic tables out at the back. We can sit outside.'

'Fab, whatever.' Frankie followed her mother round the side of the long low building. A boy sitting drinking with his parents at one of the picnic tables glanced at her, then away and back again. Frankie's mouth twitched and she straightened her shoulders.

Anna sat on one of the hard wooden benches, patting a place beside her and Frankie settled unwillingly next to her.

'You're not enjoying this holiday, are you?' Anna tried to make her voice neutral, non-accusatory.

'It's okay.' Francesca shrugged, looking again at the boy, but he seemed to have lost interest and was looking away. Her hand went self-consciously to the spot she had discovered on her chin that morning.

The sandwiches were brought by a pretty waitress wearing a short skirt, and the boy's attention slid immediately to her shapely bronzed legs. Anna watched as Frankie's colour came up and, as her daughter hid behind her long dark hair, Anna's heart went out to her. 'We could go home this evening, if you like. There's only one day left of the holiday anyway. Perhaps it was a mistake.'

She was rewarded by one of Frankie's rare smiles. 'It's okay, Mum, I know you're doing your best. You thought I'd like it here and I do. I mean, it's not grotty or anything. It's just . . . '

'I know, it's my sort of holiday, not yours. We should have gone somewhere with more young people. I've been selfish and I'm afraid I'm going to be even more selfish, Francesca.'

'I know. Millie's moving in with you and Leo. I don't want to know the details. You are thirty-four, Mum, fully adult and all that. What you do is up to you.'

'How did you know?' It takes Anna a moment to recover. She looks at her sixteen-year-old daughter and wonders just who is in charge of whom. Incredulously she repeats the question. 'Frankie? How on earth did you know?'

'It's bloody obvious. The three of you have

been going round with faces like Cheshire cats.' Francesca swigs at her cider and sits back, stretching her legs out in front of her, adding, 'Leo doesn't look straight at me any more.'

'He is human, Frankie. Perhaps he feels embarrassed.'

Francesca ignores Anna and says. 'When I come home next holiday, can I stay with Mary and John? Do you think they would let me?'

Anna nods. She thinks she may not be able to stop nodding; she feels like one of those ghastly model dogs on the back shelf of a car. 'Yes. I'm sure they would, if that's really what you want. Won't you miss Leo?'

'I'll still come and see him. I'll come and see all of you, but it's what I've wanted for a while.'

Anna finishes her drink before she says, 'That's very mature of you, Frankie.'

'Not really.' Frankie frowns, swinging her dark hair forward again.

'You don't really like me very much do you, Frankie?'

Frankie mutters from inside the tent of her hair, 'I do, as a matter of fact, Mum. It's just . . . it's just . . . not always easy. And I don't know why.'

I do but I can't tell you. Anna reaches out a tentative hand. Will Frankie allow herself to be hugged? She will. This time.

21

Francesca

So I'm here. Eighteen years old. A big grown-up student person in my first year at college, in my first term, in my first week — and I've been told I have to write an essay entitled *Success and Failure*. Huh! I could write a bloody book. Trouble is, it wouldn't be fairly divided — but Life isn't, is it?

I'm different from the others here. I try to pretend I'm not, but I know I am. It's two years since Mum started to live with her lover and her aunt. How can I tell anybody about that? Everyone else I've met appears to have normal homes, either two parents or one because of divorce, or death. I could cope with that, I've coped with that one for years. My mum is only normal in as much as she's made sure I've got clothes to wear and a trunk full of the right books. I know I shouldn't complain, she was more than generous with her time and her money before I came here, but I just wish she'd be less generous in the direction of Leo and Millie. They are all three seriously odd. I've even thought I might pretend my mother is dead

381

and tell people if she comes to visit that she's someone else, a family friend or something. But her weird living arrangements I cannot and will not explain. They don't seem to need me any more — not even Leo. It's as if they've all got their full quota of loving so they don't really need me. I'm glad I went to stay with Mary and John. Perhaps I will tell people my mother died.

I'm sharing a room with another girl, Jenny. She seems okay, a bit timid, but she's got an okay sort of a smile and she's like me . . . still a virgin! We discussed that aspect of our lives the first night we were here. Mum's told me coyly to 'be good' and she either looks at me like an anxious puppy when she says it or she goes all strained and peculiar as if there's something stuck in her throat.

I sometimes wonder about Mum. I look at the photos of her wedding to Charles, my dad, and it's so obvious she was expecting and the date of the wedding and my birth-date and everything. She must think I'm really, really stupid not to realise and yet she's got this crazy double standard thing; it was okay for her to do it, but not me. It's okay for her to live the way she does, just because she's a so-called grown-up. She just says darkly things like although Charles let her down in the end (apparently he ran off with someone and to be truthful I can't even really remember him), he was very good to her at first.

Mum won't ever talk to me openly about sex and stuff; she hints at things and talks a lot of rot about romance. Is what she's having with Leo and Millie romance? Or is it sex? And other people talk about 'being careful', I haven't really got much of a clue what they're on about. Jenny says if she ever 'does it' she'll go on the pill, but a friend of hers tried and got this lecture from her family doctor about how relationships should be kept strictly within marriage and he wasn't prepared to let her have the means to ruin herself. So she went to a family planning clinic and had to lie about being engaged just so they wouldn't go all high and mighty and moral on her. Jenny says it was so embarrassing and this friend of hers is taking the pill now, but every time she goes for a check-up she gets asked when the wedding's going to be and she has to lie.

Maybe I should go on the pill, just in case, but I haven't even got a boyfriend. I don't even know what a man looks like without clothes on, except for the statues in Florence that Aunt Mary took me to see that time.

The Beatles have brought out a new record, it was playing in the Union when Jenny and I went down for a drink earlier this evening. There's a nice-looking boy working behind the bar — he's got thick red hair and a friendly smile. He smiled at me. Someone said he's doing pottery and he plays lead guitar in the college group. He's a third year.

★   ★   ★

Who would have thought it? I've got through my first year here and it wasn't so bad. Mum doesn't know I've practically been living with Guy for most of the year, she just thinks he's a nice quiet boy about to make his mark on the world as a potter down in Cornwall. He's said he'll write, he's said he'll phone but I don't think he will. It was good while it lasted but I'm a realist and I don't want to be tied down.

Next year I'm going to play the field more. Still not on the pill, though Jenny is — and I used to think she was timid! It's a different bloke almost every week! I did go to the clinic but they were so snooty and made me feel so much like a criminal for having ordinary urges that I gave up the idea. Guy and I used condoms, don't like them much but he insisted — said he didn't want to be landed with a child at his age. Well, actually he didn't ever say that — it was just kind of taken for granted. Come to think of it, we never really discussed sex much at all. Politics yes, art yes, sex no.

★ ★ ★

So it's my final year, so many lovers, so many one-nighters, so many stupid chances taken and finally it's happened; twenty-one years old, no means of support and one baby on the way. Please God, let it be one and not twins. I found out for definite this morning. Shall probably just get the exams done and then it'll be off to the hospital; as long as I don't actually go into labour in the middle of the viva I shall be okay. Could give a whole new meaning to the word viva!

No good going in search of the father, it was a one-off, one-night stand, at Jen's twenty-first party, and we both knew it. My fault for not being on that jolly little pill, his for not being careful, but we were — very careful that no one heard us on that pile of coats in the back bedroom! Gives 'born of ignorance' a whole new meaning too, don't it? It wasn't even all that good. Guy was the best sex I've ever had. I know now that I loved him, really loved him but he's history — married and settled with a wifey in a house and working as an estate agent — all the things he said he'd never be.

Well, it's a summer of thick jumpers for me. Good job the poncho's in fashion this year. With a bit of luck I'll be able to keep the whole thing secret for as long as possible. Who am I kidding? News travels round this place as if it's got a life of its own. A life of its own — bloody hell! That's what I've got inside me. It's real, it's a child. I hope I'll do the right thing by it. I hope I can love it. Oh, how the tongues will wag. Oh, how the chaps will say, 'Well, I told you she was a good lay,' and the girls will turn away and pour bitchy scorn on me behind my ever increasing stomach and back. Oh shit! Oh shit! Oh bugger! Well done, Francesca.

★ ★ ★

Thank God I've got Aunt Mary and dear sweet Uncle John as a bolt hole to run to. They moved here to Bath when John retired. It's so cosy and so refined! Not really me, but I am glad they're here. Bath suits them well. I went to John's leaving celebrations, a service in the Cathedral — not just for him, of course, but he got a jolly good mention, drinks and strawberries on the lawns with Mary there as the perfect, perfect schoolmaster's wife, so gracious and genteel.

It's hard to believe the stories Mary tells

me about her youth, how wild she was, how she loved a man who was married to another woman. Even after all this time, and for all she's so happy with John, there's such a wistful look on her face when she talks about her 'one true love' that I know it was for real. Apparently he was a painter like me. He painted her once before he went away to the war. Mary says it was probably the realest thing she ever felt, and the look on her face makes me think that's what I want for me. I'm not going to settle for second best — not ever — even if it takes all my life to find it.

Once this baby's born and I've got myself sorted out then I'll be like Mary. She said she married John in the end because she knew she couldn't go on into old age totally alone. I think there's more to it than that. I think she does love him in her own way and they're the best of friends, but I shan't be like that; it's going to be all or nothing for me. I can see what Aunt Mary meant but I couldn't help feeling she's sold out in the end. Anyway whatever, she's made me very welcome.

The college were surprisingly good about the baby. Eventually. Had a bit of a dressing down from the principal for 'immorality'. Huh! She's a fine one to talk. We all know she's been knocking the bursar off for months. Even more immoral was her suggestion that I should have a termination. She looked at me in that fake kindly way she has and said, 'Well, of course, Francesca, there is absolutely no reason to go ahead with this pregnancy. It could ruin your life, after all, my dear.' And she coughed in what might once have been described as a delicate fashion. 'And termination *is* perfectly legal.'

I saw red. It's a wonder I didn't hit the bloody woman. I want this baby. I'm going to be a good mother. They've said I can come back for my finals after the baby's born. I shall have to. I've got to have some way of supporting myself.

Mum's been amazing. Not a mention of abortion. Not a mention of marriage. Not a single thing about our family name being brought into disrepute, just a sort of funny little look on her face when she said, 'It would appear to be a family trait.' I still haven't plucked up the courage to tell her I couldn't marry the father anyway because I'd have a job to find him and I didn't even know his name. At least she really *knew* Charles before she conceived little old me. Leo's been kind but somehow distant. I really miss him so much sometimes. He may not have been my real dad but he was such a friend when I was a little girl.

Holly House, Clifton
April, 1969

Dearest Millie and Leo,

Only another week to go and I shall be coming out to join you. Your postcards have been read with envy! I can't wait to be near La Roche again, but I know I was right to stay on here. Yes, yes — I can hear you both nagging — I know holidays are good for the soul but it's been so productive being here. I was approached yesterday by Cheryl Greenslade, you know she runs 'Slade House Fashions'. They're putting on some sort of a publicity function and she liked what I did for your publicity bash at Christmas so much she's asked me if I can do something for her. So, I hope you don't think I'm being disloyal but it would be nice to expand a little, stretch my wings etc etc. I suggested I might try and organise some local press coverage for her as well and she seemed very pleased.

Lots to tell you about various proposals that are coming in for you both. I've managed to hold everyone off, telling them you're on a much-needed regenerative break, but I think we should all be back here by the middle of May if possible, probably sooner. I'd certainly like to be around for Frankie when the baby's born. She and I have been getting on so well recently, it's lovely after all the ups and downs over the years. She came for Easter Sunday and it was a wonderful day. She's looking well and she's coping well. Maturing at last!! We went for a walk and a picnic and she came back here for a meal and stayed overnight. We seem to be on the point of some kind of a breakthrough, I really feel that bridges are being built at last. It's such a good feeling.

I've just realised I'll probably arrive before this does, but I'll post it anyway.

Love and masses of it to you both. Can't wait to be with you again.

Anna.

Extract from a letter posted to Mary from Wimborne — 1972

Thanks for the photo of Megan. She's growing up fast, isn't she? I arrived here on Tuesday, dossed down at a mate's for the night then went in search of a job the next morning. Luck would appear to be on my side! I was passing a café, sniffing the coffee smells and the hot bread smells and I saw a notice *Waitress required*. That's me, I thought so in I goes and I've got the job. It'll do me for now. I can always find something a bit better paid soon, then I can come and see Meg and you and John, and I promise I'll bring some money with me this time. How's Mum? I heard she was still living with Millie and Leo up in Clifton. I might thumb it over there one weekend too.

She wrote last week, actually it was the week before, but I'd been sleeping rough so it took me a while to get to the post office and see if any mail had been left for me. Went to a great party the other night. It was a real blast — met a really great guy. He's Irish — we talked all night. He certainly has the gift of the blarney . . .

Francesca decides to edit out the fact that this 'great guy' attempted to rape her in the early hours of the morning and stole her purse along with her dignity as more than one of his friends was present at the time. She also manages to edit out of her mind any thought that Megan might actually want her around or that Mary and John might be growing too old to easily and successfully look after a small but lively three year old.

Francesca blames her mother for being selfish and carrying on with her own life with Millie and Leo, instead of doing the decent grandmotherly thing and offering to look after Megan in any way other than financial. More often than not nowadays Anna, Millie and Leo are abroad. Sometimes together, sometimes apart. Her mother seems to manage to combine her own career and her work with Leo and Millie with consummate ease. Francesca remains selectively unaware of the effort and the planning involved, and sees only the apparent glamour as the three work and live with and around each other independently and interdependently depending on circumstances. She views them as wealthy sybarites and refuses to admit any thought that they have achieved their wealth through sheer hard work and determination. Francesca certainly envies her mother's ability to juggle her combined careers as righthand woman to the two photographers and a function organiser in her own right. Ridiculous that in her forties, Anna should be having so much better a time than Francesca at twenty-two. Francesca feels jealousy may eat her up one day.

Francesca also successfully obliterates the thought that, were it not for Mary and John's tender care and Anna's financial input, Megan would be being dragged around the country in Francesca's wake, sleeping in cars, on park benches or any unsuspecting newfound friend's floor. She folds the letter into an envelope and posts it. She has decided she likes Wimborne; she likes its broad squat-towered Minster and she feels at home in its pretty unassuming streets.

On an impulse, after posting her letter Francesca slips from the clear cold April air into the Minster and discovers to her delight that a rehearsal for a concert seems to be in progress. The building is filled with the high clear notes of a trumpet, followed by the steadier deep tones of the organ, and together the two instruments begin to weave a bright banner of sound. It's a long time since Francesca has heard such pure sounds.

A tall, heavily built young man stands in front of the altar. He has strong long fingers which press the trumpet's shining valves with an easy fluency. His eyes are a deep intense blue and his exuberant deep red hair springs out around his head in a nimbus that reminds Francesca so unexpectedly and so sharply of Megan's clouded little head that a sharp pain runs somewhere indefinable beneath her breast-bone. Megan's small earnest face wavers and dances in her mind. Then the trumpet sounds again, bouncing and shimmering along the air; it is the sound of happiness. Megan's face fades and, when the young man stops playing, Francesca stands up and applauds.

That night she is ensconced in his flat. The following morning she starts work in the café and a year later she has an exhibition of paintings which sell moderately well, but not once in the three years that she stays with the trumpeter does she ever mention Megan. She sees her from time to time, but the trumpeter never comes with her to Mary's house. Eventually, when Francesca is expecting the trumpeter's child, she leaves him and Wimborne for ever and has a termination under an assumed name at an anonymous hospital somewhere in Kent.

22

Rules are, don't meet anyone's eye. A party game in a room full of strangers. Pink card holders to the left, green to the right. Come in. Sit down. You don't mind a student being present? Rules are, you don't say 'I do.' You are a body about to be discussed. You are a woman of forty-two. The sun lights red flowers in a plain glass vase. You can see green stalks. You can see chimneys and redbrick buildings. There is sky. The view from here doesn't really matter. The white alabaster vase, the one he said was like your breasts, waits at home.

Anna lies resignedly on the examination couch. She detaches her mind from her body as the specialist, a kindly distinguished-looking man in a white coat detaches himself from the fact of Anna as a person and turns her into a thing to be examined, a machine whose monthly mechanism is ceasing to function. A machine to be discussed, not with Anna, but with the thin male student, whose extreme nervousness is rapidly turning the room into an oversized and unsavoury armpit. Anna looks at the ceiling and breathes slowly as the doctor's plastic-gloved hand explores. Anna counts and breathes and recites nursery rhymes inside her head. She is not here.

'Ah — aha!' The doctor's murmur brings her abruptly back into herself but he isn't speaking to her, he is speaking to the student. 'Interesting, very interesting. Here, would you like to have a go?' Anna knows she should say something, she knows she should lodge an objection. 'Have a go.' Is she some fairground amusement? 'Have a go!'

The student approaches her nervously and begins his examination. He will not meet her eye; he is sweating profusely and causing her huge discomfort. Anna tries to concentrate on anything but the pain and the awkward twisting and bumping, but the nursery rhymes have deserted her and she is rooted all too firmly within her body. She hears her voice strong and in command, say, 'Right, that's enough. Leave me alone.'

Taken by surprise the student backs away and Anna sits up rearranging her clothing, demanding that the student and the specialist and the young nurse all leave her alone. The student retreats into the corner of the small white room, his face redder than ever beneath its veil of acne. The specialist attempts to remonstrate. 'Miss Williams, you must let us examine you. There may be some underlying problem of which we're unaware.'

Anna's eyes blaze. 'Do you know something? I don't care if the internal workings of my body *have* gone wrong. They are mine and mine alone. Not something for people to 'have a go' with. I'll deal with any problems myself, thank you very much and now — if you don't mind — you and your little sidekick can get out and let me get dressed.'

No one in the room meets anyone else's eye. The specialist and his apprentice shuffle through the door. The nurse hands Anna a sanitary towel and, with her head down, says something about no one being afforded any dignity. Anna knows she should speak, but anger prevents her. She dresses hurriedly and leaves the room, but to reach the corridor she has to pass through the ante-room where the specialist and his student are in subdued conference. They're waiting for her.

'Miss Williams, please do accept my apologies. I think you must understand that we would like you in for observation. Do sit down — we need to discuss this.'

Anna's head comes up. 'I'm not coming near this place again!'

'Miss Williams, I don't think you can afford to say that. You are probably in need of an operation. We want you to come in for some tests.'

'Listen to me, sunshine.' Anna rounds on him. 'That wasn't a clinical examination, that was a mauling. I've got a witness!' She turns to the nurse who, with a scarlet face, is busy examining her shoes. 'I'm telling you, if that idiot comes anywhere near me again,' she points a furious, shaking finger at the student, 'if he comes anywhere near me, I will sue the lot of you.'

The tension in the room grows. The specialist clears his throat. 'Miss Williams, the words you used,' he chooses his own words with great care, 'are, shall we say, rather 'full blown'. I do admit we were perhaps,' he searches for the correct phrase, 'a little insensitive to your feelings, and I apologise. It shan't happen again. Perhaps I can telephone you in a few days and we can talk further. Or, if you wish, I can make arrangements for you to transfer to another hospital?'

The telephone on the consultant's desk rings, and when he answers it Anna seizes the opportunity to slip swiftly from the room. 'One moment, Miss Williams!' He clasps the receiver to his chest, but Anna has gone.

Leaving the hospital in a daze of emotions, walking rapidly, lost in thought, she is soon several streets away from the hospital, and gradually becomes aware that there are fewer people about. She stops walking and looks around; she has wandered into a back street of narrow houses with mean front gardens. The car park must be miles away.

Wearily she attempts to retrace her steps, becoming more and more entangled in the confusing maze of side streets. Now that anger and humiliation have subsided she feels hollow and weak and, passing a sweetshop, goes in to buy a chocolate bar. It is as she is crossing the road outside the shop, concentrating on unwrapping the bar, that a car turns the corner of the street very fast. All Anna knows is that pain suddenly splinters her mind before the world spins and turns black.

★   ★   ★

Anna is on her back, looking up at a high ceiling. It's uncomfortable to move her head, but when she shifts her gaze a fraction she sees pale blue curtains surrounding her. She decides she is on a hospital bed. The bed is a white ice mountain; beyond the curtains she can see through a gap to where other ice mountains rise. Someone coughs. Silence. Anna turns her head with difficulty; her whole body feels stiff and sore and her

399

stomach feels as though it has been kicked hard by a horse. A large plump nurse puts her head round the curtain and comes in when she sees Anna is awake.

'Miss Williams. Anna. You all right now?'

'I don't know.' Anna turns her head away and closes her eyes. But the nurse will not go away, she is arranging pillows, smoothing sheets.

'You gave us all a fright, Anna, but you'll be okay now.'

Anna opens her eyes again. The lids each feel as though they weigh several tons. She looks at the nurse, then down at her right arm and is astonished when she sees that it is linked by a fine tube to a drip at the side of the bed. Her left arm she observes without interest is encased in plaster, as is her left leg. Anna lies on her back and looks at the weights and pulleys suspending her leg from the ceiling; it doesn't seem to have anything to do with her. She murmurs weakly, 'What happened to me?' and wants to giggle at the banality of her question. The nurse reaches for a tissue and wipes Anna's tears away.

'Come on now, Anna, don't cry. It won't do you any good. We don't want you raising your temperature now, do we?'

'But what *did* happen? Have I broken some

bones? Why am I here? How do you know who I am?'

The nurse puts her head on one side and makes motherly tutting noises. 'You'll be tiring yourself out, with so many questions. We know who you are because we looked in your bag. It's all right — it's on the side table. You're here because you had an accident. A car knocked you down.'

'I remember now.' Anna thinks of the chocolate bar and the pain. 'What's happened? I mean, how badly am I injured? There's no pain — there was but it's gone away.'

The nurse looks at her sympathetically. 'There's no pain because we've given you some pretty hefty pain relief. You'll be on it for a day or two. I think I ought to get the doctor now. He can talk to you.'

'What about?' but the nurse has already backed out of the cubicle made by the curtains pulled around Anna's bed.

A doctor comes in. With relief Anna sees he is not the specialist of that morning. He folds his arms and looks down at Anna. 'How are you feeling, Miss Williams?'

'I am very tired and my stomach feels terrible. What happened?'

'I'm afraid you were haemorrhaging badly and we had to operate to prevent further

401

bleeding. Unfortunately we had no choice.'

'Operate? Operate on what? Why — what happened to me?'

'You were hit by a car not far from the hospital. You've got some broken ribs, and your left leg and hand have broken bones too. There is something else — it was an emergency, Miss Williams, there was nothing we could do. I'm afraid you've lost the baby. I am truly sorry. I'll get a nurse to sit with you a while. I'll see you when I do my rounds this evening.'

Like a conjuring trick the doctor has vanished through the pale blue curtains, leaving Anna alone. She lies quite still, enjoying the peace of the curtained cubicle, enjoying the clean white light, accepting the faintly antiseptic smell. Lulled into a feeling of security, doped with morphine, the knowledge she is being looked after is foremost in her mind.

She turns slightly in her bed and her abdomen pulls tightly. *'I'm afraid you've lost the baby.'* The kind doctor's words sound through her head and, very slowly, the meaning sinks in. He had said the word Baby. He had said she had lost a baby. She wasn't expecting a baby, she had had an examination that morning, probably an early menopause. Not a baby. Not a pregnancy. Not at her age.

She's forty-two, for God's sake, why would she have a baby now? She shuts out the specialist of the morning. There was something wrong. That was why she had been to see the man. She was reaching an early menopause. How could she have been pregnant? It can't be true — there's been a mistake.

A different nurse comes into the cubicle. She is very young, her hair tied back from her soft smooth face. She smiles at Anna and hoping her lack of experience is not on display she asks, 'How are you feeling? Shall I make you a bit more comfortable?'

Anna catches hold of the nurse's sleeve as she bends to adjust Anna's pillow.

'The doctor — just now. Is he . . . is he competent?'

The nurse straightens up and looks questioningly at Anna. 'Competent? Well yes, of course he is!'

'He said I was pregnant. He said I've lost a baby.'

The nurse is out of her depth and uncomfortable. 'I don't understand.'

'I can't have been pregnant. There must be some mistake.'

In the absence of any other authority the nurse reaches for Anna's notes and scans them, and her eyes light up. She says

403

confidently, 'It's quite definite you were pregnant, Miss Williams — it says so here. I could get the doctor back again for you if you like.' As Anna begins to weep, the nurse looks as if she would very much like to fetch the doctor back, but instead pats ineffectually at Anna's face with a tissue until Anna snaps, 'For God's sake leave me alone!'

'I'm not allowed to.'

'Get out! Just get out! I don't want anyone in here. Just go away!' Anna's voice is rising as the ward sister arrives at her bedside. The sister, a large and capable-looking woman takes in the scene rapidly. 'It's all right, Nurse Jones, you ring down to Doctor — ask him if we can administer Miss Williams a sedative. Miss Williams, please don't distress yourself, you're upsetting other patients.'

'Bugger the other patients,' Anna groans as the Sister's arms come round her, but she allows herself to be coaxed into quietness. Her head is beating its own tattoo and she feels sick and exhausted. A doctor arrives, administers a sedative, says, 'You'll sleep soon, Miss Williams,' and slides from view.

'You didn't know about the baby did you, sweetheart?' The Sister is still with her and Anna shakes her head. She is crying again. She doesn't seem able to stop crying.

'You poor girl. I am so sorry.'

'Thank you,' Anna says, bleakly because there seems little else to say.

'Try and sleep now, the sedative should help you.' The Sister draws Anna's curtains back slightly. 'I'll just be down the ward — if you need anything, ring your bell.' She indicates a white push button on Anna's bedside table before she slips softly away.

Anna lies alone staring at the ceiling. She thinks about the recent weeks and of herself and Leo one weekend alone in a London hotel. It had been like the early days of their affair; they had been mad for each other, unable to leave each other alone. Millie had been in Greece. It had been exciting. It had been fun. They had spent almost all weekend in bed and after that, soon after that, she had started to feel unwell. That she might be pregnant had not even entered her mind. Leo would have been a father. They would have loved the child. She hadn't known. There had been a life and now there wasn't one. Her face crumples and sobs shake her aching body as she lies alone in the soft semi-darkness.

When Anna wakes again, it is almost dark. Her curtains have been partly drawn and from further down the ward lamps glow above the other patients' beds. Against her curtains old picture books begin to play the

405

games she would not let them as a child; the man with octopus eyes smiles then hatches himself repeatedly. If he stood, his heads would reach the sky, he's thin and torn as paper. Someone shouts, it is Anna though she does not know it. The octopus man flakes apart and Madam Stealth in a cobweb gown creeps in. Her hooked-beaked ravens judder and perch, knowing-eyed on a hideous pot of things to burn — perhaps it's Anna, perhaps her baby, or Greg, or Cathryn. The night is a tiptoe spider.

There should be hands to hold. There are hands to hold. Someone is saying Anna's name — it's a nurse — she is smoothing Anna's tumbled hair, damping a flannel, putting it to her flushed face. Someone else is taking her temperature; she is being hurried through corridors on her bed, she is flying through darkness. Lights flash and a knight on a horse dances round a shining catherine wheel. More lights. From somewhere far above herself Anna looks down and sees she is on a bed; nurses and doctors are busy with pieces of technical-looking equipment. In a corner of the room Leo and Millie are huddled together. She focuses on them; she can hear what they're saying. They're talking about Francesca, they're talking about Francesca and Megan. She knows from their scared faces and low hushed voices that there is something terribly wrong. They are saying how dreadful it will be for Francesca and Megan and how they will break the news to Francesca about the baby.

Millie is crying. She is crying as if her heart will break. Anna wants to tell them they mustn't worry about anything — everything's going to be fine. She must help them not to be sad. A rushing sound begins in her ears; there is pressure on her body, something is squeezing the life out of her, pressing and pressing. She won't let it happen. She's not going to die, she mustn't leave them like this. As swiftly as it began the rushing stops and she plummets and wheels down through enormous dark spaces lit by explosions of light. An unknown voice says, 'She's back — well done, nurse. We've got her back.' Footsteps come and go, and Millie and Leo are there, one on either side of her, talking in low frightened whispers.

'Anna?' Millie's face is all compassion and Leo takes Anna's hand. 'Anna, darling. You're all right. It will be all right now. We're here. We're here for you, darling.'

23

Millie is visiting Mary and John. It's Christmas Eve. The house is quiet and peaceful, the mingled scents of the Christmas tree's resin, mince pies and John's after-dinner cigar fill the room. Megan, a three-year-old redhaired angel in Viyella pyjamas, has at last been persuaded to bed. John stubs out his cigar and glancing at his watch stands up. 'I hadn't realised the time. I'd better set off — Francesca's train will be arriving and there'll be no one to meet her. See you later, my dears.'

Mary smiles up at him as he bends to peck her on the cheek and Millie waves a languid hand. She is half lying, half sitting stretched luxuriously on the sofa, drinking the sherry put out for Santa and eating his mince pie. Over dinner she has drunk more than half a bottle of wine but her speech is clear. 'You take care! The roads are slippy and so is our great-niece!'

'Don't be horrid about Frankie,' Mary chastises her sister though the upturned corners of her mouth and eyes belie her words, and John turns in the doorway to wink at Millie. Mary follows John out into the hall, helping him into his dark coat and wrapping his thick yellow scarf closer round his neck.

'You really love to look after him, don't you?' Millie says when Mary returns.

'What if I do? It's in my nature.'

'Don't be hurt. I didn't mean it in a critical way. It was more of an observation than anything.' Millie swings her plump legs to the floor and stands up. Walking to the Christmas tree she reaches up, fiddling with the angel on the top, straightening baubles and bright crackers.

'You're very restless — what's the matter, Millie? Are you missing Leo and Anna?'

Millie shrugs. 'I'm not sure. I thought it would be a good idea to come here for Christmas. They seem to need some time on their own.'

'But you've always spent your Christmases together. Since . . . '

'Yes, we have. Since . . . ' Millie swings round and grins. 'It's not like you to be prudish. You've never really got a grip on the three of us being together, have you, darling?'

Mary smiles. 'Do I need to? You love each other. Isn't that what counts? And I think you've been together long enough to prove you're all really committed to each other.'

'What? We're beyond the seven-year itch?'

'Something like that.' Mary sits forward and looks up at Millie.

'Oh dear! You're wearing your intense look,' her younger sister says. 'What's the matter? What are you thinking?'

'Just that it's been a fairly ghastly few months for you, hasn't it, since Anna lost the baby.'

'Yes, 1972 is a year I'm sure we'd all like to forget. It's been ghastly for us all. Not least for Anna. May I have another drink?'

'Do you think you should?'

'I don't have a problem any more, you know, Mary. That was all a long time ago.' Millie sits on the floor by the fire, her legs curled beneath her, her long blonde hair loose on her shoulders, blow-dried into fashionable submission but already beginning to curl rebelliously round her face. The firelight softens the lines of strain and she looks briefly years younger than her age.

'Do you want to talk?' Mary fetches more wine and opens the bottle, pouring two glasses, holding one out to Millie who takes it gratefully and drinks it too fast. Mary sits and waits. Millie thinks she is like a flower waiting for the rain to fall and the sun to shine. There is no vigilance in her waiting, no patience or impatience. Mary is the calmest person she has ever known. It will be another hour before John returns with Frankie and then the house will lose its peace, becoming a maelstrom at the centre of which will be Frankie and Frankie's needs.

Millie says, 'The problem is quite straightforward. I'm jealous. Don't look at me like that, Mary, it's the truth as I see it. You see, the plan was always that there would be no children. When Leo and I were first together, back in the fifties, we talked about it then. We didn't want to have children. I've never wanted them; Leo seemed more than happy with that.'

'But he liked Francesca?'

'Yes. He liked Francesca when she was small, before she became difficult, but he always said he was glad not to have the responsibility for her. And he's right — he wouldn't have the patience. Do you remember when he and Anna — that first time — the time we were staying with you and I found out that Leo and Anna had made love, I was so angry! When Leo and I got back to London I asked him then; was it because of Frankie? Was it that he fancied himself as a family man? And he said no, it was just Anna that he wanted.' Millie smiles and watches the Christmas-tree lights reflecting in her wine. She pauses before she adds, 'You know Leo! Ever outspoken! He went on to say if

411

Francesca had not been Greg's child he might even have wanted Anna more than me.'

'No!'

'Oh yes! He couldn't hack it in those days, though. It really threw him badly, finding out about Greg and Anna.'

'And you stayed with him in spite of what he'd said to you.'

'Yes I did, because I didn't entirely believe it, but things weren't the same — how could they be? The trouble was, I loved him. I've always loved him but, as I said, things just weren't the same. We had row after row. Until it finished us.'

'But you came back.'

Millie bites the end of her fingers. 'I came back. Leo accepted Frankie's paternity. Anna and I love Leo. Leo loves us. So the merry-go-round goes on.' She puts down her glass and Mary sees how tired Millie is as she adds, 'Times change, we grow older and hopefully wiser except apparently for one thing. I used to be such a jealous woman and that's the awful thing, Mary. I've realised in these last few months I still am a jealous woman, no matter how hard I try not to be. It won't go away.

'I thought when I ran away and took refuge in retreat at Briancon, that I'd dealt with all those feelings of jealousy and anger; I really believed I'd grown stronger than those kind of feelings. It was a part of myself I really worked on. When I came back to England at first it wasn't too bad, but then it all started up again, seeing Anna with Leo. Being around them was hard, but then something wonderful happened and we were all together and it's worked for us. It's worked so well for all these years. The three of us have been so happy, no jealousies, no problems — and then — the baby happened and it's spoiled things and — oh shit! I didn't mean to cry. I feel so selfish for being jealous when Anna's been through so much.'

Mary slides from the sofa and sits with an arm round Millie's shoulder. As Millie wipes her eyes with the back of her hand, Mary passes her a handkerchief and looks at her white-faced sister; she strokes her hair and her arm. 'Don't be so harsh on yourself, Millie. It's bound to have hit you hard.'

Millie nods and wipes her eyes. 'It has. And I haven't been able to say anything to anyone about it. Not really. The stupid thing is that it wasn't meant to happen; they didn't plan to have a child. They weren't trying to deceive me.

'Anna always said she didn't want another baby, not after Frankie. She's had such problems over the years with her, not just

Greg being her father, or maybe yes, the fact that Greg was her father, it made things so difficult for Anna. You know only too well how damaged Anna was by the affair with Greg. Heaven knows, you've picked up the pieces so many times. I think she's never been able to connect properly with Frankie, not since Frankie was a very little girl. I'm sure Anna worried that with any further children she would have the same problems. She's said more than once she couldn't face another pregnancy. She was so frightened of what it might do to her mental health — you know how fragile she is — and there's the irony. Anna's been so depressed and so low since the accident and she finds it so hard to get about; her body took such a pounding she's taken a long time to recover, and Leo's had to give her so much attention that it's brought the two of them so much closer. Mary, I have to tell someone . . . ' Her voice is an anguished wail and she begins to sob loudly, snuffling hard into Mary's handkerchief, muttering, 'Oh hell. I'm sorry.'

Mary holds her and waits until Millie is calmer, before she says, 'What, darling? What do you have to tell someone?'

'I have to tell someone.' Millie bites her lip. 'I have to tell you how frightened I am. I'm afraid that they don't need me any more. I'm afraid that Leo and Anna are going to be just the two of them without me. I feel as if I can't relate to Anna any more. To be absolutely honest, I feel I've got no real part in their lives.' Millie struggles to her feet and refills her glass. 'You must think I'm very self-pitying.' She stands on the hearth rug clutching the stem of her glass, her knuckles are white.

Mary watches her. 'I don't think you're self-pitying at all. I think you're wise to give them some time to themselves. If you are jealous it's natural and human, and at least you're aware of it. You all need more time to digest what's happened. You're very welcome to stay on after Christmas if you want to, but perhaps you won't want to?'

'Can I let you know tomorrow?'

'It doesn't even have to be tomorrow. It could be in a week's time, if you like.'

Millie's smile wavers like reflected water. 'With Frankie in the house! You expect me to be able to think!'

Mary stands up and hugs Millie. 'I've told you — don't be horrid,' but she's laughing and Millie returns her hug saying, 'I'll try not to be horrid, I promise. Thanks for listening to me. I think, if you don't mind, I may go to bed. I don't think I can face Francesca tonight.'

Mary kisses her youngest sister. 'I don't blame you. Goodnight, darling. Sleep well.'

★ ★ ★

On Christmas morning, helping Mary with lunch preparations, Millie refuses a glass of sherry and says, 'I'm going abroad for a month or two. I've always fancied doing a photographic piece on the beauty of the fjords.'

Mary raises her eyebrows. 'Really?'

Millie smiles her usual lopsided grin. 'No, but I'll think of something! I might go and stay near La Roche first. It usually steadies me.'

Mary nods. 'That's a good idea. It always steadies me, too. I think it's the same for us all. It's where we really belong.'

Postcard from Paris — February 1973

Hi, Leo and Anna! I've decided to travel up slowly through France. Being near La Roche was tremendous — wish you could have seen it. I paddled! Have freelanced a bit for the papers here, so I'm earning my way. Will let you know when I have an address. Take care of yourselves.

Love, Millie.

Holly House, Clifton
March 1973

Darling Millie,

Leo and I were so pleased to receive your cards and it's good to know you're finally settled. But why do you never phone?? We want to hear your voice!! Don't you have a phone in the apartment? I'm sure Oslo must be well supplied with phones. This is unfair, we miss the sound of you around here — it's too quiet!! Hurry up and finish your project then you can come home.

Leo has been busy working for various local periodicals and as a tangential result has found himself sucked into the local tennis club. He's out playing now and guess what? I'm going to start playing again soon. I've been doing press-ups in secret in the bathroom in the mornings and taking long walks across the common and I know I'm physically fit again — at last.

On a serious note, Millie, I want you to know I never wanted to drive you out. I do know how hard things were for you, but we both miss you very much and we love you. Come back to us soon.

Anna.

Postcard from Oslo — March 1973

Thought you'd like this view. Thank you for the letter, Anna, it was very much appreciated. I'll be back. Don't worry.
Millie.

Postcard from Stockholm — April 1973

I was in Helsinki at the weekend! You'd have loved it. I miss you both. Great to know you won the tennis match last week, clever darlings. It's wonderful to know you're so fit, Anna, it must be such a boost to your confidence. I'm leaving next week and going on to Copenhagen, but coming home very soon, I promise. Love, kisses etc.
 Millie.

Postcard from Clifton — May 1973

MILLIE! How long does a project take? When are you coming home? What do *you* think of as soon? Have you forgotten how to write? Is your telephone-dialling finger broken? If you wish to answer any of the above questions, then please respond on a postcard, or the back of an old envelope, or a cigarette carton. WE MISS YOU!!
 Love, and lots of it, Leo.

It is summer. Leo and Millie are playing badminton on the lawn of the rented holiday house in Cornwall. Millie's series of Scandinavian photographs is under consideration by a travel publisher and they have suggested she might do more in the near future. She is considering the proposition in a half-hearted way, but people have always meant more to her than places and she doesn't want to leave Anna and Leo again so soon. She has been back for almost two months now and the three have resumed their old roles. Almost.

It's early evening and Anna sits watching the badminton game with suppressed agitation. They have spent the day sunbathing and swimming and, at Leo's insistence, Anna is sitting curled in amongst the cushions of the large garden swing. She has recently had a bad bout of flu and has been tired ever since. Leo and Millie have noticed and worried that she has grown thin and strained, and it was Millie who suggested and booked the holiday.

Anna shifts in her seat. She is growing restless; the other two keep telling her the holiday has done her good, so why doesn't she sleep at nights? And why does every meal she eats make her feel sick? She looks down at her brown arms and turns the palm of one hand over, contrasting its paleness with the back of the other. Her fingers look like spiders, she doesn't want to look at them. In a minute or two she might perhaps suggest that she should take a turn with the racquet. She thinks of the baby, as she does every day.

It would have been a month old by now. She would have had a pram, here beside her on the lawn. It would have been a beautiful baby, she would have enjoyed being pregnant. There would have been no fear, no need to hide or distort the truth. Leo could have been a wonderful father. He would not have run halfway across the world. He would have had no need to go so far from her, so very very far. Fatherhood would have meant a new beginning for Leo, not an end of him as it had been of Greg. It would not have been in the least like last time. She would have been so proud and Leo would not have run away from her: Millie would have learned to love the child; it would have had so much love from all of them. This is the treadmill of Anna's thoughts and it troubles and erodes her every day.

Anna stretches her arms above her head and her fingers touch the sun canopy. A slight sound behind her makes her stiffen and turn her head. She stifles a scream. The trees behind her have moved. She has been aware for the last couple of days that things in the garden have been changing, but she has decided not to tell Millie and Leo.

Leo runs near, in pursuit of the shuttle-cock. 'Are you okay, Anna?' His long athletic body comes to a halt beside her, his soft greying hair is ruffled above his tanned face. He looks so handsome she needs to touch him.

'Yes, I'm fine,' she reaches for his hand, 'but take care!'

Leo laughs. 'I shall mind my poor old bones. A forty-third birthday is no joke!'

'I mean it.' Anna is so forceful that Leo hesitates, coming to sit beside her on the swing.

'Aren't you coming back to play?' Millie calls from the other side of the net. She swipes her racquet at a passing wasp.

'Yes, in a minute.' Leo waves his hand, turning to Anna. 'What's the matter, Anna?'

'Nothing. Go back to your game, I'm all right.' She touches his hair.

'Is Anna okay? Are you, Anna darling?' Millie begins to walk towards them, narrowly avoiding a tree which has glided nearer to the net. Anna is puzzled. Why didn't Millie see it?

'Yes. I've told you I'm fine. Keep playing. Please.' Anna knows it's important that they keep playing; that way they will be safe.

'Are you sure you're all right?' Leo bends and kisses her before running back towards

Millie across the daisy-starred grass to continue the game. From time to time both Leo and Millie glance over to where Anna is sitting unnaturally still. Millie mouths the words, 'Is she all right?' Leo answers with a shrug. The two continue their game uneasily. 'We'll go in soon, Anna,' Millie calls, diving for and missing the shuttlecock.

But Anna doesn't reply. Millie wonders if she's fallen asleep — it's difficult to see against the setting sun. Anna is still watching the trees and still silently urging Millie and Leo to go on with their game. The trees have crept closer to the house. Surely Leo and Millie can see them. They are waving their branches; their fearsome greenery is too lush to be trusted. Anna lets out her breath. Thank goodness, now they are tiptoeing away. Who knows but they might have talons beneath those long green skirts. It is not so much a tiptoe as a long oily glide, a slide and a slither, with their great weights bearing them away. The youngest and slimmest tree turns over its phallic shoulder for one last greedy look at the house. There is no more need to threaten, no need to bully; it sees with satisfaction that the ivy is doing its work well. By the time the moon is up the house will be devoured; perhaps the fretwork gallery might remain, but nothing more.

As if it knows its fate already, the house has thoughtfully moved its windows up as far as they can go. Soon in order to allow the house to breathe a little longer, the windows may have to become skylights then they can reflect the sky and the clouds like broken wings. The moon is up already, it looks pale and nebulous. Anna's heart beats faster; she knows that with the fall of night the crack and cry of breaking glass will fill the air before the advance of emptiness.

Unaware of their danger, Leo and Millie go on playing, lofting the tiny shuttlecock. If they're wise, if they can keep the score at nil the trees will go on gliding, creaking and gliding away, eating their shadows until the moon is up. Up like the shuttlecock. Already Anna's arms are aching with the will to keep the shuttlecock in play. She must call to them, but the words won't come. Do they know they cannot stop? Are they wise to the fact that three years ago, all of this was houses, as far as the eye could see and now there is nothing but green, and every year the trees grow bigger, their need to dominate more urgent.

Millie throws down her racquet. 'Oh! I've had enough. I'm worn out. Let's go and have a drink before supper.'

'Keep playing, you must keep playing!'

Anna calls. She is breathless with her need to stop the trees. She has taken the precaution of wearing her best dress, rose-coloured. Just in case. You never know — it only needs the world to turn, or the moon to fall and she never trusted that hedge.

'Slave-driver! We'll be exhausted.' Leo turns round laughing, but the laughter dies on his lips. Anna is running towards a large conifer and she is screaming obscenities.

'What the hell . . . ?' Leo drops his racquet and in seconds he and Millie are beside Anna, but she doesn't seem to recognise them.

24

A year has passed and the doctors have said Anna is doing well. She feels well, out here in the air, alone for the first time in months, walking across the park hearing light talk amongst strangers, and knowing they are not talking about her. People don't talk about her. She knows that now.

She has always loved this park. It is Victorian, well planned and full of wide spaces, the kind of park she never played in as a child, but children in story books and picture books do. So she felt she knew it well even before she and Millie and Leo moved into the house in Clifton. The park is one of the reasons why she loves their house. From her room she can see the winding paths, and sense the space; she loves the stubby, black and shiny lamp-posts. It gives her pleasure to be out walking amongst it all.

In an hour the lights will come on. Millie and Leo are at home now waiting for her. Soon she will walk back down the hill to them, and they will want to continue with their peaceful lives; it will be as though nothing has ever interrupted them. They will not talk about the baby, or her illness, and even though Anna may want to talk about it, Leo and Millie will tell her it isn't good for her and she will try to see the sense in that. They will look across the table at one another and feel safe. Anna draws a deep breath. She knows that since the baby, Millie has found it hard to be with her sometimes. Though Millie visited her assiduously in the clinic; though she has cared for her tenderly since her return home, never letting Anna become over-tired, protecting her and nurturing her; deep in her soul Anna acknowledges the shadow of the baby will always lie between them. She knows it and she grieves over this knowledge when she is alone.

As the evening begins to close in Anna quickens her pace, pushing aside dark thoughts, revelling in the sense of air and sky around her. She is up above the city; she can look down on it if she wishes, but chooses not to do so. Instead she focuses on the birds flying home across the pale sky. Her thoughts become distracted and as light as feathers, as light as leaves, as light as she feels. She realises she is hungry and turns for home.

Reaching the house she lets herself in, hanging her coat up and calling, 'Hi! Are you in?'

'Down here, Anna.' Millie appears at the

foot of the basement steps. She is wearing a large butcher's apron and her face is rosy with the heat of cooking.

'Smells good! I'm starving!' Anna smiles. 'Where's Leo?'

'In his study. Do you want to give him a shout? We can eat now if you like.'

Anna runs quickly upstairs to Leo's study and puts her head round the door. 'Hello, my love.' He stands up and throws his arms round her. 'Did you have a good walk?'

'Wonderful. It's so peaceful out in the park, you should have come with me.'

'If I'd come with you, it wouldn't have been peaceful. You mustn't tire yourself.'

Anna pulls away from him. 'I don't tire myself. I've got masses of energy, probably more than you have, old greybeard!' She runs a finger over Leo's recently grown beard. He takes her hand and leads her out of the room.

'You don't like the beard, do you?' he asks.

'Not sure. What does Millie think?'

'What does Millie think about what?' She meets them on the stairs. 'I was coming to see where you'd got to. The food's going to spoil if we don't eat soon.'

'Let's eat downstairs, it's cosier than the dining room.' Leo pats Millie's ample rear with his free hand and she laughs up at him.

Anna momentarily feels excluded, but she covers her hurt as she smiles and says, 'I was talking about Leo's beard.'

'It hides some lines,' Millie grins. 'Makes him look distinguished.'

'Talking of distinguished, did you know the critics are saying that in *Our City Life* we've produced a seminal work,' Leo says, sitting down, fingering his beard, looking from one woman to the other.

'Well done,' Anna begins to serve pasta.

'Well done! Is that all you've got to say?' chides Leo.

'Sorry. I mean it's terrific news.' *And you two are growing closer, leaving me behind.* 'I'll fetch the salad.' Anna gets up clumsily, banging into her chair.

'Sit down, Anna. I'll do it.' Millie brings fish and salads to the table and begins to serve the food deftly. 'You're a bit quiet, Anna. Everything all right?' She is watching Anna covertly, but Anna knows Millie very well; she tries not to sound antagonistic as she replies, 'Everything's fine. I've been thinking, that's all.'

Leo pours wine, takes his plate, watches the two women. 'What's happening? Is there an argument?'

'No. No argument. I just want to tell you what I've been thinking and I know you usually try and stop me, but it's important. Will you listen?'

Millie throws a glance at Leo.

'Don't look at each other like that. There's no need to. I just want to talk.'

'Okay.' Leo raises his glass. 'Tell us what you're thinking.'

'The doctors have said in a month or two if I continue to be well, I'll be able to start travelling with you both again.'

'I know,' says Leo. 'I think we should start with something on peasant life — perhaps the Greek islands?'

Millie is abrupt. 'What a cop out! Leo, we can't let Anna . . . ' she trails off.

'It's okay, Millie, you were going to say I'm coming between you and your work and you're right.'

'Oh hell! I'm sorry, Anna. I didn't mean anything by it.' Millie's mobile face registers a swift transition of emotions.

'It's okay.' Anna helps herself to more food. 'You've managed without me for a year and Anthea is a very capable assistant.; I was thinking it might be wise for me to break away from your work altogether and think about resuming and rebuilding my repertoire as an organiser of functions and festivities. Perhaps a career completely of my own is just what I need.' *God knows I need something of my own.*

Leo clears his throat and says, 'It is only your career that you're wanting to alter, isn't it?'

Anna smiles from one to the other, hoping her smile covers her fear of losing them. 'I love you both very much, but I think if we're honest we all know things won't ever be exactly the same.'

Leo's dark gaze is nervous as he says, 'Perhaps not, but it doesn't mean we can't all work this out.'

Millie fiddles with her food. 'What do we all want to do?'

'About us?' says Anna.

'Yes. It's not working right, is it?' Again Leo's hand goes to his beard. 'The dispute over my beard isn't really about the beard, is it?'

'No,' says Anna.

'Anna, you mustn't be jealous,' says Millie. 'Leo and I were bound to be closer after . . . '

'Yes, I know. After my year at the funny farm.'

'Don't!' This from Leo. 'Don't say that, Anna.'

Anna says, 'I want to stay with you both, I want to be with you, but since all that's happened it's going to be difficult.'

'It doesn't have to be,' says Millie. 'If we all

try and all look after each other, it can be all right again.'

'But that's just the point, Millie. Looking after each other. Not you two looking after me. Equal shares, we always said that. About everything.'

'But the baby wasn't equal shares!' Millie blurts before her hand flies to her mouth. 'Oh Jesus! I'm so sorry!'

'Millie!' Leo's face is anguished. 'That was unforgivable.'

'And so was the two of you having the baby.'

'But it was never intended. Millie, you know that.'

'Yes, I do. I do, but can't you see what it did to me? I felt so excluded!'

'And I feel excluded now!' says Anna.

'Do you? Do you really, Anna?' says Millie.

Leo groans and pushes his plate away. He stands up, tall and slim above the two women. 'This is ridiculous! It's all old ground. I thought we were sorted out. I thought we were all right,' he thunders.

Anna is on her feet beside him. 'Sit down, Leo, please sit down.' She is so calm the other two look at her in surprise and Leo subsides into his chair. Anna sits beside him, holding his hand and reaching out for Millie with her other hand. 'It's okay, I've had time to think

431

things through. It's okay. We can make it okay. If we want to.'

'Do you really think so, Anna?' says Leo.

Anna nods and the corners of her mouth lift. 'Yes, I do. I want to tell you how I really feel, and so far you haven't let me. Honesty, that's what we've always promised each other, isn't it? For better or for worse — honesty.'

Millie and Leo are sitting very still. Millie has forgotten to remove her apron and the butcher's stripes rise and fall swiftly as Anna continues. Feeling her way for the right words, she says, 'I like — I love — being with you both. You've given me strength, you've helped me through a terrible time, but now, if you can, it's time to let me try my wings at last, and not just me. You too, both of you. I know how hard the last year has been for all of us, not just for me. I want space and room to grow. We all do, we need it if we're to survive. I want that for all of us. I hope you'll understand.' She lets go of their hands and looks from one to the other.

Leo lights a cigarette, and draws on it hungrily. 'You're not talking about us all splitting up? You're not even thinking about it?'

Anna notices the agitation of his hands; he plays with his knife, with his cigarette, with his glass. She shakes her head, as she leans

432

over and kisses him. 'I love you both too much.'

'And I love you both too. We'll be all right if we give each other some space.' Millie stands up to fetch more food. She stoops to kiss the top of Anna's head as she passes and looks for wood to touch.

25

Extract from a letter posted to Mary from Miami — 1979

I almost forgot to wish you Happy Birthday, dearest Mary, and Happy Anniversary too for last month. Yes, I take your point, at ten years old Megan must be getting too much of a handful for you and John, and perhaps it is time that she had more young people around her. I couldn't agree more. It's so good of you and John and Mother to offer to pay for her boarding school. I don't know what I'd have done without you all. Mike left me, he wants kids. Found out about the reasons why I can't have any and that was that. I'm coming 'home' to England for a while in about a month; perhaps we can talk more then. I'm looking forward to seeing Meg — it's been too long.

Francesca.

Megan
Mummy came home yesterday; she looks very brown and a bit scraggy. Her face has got funny dark shadows under the eyes though her eyes are still pretty — they make me think of the sea down in Cornwall in the summer. I drew a picture of her, she said it was good but it made her look like a gypsy. Then she laughed and kissed me and said I must be a good drawer because she is, and Granny Anna's daddy was. Mummy's a very sudden swoopy sort of a person. I know she's my Mummy but she doesn't feel like she is. Auntie Mary's a real Mummy. Auntie Mary said Mummy was coming home to see me but I don't believe her. I know the real reason — it's to send me away to boarding school. Granny Anna came to tea too. She's lovely, ever so pretty and not a bit like some of the other girls' grannies. She's not old for a start. I asked Auntie Mary how old Granny Anna is, and she said forty-nine but I don't believe her, she must be years younger than that. Mummy looks nearly the same age as Granny. She says I've got to go to boarding school but I don't want to go. I want to stay here. Auntie Mary says I can come back in the holidays; she says this will still be my home and Uncle John says he'll buy me a new bicycle for when I come home at

Christmas, but I don't want to go. I asked Mummy where she was going to be and she said in a commune in London. I don't know what that is but she says I can't go there either.

Mary

The attic is warm beneath the tiles. It's full of unwanted things, a settee with stuffing coming from its back, cobwebs, childhood toys — mainly Megan's, but a few of Francesca's, and even some of Anna's. So many years of looking after other people's children. And now it's time to let go and devote myself to John; he's going to need me so much in the coming months. The water tank in the corner gurgles as John runs his bath downstairs. It's not often I come up here any more, but I like to know it's all present and correct.

Poor little Megan. I can't help wondering if John and Anna and I have done the right thing by her, but it seemed the only possible solution. Knowing John is so ill and likely to become a great deal worse before too long, I couldn't bear the thought of dear Megan being around to see him deteriorate. She has enough to cope with having Francesca as a mother. I know it's not all Francesca's fault,

436

but it's such a tangled mess we must all do what we can to make the best of things. In view of Frankie's track record as a mother, I knew she wasn't going to be suddenly reformed and offering Megan a settled home. Right from the day Megan was born it was as if Frankie just rejected her. And yet she'd wanted the child, she really had wanted her. It seemed like depression but when it went on and on and Frankie would never discuss it, for John and I to take Megan in seemed the only course of action, either that or stand by and see her totally neglected.

I used to blame myself for stepping in too quickly, and perhaps I did make it too easy for Francesca, but how could I stand by and watch her drag a tiny baby along in her hectic way of life? I couldn't bear to contemplate Megan living in the back of some old car, or making do in a squat somewhere. It was as if, when Megan was born, Frankie wanted nothing more to do with her. She'd always been reckless, but after Megan came along she seemed to get worse, not better.

Anna, of course, blames herself. She's always said Francesca behaves as she does because somehow she guessed about Greg and it had blighted her life, making Frankie fearful of having any more children and fearful of what the future might hold for

Megan. Certainly Anna is right when she says there is something twisted in Francesca and I do believe, though it's a desolate thought, that on the day Megan was born something died in Francesca's soul and the reverberations go on and on.

Francesca has taken Megan out for the afternoon. I didn't really want her to, but it is two years since she was here for more than a day at a time and I always hope that spending time with Megan may make Francesca appreciate her own child more than she does. I feel so angry with her and yet so sorry for her, though I don't believe she has ever understood or had maternal feelings. If she had, how could she have had all those terminations. Why the devil couldn't she use contraception like any normal person? And now she's gone and lost this man, Mike, because of it. Though she's now declaring, as she does at the end of all her relationships, that he wasn't the right man for her. That's probably my fault.

I sometimes think I made Frankie hope too much that she would find there was one true love for her. Perhaps I shouldn't have told her about my own love, yet that's egotism. I still dream of Bryn sometimes, still wonder what happened to him, but I suppose it's best not resurrected. It's all so long ago. So very long.

If only he'd lived, who knows what he could have achieved. I come up to the attic sometimes and unwrap his painting of me. What a strange, shy-looking girl I was — and yet he made me something else too, something I never believed I was, until he painted me.

Francesca has been painting again recently — nothing spectacular, pot boilers if we're being brutally honest, but they sell fairly well on the flea markets, well enough for her to make a living and buy dope if I'm not mistaken. The minute I talk to her about settling down, that old haunted look comes back into her eyes. If only she would stay. If only she would face up to her responsibilities more. If only Anna were at home more. If only.

26

Postcard from France — November 1981

Bonjour, Anna-Gran, you were right — I love France! Miss Hughes is taking us to Paris at the weekend and we're going to the Louvre. Am practising my French *beaucoup*. Good old Auntie Mary really kept me on top of it so I've an unfair advantage! I thought you might like the picture on the front of this card. It is La Roche, isn't it? It looks like all the photos. I found it on a 'junk' stall. See you in the Christmas hols.
   Love, Megan. XXXX

On her way to her office, hurrying because she is late, Anna stoops to pick up the post from the hallway of Holly House. She stuffs it into her briefcase and lets herself out of the house. It is cold. Winter is coming. The trees in the park show clichés of black lace branches to the grey sky.
   Anna tightens her coat belt and pulls her hat lower, as she hurries through the streets of Clifton to her office. She passes the coffee house on the corner, and waves to André,

who pauses in the act of wiping a table to wave back. Anna decides she'll call in later for coffee and practise her French with him. He's always pleased to see her and enjoys conversation in his native language. For her part, Anna finds it good practice. Recently Millie has only spoken in English and Anna worries that she might be forgetting her roots.

Anna arrives at her office and unlocks the heavy front door. The feel of the keys in her hand, the sight of the black and white tiled vestibule and the clipped miniature laurel bush, all fill her with an enormous sense of achievement and pride. She has worked hard in the last nine years to establish herself and she stops for a moment to admire the shining brass plate engraved with her name *Anna Williams* and below that, *PR Consultant*.

Anna slips out of her coat and hat as she passes through to the inner office; her secretary has not yet arrived and Anna enjoys the quiet of the high-ceilinged rooms as she does every morning before the rush of her day begins. Leo and Millie are as pleased for her success as she is herself. Anna has long since ceased to see herself as whole only when part of what Mary refers to as their 'unholy triumvirate'.

Anna puts her briefcase on her desk and

opens the lid. She takes out the handful of post from home and shuffles through it — a few bills, a letter from an old friend and a postcard from Megan. Anna smiles when she recognises the child's handwriting and idly turns the card over before reading it. She sits down heavily and brings a shaky hand up to her mouth. The front of the postcard shows a painted familiar scene. The scene is the cottage and the beach below La Roche. She peers closely at the postcard; the reproduction is not good but she can just make out a faint signature. Reaching into her desk drawers, Anna rifles through them, hurling things to the floor in her impatience, until at last she finds what she is looking for — a magnifying glass, bought as a joke by Leo when Anna complained of no longer being able to read small print.

Anna moves the magnifying glass to the card; the signature is unclear but she can make out the letters *Br . n W .. lia . s*. She has no doubts at all, the artist is Bryn Williams, her father, whose dates are given as 1900–1964. Anna drops the magnifying glass. 1964. He didn't die until 1964.

When her secretary arrives, the office is deserted and Anna has left a note; *Sorry, something unexpected came up. Will ring you this evening.*

Christmas, 1981

Dear Miss Williams

In response to your recent enquiry concerning the artist Bryn Williams, your late father, we now have pleasure in being able to inform you that the late Mr Williams lived and worked in the South of France from the end of the 1950s until his death in 1964. He was particularly fond of an estate known as La Roche, producing numerous paintings of the area and selling largely to tourists.

The reproduction which you sent to us and which we now have pleasure in returning was taken from a painting bought by the local museum. We are able to supply you with the name and address of a local woman who has been particularly helpful to us in supplying Bryn Williams's paintings for reproduction, and I am happy to report that she has stated that she would be more than happy to meet you. Should you wish to do so, please contact us again and we can make arrangements to put you in touch.

Mary

Winter. My sixty-eighth birthday. The first since John's death and I am, I think, mostly managing. The fountain in the garden is frozen. I look at it and wonder if the water freezes suddenly, or if there is a gradual cessation of movement, until at last there is no more. We walk in the garden, Megan and I; the sun is low and deep red beyond the end of the lawn. Every tree is weighed down with snow and the shadows are deepest blue. Huge icicles hang like organ pipes from the gutters. The garden is almost unrecognisable.

Our footsteps creak across hard-packed snow and we throw crumbs for the birds. The air feels cold in my lungs as Megan and I walk arm in arm, slipping and sliding together until we're laughing like two young girls, instead of one young one and her rather elderly great-great aunt. It is then that I tell her about the postcard that she sent to Anna. Megan is astounded when I tell her it was of a painting by her great-grandfather.

'Fancy that!' she says, her lively face radiant under her mass of dark red hair. She's such a pretty child. She turns to look at me. 'Do you think perhaps it was him trying to contact me? Wouldn't that be wonderful! It's because of him I can paint and draw, isn't it, Auntie Mary? Isn't ancestry a funny thing! I lie in bed sometimes and I think about all the people who have been in this family before me. Doesn't that sort of thing fascinate you?'

'Yes.' I know I should say something more, but feel like a rabbit in a trap.

'Aunt Mary, why don't the family own La Roche any more?'

'An estate like that costs a great deal of money to keep running.'

'Don't you miss it?'

I look around at the English winter scene, and for a second my heart feels not unlike the frozen fountain. 'Sometimes I do.'

'Oh! Now I've made you sad.' Meg kisses me on the cheek.

'Well, now you've made me happy again.' I return her kiss.

'Do you mind talking about La Roche? Was it very beautiful?'

'I never mind talking about La Roche. Yes, it was very beautiful, but after Maman and Papa, your great-great-grandparents, divorced before the war my Papa decided to sell up. We were almost all grown-up and besides, he had some big gambling debts to pay.'

'Gambling!' Megan's face registers wonderment and a kind of glee.

'I'm afraid so, darling. I believe the family home was used as offices and is now a girls' school, and my Papa lived the rest of his life in a very comfortable apartment in Marseille.'

'Auntie Mary, who was my daddy?'

'Hasn't your mum told you?' I feel my way carefully.

'Not really. She said he was someone who wouldn't marry her.'

'Then if that's what she says, I think that's what you should accept — don't you, darling?'

Megan shrugs. 'I suppose so, but I just wonder sometimes if he was someone special to her. I do hope he was, because it must be so good to have someone who's special to love you, don't you think so?'

'I do, Meggy.' We walk for a while in silence and I think of Bryn's painting on the postcard and wonder as Megan does, if perhaps it *is* a message from him.

'Auntie Mary, do you remember that time when Mummy got out the photo albums and showed me a picture of Anna-Gran's brother?'

'Not really, darling. Let's go in, it's getting cold.' I'm such a coward.

'You must remember. She said such a strange thing about it. She said he was my grandad. What made her say that?'

My laughter sounds false even to my ears. 'Goodness only knows! You know how your mum's always inventing stories to suit herself.'

'Is she?' Megan's eyes are round. I look

446

away across the garden to where birds are swooping down for whatever food they can fight for. Their wings send up small clouds of powdered snow. Which is worse, to have Megan believe her mother tells lies or that her beloved grandmother committed incest. 'Yes,' I say brightly, 'your ma's a bit of a scallywag at times. There's no harm in it though, she just likes to wind people up. Shall we go inside now?' I dislike myself as I resort to bribery. 'There's a chocolate cake and the fire's lit.'

Megan starts to run. 'I'll race you,' she calls back to me, her voice high and childish in the clear air. Crisis, ever a transient thing, has passed for now, but the day has lost some of its shine and the intense cold is making my head ache. As I pass the fountain I look at it again. How could I have been so foolish as not to turn it off. We shall have a burst pipe. This house and the garden are getting too much for me. It's time I moved.

★   ★   ★

Phone call from Anna to Mary — March 1982
'I thought you and I might take a pleasant outing in a few weeks.' Anna's voice is light and Mary senses that she is smiling.

'Really? Where to, darling?' Mary imagines shopping in London, or walking in the Yorkshire Dales. Knowing Anna it could be either, or anything between the two. Whatever it is, it will revive Mary's flagging spirits. The winter has been particularly difficult and her health, normally so good, has been fragile.

'Try and guess! No, don't try and guess. I'll tell you. I thought we could go to La Roche.'

'La Roche!'

'What do you think? Will you come with me? I can't think of anyone I'd rather go with.'

Happiness lifts Mary's voice. 'I'd love to come. Thank you, Anna. Thank you so much for asking me,' and arrangements are made for a meeting to discuss details.

Mary goes into her garden and sits on the bench beneath the rose arbour. She watches the fountain, miraculously undamaged by the winter frosts, and flowing freely once more. A hot-air balloon floats high above her, like a token of sky, the basket slung beneath a balloon painted with rainbows and birds, so it is as if a piece of heaven has been uncorked and flung free. Mary wonders if somewhere an exact balloon shape is waiting to be plugged. She tilts her head and calls, 'Hello!' and waves her hand, but the balloon is too high. The silk bellies and drifts on, leaving Mary caught and trembling with it.

Letter from France — spring 1982

Dearest Millie and Leo,

I can't believe it — we're actually here at last! La Roche is as lovely as ever. The spring flowers are something I'd never seen before, but I know you talked a lot about them, Millie. You were right — they are amazing. So I'm taking photos all the time (not as good as either of yours, of course!).

The house has been heartbreakingly neglected — new paint is badly needed. The headmistress of the school here has been very kind in allowing us to look around. She has explained that she feels responsible for the neglect, but as she shrugged so charmingly and told us, it's self-evident there's not a great deal of spare cash. She intimated that she is thinking of selling up. A point which I shall return to soon!

The grounds are very overgrown, except where lawns have been mown to make playing spaces for the girls here, and Mama and Bryn's cottage is little more than a ruin, used to keep unwanted junk in.

I'm so glad I brought Mary out here — she's positively rejuvenated! Not at all fazed by the state of the place, just incredibly pleased to see it all again. Mary and I walked on the beach, which hasn't changed at all, then we drove out to a restaurant recommended by the headmistress. It turned out to be in Monsieur Becque's old house, which is now a kind of country club!! Poor old Monsieur Becque — turned down by Mama and then Babette left him. After that, he sold up and went off round the world. Rumour has it he married some Tahitian maiden, but I think that is just rumour! Today we meet Madame Hubert. I'll finish this letter after our meeting.

Now about the fact that the school is probably selling up. I've conceived a plan — you'll probably think it foolhardy — but I'd love to buy La Roche. I know it could take a lot of time and planning but to buy it, renovate it, and use it for ourselves and our friends would be so wonderful. I would close down the PR business in Clifton. You two could run your careers from here. There's ample space for darkrooms! I would run La Roche as a holiday letting business and, when it's time, we could retire here in style. I'm not joking — it would be so right for us all. Please let's talk about it when we get back.

Later

Well, what can I say? Madame Hubert was amazingly helpful. Apparently she met Papa Bryn in 1956; the years from the war until then seem very foggy. I think he was quite badly injured, lost his memory for a while. Then, when he got his memory back, he had no apparent wish to find any of us again. That's the bit that hurts even now, even at this distance, but — well, we all know parts of life can hurt too much, so I have to accept that was his decision. His war experiences had made him restless and he was bumming about on the Continent generally, unable to settle — that sort of thing. Anyway, it seems eventually he came back to this part of France and rented a room at Madame Hubert's house. It was she who suggested he try selling some of his paintings to pay his rent. I think that must have been before she fell in love with him — because it's pretty obvious she did. Much to his surprise and delight he got quite a local following in the summer with the tourists; the postcard publishers paid him quite well too. It was enough to keep him and enough to give him money to buy drink — which Madame H. said was what killed him eventually, that and the fact that his wartime experiences had taken quite a toll on his health.

Madame Hubert has some of his paintings in her house; she was very kind and asked us if we wanted any, but we said no she should have them. After all, they weren't part of our lives. Bryn had opted for them not to be. She didn't say so in so many words, but I'm sure they had been lovers.

And now, I feel strangely flat. I have a photograph of him, but apart from the eyes it's like looking at a photograph of a stranger. I shall give it to Megan — she may want to know what her great-grandfather looked like as an elderly man. I'm not sure what I hoped to feel, but it doesn't really matter. I know my memories of Bryn are still good ones. Perhaps it was silly to try and resurrect something that was never mine to resurrect. Mary and I are going to travel around a bit before we come home. I'll ring you when we decide to return.

Love, and lots of it — Anna.

Mary
La Roche in the late-evening sunshine, just as I remembered it . . . the wind in the trees and the sun going down. So many memories

452

— not all good, but more good ones than I thought there would be. I'm glad Anna has at least thought of buying the house. It's not as mad a scheme as she thinks it is. I've made the decision she shall have the money when I die — it will help her, and Millie and Leo too. They should all be at La Roche. It's the place for them; La Roche deserves them.

Madame Hubert — who did she remind me of? Would it be foolishly egocentric to say myself? She came into the room and I knew — it was like looking in a mirror. She is slightly younger than me, perhaps a little less cultured (what a snob I am!) but still very alike. She was extremely surprised and almost shocked to meet me, she said, because it was thought I had died. That was an ice-breaker, when I said I was pleased to report I had not!

Whilst Anna was looking through Bryn's paintings, Madame Hubert and I had the chance of some private conversation. I asked how she had known of my existence and she said Bryn talked of me often. She told me he had tried to trace me when he came back. He even went to Lyons and tried to make contact with some of the other Resistance members of The Group, but many had moved on, or were dead and no one seemed willing to talk; there was no one who remembered Bryn — and why would they? We kept our love so secret it was only a close few who really knew the truth about us.

Somehow Bryn got hold of the information that I'd been killed in the last attack on the printing works. My blood runs cold, even now, to think how narrowly I missed losing my life that night. It was a terrible attack — machine guns and mortars and no survivors. Whoever told Bryn about it would not have known I was not there when it happened. I went to ground for days afterwards, I was so traumatised, and then I fled to Paris. How was Bryn to know I only missed the others' fate through having pneumonia! One of life's perpetual ironies.

When Madame Hubert told me of all this I wanted to cry, and I could see there were tears in her eyes too. She confided that she had loved Bryn and I'm truly glad for him that he found love at last. She told me he had some bad experiences in the war and it made him difficult at times. His paintings could have been so much better if he'd worked at it more. If he had been with me, I would have helped him. I wouldn't have let him drink his precious life away, I would . . . but what's the use? These are the thoughts of a foolish girl. I expect Madame Hubert did her best. When she told me he could be difficult I knew from the sadness in her demeanour there was more than understatement there. Perhaps I might not have been able to love him during those times. I think Madame Hubert knew. She was very kind.

I've done a lot of hard thinking since we came back to England and I can see now that Bryn and I were never meant to be. What we had was beautiful and I shall always be grateful for that. When I think about how alive I felt then, it makes me realise I've been unchallenged for too long. It's time I threw myself back into life. I've been too quiet since John died.

I had thought if I came to the museum I might be able to sit and write, to assemble my thoughts about Bryn, about France, about La Roche, and about my life. I tried the café — small, noisy, tables too close together. I'm now in a room full of paintings all over 400 years old; all making me see how bad Bryn's work was, but I don't care. The custodian keeps coming to look at me. I find myself feeling guilty, but she needn't worry — there's only one painting here I'd really want and I think that although small, it still wouldn't fit under my jumper. *Portrait of a Young Man*, dated 1565. I see the insolence in the way he stares that isn't really insolence at all, but bravado, the soft down on his upper lip, baby soft and never shaved, dark eyes beneath winged dark brows, a high intelligent forehead, a mouth, irresolute. The son I never had. The son Bryn and I could have had. If you saw this youth today with an earstud and a Walkman he wouldn't be out of place.

The custodian's staring at me again. I can't stand her a moment longer. I get up and wander into a further room; the paintings in here are more modern, but apart from a beautiful Renoir pastel there's nothing else to excite me. The loos are about the best thing in this museum — dark oak doors, shining brass bolts, frosted glass, a marble floor. How disappointing that the seats are plastic, though in the interest of hygiene I'm rather glad they are.

27

Finding the portrait was a shock. Anna had said I could have what I wanted from the house. It was winter and cold up in the attic. There was a lot of junk, nothing of any value and then I found it, wrapped in heavy canvas, tucked in behind the other things — and yet it looked as if it had been out recently. There was no dust on it at all; I think that's what made me notice it. God! What a shock when I opened it and there was darling Mary in all her glory. And it was glory. I knew straight away that whoever painted it must have loved her very much. They'd caught the essence of her — all the shining qualities of her, all her vulnerabilities. And then I *knew* who'd done it. Everything fell into place. Mary and my great-grandfather, Bryn Williams.

Somehow I couldn't show it to Anna, it seemed wrong. I thought it might be too much for her. I waited until she was out of the house then I took the picture, but now I don't quite know what to do with it. It's a bit like stealing. Perhaps it should belong to Anna — after all, Bryn was her father. But I love it, I love owning it, it's one of the few things he painted really well. He and Mary should have stuck together. Who knows what would have happened? They might have produced a brood of their own — perhaps a whole new painting dynasty would have been founded. Perhaps it was anyway!

Came down from London for the funeral. It was okay, better than I'd thought it was going to be. Couldn't get over how small the coffin looked under all those flowers. Mary's boys had done her proud — there were quite a few of them there, those deep uncertain voices singing the hymns, all a bit too much for me, a bit too much for everyone. I went back after to Holly House with Anna and Millie and Leo. Ma couldn't make it to the funeral, but sent an enormous overblown wreath thing.

It was good to be with the three of them again — the triumvirate as Mary often called them. I shall miss her so much, we all will. Her boys at the youth centre certainly will. How she managed to persuade them to take her on there as agony aunt-cum-playleader-cum whatever needed doing I'll never know, but once Mary had made up her mind there was no stopping her. She was incredible. She's such a loss; it's going to be so odd without her.

I sometimes think I could be happy to live at Holly House for ever, though it looks as though things are going to change. It's a shame, I love this house so much — all very English provincial — the green front door, camellias in tubs, white railings, polished brass lion knocker and letterbox. Dried flowers, parchment shaded lamps and the view of the bridge. It's so much quieter here than London.

The evening meal was lovely, a sort of haven with the three of them, my archangels, my guardians. Anna's just so full of vitality since she's given up her PR business. Millie and Leo take care of her when they think she won't notice. They all take care of each other when they think they won't notice! Can't believe Anna's sixty, can't believe any of them are, they're all so full of life. I thought Leo looked thinner than last time I saw him, but still very, very handsome. Twenty-six years they've been together now; the neighbours accept them, they have some good friends. Millie still travels, still has a full appointments diary and though Leo works less in his own right he goes with her as a companion and assistant nowadays. He hasn't worked much for himself in the last year and come to think of it, he really doesn't look very well. He's always been slim but he's verging on being thin — however he's still got absolutely incredible eyes and that mouth! He's still gorgeous! I do hope he is okay; nobody said anything to indicate he isn't.

Over the meal they were all talking about La Roche. It seems Mary told Anna shortly before she died that she was leaving her everything and Anna wants to sell up at Holly House and move out to France. She's wanted to for a long time — about eight or nine years now apparently — but the other two have previously been putting up resistance to the idea. Now it seems La Roche is likely to be coming up for sale. The school that was there has finally gone out of business. Millie and Leo are still not sure about it, but Anna is fairly determined.

Phone call from Anna to Megan — April 1992

'I'm afraid it's bad news, darling. Leo died last night — we were both with him.'

'Oh God! Oh Anna! I'm so sorry, so

460

terribly sorry. Is there anything I can do?'

'Perhaps if you can manage it, you could come down for a while? Millie's taking it very badly. I thought she would — she wouldn't even acknowledge he was ill and he was for so long, so very long before he even told us. And then all these months it's been so hard.'

'Poor Leo. Poor all of you. I feel so useless.'

'You're not useless, it's good to have you to talk to, darling. Oh God! Megan, if only he'd said something sooner, if only we'd noticed when he first became ill.' Anna's voice breaks.

'I'll take some time off, of course I will. Are you going to be all right until I get there?'

'I'm okay, I'll be okay.' Anna's breath wavers audibly. Megan can hear the fight for control before her grandmother adds, 'I think I'd prepared myself for this. It's Millie I'm really concerned about. Darling Leo, he was so brave, so very brave right to the end.'

'I'll come, of course I'll come. When's the funeral?'

'I'm not sure yet. I'll let you know. I must go — Millie's calling me.'

★ ★ ★

Millie looks from her bedroom window down towards the river. She has been sitting in Leo's study all afternoon. It was so quiet in there. So peaceful. She had found a copy of his book on Somerset and the Levels, his first ever, the one she had helped him with when they were young, when they first met. So many years with Leo. For most of the afternoon she has sat with the book on her knee staring blankly at the front cover. Now she has left Leo's room. Leaving the book on his desk she came out and closed the door very gently behind her and walked through to her own bedroom. She looks at the river and she looks at the bridge. The ground begins to slope away steeply above the river to where the massive pink brick structures hold back the high cliffsides and the steel inverted bows swing in languid graceful curves between two grey towers. The vertical struts look like unplucked harp strings. Lower down there is a fretwork like frosting on a cake; from this distance the huge bridge looks no stronger than silver ribbons.

Millie can see people crossing to and fro, their heads no higher than the parapet. She knows how far, how infinitely far it is from the parapet to the river below. Evening will be the best time. Anna will be with Megan this evening. At this time of year it is easy to see the bridge because the branches of the trees are only just coming into leaf; the twigs still make patterns against the grey sky and a few sea birds fly over a world that without Leo is empty and meaningless. Millie knows there is a notice on the bridge, she has been down and read it several times in the past week. It advises the desperate and desolate to ring the Samaritans. She thinks she will not bother. It will be easier to jump.

Holly House
June 1992

Darling Megan,
Thank you for all your help, sweetheart, in the past dreadful weeks. I don't know what I would have done without you. I thought you should know that the house has a buyer and as soon as the sale goes through, I'm going to France. I shall make arrangements to live as near La Roche as possible and be in a good position both financially and physically to put in a bid. It's terrible here without Leo and Millie and I do hope you understand that I simply cannot contemplate going on here, not only in the house but even in England. It would seem that the doctors were right — I half thought, more than half thought, my demons would come for me but no, I'm here and as whole as I can

be without my two darlings, and I'm quite convinced that's more than partly thanks to your kindness. Come and see me again soon if you can.

All my love, Anna-Gran.

28

Letter from Megan to Anna, received in a package two days before Megan arrives for her exhibition in France.

August 15, 1998

Dearest Granny-Anna,

This is a very difficult letter for me to write and probably even harder for you to read. I hope you will forgive me, but I felt before I came to see you and before the exhibition in Toulon, it was important that you receive this. As you know, Ma — back in Britain for a while — told me to bring this package with me and give it only to Jean-Baptiste and to no one else. I'm sorry, Anna, it had nothing to do with me but Ma had been making such a big deal out of the package I was afraid it contained something that might hurt you. I know to my own cost how hurtful she can be, so when she'd given it to me and gone, I'm afraid I opened the parcel and I have to confess, I am so very sorry, but I read your brother's diary.

Anna, please, please don't be angry. Please forgive me for what I did. I feel stupid and small and like the very worst kind of snoop, but I didn't know what else to do. I wanted to protect you and not to indulge Ma, and though perhaps I have no right to comment I want to tell you — because I feel it's important that you know — that I wept when I read your brother's story. You poor, but so rich creatures, to have loved each other as you did. It's a love story from start to finish. I've known for a long time how Greg died, and all I can do now is send you my deepest love.

If you don't want to see me when I come to Toulon for the exhibition — which is unstoppable now or I would hesitate to even set foot in France after what I've done — I shall understand and I shall make arrangements to stay in a hotel and fly straight out again when the exhibition is over. If you do forgive me, and I hope so much that you do, I shall perhaps see you at the exhibition. If you're not there I shall understand.

All my love, Megan.

Anna is in the cottage when the postman arrives; she still has not summoned the

466

courage to pack her belongings and go. All morning she has prevaricated, finding small unnecessary jobs to do. The postman smiles and says good morning as he hands a small package through the open door.

'Thank you.' Anna glances at the handwriting, Megan's handwriting on the outside of the brown paper. She glances out into the garden. There is no sign of Jean — he must be swimming or up at the kitchen garden. He has stayed overnight again up at the house and has not been around all morning. Feeling like a criminal, Anna slips back into the living room and tears the wrapping from the package. A small battered leatherbound book falls softly to the floor. Anna recognises the diary instantly: how could she not — she gave it to Greg for his sixteenth birthday. Megan's letter slides from the brown paper and Anna crouches on the floor, protective as a mother bird beside the diary, as she reads her granddaughter's letter.

The morning creeps slowly on and Anna reads and re-reads her brother's diary, turning the pages, looking and looking at the faded writing. Sometimes she does not read at all, but sits staring into the past of fifty years ago. There are times now when it is difficult to recall Greg's face, and it is only in her dreams that she ever hears his voice. Their love affair was so long ago. Greg is frozen in time for ever.

Paws comes to sit beside her, looking anxiously at her mistress's face, curling in close, aware of distress. Disturbed by the cat, Anna puts the diary down for a moment, long enough for her to remember something. Cautiously she turns to the back of the book and runs her fingers over the lining plate of the back cover. As children she and Greg used to pass secret messages, slipping notes under the final fly leaf, sticking them down with precision. Anna is certain there will be a message for her. She goes to the kitchen taking the little book with her and fetches a sharp knife. With infinite care she slits the page and sees she was right; there is a single sheet of paper folded tight, tucked in between the endpaper and the back cover. Anna's tense fingers feel for the paper's edge. At first it won't come. With her tongue protruding between her teeth, Anna tries again; there is a slight tearing sound and the paper is free. She knows she is the first and only person to see this since Greg placed it there. Her palms are sweating as she unfolds the piece of paper and reads.

Play no sad music.
Beat no drums.
Remember me with joy
when my time comes.
Wear red at my funeral
sing the songs I loved
throw a giant party
wear no hats or gloves.

Anna, there should be more but my head is pounding and I can't think straight. If you ever find this, I want you to know how all morning Auden's 'Stop all the clocks' poem has beaten and beaten in my brain until the only way I can stop it is with this pathetic tired little jingle, and poor though it is, it might just convey something of how I feel. It is not my intention to die, nor is it my intention to stay alive. I simply exist. New Zealand is a land of opportunity, but I want none of it. My head and all my limbs ache most days, but not so much as my heart. I know if I go on as I am doing I shall not last much longer. Anna, you have reason to go on — you have our child. I hope and pray for you both that you and she can love each other and be happy. I wish you had come away with me when I left. Living in a country so far away from home I think of how we might have survived. Seeing how Babette and Olivier live side by side truly as sister and brother, I have regrets; perhaps you and I could have gone on knowing each other into a peaceful old age if we had obeyed the rules as they have done. Yet, even as I write I know that's a lie. We loved each other too passionately, we wanted too much, and it saddens me more than I can bear to know that because of our love I will never see you again. I want you to be proud of our child. My sweet, sweet girl, if ever you find this as I hope you do one day, I want you to do one thing for me, and that is to think of the happy times we had. I mean it when I write remember me with joy, because that is how I will remember you. I love you.

Anna

At last I lift my head, and stretch my cramped limbs. I want so desperately to cry, but no tears will come. I make my way to the stairs: I know what I have to do. For Greg, for myself and for Francesca. I climb the stairs, each one so high I can scarcely lift my legs but at last I am at the top, where I pause for breath which seems as reluctant as my tears to come. My heart is hurting. Jean is out — I hope he stays away until I have done what I have to do.

470

I go to my dressing table and, crouching down, I reach into the recess below it and take out my daisy box. I shall not need it now. Back downstairs and out into the garden, collecting the diary and Meg's letter as I go, I make my way to a clearing, out beyond the gate. I have matches.

The fire takes a while to light, but soon I am fearful for the trees nearby; it has been a long hot summer. I sit watchful and fearful beside the pyre I have made, until there is nothing but flakes of grey that turn to dust as I grind and grind at them with a large flat stone. I look up and see the sun is well past its zenith and still I have not cried. Tomorrow I shall leave.

29

Megan

The suddenness of a complete rainbow, the sunlight unexpectedly hot and brilliant lighting the houses, and the trees are a garish green against a black sky; a perfect arc of soft glowing colour, and somehow it's important that it's whole. Ma and I are out on bikes in the countryside. She's come to Aunt Mary's for one of her weekends. I follow her wet back tyre, splash splash shaking off the wheels. She's pedalling along in front, her head up, her long hair whipping and flying in the wind. I'm eight years old, still enchanted by her, still full of illusions — perhaps she's a princess. She has princess's eyes and her hair is nearly blue it's so black. She's wearing scarlet, she's a gypsy princess that's why she can never stay for long; she has to keep watch over her realm. We stop off at a pub and when I go to the loo, I look at myself in the mirror above the wash handbasin. I don't look like anyone I know — not Mary, not Anna-Gran, not Ma. Perhaps I look like my dad? We eat our sandwiches, we hardly ever have anything to say to each other, but made bold by the day's freedom, I ask, 'Who do I look like? Is it my daddy?'

Ma looks at me for a moment or two, then she draws in her breath. I think she might be going to be angry with me, but she's not. She smiles and it's just like the rainbow outside, all soft and warm but what it touches gets lit up too harshly. 'No, you don't look like your dad, you look like your grandpa.'

I'm puzzled. I've seen a photograph of Grandpa Charles, I know he left Anna a long time ago, when Ma was too little really to remember him. 'Do I? Do I look like him?'

Ma nods, her long silver earrings swing vigorously. 'Just like him. I'll show you when we get home, but it will be our secret.'

When we come out of the pub the sun has gone in and black clouds lash stinging rain in our faces all the way back to Mary's house.

Later, when we're warm and dry by the fire that Mary has lit specially for us, and Mary is making the tea, Ma reaches down a photo album. I've never seen it before. Its pages are heavy and creamy and there's a musty smell as she turns them. She points to different people in funny old-fashioned clothes. There's a tall slim boy with a big wide smile; he's looking at the camera and laughing. I recognise myself — he looks so like me. I've never seen anyone else look so like me!

'That's him.' Ma points.

Mary comes into the room; her voice sounds odd. 'That's who, Francesca? What are you showing Meggy?'

'Oh, just some old photos. She wanted to see one of Greg.'

Mary's face looks funny; it's gone a sort of yellowy colour under her tan. She says in the same odd voice, 'Can I have a word please, Francesca?' Only she's not asking her, she's telling her and she leaves the room.

Ma pulls a face at me and takes the album out of my hand as I object, 'But he's Anna-Gran's brother — he's the one who went to New Zealand and never came back.'

'Oh, he did come back . . . '

Mary's voice from the kitchen is sudden and loud and makes me jump. I've never heard it sound like that before. It's like a knife going through me. 'Francesca. Will you come in here. Now.'

Her voice is shrill on the word 'Now,' and Ma puts the album away and goes through to the kitchen. I can hear angry voices. I feel sick. I hate it when the grown-ups get angry. I want to look at the album again, but Ma has put it up on a high shelf and I would have to stand on a chair to reach it. I don't want Auntie Mary to be angry with me too. The next time I go to the house the album has been moved. I daren't go looking for it. I don't want Mary to hiss at me the way she is hissing at Ma now in the kitchen. I can hear odd words, 'How could you, how could you,' Mary hisses and Ma mutters something back.

Mary's voice is loud. 'Far too young.'

Ma says, 'She should know.'

Mary says, 'I'm sorry for you, but don't be ridiculous. She should . . . ' Her voice drops away too low for me to hear anything. I don't know what to do. I think I should put the radio on, or leave the room. I don't want to listen to any more. Then Auntie Mary calls to me to go and wash my hands and when I come back downstairs it's just Mary and me having tea. Mary says Ma's gone out to meet some friends; this is a surprise and when Ma comes in much later to look at me when I'm in bed, I pretend to be asleep but I can smell cigarettes and whisky on her breath. She bumps into the door on her way out of the room and I hear her dropping things and swearing as she gets undressed in her own room.

Ma never talks to me again about Greg. I try once to have a conversation with Auntie Mary. It's on her birthday; I've gone to see her and we're feeding the birds in her garden. It's snowier and colder than I've ever known it. I try to talk then about Greg

475

but somehow that memory's all muddled up with running in the snow and chocolate cake for tea.

Later, when I'm about fourteen, I ask Mary who Greg really was. She says he was Anna-Gran's brother and he went away to New Zealand — but those are just the things I already know.

'When did he go?'

Mary is vague. 'Oh some time, a long time ago.'

'Ma said he came back.'

Mary bites her lip, turns her back, is very busy across the other side of the room straightening curtains that are already hanging straight.

'Did he come back?' I persist.

'Yes, he came back, but he died.'

'A lot of people died, didn't they, Aunt Mary?'

Mary sits down and runs her hands through her hair. 'Yes, a lot of people died.'

'Mary . . . if Greg was Anna's brother, he couldn't have been Ma's father, could he? It would be,' I hesitate, unsure if I've got the right word, 'it would be incense, wouldn't it?'

'Incest,' Mary corrects automatically, but her face has gone very still. 'Yes, darling, it would be incest. How are you getting on at school at the moment?' She stands up and

476

without waiting for an answer begins to lay the table.

Francesca
It was dark in the attic. I'd been restless all morning. I was a twenty-one-year-old unmarried mother, damaged goods, a fallen woman. The baby was due some time in the next week. It had been a long and lonely nine months. Cut off from my friends, unable to start my career. Made to feel lucky not to have been put in a home for wayward girls, or to be threatened with having my baby taken away from me for adoption. We had worked out a plan between us. Mary and John had been more than kind and compared with some I knew I had been lucky, but life was slow and tedious.

Mary and John were out shopping. It was probably foolish to climb up to the attic in my condition as we had euphemistically termed it. 'My condition' — it sounded like an illness, and yet I'd never felt so well in all my life. Mary had been so good about everything; she'd lied for me to the neighbours, and told them all my husband was a sailor on a tour of duty. Of course, when Megan was born that little lie came tumbling around our ears, and we had to invent a 'death' for my

477

'husband'. So then I was a romantic young widow in the eyes of the neighbours.

Mary and I had some arguments. I used to shout, 'God! Why is the world like this? I'm not ashamed of what I've done, but everyone else seems to think I should be,' and Mary would reply that everyone didn't include her and Mum, but they were protecting me from scurrilous tongues. I used to wonder how Mum and Mary were so intuitive, and thought how special they were to know just how I felt. Then I found out.

That was the day I decided attics are places where only the brave should venture. There was a painting up there, and what a revelation that was, to see Mary as utterly naked as the day she was born and so alive and sensuous as I'd never even suspected she could be! I knew even before I saw the signature who had painted it. It was Bryn. So, sweet innocent Mary had had an affair with her own sister's husband. No wonder she knew all about life and love with a capital 'L' — and to think I'd been impressed by all that romantic guff about one person and one only in her life. What a dark horse.

There was worse to come. I found a box with a load of old books and clothes inside it. Men's clothes and an ancient teddy bear and a small leatherbound book. I nearly missed it;

I wish I had. It was a diary kept by Greg, Mum's brother. My father. I thought it was innocent, just the diary of a schoolboy and took it down from the attic and sat in my room reading it. It amused me until I got to those pages. Then it was horrible. It was the worst thing I'd ever read. I literally thought I was going to be sick but I couldn't stop reading, it was like a terrible fascination. I read it all, right to the day before he left for New Zealand.

Flick, flick go the pages of my little flicker book and the pictures make sense. My mother is naked with Leo. It is dark in the room apart from the fire. My mother is saying something to Leo about her brother. About me. Leo's hand is on my mother's back. I wanted a drink of water. Soon after that Leo went away, only to return a few years later to my liberal mother with her liberal lifestyle, living with her young aunt and their mutual lover. The three of them living together was as nothing compared to this. Finding the diary made me hate my mother as I didn't know anyone could hate. It began to eat at me on that day.

When Mary came home I said I had a headache; it wasn't a lie, and I went to bed. I lay awake all night going over everything I had read. The next day I went into labour with Megan. It was a long and dreadful labour. The pains went on for hours and hours, and all the time she was being born all I could think of was what I had read the day before. When Megan was born I was terrified to look at her for fear of what I might see. If I had escaped unharmed, would my baby be so lucky? I wouldn't believe them at first when the nurses said she was perfect. When my mother came to see me, I wouldn't talk to her but lay facing the wall. They all thought it was post-natal depression. What did they know. No wonder Mum had hardly flinched over my little 'sin'; it was as nothing compared to hers. How could she. Her own brother.

It was a year later that I confronted Mum with it. She had called to see me and Mary about my 'behaviour'. Like some bloody angelic social worker. Mary had contacted her, worried about my tendency to stay out at nights. I'd told Mary I had a right to live my own life. She'd told me I had responsibilities. She said she and John didn't really want to have to look after Megan but I was giving her little choice. Exactly my intention. Soft-hearted Mary, the easy touch. I knew she wouldn't stand by and let Megan suffer. Besides, she'd been in on the deception about Greg all along. She could pay some of the price. I was bad to Mary. She didn't deserve the way I behaved. I'm glad I made my peace with her before she died.

More pages turn. Here comes Mum, fresh from a trip abroad with Leo and Millie. Bringing a teddy bear for Megan and a lecture for me. But I'm ready for her. We're out walking, through the local park. It's spring. Again. Daffodils are out, weak sunlight breaks through clouds, the silvery patterns that, as a child, I thought were God's fingers ray out from the underside of a cloud. Every cloud with a silver lining. I don't think so. Mum is pushing Megan in her pushchair. We've done all the stuff about me behaving badly and Mum has concluded her speech with, 'I don't know why you're like you are. Perhaps you should see a doctor. It could be that you are depressed, darling.'

I'm not looking at Mum as I say, 'Greg was a good brother, wasn't he?'

I slide my eyes to see what effect I've had. Her face has gone absolutely wooden, and she says, 'Yes. He was a good brother. Do you think we should go back now? I don't think Megan wants to be out here any more.'

I glance down at Megan, who is sound asleep. Mum turns the pushchair and begins to walk away from me, but I'm too quick for her. I put a hand out and catch the pushchair's handle. Mum falters and looks at

481

me; she's in flat shoes so she's looking up at me. Neither of us says anything, but her face isn't wooden any more. I hear my own heart thundering in my ears as I say, 'Do good brothers and sisters often have babies together?'

Mum has stopped walking and she is holding onto the pushchair as if it's a Zimmer frame. She doesn't look healthy any more and the fine lines around her eyes are showing. I can see what she'll look like when she's old. I realise too late that I'm afraid of what I've done. I think she might actually be about to have a heart attack. Her breathing is laboured and her head is down. Then, as her head comes up I see how angry I have made her.

'Just what are you saying, Frankie?' She is cold and distant. It's far too late to say I mean nothing. Nobody says what I have said and means nothing by it. I'm trembling but I say, 'I couldn't go on, Mum, I had to tell you. I had to let you know that I know, and I had to make you see what it's done to me. I can't mother Megan properly; I don't want to be with her. I can't seem to relate to anyone. As if it wasn't bad enough you living as you do with Leo and Millie, as if it wasn't bad enough thinking I was being brought up by Mary and put into a boarding school because you couldn't cope easily with life, I thought

— I *really* thought it was because Charles had died. But no. It's because my father was your brother.'

'I'd like to go back to the house.'

'Is that all you're going to say!'

'No, but I'm not prepared to discuss this here, it's too public.'

I look around — there's no one else in the park. I say, 'It might be less public here than it would be back at Mary's house.'

Mum's mouth is tight, but she nods. 'All right. We'll sit over there on that bench and I'll talk to you.'

I watch her walking ahead of me to the bench. Part of me reluctantly acknowledges that she is brave, but a larger part of me still hates her.

We sit side by side. Formal and chilly. The sun has gone behind the clouds. Megan stirs and Mum adjusts the pushchair blanket.

Neither of us speaks at first, then Mum says, 'How did you find out?'

'So, it is true?'

In a low voice she says, 'Yes. It's true. You haven't answered my question. How did you find out?'

I've thought this one through already. I don't want her to know about the diary. To admit I'd found and stolen it would put me in the wrong; I don't want that. Just now I

483

have no intention of using it against her. I just want to appear totally self-righteous. So I say, 'I worked it out.' Will she be so busy with her own guilt that she's willing to believe me? She's sitting slumped, but she rouses and looks directly at me, her eyebrows raised, her expression wary. 'You worked it out? How?'

Steady, Francesca, don't rush your explanation, stay calm. I shrug. 'It wasn't that difficult. It's taken a long time, but you've left a lot of clues over the years.' She is watching me, listening intently. I say, 'Mostly it's the way you don't talk about Greg.' She draws a breath and looks down at her hands. It's easier without her staring at me. I continue, 'You see, Mum, you do talk about all the other relatives, but never your brother — and if his name does come up, you go too quiet. So I've always known there was something wrong. I've seen the photographs of him as a baby and Megan's so like him. But most of all I've worked out just when he left for New Zealand. It was when you were pregnant with me. I'd already realised I was born too soon after your wedding to Charles. Then there are no photographs at all of you for about a year when I was tiny. I asked Mary about it once and she said you were ill — having one of your 'fragile times'. I've never told you before, but I went to Brockley churchyard. I found Greg's headstone. I know when he died. It's when I was one year old and you were ill. I'm not stupid, Mum.'

I'm beginning to think I've said too much, made the explanation too elaborate, but she's crying and I know she's so wrapped up in herself I've convinced her. I get up and walk away from her, taking Megan with me, leaving her sitting there in the park. I make sure I'm out when she comes back to Mary's. After that we have a long series of appalling rows, until we're both exhausted and there really is no more to say.

30

Letter to Anna Williams, to be opened only in the event of the death of Francesca Browning:

Outside Holly House
August 22, 1998

Dear Mum,

In spite of having Greg as her grandfather, and me as her mother, my daughter Megan has grown into someone very wonderful, both as a person and an artist. She's arrived in Toulon safely, you have seen her. You will be with me tomorrow and, to my immense surprise, I am glad. I am visiting Holly House. I am sitting in my car outside. It feels strange, but it seemed like the best place to come and think, though I never really knew it when you, Leo and Millie, the 'idyllic three' lived here. I never came near the place really.

In my driving mirror I am watching a newly registered Merc. A woman climbs out, expensive raincoat, fashionable haircut — a young grandmother like I might be if I manage to survive long enough to see Megan's baby. Look after Megan and her baby for me. The woman is clutching a stuffed toy duck; it's wearing a yellow sou'wester and a foolish grin — the silly creature is dangling upside down from her hands. I watch the woman collecting more and more things from the back seat of the car — bags, bright wrapping paper. I feel curiously comforted that someone with such clearly abundant money should be no more organised than I am. I hope you can organise me, Mum, in these last weeks. The woman has had to close her car door by bumping it shut with her bottom. The toy duck is tucked under her chin. I hope its recipient appreciates the hard work it has caused! I expect you to buy sensible toys for Megan's child. The woman has gone into the house and the street seems very empty. I wonder if Leo and Millie might haunt the house. It was a strange arrangement, but you were happy. Perhaps I should have settled down. Perhaps I should have found a man to stay with 'for ever'. But for ever isn't going to happen now.

You know I've had all the tests. You know the doctors say my lungs are irreparably damaged. It's what I thought it was — the big C — and I have to find a way to face that. If that way involves my mother, then that's how it's going to be.

When Megan said she was going out to La Roche to meet your new man, and how you were full of delight at being so much in love, I was so angry. I tired myself with my anger. When I gave Megan Greg's diary, sealed into a box, with strict instructions that only Jean-Baptiste must open it, I thought if I built it up enough Meg would think it was just me being melodramatic and humour me, as she so often has. I didn't expect her to open the box and send it to you. She's braver than I am; you are both braver than I am. I'm a coward and because I'm a coward and don't want to face what's left of my future alone, I've agreed to let you come here.

Yesterday afternoon you phoned from Toulon. Megan had told you I'm ill. At first I was furious with her, then I was astonished by you. I have been astonished by you in many ways throughout my life. This time I was astonished that not only do you want to be with me, you actually wanted to talk to me about the diary. I nearly put the phone down. I think you knew I did because of the way your voice hit that insistent calm note.

Of course, as soon as you mentioned the diary I knew the whole thing had backfired on me, but I also knew that wasn't why you were telling me about it. You were infuriatingly calm, as only you can be. You told me you should have known all along that was how I knew. I wish you had. I wish I had known all my life about Greg — that way we could all have been saved a deal of trouble. You said you had read the diary; you said you had Greg's letters and you had read those too and then you had burned them all. They no longer exist. You say you feel free. I didn't ask you about Jean, but I hope, to my amazement, that he is with you when you read this.

This may be as big a shock to you, Mum, as it is to me, but I want you to know that sitting here outside Holly House in the warmth of my car, I am laughing. Why? Because only you could react as you have done.

I shall not leave this for Megan to find. She is not to be trusted with private mail and packages! Instead I shall post it this evening, before I change my mind, to my solicitor with instructions that you only read it on the event of my death.

Love to you from Francesca.

31

Anna

A small crow has fallen from a tree and is haunting the cottage garden; its presence makes me uneasy. I have been aware of the bird for several days now, flapping out of unsuspected corners, sitting amongst shadows disguised as a black plastic flowerpot or a scrap of rags. This morning, the morning I have chosen to leave, the crow sits by the car, a huddle of nothingness. As I check the car's oil and water, the crow lifts heavily over the garden gate before falling back to earth. Yesterday it was tapping at the kitchen window; it made me shudder with its ungainly beak half the size of its head, and its ugly dusty feathers. Unlike its vagabond brethren up in the trees it is silent. There is menace in its disfigurement and in the constant coarse chuckling of the others occasionally flapping out of the trees like badly designed planes; they are too heavy to be real birds and their noise is incessant. All the past endless night the injured bird has lurked in a corner of my mind — a message best not deciphered. Perhaps when I have gone, Jean will come and shoot the bird.

La Roche is very beautiful in the early-morning sun. Through the gaps in the trees I can see its lovely old cream walls reflecting the morning light. I thought I'd come home for ever when I came here. How arrogant can anyone be. Paws has followed me out to the car. I can't take her with me, but I know Jean will treat her well. She has gone to sit in a patch of long grass, half-hidden and protected by the shade of an overhanging tree. Crickets and butterflies land unheeded close by. The heat is their safeguard; it is as if they know Paws is feeling indolent. I can hardly bear to look at her. I squat beside her for a moment stroking her hard little head and watching the play of insects amongst the long grass stalks. An ugly black fly crawls across a patch of bare earth and without compunction I squash it beneath the heel of my canvas shoe. The thought arises that if butterflies were dangerous or disease-carrying, would it be possible to kill them with so little regret? A green glitterati beetle ambles past and as if I want to preserve everything about this moment, I notice every detail of the iridescent sheen on its wingcases. Paws butts her head trustingly against my leg and I get quickly to my feet.

I go back towards the cottage intending to

pack, but Jean is coming through the garden gate and I think I have never loved him so much as I do at this moment. I know I can't leave without telling him, but I don't know how to tell him and the longer I delay the harder it will be. He smiles. The dark shadows under his eyes tell me he has had no better a night than me.

'Good morning, Anna.' *My lover, my best friend — so formal — is that what we've become.*

'Good morning, Jean. How are you? Would you like some coffee?' This is ridiculous. We sound like polite neighbours — we *are* polite neighbours. He lives at La Roche and I live in the cottage; after today we won't even be neighbours. I will be a woman he once knew.

'Coffee? No. No, thank you. I thought I'd just come and see if you were all right.'

'Sit down.' I gesture towards the garden chairs as if they are unusual exhibits in a museum. Jean looks at them as if he has never seen them before, so perhaps they are unusual exhibits in a museum. He says, without sitting down. 'You look as if you're dressed to go out?'

'Yes, I suppose I do.' I see him look at me as if he would like to read my mind. He's always been good at reading my mind. Always? We've scarcely known each other.

Not in chronological time, but in terms of personal destiny — well, that's a different story, irrelevant now. I decide to save him the trouble and launch unrehearsed into what I have to tell him.

'The diary came yesterday. Megan sent it.'

'Oh.'

'Is that all you've got to say?' *Unfair of me.* Jean shrugs. 'I don't know what else to say.'

'I burned it.'

'You burned it?'

'Yes, and some other things.'

'You didn't have to burn it.'

'I did.'

'Are you going to leave me, Anna?'

This is too sudden. I didn't expect it and I counter with, 'Are you going to leave me?'

Jean waits slightly too long before he says, 'I don't think so. I'm confused. What happens now? Is Megan still coming?'

'I don't know. She'll be in Toulon the day after tomorrow for the exhibition. After that, I don't know.'

'It's all a bit of a mess, isn't it?'

I laugh, a sudden almost shocking sound; it takes us both by surprise. 'You could say that. You could say it always has been, Jean, I have to go.'

'Like hell you do. You don't have to go, Anna, we can get through this. At least stay

493

until Megan has been. Please, Anna. Why do you feel you have to go?'

'Because I simply can't bear to think of your disapprobation. Whenever we're alone together this is going to come between us.'

'Not if we don't let it.'

'How can we not let it?'

'Anna, for Christ's sake, it's fifty years ago!'

'It doesn't really matter how long ago, does it? The fact remains I didn't tell you and I should have done.'

That stops him. I see his face tighten, his cheekbones stand out, two hard edges, above which I see there is no kindness in his eyes. We face each other in silence and I watch the heavy clouds, which have been banking themselves all morning behind La Roche's roof tiles, as they blot out the sun. The trees turn their leaves backwards, showing their silvery undersides in a sudden eddy of warm wind. Jean continues to look at me but his eyes slide away from mine and his large square hand is at his mouth as he says again, 'Stay, Anna, at least until Megan has been. I think things will work out.'

I stare at him in despair. How can the easy *patois* of constant communication have become as dead a language as Latin? Nothing is taken as read. I feel I am wearing the thinnest of emotional clothing and, as if we're afraid we might bruise one another, we have not once touched each other since this conversation began. The air is so thick it feels like fur pressing against my face. Each movement is an effort, and a weight is pressing on my chest. Sweat trickles down my nose and my neck; my clothes are sticking to me. If Jean will not listen to the direct approach I must after all resort to trickery.

'It's so hot, shall we swim?' I say.

Unsurprisingly Jean looks amazed by my complete *non sequitur* but nods. 'Okay. Yes. Okay — if that's what you'd like to do.'

'You go ahead and get changed. I'll come in a minute. I just want to make sure Paws is okay.'

Without answering Jean leaves the garden and goes into the cottage. Now will be the best time to go. If I am quick it will be easy to get in the car and drive away. I could ring him when I get to Paris. He wouldn't expect me to leave that way, he would go to Marseille airport to look for me. It would be too late by then for him to catch up with me. Jean looks out of the bedroom window. 'Are you going to get changed?'

I force a smile. 'Yes,' and I go inside.

Jean is sitting in the living room in his bathing shorts. He seems very large in the confines of the small room. 'I'll wait for you.'

I see my opportunity slipping away from me. 'It's all right, you go ahead. I'll catch up.' Perhaps my face is telling him more than I want it to because he stands up and puts his arms round me.

'I love you, Anna. I'm sorry if I've been judgemental.'

I want to give in, but I'm so convinced that our happiness would be shortlived I stand rigid beneath the pressure of his arm. Uneasily he drops his hand to his side. He looks awkward and unsure of himself, but I force myself to say, 'At least being judgemental proves you're human! I've sometimes thought you must be some kind of a saint,' but I can't look at him as I say it.

'Am I to take it from that, that I'm forgiven?' The sarcasm in his voice is the point I hoped I would goad him to.

I say, 'Don't be so bloody patronising. Why should I forgive you!' *Good girl, just like the lines of a play.*

Jean looks at me incredulously. The hurt in his eyes is terrible as he says, 'Patronising! How can you say that! I want us to be together because we're friends.'

It's because I'm your friend that I'm leaving you. We'd only end up hating each other if I stayed. 'I'm not so sure that we are friends.' I turn my back on Jean and speak my

496

lines through frozen lips. A second later, just as I expected to hear it, the back door slams. I know him oh so well, but I tell myself that when Jean gets used to the idea he will be better off without me.

I climb the cottage stairs, walking up slowly through the emptiness of the house. From the landing window I can see Jean walking down to the sea. He is walking like a drunkard. Or a blind man. I mustn't think about him; it will be better this way. I will write to him from England and soon he will be glad that I've gone and after a while he will learn to forget me.

It's so hot I can hardly move but I know I must. Perhaps a shower will cool me down. I should have time now for a shower with Jean out for his swim, but I must be quick. I strip off my clothes and wash myself. I turn off the shower and move into the bedroom. I won't think about Jean. I have to get out of here. It's unusually dark in the room and I have to turn on the light. The clouds are turning the sky blue-black: there's going to be a storm. Still naked I reach down my suitcase and begin to throw clothes into it, not really caring what I take and what I leave. I don't cry at all. There will be time enough for tears later.

When my case is full I struggle into briefs and a clean cotton dress; they cling to my still wet skin. I pick up my case but as I cross the landing it's so dark outside now that I cannot help one final look. Jean should not be swimming when the air is so thick and the sky so dark. Any minute now, surely a storm will start. From the window I can see where Jean would be swimming in the swelling waves of the bay. My heart seems to turn over, and fear touches my stomach. There is no sign of his strong body cresting the waves. It would only be a madman who would swim in waves that high. They are mounting and swelling one on top of the other. I can't ever recall seeing the water running so high. Its steely rolling back rises higher even as I watch and, along the horizon, I catch the first long-tongued flicker of lightning. Thunder rumbles in the distance and I feel sweat break out along my upper lip. Why can't I see Jean?

Frantically I lean out of the window. Wind lashes my face as I twist my head round, craning to see further along the beach. He's not in the water and he's not on the beach. Where can he have gone, dressed only in his swimming shorts? Large drops of rain fall, slow and separate at the start but soon becoming a deluge through which it's impossible to see further than a few inches. I pull the window shut. The world has slowed down. I leave my case on the landing. I am running down the stairs through thick treacle. I must find Jean.

As my foot touches the bottom step a violent clap of thunder breaking almost overhead transfixes me. The room turns totally black for a split second before it is brilliantly lit in a white and terrifying light. A jagged splinter of lightning slashes the sky from top to bottom. Every pane of glass in the house rattles as the wind rises shrieking and moaning through the nearby trees and beats itself furiously against the little house. It feels as if millions of tiny unseen hands are hammering to be let in. The noise is enormous. Petrified, I cling to the banisters.

Another flash of lightning illuminates the room and the back door bursts open. I scream as Jean seems to be flung in on a rush of air and sound. He has to fight to close the door and I come to life, running across the space between us to help him; the strength of the wind is unbelievable. Jean's strong hip is against mine, water streams off him soaking my dress as we push together with our arms outstretched and our heads down to close the door. I feel my fingers might break with the strain. At last we battle the door closed. Jean pushes the bolt home and stands barefooted on the tiles of the kitchen floor with water still streaming off his hair and body.

Through the gloom I can actually see the whiteness of his teeth as he grins.

'*Merde!* That was a close shave!'

My throat is tight and all I can say through a tumult of feeling is, 'Jean! You're here!'

'So it would seem. Could you get me a towel? Or are you going to use your dress?'

Jean almost laughs as I look down at my soaked dress, and I say indifferently, 'It's only a dress — it'll dry. I'll go and fetch you a towel.'

I run upstairs picking up my suitcase, pushing it into the depths of the wardrobe, returning to Jean with a heavy white towel and his bathrobe. He takes the towel and rubs at his hair until it stands in crests on top of his head. The muscles in his arms and back move, lit weirdly as lightning flickers on and off and thunder roams hungrily round the sky directly above us.

'Anna, I want to ask you something — ' but the sentence remains unfinished as thunder crashes again and again, and lightning rips the darkness apart. A high-pitched whistling sound tears at the air and I scream and cling to Jean as the trees around the cottage cast sudden huge shadows into the blue-white light of the kitchen. The hair on the back of my neck lifts as an eerie tearing sound screeches fast along the air towards us. Jean holds me close and soothes me like a child as he says in a not quite even voice, 'That was close. I think a tree's been hit. Are you all right?'

'I think so.' I move away from him and go to the window. Already the sky is lighter. I can see ragged edges to the clouds trailing out like plumes of smoke as the storm passes on its way inland. Pale blue sky opens up in its wake. Without speaking we move around the house opening windows, letting in the fresher air, watching how the sunlight glances off the rainsoaked garden. I can hear Jean moving about upstairs. When he comes back, he has changed into a clean shirt and slacks.

He walks into the kitchen and says, 'Will you come out for supper with me, Anna? We could go to Monsieur Becque's old place,' and his big hands clench and unclench and I know he has found the case. Once he would have told me that he had. Now I watch his hands.

'I don't think I want to eat out, but we could have something here. I'd like that.' The case is still my insurance policy but I see no way of eluding Jean this evening.

★ ★ ★

501

We gather ingredients from the fridge and the larder. Cheeses, ham, good bread, some salad and some wine. There is even half an apricot tart, left over from our picnic.

I discover I am hungry and so, it would appear, is Jean. We sit in the kitchen where we have sat for so many meals together. The food is good, the conversation light and unexpectedly easy. We are talking everyday talk, like any couple might. It is towards the end of the meal that, mellow with wine, I find myself speaking of my Aunt Mary with great fondness.

'She was a wonderful person, Jean. I wish you could have known her. They were good days with Mary, always good days.'

'I thought you said Megan lived with her at one time.' Jean's gaze flickers away from me. I try to read his face but can't. I pour more wine as I reply.

'You're right. Megan lived with Mary and John for a long time, then Megan went to college. Mary had been a widow for a while. She was lonely and needed something to do and, being such a loving person, she needed someone to care for. So she took on the down-and-out boys at a youth centre in Bristol. They adored her, and not one of them ever traded on her goodwill. They wouldn't have dared! After the boys started coming to

Mary's house, Megan spent a lot of her free time with me.'

'Mary must have been a tremendous person. I think you may have inherited a lot of her character.' Jean smiles. 'So, did Megan actually live with you all?'

'All?' I play for time. I'm like a small boat heading for unseen rapids. In the last few moments something indefinable in the atmosphere has altered; it would not be overstating the case to say the air feels charged.

'Yes, you and Millie and . . . and Leo, of course.' Jean attempts a teasing tone, but though his mouth smiles, his eyes do not.

I feel myself flush. 'You don't mind that Millie and I . . . shared Leo?'

'No, it's not that — I've never minded that. It's something you said. You told me you could not bear my disapprobation and that's why you were thinking of going. Anna, don't deny it, please. I saw the suitcase and I think you are so much braver than me.'

'Braver?' I feel dizzy as I look across the table at Jean. Braver, what is he talking about?

'Yes. You had the courage to pack and to think of going. I saw the suitcase so you can't deny it. Though I too cannot bear your disapprobation, what do I do? I sit on the fence. I hedge my bets. I make no move.'

'Jean, what are you saying? Why should you think I would be condemning of *you*? It's me that's done wrong.'

His face is agonised. I see he's almost crying as he says, 'I've reacted so badly to everything you've told me. You must think I'm totally unfeeling. What I said about Francesca being angry with you and that she must hate you — I had no right to say that. Me! I've always thought I was so strong on not judging people and letting them run their own lives, and the first time you come to me with a real problem, what do I do? I let you down. How can I do that to you of all people! And you know what's worse of all?'

'No.'

'I realise I am smallminded, mean and filled with stupid petty jealousy. What troubled me most about all of this? It wasn't *your* feelings, it wasn't what agonies you and your brother must have gone through. It was that Leo knew and that I didn't! I love you, Anna. You are a wonderful, strong person. Me — I am nothing.'

He's pushed the remains of his meal away from him and is standing up. Stooping slightly he comes round the edge of the table and walks towards the back door.

'Where are you going, Jean?' I'm on my feet now. I put out a hand to stop him, but he brushes me away and almost runs down the path and round the side of the house. I run after him and shout his name, but already he's in the car and driving away.

I hear the car moving up through its gears and know he's heading out along the coast road. It will be wet and slippery after all the dry weather we have had. I think about how the waves will be smashing onto the rocks and I pray to any deity that might be listening, to keep him safe. A light rain begins to fall and as I go back into the cottage I realise that I have not seen Paws since this morning.

I clear away. Wash and dry two plates, two sets of cutlery and two wine glasses and wonder if I ever will again. Even when I am in bed listening to the night sounds outside the open window, I still cannot cry. I lie for hours with hot eyes and watch the illuminated hands of the bedside clock move ponderously through the hours.

I must have slept because the phone wakes me. My head is aching, my legs are heavy. Raw-nerved and edgy I stumble downstairs. Certain that I'm going to hear a terrible message about Jean, I snatch the receiver from its rest. A high-pitched tone buzzes through my head. Disengaged. Slumped and weary, I replace the receiver. There was no phone call; my tired mind has invented it. The storm has put the line out of action.

Mary's old case clock on the wall strikes the hour. Six o'clock. I might as well get up. Passing the kitchen I notice that Paws's food has not been touched. I make hot tea. Sipping at its reviving warmth, I go out into the garden in my nightdress. My bare feet make dark marks across the silver dew on the lawn. A slight mist is already rising from the garden and the surrounding trees. I shout for Paws repeatedly into a quiet broken only by the early-morning crows.

I hope Jean has returned to La Roche in the night. On an impulse I go back indoors and shove jeans on over my nightdress, tucking its bulk in round the waistband. I push my feet into my old sandals and locking the cottage door behind me, I hurry through the trees up to the house.

There is no sign of the car, but still I run round to the front door and hammer on it. I step back and look up at the upstairs windows, Jean always sleeps with the window open. The house looks back at me, shuttered and empty. He must be with friends. Perhaps he has gone to Marseille and stayed with his old friends there. I close my mind to the thought of the wet roads and of Jean's distress when he left last night. Should I walk into the village and try to contact the police? How soon does someone become a missing person? Perhaps he has come back to the cottage. If he hasn't, he may do so later in the day. I should be there, just in case.

I'm walking back to the cottage when I find Paws. I didn't see the tree on my way to the house, but coming from this direction I can easily see the clearing over to my left that its ruination has made. The huge tree hit by yesterday's storm has ripped a hole through the canopy of pines, crushing and breaking smaller trees and bushes as it fell, upending itself so that its roots show white and ghastly amongst the raw orange-red earth still clinging to them. I go closer, overawed by the power that brought this giant down. That's when I see Paws. There's only one mark on her soft greyness, where a passing branch must have caught her head. She lies with her small body twisted and still, a deep gash running from below her left ear to her amber-coloured nose. I pick her up and carry her home. I find a spade and bury her deep beneath the lilac tree. That's when I start to weep.

32

Anna is waiting in the airport lounge. Soon a plane will fly her to London. From there she will take the train to Bristol. She is on her way to be with Francesca. Francesca will need someone with her; she cannot be expected to go through any more tests or treatment alone. In a phone call from Megan's hotel in Toulon Anna has persuaded Francesca to permit her to come. She has reminded her daughter of how much support Leo needed, and Francesca has replied, with savage humour, that perhaps there are times when everyone needs a mother and, if Anna really wants to come then there is no way Francesca can stop her. It is a start. Before the inevitable end.

$\star$ $\star$ $\star$

The exhibition hall was larger than Anna had expected. Setting off very early in the morning she had made her way to Toulon, travelling on foot as far as the village. Carrying spare shoes in her bag, she had arrived hot and thirsty outside Monsieur

Bertrand's *épicerie* just as he was opening the pale sun-bleached shutters for the day. He had been surprised to see her. 'Anna. Good morning. You are very early — and on foot? Where is the car?'

Anna had smiled and lied, 'It's broken down and I really have to get to the station. Please could Guillame take me? Can you spare him?'

'But of course. Why didn't you phone? He would have come out for you.'

'The line's still not working after the storm.'

'Of course, ours too.' He turned his head to shout into the back of the shop, 'Guillame! Madame Anna needs a lift to the station!' He had gone into the cool darkness, redolent with cheese and fruit, and returned a moment later with a chair and a bottle of ice-cold water and a glass. 'Here, you look thirsty — sit and drink. Guillame will not be long.'

Anna had blinked hard. 'Thank you.'

⋆ ⋆ ⋆

The train had been delayed and the journey seemed so long as Anna stared into space and wondered where Jean might be. Perhaps she should not be going to the exhibition;

perhaps she should wait at home in case he came back. She had not known what to do that morning and her sleepless night had left her unable to make any sensible decisions, so she had dressed and come on this awful journey to be with Megan.

Although she had dressed carefully for her journey, by the time Anna arrived outside the exhibition hall she was hot and exhausted. She paid off her taxi and stepped out into the welcome shade of large plane trees. The stone steps of the hall were blindingly white in the sun and the contrast between shadow and sunlight hurt her eyes. She fumbled in her bag, cursing softly because she had forgotten her sun-glasses. Feeling small and insignificant, Anna walked up the steps and into the coolness of a wide vestibule. An officious doorman stepped forward. 'I'm afraid entrance is by invitation only.'

Anna quailed in front of his authority. 'I have an invitation, here in my bag,' but when she looked it was not there. Dear God, was nothing going to go right today!

'I'm sorry, Madame.' The doorman smiled, but his outstretched arm was a barrier against which Anna felt she had no power. She tried once more. 'I'm the artist's grandmother. If you could send a message inside I know she

510

would come and verify that.'

'Indeed, Madame?'

'Indeed.' And suddenly Megan was beside her, smiling with Greg's eyes and Greg's smile, and Anna's vision lurched and settled as Megan became Megan, dear and familiar, sweeping her along into the hall where, already in the vast white space, there were at least fifty or more people — well-dressed, suave, monied people, milling enthusiastically around Megan's paintings, each one of which glowed with vibrant colour.

'Darling Anna, I didn't think you would come. You're so late — are you all right?'

Anna had smiled, her tiredness temporarily forgotten. 'Nothing would stop me coming, darling, and why didn't you tell me about this?' Her hand briefly caressed Megan's rounded belly. 'When's the baby due? You're looking well — are you happy?'

'In three months. Yes, I am well. Yes, I am happy. But you, Anna? What about you? We can't talk here, but . . . the package . . . I was so sure you weren't going to come.'

Before Anna could reply Megan was approached by a reporter. She hugged her grandmother. 'I've got to go. I'll come back soon then we can talk. I hope you'll like the pictures.'

Left to herself Anna wandered amongst the

paintings. Examining each one at close quarters she observed scenes of domestic life, each quite breathtaking in its apparent simplicity, almost disguising Megan's superb technical skill. Vivid colours sang out of each canvas. There was a beautiful painting of dear Mary, whose arms encircled many children, known and unknown. Tears pricked at Anna's eyes and her throat was sore with the effort of not crying. As she walked on from painting to painting she realised that each scene was a depiction of aspects of motherhood, ranging from a tender, almost Madonna-like triptych to a startling image of three generations apparently locked in fierce combat, but on closer examination seeming to be a circle of dancers. Anna recognised herself and Megan and Francesca and stared in wonder at the picture. Were they dancing? Who was in charge of the dance — or was it a fight? She moved away, hoping to find comfort in a self-portrait of Megan, in profile, her clearly pregnant belly cradled by her own arms. Clever Megan. The white room seemed to spin; it was difficult to breathe.

Anna looked round for Megan, but she was on the other side of the room. The crowd was increasing and the steady hum of many voices sounded like a great hive of bees. Fighting panic, Anna sank onto a padded red-leather bench in a small alcove. From here she could listen to snatches of conversation floating towards her like flotsam. How well people spoke of the paintings; the growth of small red dots beside the canvases indicated sales were rapid. Anna leaned back against the wall. Megan would not have meant to shock her or to hurt her. She painted life as she saw it and she was right to. It had been a long day. Anna closed her eyes.

She was woken by Megan coming to sit beside her.

'Oh my goodness. What time is it?' The hall had almost emptied. Guiltily Anna sat up and stretched, rubbing her neck. 'Your guests must have wondered who the old hag in the corner was. I'm not in my dotage yet, thank God, but here I am falling asleep in the middle of the afternoon. Whatever must you think of me, Megan?'

Megan's smile was concerned. 'It's all right, Anna, don't worry. Most people have left, it's almost five o'clock. Are you all right, darling? Oh my God — I've caused you such pain, haven't I? You look done in. Please will you come back to my hotel?'

'You booked into a hotel? You didn't have to.'

'I thought after I sent the — ' Megan stopped and bit her lip.

'Yes, I know, but you could have come to La Roche.'

'Anna, you do look exhausted. I'll take you to the hotel. You look as if you could do with some tea, or a gin perhaps?'

Megan

I'm here at last on the tea-time terrace. I can hear the sea; I can hear the birds. No wonder Anna wanted to live here, it's delightful. I made the decision not to put Bryn's portrait of Mary into my exhibition. I realised it would have been inappropriate. I gave it instead to Anna yesterday evening. We had eaten in the dining room at the hotel and had coffee upstairs in my suite when I decided that the time was right. So I went out to the car and brought the package in.

Anna looked up as I came back into the room. She's so pretty, and somehow so vulnerable. From what she's told me, she's had a really rough time in the past few days, and I knew it was about to get much rougher. I suddenly wasn't sure whether to give her the painting or not, but it was too late. She had seen the parcel and there was nothing I could do, so I held it out to her.

'This is for you. It was Mary's. It's something I feel you should have.'

I handed it to her and watched her unwrap it. I thought I'd upset her, she was quiet for so long. I felt certain I'd done something I shouldn't, but at last she looked up and there were tears standing in her eyes. She smiled; her lovely face lost all its fatigue for a moment as she said, 'Bryn painted this, didn't he? Thank you. I always knew Mary loved him and I'm glad my father had someone he loved so much. May I keep this?' She paused and the room seemed very quiet. I knew what she was going to say before she spoke.

'I destroyed the diary, you know.'

'I wondered. You minded that I read it.'

'I did at first, but it doesn't matter now. I'm glad you knew the truth. You're really very good at the truth. Your paintings show that. It's better that way.'

'I'm sorry if I shocked you.'

'You must paint what you know.'

I poured a brandy for Anna before I said into the awkwardness that had fallen between us, 'Do you think Jean will be back?'

'I don't know. I've told myself repeatedly if he'd been in an accident I would have known by now. I hope he comes back. If he doesn't, then I shall have to manage. God only knows, I've managed far worse things in my life.' Her mouth and eyes had gone tight in her white face.

'I feel it's my fault.'

She reached over and patted my knee. 'Not your fault at all, my dear. I should have told him about my past when I first realised I was in love with him.'

'And are you still in love with him?'

'Oh, very much so. But I'll survive.' She sipped her brandy without looking at me.

We were quiet for a while, then Anna asked the question I knew was inevitable.

'How is Francesca?'

I tried to put her off. I told her, 'Ma doesn't look well. She said something about some tests, but when I tried to pursue it she shrugged it off.' Anna leaned forward and now she was looking at me. I hurried on, trying to make her laugh. 'You know Ma — she never really changes. She kept eyeing my Tom up, and asking when he was going to make an honest woman of me.'

'And is he going to make an honest woman of you? Perhaps nowadays it isn't necessary?'

'Oh, Anna! I seem to be putting my foot in it all over the place.'

But although she looks so tired and there was regret in her voice, I knew she meant it when she said, 'It's all right, Megan. I understand things are very different nowadays — not so different that Greg and I would have had what we did condoned,' she bit her lip, but continued steadily enough, 'but still, you're twenty-eight, you're successful and you've chosen to have Tom's child. Will he be with you when the baby's born?'

'I hope so. I'd like him to be.'

'And then?'

'And then we'll see. We may choose for me to bring this baby up alone, or we may choose to stay together.'

'I hope you do stay together — if that's what you want, darling.' She gazed across the room at Mary's portrait, then said, 'Meggy, you told me Francesca was having tests — what kind of tests?'

I'd been dreading the question. Ma had sworn me to secrecy, but perhaps secrets aren't such a good idea after all. So I risked Ma's wrath and I told Anna about the cough and the pains and the loss of voice, and how I'd persuaded Ma to go to the doctor's.

'It's cancer, isn't it?' Anna's voice was quiet.

'Yes.'

'Just like Leo.' She started to cry then and I knelt beside her, holding her hand and stroking her hair.

'She didn't want me to tell you, Anna.'

'I'm glad you did. I'll go to her tomorrow.'

'She might not want you to.'

'I know that,' Anna said grimly, wiping her eyes. 'It's a risk I'll take. I'll ring her — there are other things I need to talk to her about before I actually see her.'

★ ★ ★

So, I'm here at La Roche for a few days. Next week I'll go home so Anna and I can be together with Ma; she'll need us both.

Jean has been here. I liked him enormously. Anna will be at the airport by now. If Jean is quick enough he may catch her there before she leaves.

★ ★ ★

Anna is waiting in the airport lounge. Soon a plane will fly her to London. From there she will take the train to Bristol. Ostensibly reading a magazine, in reality Anna is thinking of Francesca who cannot be expected to go through any more tests or treatment alone.

Anna lays her magazine to one side and is startled to hear her name called over the Tannoy. 'Miss Anna Williams to the enquiries desk, please.' She glances at her watch. A few moments ago her plane had been announced as delayed by half an hour, but these days

518

travelling makes her anxious; she would prefer not to leave the lounge. Her name is repeated. 'Miss Williams, travelling on flight 2002 to London, please call at the enquiries desk.'

Reluctantly Anna gets to her feet and makes her way through the crowded airport looking for the enquiries desk. Across the swarm of heads and the general hubbub she sees Jean. He is still wearing the slacks and shirt he left in two days ago, there is a growth of stubble on his chin and his eyes are dark-rimmed, but he has never looked more wonderful. Happiness is filling her up. She is pushing through the crowd towards him until she is in a space and running like a young girl.

THE END

We do hope that you have enjoyed reading this large print book.

Did you know that all of our titles are available for purchase?

We publish a wide range of high quality large print books including:
Romances, Mysteries, Classics
General Fiction
Non Fiction and Westerns

Special interest titles available in large print are:
The Little Oxford Dictionary
Music Book
Song Book
Hymn Book
Service Book

Also available from us courtesy of Oxford University Press:
Young Readers' Dictionary
(large print edition)
Young Readers' Thesaurus
(large print edition)

For further information or a free brochure, please contact us at:
Ulverscroft Large Print Books Ltd.,
The Green, Bradgate Road, Anstey,
Leicester, LE7 7FU, England.
Tel: (00 44) 0116 236 4325
Fax: (00 44) 0116 234 0205